FIFTEEN POSTCARDS

KIRSTEN MCKENZIE

SSP

First Published 2015 by Accent Press

This edition published 2021
by Squabbling Sparrows Press

ISBN 978 0 9951170 51

Squabbling Sparrows Press

ALSO BY KIRSTEN MCKENZIE

The Old Curiosity Shop Series

FIFTEEN POSTCARDS

THE LAST LETTER

TELEGRAM HOME

Standalone Novels

PAINTED

DOCTOR PERRY

THE FORGER AND THE THIEF

Anthologies

LANDMARKS

NOIR FROM THE BAR

To David Brettell, my father,
who gave me his love of antiques.

To Geraldine Brettell, my mother,
who shared her love of reading with me.

To Fletcher McKenzie, my husband,
who loved me enough to encourage me to do this.

To Sasha and Jetta, my daughters,
who I love, just the way they are.

FIFTEEN POSTCARDS

POSTCARD #1

31/12/39

Dear Phil

> *Wishing you a Happy New Year, wherever you may be.*
>
> *I'm baking a cake today, and I wish you were here to taste it, to tell me that it's simply the best you've ever eaten.*
>
> *Nothing tastes any good without you, so I have no idea if it is the best.*
>
> *Stay safe.*
>
> *B xxx*

THE OLD CURIOSITY SHOP

In a cramped little street, in a dusty corner of London, stands a set of two-storey brick facade shops. An architectural relic from last century, untouched by the bulldozers of modern developers. A greengrocer, a boutique, a gentleman's tailor, the ubiquitous Chinese dumpling shop, and *The Old Curiosity Shop*, an antique shop named after the Charles Dickens classic of the same name. A shop passers-by would wonder if anyone ever went in or whether they ever sold anything.

And inside the crowded little antique shop, you'll find a treasure trove of discarded history: towering stacks of china plates; bundles of old newspapers announcing the armistice with the surrender of Italy and that man has landed on the moon; unloved gifts; and abandoned childhood memories. An extraordinary melting pot of treasures from many cultures, mingling with the more mundane domestic items to create an idiosyncratic mix; part shop, part museum.

Through windows smeared with street dust, you'll see a young woman, dressed in jeans, a shirt, and sensible leather loafers poring over a bundle of black and white postcards, her wavy brown hair tucked behind her ears.

The girl behind the counter, Sarah Lester, an antique dealer, pawnbroker, and sole proprietor of *The Old Curiosity Shop*, thumbed through the postcards until the one about the cake caught her eye. Age fading the ink, the words on the lines shrinking with time.

After reading the postcard she'd picked up out of an old Huntley and Palmers biscuit tin, Sarah leaned back on her stool, her eyes sad. She glanced at the old porcelain beehive mixing bowl waiting on the counter for a new owner-somewhat battered, with two decent gouges out of the sides, the perfect size for a family. As an only child, family was the one thing missing from Sarah's life, another reason she adored reading tatty old postcards. The sentiments written on old-fashioned postcards weren't on Facebook or Twitter. People didn't feel the same way about friends and family, life got in the way. But when postcards ruled the letterboxes of the masses, people used them to express their love for each other — in her opinion, anyway.

When Sarah was thirteen, her mother vanished, a mystery the police had never solved, and about which the neighbours still gossiped. With no suspects or motivating factors for her mother's disappearance, the police considered it a 'cold case'. They'd told her that her mother was last seen in the shop tidying up before the busy Christmas season and her father had left the shop to pick up lunch. When he'd returned, his wife had vanished leaving the shop unattended, and everything in its place-the till untouched, the jewellery still sparkling in its cabinet — there was just a mother-sized void.

For years, the police issued annual press releases on the anniversary of her disappearance, saying much the same thing: appealing for witnesses or new evidence; that they were committed to solving the disappearance. With no leads, they assumed her mother had walked to start a new life with another man. Her father refused to believe this, insisting there was something far more sinister at play.

As a result, she'd been lovingly, but suffocatingly, raised by her desolate father. She'd done well at school and, influenced by the surrounding antiques, she'd studied at Oxford University, getting her degree in Late Antique and Byzantine Studies. As a teenager, she wasn't the best correspondent with her father. Sometimes weeks passed where they didn't speak at all. He was busy, she was busy, and, just after her twenty-first birthday, she'd received a call from the police. The shop had been unattended for several days and neighbouring shopkeepers, concerned that something was amiss, had contacted them.

Sarah returned to London and, with the help of the police, broke into the shop. With no sign of her father, nor of anything suspicious, they'd checked the family home in Raynes Park. The house backed onto Malden Golf Course as the only thing her father loved more than antiques was golf. She half expected to find him slumped over his golf clubs in the garden. But, just like her mother, he'd vanished.

The police opened another missing persons file, and although the shop was profitable and they hadn't found a note, the police suspected suicide due to the delayed reaction to his wife's disappearance, coupled with stress brought on by declining sales — exacerbated by the success of Internet auction sites. They were confident a body would turn up in due course, probably in the Thames. Sarah did not share their belief. Although her father steered clear of technology, competition from the Internet didn't faze him, and she knew he would have embraced selling online. Every day she wondered where he was, and what had forced him to leave a daughter and a business he loved.

With no one to run the shop, Sarah resigned from a brief stint as a junior cataloguer at a minor auction house to take over the business her father started in the Seventies. The convoluted process of managing her father's business, and having access to his accounts, even his bills, had taken years to complete. After a Coroner's Inquest declared her father dead, Sarah inherited the Raynes Park house, the block of commercial buildings containing *The Old Curiosity Shop* and its stock. She'd sold the family home to pay off the debts, choosing to live upstairs to minimise her overheads, like her parents had before she was born.

THE MIXING BOWL

The Old Curiosity Shop was disorganised and overfull. Her father's record keeping almost non-existent and his stock records indecipherable, but somehow he'd been profitable, due to clever buying, a stable of regular customers, and his mantra of 'Leave something in it for the next guy'. She'd tried following his lead, but without him to guide her, she'd seen a downward slide in profits for the seven years she'd been running the shop. All the Global Financial Crisis had achieved was that people were keener to sell than they were to buy.

Reading postcards distracted her from her troubles, much like gambling or knitting distracted others. She'd found these postcards tied in a bundle in the old biscuit tin from a deceased estate she'd bought. The solicitor's acceptance of her offer for the estate had surprised her, as even *she* considered her offer on the low side. The house was a fair way out of town, and transporting the contents back would have been time-consuming, so she'd come in low. Her father wouldn't have given the transport a second thought. He'd have made the perfect offer and got down to the business of moving the stock on expeditiously and profitably. How he'd turned over his stock so fast was a mystery.

With mixing bowls, postcards, and thoughts of declining profits distracting her, she didn't notice an elderly man entering the shop, until he placed a cardboard carton on the counter. Yelping, she fixed her startled stare on the man.

'You made me jump!'

The old man replied, 'Sorry, I didn't mean to scare you, but I found these in my mother's house. I didn't want to throw them away if they are of use to someone. Will you take them?'

Sarah only just refrained from rolling her eyes; a bad habit. *The usual drill, no doubt. He thinks he has valuable heirlooms.* She'd have to tell him his stuff is mostly worthless, and then she'd offer him a ridiculously low price. He'd squawk and postulate that whatever was in his box was worth hundreds of pounds.

Sighing, she hopped off her tatty stool to lift the flaps of his cardboard box. The pungent scent of mothballs and silverfish assailed her nose, and what met her eyes confirmed her thoughts.

A jumbled mess of mismatched crystal glasses wrapped in newspaper, two pairs of old spectacles — possibly with gold frames, a ribbon-wrapped bundle of photos, odd cutlery, several pieces of a Victorian dinner service, and a trinket box filled with costume jewellery.

After a quick mental calculation, she asked, 'How much were you expecting?'

'Nothing,' he replied. 'I didn't want to throw them away, in case they were any good to anyone. My mother liked things to be used...' he trailed off.

Sarah, who, in good conscience, couldn't take them for free from a man who looked like he was barely surviving on a pension, offered him fifteen pounds.

Surprised, the stooped man accepted her money and limped from the shop, the door closing behind him.

A quick coffee and then I'll get onto this lot, she thought. A caffeine hit helped when she had to price up a pile of odds and ends, or rubbish, depending on how generous she was feeling. They were rarely of any worth. She may get the odd set of Waterford whisky glasses, or an exquisite gold filigree brooch, but mostly it was old dinner sets and cutlery given as wedding presents forty years earlier, unused and kept for good, then sold by their ungrateful children.

A steaming coffee in hand, Sarah returned to the scratched counter, half-covered in old novelty pencil sharpeners, a pair of Edwardian vases of dubious taste, postcards requiring sorting, chinaware from the estate lot she'd just purchased, and now the old man's carton. Sarah pushed her wayward hair behind ears decorated with tiny, diamond studs. No fancy cascades of Tiffany's pearls or bewitching rubies the size of cherry tomatoes here in *The Old Curiosity Shop*.

As she read the next postcard from the *Huntley and Palmers* tin, two middle-aged women, dripping with ostentatious jewellery, entered, marvelling loudly at the array of treasure inside.

'Oh, your shop is *such* an Aladdin's Cave, however do you manage the stock take?' the women trilled.

Sarah grimaced. Their question at the top of the 'Five Most Asked Questions' list she kept in her head. The rest comprised:

'You wouldn't want an earthquake in here, would you?'

'Who does the dusting?'

'Do you ever sell anything?'

And her favourite, *'How do you know where everything is?'*

Swallowing her frustration, she answered, 'Everything has a stock number, which I mark it off in the register.'

The coiffured women looked astonished, and, after asking the location of the English china dinner plates, happily started ferreting through the racks of plates. Sarah left them to their own devices and continued reading the postcards.

All written in the same elegant hand, addressed to 'Phil' and signed by the mysterious 'B'. The fronts of the cards contained photos of scenic shots of sheep grazing, brooks bubbling, and anonymous church steeples. The postmarks on the reverse sides almost illegible.

Sarah cursed the lazy mail clerks who never checked if their franks were legible on the mail leaving their post offices.

The women interrupted her again as they carried a pile of china to the counter, slamming it onto the countertop. Sarah winced, but they were undamaged, and she put through a sale for twelve mismatched plates. The women bubbled as they told Sarah they'd planned a charity dinner with a 'vintage' theme, and how different it would be, predicting afterwards that their friends would flock to her store to copy them.

Sarah nodded, smiled. 'That sounds wonderful, I may have to try that myself!', to which the women beamed.

They didn't realise every other woman of a certain age was following the same craze this summer. Once it appeared in *Vogue Living*, all the 'ladies who lunch' raced in to copy the latest trend, thinking they were the only ones clever enough to source their themed crockery from an antique shop.

After wrapping the plates in newspaper and the ladies left, she found the postcards jumbled again. In a fit of frustration, Sarah scooped them up, dumping them into the mixing bowl.

The instant those postcards landed in the bowl, the millisecond Sarah's hand brushed the battered surface of the porcelain bowl, the impossible happened.

Sarah Lester disappeared — leaving no sign she'd ever been in *The Old Curiosity Shop*.

POSTCARD #2

19/6/40

Dear Phil
They've asked us all to knit winter socks for you boys. If I were to knit
something, it would probably end up hobbling you! So instead I've collected some
wool for Miss Swiveller. She has a much better idea of what to do with it than I.
I can't imagine that you'll be there for another winter, so I'll stick to my
embroidery. My flowers are really quite beautiful and remind me of our last
spring together.
Stay safe.
B xxx

THE KITCHEN

*S*he reappeared, slumped over the vitrified mixing bowl. The same bowl from her shop counter, except here its age was disguised by its contents, half-mixed egg whites still runny, a wooden spoon abandoned in the mixture. The bowl was brand new, in perfect condition. Every kitchen in England had at least one; larger kitchens had several, at least they did in the 1890s...

Through Sarah's sudden headache, she could swear she could smell baking. *Thank God that new bakery across the street has opened,* she thought. *There's nowhere good around here to get lunch, only noodle houses with dodgy council hygiene ratings.* She shook her head to dispel the pain, kneading her eyes with her knuckles. It refused to budge. Someone was screaming the name Betsy over and over. Damn halfway houses, they were everywhere around the shop-a leftover social experiment from the previous Government. A failed experiment. She moaned as the ache travelled through to the back of her skull.

Head resting on her arms, she willed the pain away, until someone poked her so hard in the ribs she jumped up with a scream. A scream cut short at the sight in front of her.

Gone was her antique shop filled with dull brass and flowery china. Instead, she found herself in a large kitchen dominated by a black hearth, gleaming copper pans hanging on the walls, and racks of crockery — and an angry woman brandishing a bone-handled carving steel.

'Stop that noise, you'll wake the dead. Get back to mixing those egg whites before I poke a hole right through you!' said Cook, before disappearing through another door.

Sarah slumped to the scrubbed kitchen table. *My headache must be worse than I thought; now I'm hallucinating.*

But if she *was* hallucinating, it was vivid, especially the scent of burning bread. *Burning bread?* Sarah looked up to see plumes of smoke billowing from the coal range. In a panic, she searched for anything she could use to open the door. Grabbing the nearest cloth-white and heavily starched and wrapped it around her hand to wrench the range door open. Smoke poured out as she reached inside to remove the charred remains of a loaf of bread.

Feeling proud of herself, she turned to place the burnt loaf on the table, only to find three strange faces staring back: Cook; an uptight older man in a severe black suit; and a handsome young man with a trace of a smile.

The heat of the loaf seeped through the linen cloth, burning her hand and jolting her back to the present. Not her *normal* present, which was in a cluttered, musty antique shop, but her current, peculiar present in this kitchen, somewhere in the late 1800s.

'Betsy!' the woman screamed at her. 'The tablecloth! Oh my Lord, what *have* you done?'

'Cook, is that the bread for supper? See that this is rectified.'

With that, Mr Sutcliffe, the disapproving gentleman in black, wheeled on his polished shoes and left the room.

Sarah or "Betsy", as she was being addressed, collapsed sobbing to the table, muttering through her tears about her headache, that she didn't know where she was, how everything was so confusing, clutching her head with one hand and the ruined tablecloth with the other hand.

The two remaining strangers exchanged startled glances. After passing the burnt bread to the young man who'd witnessed the melodrama, Cook bathed her burnt hand, muttering soothing words. After several minutes, she encouraged Sarah to her feet, guiding her from the room.

Cook escorted Sarah upstairs and down the corridor to a bedroom, removed her sensible sturdy black boots, and placed her into bed, laying a light eiderdown over her.

'You rest, young lady, and if you are no better by breakfast tomorrow, we'll call for the doctor,' said Cook, as she left Sarah alone in the room, lit only by a high window leaching watery sunlight onto the scrubbed wooden floor.

THE MAID

*S*everal hours later, after a dreamless sleep, Sarah raised her head, conscious of the saggy mattress, to take in the solid functional furniture, and the complete absence of anything she recognised. *Except, perhaps, for that chair in the corner. Haven't I seen that somewhere? Heavy green velvet, the colour of spongy moss under an oak tree.* Yes, she was sure she'd seen it amongst the furniture her haulage company had picked up from Elizabeth Williams' estate, the one the mixing bowl and postcards had come from.

Sarah buried her head into the starched pillowcase. Where was she? What had happened, a blood clot in the brain? There was no way she could be living this life, in this time. She felt transported back a hundred years.

Bracing herself to investigate her new reality, she slipped out from under the covers. Up on tiptoes, she peeked out of the window. The cityscape she saw was not the one she walked through on her way to the local markets every weekend. She gaped open-mouthed at the scene outside — carriages, ladies in long skirts, men with black hats, and smoke from a thousand chimneys. She screwed her eyes shut, rubbed them and caressed her aching head, before opening her eyes and taking a second look. The view hadn't changed. If she were to describe what she saw, she'd have said it was a scene from one of Charles Dickens' novels. His original work, not a Hollywood adaptation.

What *had* she gotten herself into? She swallowed with difficulty as she viewed old London with her modern eyes. Her fear overshadowing the miracle of her transition.

'Oh!' she screamed, before clamping a hand over her open mouth.

All the pennies in England dropped. *Mum and Dad! This must be what happened to them.* Her heart sang with joy. For although she'd refused to believe either of her parents had run off or committed suicide, there was that tiny locked door in everyone's mind behind which they keep their darkest thoughts. And in that hidden place, she'd harboured an absolute fear that her parents had abandoned her because she was a disappointment to them both. But this extraordinary turn of events must have been how they disappeared. They must be *here*, somewhere!

She leapt out of her saggy bed, flushed with joy, her rose-tinted glasses on her face. It was through these she caught sight of an embroidered sampler on the wall. She touched the fine thread-work, awed by such a beautiful piece. She only ever saw the faded, damaged ones at work. The best ones never made it to her store; they went straight to the big auction houses.

Her excitement over finding her parents pushed to one side. The curse of being an antique dealer; even the smallest treasure can sidetrack the thrill of the chase, the fleeting possibility of that one find to eclipse all others — to become the stuff of legend in the circles in which she travelled. This sampler was an absolute masterpiece — a short bible passage with detailed plant and animal illustrations, dated and with the name of the embroiderer: 'R. J. Williams. 19th of June 1726'.

She knew other antique dealers had contacts in the Victoria & Albert Museum who would pay thousands of pounds for a piece like this. Museum people never set foot in *her* little shop, but calling them with a query...

If only she could take it home. If there was a way home. Her father would've known the perfect person to sell to for the best price; he'd been such a wheeler-dealer. The familiar prickle of tears when she thought of her father did not appear, no doubt due to the certainty she was about to bump into him in this grand house the minute she left the room. Meanwhile, she'd just examine the embroidery a bit closer.

Sarah lifted the frame from the wall, certain that it wasn't the original frame, more like someone had tried to make the sampler fit the frame, and not *vice versa*. Larger than average and tacked to the back of the oak frame. Easy enough to remove the embroidery to see if there were further illustrations hidden by the ill-fitting frame. Sarah pulled the tacks out to examine it further.

Footsteps in the hall made her jump.

'What *am* I doing?' she muttered under her breath.

She thrust the frame back onto its hook and, with no time to return the sampler to its original home, she thrust it deep into her skirt pocket. Guiltily, she realised she was considering stealing from people she didn't know, from a time where she didn't belong.

A gentle tap-tap-tap pulled Sarah into the 1800s 'present'. Crossing a colourful rag rug, she opened the door, the rolled-up sampler digging into her thigh. Sarah prayed Cook wouldn't notice the empty frame behind the door. However, Cook had no reason to come into the room so Sarah's dalliance with the sampler remained undetected, for now.

'Right then, I suggest you make yourself presentable. We have important guests arriving this afternoon and you must be immaculate, or Sutcliffe will make both our lives miserable. You're late and I've already covered for you this morning, which I won't be doing again unless you're at death's door, if he'd even have you. Now quick smart.' Cook turned and hurried down the narrow corridor.

Sarah closed the simple white door, leaning her forehead against the wall. On the washstand in the corner was a robust china jug and basin. Her professional side refrained from checking the underside of the jug for the maker's mark, although tempted. She poured water from the jug into the basin, splashing some onto her face as she decided to use this nightmare as a learning experience. Something to be used in her work. The Victorians had something for everything, and half the time she was clueless about what things were for. Google and all world's reference books were no substitute for living in the Victorian era.

In a chest of drawers, she found a clean shirt identical to the one she had on and changed. There was nothing she could do about the creases in her apron and skirt, apart from hoping they'd fall out before she found the kitchen. She was certain she'd find her parents before there was any need to worry about flaws in her uniform.

Sarah spied her, or "Betsy's", black leather boots, and pulled them on. She took a punt whether to turn left or right down the uncarpeted hallway, and turned left, which always worked in those frustrating tourist mazes dotted around England.

Following the sound of voices, she found a short flight of stairs leading down to the kitchen. Thankful she'd passed her first test, she paused just before the doorway to the kitchen to examine the tableau inside. At the floured bench with her strong arms was Cook, her white hair pinned out of the way. At the large pine table sat the inscrutable Mr Sutcliffe, reading the paper and sipping tea from a china cup, his shoes polished within an inch of their lives. Another girl, dressed the same as Sarah, sat perched at the end of the table, mending the shoulder seam of a gentleman's coat. Alas, no sign of her parents. Sarah debated whether she should ask if they were there when Sutcliffe noticed her in the doorway.

'Ah, Betsy, you've joined us. You inconvenienced us all by your absence this morning. Young Adelaide undertook your duties besides her own,' he said.

'Dinna fret, Betsy, I know ye'd do the same for me,' Adelaide, the other maid, said in a broad Scottish accent. 'Are ye feeling better now?'

'Yes, thanks for covering for me.' Sarah replied, wondering if her modern accent would give her away as an impostor.

'Sit down, sit down,' Cook fussed, plonking a cup of tea in front of her.

'We have lots to do before her Ladyship's guests arrive. The parlour must look perfect, and you'll help Adelaide with the tea things. We need you in top form, so no more headaches or mistakes. This afternoon is to gauge if the woman visiting is suitable for our young Lord. We can't do anything to ruin the impression her Ladyship is trying to make. The girl has an immense fortune behind her as an only child, but she's not quite from the right family. Oh, but the money! Her Ladyship hardly knows what to do.'

Flustered by the importance of the afternoon tea guests, Cook rambled, flour flying all over the kitchen as she punctuated the important points with energetic arm waving.

'Gossiping like a scullery maid? As if the daughter of a *trader* is suitable for Lord Grey. Your efforts in the kitchen will not make Lady Grey change her mind about that,' sneered Sutcliffe, brushing specks of flour from his suit as he left the room with a look of distaste on his face.

Shocked into silence by Sutcliffe's outburst, it would be the only time Sarah would ever see Cook silent.

'Well, I never!' Cook spluttered. 'This family needs the money more than it needs to keep its family line pure by marrying only titled folk. I never...'

Cook muttered away as she disappeared into the depths of the scullery.

Sarah looked at Adelaide, who sat nonplussed at the table. Adelaide smiled. 'They never change do they? Ye'd think us all for the poorhouse, the way Cook carries on. Och, I know the old Lord Grey lost a deal of their money, but *really*, they're not destitute, are they? They could sell off one of their houses or some silver. I'm so sick of polishing it, anyway. The old lady will give her approval, he'll marry the girl, the lucky thing! And the family's future will be safe. Beggars canna be choosers. Right, I'm off upstairs. I'll meet you in the parlour, after ye've finished yer tea.'

Sarah sat alone in the kitchen, considering her current fate as "Betsy". She worked for a titled family, but down-at-heel, which explains why she'd only counted four servants, including herself. Maybe five-the young man she'd seen the day before, but perhaps only a tradesman, as she hadn't seen him today. Nor had she heard the others refer to him. There had been an elder Lord Grey, but he was dead, leaving behind a Lady Grey and a young Lord Grey. Old enough to marry though. And now she was to clean house and serve afternoon tea to an eligible daughter of a wealthy trader. As far removed from selling antiques as you could get.

Carrying her cup to the sink, she wondered how much of the crockery had been through *The Old Curiosity Shop*. So much of it seemed familiar, albeit newer and in better condition! Sarah rinsed her cup, leaving it on the draining rack and headed in the same direction as Adelaide, hoping she'd be able to navigate her way through the house without running into Lord or Lady Grey, unless they were her parents...

POSTCARD #3

21/9/40

Dear Phil

You'll never guess what's happened here. An Indian man has opened a wee shop in the village. It smells so divine, but so many people are appalled (not me).

His name is Mr Singh. He has a wife, but I haven't met her yet.

Have you met anyone exciting in your adventures yet?

If you meet any Indians, can you ask them if they know Mr Singh in the village? He's almost as famous as the King I expect now!

Stay safe.

B xxx

THE STUDY

*H*er efforts in finding her way to Adelaide and the parlour was an exercise in art appreciation, and a 'How To' guide for home decor enthusiasts. Lady Grey's home was *beautiful*. Pure elegance and simplicity, the art more suited to the National Portrait Gallery than to the walls of a private home. Heavy gilt frames filled with lifelike oil paintings hung above occasional tables groaning under ornate bouquets of lilies and roses spilling from priceless Lalique glass vases.

Sarah imagined the set dressers for *Downton Abbey* could have used this home as the blueprint for their show. She'd been lucky to sell pieces to ITV for their programme, and she always got a tiny thrill when she caught sight of her writing box on the show, or the inkstand in the study. Those were from her shop. Not valuable, but mentioning it to her customers always pleased her, and it gave the shop a dash more credibility.

She was so busy taking in the art she tripped over a kneeling Adelaide as she rounded the corner. Both girls lay giggling in a tangled heap on the parquet floor, Adelaide's polishing cloth abandoned at the bottom of the staircase. They'd both been so startled when they'd fallen that they'd screamed, before dissolving into fits of laughter and, with the high ceilings and uncarpeted hall, the sound amplified, travelling further than it should.

Their cries brought a pair of thundering boots down the stairs, and the sound of a man yelling in surprise as his foot slipped on the polishing cloth, leaving a dishevelled young man prostrate on the floor next to Adelaide and Sarah.

'Oh!' he exclaimed, shaking his head to dispel the shock of finding himself on the floor. Laughing, he leapt up and offered his hand to pull the girls to their feet. Sarah reached up and grabbed his hand.

'Thank you. Imagine if Lady Grey found us! What would she have thought? You, cavorting with the maids at the bottom of the stairs!' she chuckled.

She smoothed her skirt, laughing at the ridiculous picture in her mind, not noticing that Adelaide hadn't taken up the offer of his gentlemanly hand.

Adelaide scrambled up, averting her eyes.

'Sorry, sir,' she whispered, trembling as she picked up her cloth, tears threatening to escape her eyes.

'Adelaide,' he said in an exasperated voice, 'You do not have to treat me the way my father expected the staff to treat him. We've known each other since we were children, we are friends. It's nothing, don't worry. See, even Betsy has transitioned to the new style. Why, Betsy, I swear your turn yesterday must have knocked sense into that head of yours, now you're capable of talking instead of treating me like the Pope, all that bowing and scraping. So wearisome, enough to drive one mad.'

Sarah's eyes widened. *This must be the young Lord Grey. He* had been the young man in the kitchen yesterday who'd seen her incident with the bread, and now he'd fallen at her feet at the bottom of the staircase, and here she was making smart comments. Why she'd ended up as the maid Betsy in old London was beyond her comprehension, but making Betsy a more confident and outgoing one would not end well.

'Oh, well, um, so sorry about your fall. I think Adelaide and I have to finish the parlour before, um, before your fiancée arrives…'

'My what? I think not.'

Lord Grey's face turned to stone. The happiness and light gone from his eyes.

'You carry on, I need to speak with my mother. As I've told her before, I will marry whoever I choose.'

With that, he ran up the stairs, disappearing from sight around the curve at the top.

Adelaide's tears spilled over.

'Oh, why did you say that, Betsy? Why?'

Adelaide scurried away, leaving only her sobs behind. Sarah stood puzzled. Putting her foot in it seemed par for the course, and if she didn't watch her words, they'd fire her, cast her out into the world without the safety net of a job or a family to help her. She was so ill-prepared for making it on her own in nineteenth century England, she was sure she'd starve to death if they fired her. What she *needed* to do was find her parents. Every girl needs her dad, regardless of how old she is, or which century she's in.

Following Adelaide, she committed to keeping her mouth shut, until she found her parents. No more modern-day curses or uncomfortable comments. She'd be mute, except where politeness required her to comment. Do her job, with no laughing or pulling frames off the walls or checking makers' marks on the bottom of chinaware, just be *Betsy*. Her safest course of action was to shelve *Sarah* until she found a way home.

She opened the first door she came to, expecting it to be the parlour. She stepped through, and found herself in a wood-panelled study, not the parlour, with no sign of Adelaide.

With lush curtains pulled tight against the morning sunshine, protecting the books lining three of the walls, a giant roll-top desk took centre stage, gleaming with years of polish rubbed into the grain. There were four museum-quality display cases placed equidistant around the room. Interest overtook caution, negating her decision of only moments ago to shelve Sarah and to be Betsy, as she peered into the nearest cabinet.

She didn't imagine Betsy the maid *ever* examining the contents. But Sarah had a natural curiosity, kindled by her father's love of everything old and *potentially* valuable.

There, nestled in velvet hollows, sat a pair of jewelled Indian *katar* — daggers, often referred to as 'tiger knives'. She'd seen them come up for auction when she'd worked as a cataloguer but never a pair, and never of this quality. At first glance, they appeared identical, but on closer examination, she saw the engraving on the two hilts was complementary. *The red stones must be rubies* - and the inscribed scenes on the blades were stunning. *Imagine the worth of these now,* she pondered. They were genuine tiger knives from the sixteenth century, not the replicas made for English tourists two centuries later.

Sarah tried lifting the cabinet's locked lid. With no consideration of the consequences if they caught her, she ferreted through the little drawers of the desk, looking for the key. Her efforts rewarded a short time later, for in the third drawer was a tiny brass key in an ebony box.

Sarah slipped the key into the lock of the cabinet; it fit like a silk glove over a lady's hand. It gave a satisfying pop, and she lifted the lid. Without the glass distorting the luminosity of the stones, they glowed with old warmth, tantalising her with the tales they could tell, if only they had a voice. The precious stones themselves were valuable, but here, set in the old *katars*, their value became immeasurable.

Sarah lifted one out, marvelling at the perfect balance of the dagger. She ran her finger along the intricate engraving, following the line of what she presumed to be the Ganges River, alongside which were depictions of tigers and elephants along the riverbank, trailed by monkeys. The engraving from one *katar* spilled over to the second. Each illustration complete in itself but both together told the complete story. Not an illustration she was familiar with; Saakshi, her friend from university, would know — she'd have to ask her, *if* she ever got back to England, *her* England...

Sarah was so intent on admiring the fine engraving, she did not notice the door opening, until a shaft of light from the hall fell onto the desk. In fright, she dropped the *katar* onto the Persian rug which muffled the thud of the weapon as it landed.

'Lost something?' a man's voice queried.

To her immense good fortune, the back of the desk shielded the cabinet from the doorway, so the fact it was open was not obvious. After recovering from the shock, she straightened, and closing the cabinet she replied, 'I was cleaning the study.'

At the door stood a man unknown to her. He entered the room, looking around as if for the first time. As he stood with his back to her, surveying the bookshelves, Sarah knelt to retrieve the dagger, concealing it behind her skirts, willing the stranger to disappear.

'I'm surprised you're in here,' he said. 'Father never allowed servants in here when he was alive, unless he himself was in here to supervise, just in case one of you pilfered his treasures or damaged these damn books of his.'

Sarah moved towards the desk, hoping for an opportunity to slip the dagger under the paperwork. What response should a trusted housemaid give? She scrambled in her mind for something suitable to say.

He moved towards her.

'Come now, Betsy, you know you're not allowed in here. What are you doing, snooping? Or were you looking for money?' He laughed.

'As if my father would ever leave his money unguarded, my brother even less so. Well then, Betsy, you like your job here, don't you? You've been here a long time, it's time we got to know each other better, don't you think? Come to Benjamin, now. I want us to be friends.'

Benjamin moved nearer, close enough that the stench of stale alcohol reached Sarah before he did. With unexpected speed, his eyes bright with alcohol and desire, he grabbed her hand, bringing it up to his lips, crushing her fingers with his brutish ones.

Extricating herself from his grasp proved harder than expected.

She'd still not said anything, worried about her position in the house, and her future self. What if he raped her here, what on earth could she do? You didn't 'go to the police' in those days. As the maid, the fault would be laid firmly at her door. She tried twisting away, just his other arm circled round her waist, pulling her closer to him, his bristles rasping against her skin as he nuzzled her neck.

Her position would be worse if he found her with the dagger, meaning she couldn't use both her hands to stop him, encouraging him further.

'Please stop, please, please stop' Sarah begged, pulling away from his clumsy embrace. 'Stop, stop, stop,' she repeated over and over, the volume increasing with each desperate utterance.

Trapped against the desk, Benjamin thrust himself against her, his grip cutting the circulation in her hand, which he held tighter than Croesus held onto his riches. With his other hand, he fumbled with her skirts, which were plentiful and voluminous, and he was finding it difficult to navigate them one-handed. With a satisfied grunt, he found what he was looking for, his bloodshot eyes smiling at the thought of imminent conquest.

Sarah screamed, and swung her free hand towards him, the one still holding the *katar*. With a satisfying thwack, it collided with his head and Benjamin crumpled to the ground, like a soggy cardboard box giving up its usefulness. Sarah scuttled to the other side of the desk, plunging the *katar* deep into her pocket, stifling her sobs with her free hand.

The study door swung open with a crash. Lord Grey stood there with a thunderous look on his face, making clear his feelings about the scene confronting him.

'Out!' he barked at Sarah, leaving no room for misinterpretation.

Sarah sidled out past Lord Grey, but not before he stopped her to inspect her face, noting her tears and the fear in her eyes. His face softened, and he moved aside to let her pass. He entered the study, closing the door behind him.

Sarah stopped to look at the door. Whatever was happening in there, she wanted no part. She feared Benjamin Grey didn't take rejection well.

She opened the next door she came to - the parlour. Adelaide had afternoon tea laid out, and the room was immaculate. A short rest was what she needed before facing the rest of the day, she thought, collapsing into one of the delicate Chippendale chairs.

POSTCARD #4

1/11/40

Dear Phil
It seems like you only just left, yet so many things have changed since you've been gone.
The dressmaker has closed up. She couldn't get any new fabric in. So we're all going to get together and do some swapping of clothes and unused fabric. I'm not sure that I can even remember how to sew.
Winter has really set in, so I'm not out and about too much.
Stay safe.
B xxx

THE FRIEND

*A*s Sarah sat on the Chippendale chair, giant pliers squeezed her head, the blinding pain making her moan in agony. Rough hands shook her shoulders.

'Sarah, Sarah, are you OK? Can you hear me? Sarah, wake up, please! Shall I call an ambulance? Sarah…'

Sarah opened her eyes. Lines of shelves stuffed with books filled her vision. This wasn't the parlour. She closed her eyes, shook her head, and opened them again. She was back in her shop. Her closest friend, Patricia Bolton, shaking her awake. Friends and neighbours since Patricia had taken the lease next door to showcase her own fashion label, Blackpool Love, Patricia was a minor fashion celebrity-thanks to photos of 'A' list celebrities wearing her clothes appearing in the national gossip magazines.

'Are you OK? I've never seen you asleep on the job. You're just asking for a robbery! My God, how many people came in with you asleep? Is anything missing?'

The words tumbled out of Patricia's mouth, tripping over each other as her head swung from side to side looking for evidence of a robbery.

Sarah took her hands away from her head, half expecting the shooting pain to return. She looked at Patricia and laughed.

'Oh, Patricia, I can't believe I fell asleep either. You'll never believe the dream I had. It was so vivid! I could taste the flour and the heat of the fire was so real. I've no idea of the time. What's the time?'

Sarah stood up and tried to focus on the only modern thing in the shop, a wall clock decorated, ironically enough, with pictures of Victorian children's toys. Patricia stood staring at her, lipstick-painted mouth wide open. Sarah waved her hands in front of Patricia's face.

'Patricia, hello? What's the time? My clock has stopped. Must need new batteries. Hello?'

Still gaping fishlike, Patricia answered, 'It's four o'clock. But seriously, what *are* you wearing? Where did you get that glorious shirt? Who made it? You promised you'd only spend your money on my clothes!'

Patricia Bolton was a fantastic seamstress, and a genius pattern designer, but she'd never seen such quality cotton before, hand-done. She fingered the fabric of Sarah's shirt, caressing it as you would a newborn chick.

Sarah moved in front of a Georgian hall stand, old water damage rendering it impossible to sell. In the cloudy mirror, she saw her reflection dressed in a buttoned, white cotton shirt and a long, black skirt. She touched the wispy bits of hair escaping from old bobby pins and ran her hands over her hips, stopping after feeling a bulky lump in her skirt. Shocked into silence by the Victorian outfit, Sarah couldn't believe it when she put her hand in her pocket and brushed over the *katar*, and there underneath, the sampler.

'Where. Did. You. Get. That. Shirt. From?' Patricia demanded.

Thinking quickly, Sarah replied, 'It was in a trunk of goods from that last estate I cleared. You know, the Elizabeth Williams one. It looked my size, so I thought I'd try it on.'

'Wow. She must have had a wonderful wardrobe. When you aren't doing your Mary Poppins impersonation in the shop, can I borrow it? I want to copy the pattern. I've just had the best idea for my next collection. It will amaze everyone! I'll use stuff from your shop as props, we'll make the showroom all Victorian, ivy everywhere, big vases, candles. I'll invite all the names. It'll be huge on the Net. I'll get someone to live blog it, put it on Twitter, everything!'

Sarah laughed and put her finger on Patricia's lips.

'Hush! You're talking too fast! Yes you can have the shirt. I was just playing dress-ups and got carried away. The skirt, too and you can use anything from my shop you need. Put together a list and I'll set it all aside. But you're getting ahead of yourself, you need to design the clothes before you plan the runway show!'

Patricia wasn't listening — she was already designing her collection, with the shirt as inspiration.

Sarah took Patricia by the shoulders and steered her out of the shop.

'I'll get some sleep, then I'll wash it and drop it over to you tomorrow. I'm just tired. Falling asleep at work was stupid and I promise not to do it again!'

Patricia, lost in her own world, waved, and skipped into her own shop, the bells above its door tinkling.

Sarah shut her own door, and switched the sign to 'Closed', pushing home the deadbolt. Living above the shop had its advantages — quick locking up, and even faster getting home-through the rear door and up to her flat. Sarah headed upstairs in a daze and sat on her kitset couch. She laughed, amused at how bizarre it would be if she turned up in the middle of a production line in Sweden. Nothing happened other than something digging into her thigh.

'Argh.'

She leapt up, trying to find the pocket in her skirt to retrieve the *katar* and rescue the precious embroidery. *Far too much fabric for one skirt.*

Her hand found the opening, and she withdrew the weapon and sampler, which had escaped unscathed from its close encounter with the blade. Heart fluttering, she laid out the sampler on the coffee table, smoothing it with trembling fingers. The colours were gemlike, with a deep iridescent glow identical to the rubies embedded in the katar's hilt, which lay ignored on the other side of the table. Such tiny stitches. So perfect, and valuable.

Sarah moved the lamp closer to the table. She had to take photos of the embroidery and needed better light. She grabbed her Canon from the sideboard and shot a series of photographs. In her mind, she'd sold the sampler through Christie's, or to the V&A, or the British Museum. She'd already mentally spent the money from the sale -a replacement shop counter the priority, followed by a new sign-written van. Duct tape was the only thing holding her old van together. A good-looking vehicle could only help to improve her reputation around town as a serious dealer, instead of just a girl who'd inherited her father's business.

She loaded the photos onto her laptop, picked the better ones, and fired off quick emails from her personal account to textile departments at Christie's, Sotheby's and Bonham's asking them to get back to her if they were interested in auctioning the piece for her. The emails contained minimal information about herself as she didn't want her job to influence their replies. She slipped the sampler between the pages of the huge world atlas she'd won as the Geography Prize in her last year at school. It was the only book big enough to hold the whole piece flat.

And now the *katar*. This was a different story. How could she sell just one when somewhere its twin existed? No antique dealer would split up a pair. She'd never meant to take it, to split it from its twin. She'd broken an unwritten antique dealer's rule. It was akin to owning a pair of Ming Dynasty vases, and giving one away, decimating the value. But had time lessened the impact of separating the pair?

Sarah kneeled at the table, chin in her hands as she considered what to do with the knife. It was valuable, more valuable than the sampler. More desirable. She'd auction that too, she didn't want to keep it - the memory of what Benjamin Grey tried to do to her still raw. But which auction house? Christie's was better, given their worldwide network. They'd have wealthy Indian collectors on their books, and the usual institutions who'd bid high for something so unique.

She picked up the *katar* and started photographing it. The photos showed in perfect detail the engraving of the monkeys. Sarah's judgement was clouded and couldn't wrap itself around having committed a crime. While *technically* she'd stolen from the home of Lord Grey, is a theft which occurred over a hundred years ago still a theft? The only time she'd stolen something before was when she was seven — a packet of thumbtacks from the local hardware store with a friend. She'd felt so guilty, not only had she thrown them away before getting home, but she'd been in such a state she'd thrown up, and confessed everything to her horrified mother. The next morning, her mother had marched her back to apologise and to pay for the tacks. The mortification enough to make sure she never stole again, until now.

Sarah took off Betsy's clothes, folding them carefully as she realised she'd have to hand wash them — no point trusting the launderette with such quality garments. She needed a shower and bed. The practicalities of how she became someone called Betsy, in London in the 1800s, wearing clothes that weren't hers, and being assaulted by the brother of a Lord, were too fantastical for her to process until after a decent sleep.

She loaded the photos into a carefully worded email to Christie's Auctions in London and hit the 'Send' button. In her haste to get it off before the close of business, she clicked on the tab for the Costumes and Textiles Department instead of Indian and South-East Asian Art.

A mistake of no clear consequence…

POSTCARD #5

22/6/41

Dear Phil
Sad news from home, I'm afraid. The Quilp brothers from next door are both
reported as missing in action. Missing is better than killed, I suspect, but Mrs
Quilp does not agree.
I'm sitting at Father's desk writing this. It has the best natural light for writing.
I've lost count of the number of postcards I've written at this desk now. I pray
each day that they have all found their way to you.
Stay safe.
B xxx

THE LORD

*L*ord Edward Grey seized his brother by the shoulders, pulling his unconscious form off the floor. Disgusted, he threw him down again, and running his fingers through his sandy hair, he slumped into the chair in front of his father's desk. Correction, *his* desk now; Edward was having difficulty coming to terms with his new position, and his familial responsibilities. He slammed his hand against the wood.

'I should have left you in India to rot. That's all you're good for,' he addressed his prone brother.

The two brothers stayed in the study, one conscious, the other not, their bond damaged even further. Threads frayed by the trouble in India were now giving way one by one. Today's antics had broken another of those threads. How their relationship could recover from the damage caused by his brother's behaviour, Edward was uncertain, but he couldn't let him harm the family's reputation any longer.

Benjamin stirred on the carpet, moaning. Edward, who'd been perusing his father's papers, paused, stood up, and leant over the desk. Benjamin's face contorted in pain, but Edward had no sympathy for what had happened to him. The maid had delivered a just punishment to his brother, and it was a far better result than what could have happened to her.

'Jesus Christ!' came an exclamation from the floor, as Benjamin pushed himself into a sitting position, pain sending a thousand shooting stars into his skull. He probed his head gingerly, fingers brushing over a swelling the size of the Pyramids. After making it to his feet, he caught sight of his brother at the desk.

'Oh, it's you. You could've given a chap a hand, instead of leaving me on the floor.'

'So tell me, Benjamin, what put you there?' grimaced Edward.

'That little tart. Mother will fire her; can't have the likes of her working for the likes of us. Hussy. She's always fancied me. You should have seen her throw herself at me and I fell against the desk when she accosted me,' explained the other, with all the innocence in the world.

'Mother won't be doing anything of the sort, Benjamin. The likelihood of her believing your fabricated story is negligible. You'll stay away from Betsy, or the only person being thrown out of this house will be *you*. I'll see that the Army takes you back, regardless of your last performance. For Christ's sake, Ben, you're a Grey — behave like one, instead of a heathen from the colonies.'

Edward stalked around the desk until he was standing face-to-face with his brother.

'If you cause Mother any more grief, I'll march you to the closest Navy vessel I can find and, so help me, regardless of where it's going, you'll be on it!'

With that he left the study, slamming the door behind him.

Minutes later, Benjamin slunk out of the study. Neither brother had noticed the space in the display cabinet where the *katar* had, until recently, lain next to its mate.

THE HEIR

After leaving his brother in the study, Edward sought his mother. He found her with their housekeeper in the dining room planning the week's meals, and fine-tuning the serving of afternoon tea for his future fiancée and her aunt.

Standing in the doorway, he could tell his mother was not the same woman she'd been before his father died. The late Lord Grey kept the exact nature of their financial woes to himself, no doubt certain he'd be able to gamble the family out of debt. But after his death the creditors came calling, throwing his mother into complete turmoil. Although not incapable of understanding finance, his father never considered it a woman's place to handle money. He'd allowed her to spend it, but, outside of the day-to-day running costs of the household, she never knew how he came by it, nor how he spent it. And she was oblivious to the gargantuan debt into which he'd gambled the family.

Edward had watched his mother turn the creditors away at the door, instructing them to put their demands in writing. Taken aback at her cool demeanour, they'd left her in peace for longer than most. That grace period was over and letters of demand piled up on his desk.

His mother, unable to meet any bills without selling off the family's holdings, had seized upon the idea of marrying him into money.

Seeing her flustered over which porcelain to use for entertaining a potential wife tore at his heart and he cursed his father. For most of Edward's life, he assumed he'd marry a nice girl from a titled family. But most noble households needed money too, to support their vast estates and crumbling mansions, and his family had none. So, they needed to marry him off to a trader's daughter to secure a future for his mother and to save their family name. Selling her beloved house or jewels would kill her. He could see that now.

He walked into the dining room, put his arms around her, and planted a kiss on her head. Surprised, she turned around and, unnaturally for her, returned his hug. The housekeeper, Mrs Phillips, barely concealed her surprise at this display of affection, and turned away, busying herself with refolding the folded napkins.

'Thank you, Mother,' he said, and left the room. His thoughts of chastising her for arranging his marriage quashed by thoughts of the greater good of the family.

Returning to his room, he sat in his leather button-back chair by the window, brooding over the day's events. His brother was a problem and getting further out of hand. He berated himself for involving himself in the 'India trouble'. If he hadn't intervened, his brother would be of no concern. He felt his responsibilities as the eldest child acutely and ignoring Benjamin's troubles had not been an option.

As Lord Henry Grey's heir, he'd lived a charmed life. He'd graduated from the Royal Military Academy at Sandhurst, earning his officer's commission. His rank had been hard-earned, not bought like so many of the commissions of older officers serving above him.

Though his service was during a time of peace in England, his regiment deployed to India where he saw action during minor skirmishes along what would later become the border between India and a new country, Pakistan. Respected by his subordinates, and his superior officers, his valour at the battle at Nilt Nagar saw him awarded a Victoria Cross for his bravery.

The only stain on his record was because of the actions of his brother. An alcoholic reprobate like their father, Benjamin Grey followed his brother into the army, primarily because there were insufficient funds to support his penchant for whoring, drinking, and gambling. In one of their father's more lucid moments, he'd instructed his youngest son to join the army or face being disinherited. Benjamin Grey, while lacking the finer social graces of his elder brother, realised that a firstborn son and heir undertaking active military service overseas might never make it home to take up his inheritance. That was enough of an incentive for him to agree to join. Ben expected the British army to face little conflict, and so his chances of seeing active service were low. That was until his regiment also deployed to India.

While both brothers were in India, they'd had nothing to do with each other. They were in different regiments; Edward was away with the 5th Gurkha Rifles at the border with Pakistan, and Benjamin weaselled his way into a cushy position with the Indian Staff Corps, where he supplemented his income by selling army supplies to the locals on the side — an activity for which he avoided detection for most of his service.

It wasn't just black market rifles and provisions which tarnished the Grey name; it was Benjamin's after-hours activities with Indian women that saw him subject to a court martial, with the potential outcome of the death penalty. Selling weapons to rebels and raping the daughters of the locals was not acceptable for a member of the British army.

Granted immediate leave by his commanding officer, Edward Grey made his way to Calcutta to help his brother. Their father had, during his prime, been an influential man in the House of Lords, and many senior officers of the Indian Army were personal friends. Through his written intervention from London, and Edward Grey's reputation, the army spared Benjamin Grey's life. Stripped of his commission, Benjamin received a flogging, the staggering number of fifty lashes-the maximum allowed.

The stain on their family made their father lean on the bottle, with his demise following swiftly. The new Lord Grey returned to London to his new position and responsibilities. Returning with him was his disgraced younger brother, dishonourably discharged.

THE EMAIL

*S*arah woke from a pleasant dream of her appearing on *Antiques Roadshow* with rare silverware from a Royal estate in the seventeenth century. She took a while to wake, and snuggled under the covers with a smile, wallowing in the remnants of her illusion. When she surfaced, the pile of folded Victorian clothes at the end of her bed, the first thing she saw.

With unusual speed, she showered and dressed in her more practical jeans, a plain white cotton shirt, and a pair of ballet flats. She vaulted down the stairs, two at a time, grateful her customers never had to ascend them, as the old threadbare carpet had worn right through, showing the original flathead tacks that had held it in place for years. *I must replace it when I've got some spare cash.* She grinned to herself as she considered the sale of the *katar* — that might give her enough money to do everything she'd wanted for so long. Even when her parents worked here, these stairs were a potential death trap. She suspected most of the carpet had worn away even before her parents had lived above the shop in the Seventies.

Flicking on the lights, she half expected to be back in Betsy's kitchen, but no, the shop was just as she had left it — just as her father had left it to her: piles of unpriced goods on the counter; boxes of uncatalogued stock tottering on the floor, reminiscent of haphazard Roman ruins.

Her stomach complained at its emptiness. Sarah stepped around everything and left the shop on a mission to the bakery across the road.

With a steaming takeaway cappuccino and a sticky bun-her absolute favourite, Sarah slipped behind the counter, with the battered 'Closed' sign still on the door. She needed to get this stuff priced up for the weekend rush, but hesitation stayed her hand.

A gifted procrastinator, she checked her emails, 'just in case' an answer had arrived from one of the auction houses. She logged on, and bingo, one *actual* email hidden amongst spam messages offering 'Help With Marketing', 'Sexy Housewives', and 'Penis Enlargements'.

Dear Miss Lester,

Thank you for your email. We have contacted some of our clients who collect such examples and have at least three interested parties.

If you could let us know your address, we can dispatch one of our specialists to uplift the sampler which will avoid any additional stress on the threads, and the fabric itself, due to incorrect handling.

Yours sincerely,

Andrew Harvard

Senior Specialist Costumes and Textiles

Christie's

The cheek, she thought. *'Incorrect handling'.* What rubbish is that? Do they think she's a novice who found something in her grandmother's attic? Her hackles rose against Andrew Harvard. *Moron.* No mention of the *katar* though. Odd.

Sarah slammed shut her laptop, making a mental note to reply to *Mr* Harvard tonight. They sounded interested, but after his condescending email, *he* could wait. *That'll make his private clients anxious,* she grinned.

With a fluttering heart, she pulled the postcards out of the mixing bowl. She planned to sort them into chronological order before she opened for business. It didn't take long because there were a number from other people mixed in with those signed 'B'. The postcards needed categorising and pricing, after which the aficionados would pore over them, the compulsive collectors, each looking for those special cards to fill the gaps in their collections. Half were unused. Even back in the day, good intentions to write to friends and family failed.

There were fifteen postcards addressed to 'Phil' from 'B'. Was that the extent of their relationship, she wondered? Had there been more? They were signed 'B', not 'Love, B', or 'Best Regards, B', or anything else telling, but they were full of references to love between the two correspondents. Nothing gripped Sarah more than a good love story. She often cried in movies and during poignant commercials, and now she found herself welling up over a pile of postcards.

She held one in both hands, turning it over, perhaps the front would offer more clues? It was an actual photo postcard of Salisbury Cathedral. From that she guessed 'B' could have been from Salisbury. She could have been just visiting but, for now, Sarah wanted to imagine 'B' living in the historic city. Wait! Phil's name was on the other half of the card. 'Mr P. Williams' — *these* postcards were from the Elizabeth Williams estate so was Phil related to Elizabeth Williams? Sarah needed to plot everything she knew about the Williams family to work out the relationship. She'd taken a short genealogy course after she had finished secondary school, when she thought it might help with her half-baked dream of becoming a private investigator which turned out to be a short-lived career path, given how bored she'd been during work experience with a firm in London. Following men cheating on their wives was not something she enjoyed. Still, in hindsight it was beneficial, especially now.

Signing into her favourite genealogy site, she started a family tree, plotting on it Elizabeth Williams, but didn't add Phil to the tree until she found confirmation of his place in the family. She fumbled through her paperwork looking for her purchase book, thinking she might find further information about Elizabeth Williams from the estate documents.

There weren't any *known* relatives, which was why she'd been able to bid on the complete estate, excluding house and grounds; which were being sold as separate entities. Distant relatives turned up at a deceased estate like vultures hovering over carrion, stripping a house of anything they perceived as valuable in mere moments. But in this case, the solicitor couldn't find any kin, distant or otherwise. The house itself was up for auction, now she'd emptied it of its contents. Despite dozens of boxes being packed before she'd arrived, it still took several hours to finish packing up the contents of the house and its various sheds. She'd called in a removals firm to haul off the furniture, which was going into storage until there was time to appraise it. The timeframe set by the solicitor for clearing the house had been tight, but she was sure she'd got everything, and when she came to unpack, she prayed there were treasures hidden amongst the dusty relics of Elizabeth Williams' life.

She needed to price the new stock before she mixed up the lots. The last thing she wanted was a prosecution for poor record-keeping. If she lost her Second Hand Dealer licence, she'd lose her livelihood, so she had to get things sorted.

Sarah's rational brain considered the possibility she had touched something hallucinogenic when she was sorting through the Williams estate, and in a drug-induced haze she'd dressed herself in clothes from it. That supposition held true until she remembered the exquisite piece of embroidery upstairs, nestled between the pages of the Congo and the Horn of Africa. And the *katar*, hiding in a Tupperware container in the freezer. There her theory failed.

She groaned knowing the cataloguing still needed to be done, if only to find more clues as to the identities of 'Phil' and 'B', and — a long shot — of discovering a way to her parents, if they had vanished into time the same way she had.

The first item she picked up was a battered pewter vase. It held no mysteries; it appeared English-made, and stood crooked, so not the best vase to use for a Valentine's Day rose.

'I wonder if Phil ever sent her flowers?' Sarah mused.

Maybe if he had, 'B' used a similar vase, they were as common as muck, but worthless, unless they were genuine Art Nouveau and had the magical 'WMF' mark from Germany's *Wurttembergische Metallwarenfabrik* factory, which increased the value by two hundred pounds, but, *typically*, this one didn't have the required mark. She slapped a price sticker of eighteen pounds on the base and moved it to the right-hand side of the counter — that was her system. Everything unpriced was on the left side by the old till she used, and everything priced she moved to the right side, waiting for a suitable moment when she might find a home for it on an already cluttered shelf.

The phone rang, distracting her again from her pricing.

'Good morning, *Old Curiosity Shop*, how can I help you?'

The voice on the other end was distant, and hard to hear.

'I'm sorry, it's a poor line. Can you repeat that?' Sarah said.

Often, calls were from the elderly, so she had to exercise patience on the phone. Her younger clients preferred sending emails; she'd even received texts from people wanting to sell to her.

'No, we don't trade in old televisions. I have limited space, so I try to stick to antiques-'

The woman interrupted, insisting Sarah buy her household goods.

'No, I'm sorry, I only buy *antique* furniture. No, I don't know who else might want to buy your wall unit. Sorry.'

Sarah hung up. Her advert in the local paper said she bought and sold antiques, yet that didn't stop at least one call a day from people trying to sell their old heaters, televisions, and obsolete CD players.

Now sidetracked, Sarah walked over to a battered old steamer trunk packed by the solicitor's staff, its contents a complete mystery. Anticipation was the best part of the job, and heaving open the heavy lid reminded her of plunging her hand into the lucky dip at the annual village green fete hoping something valuable was inside.

POSTCARD #6

5/1/40

Dear Phil,

The biggest news in the papers this week was the sale of the most stunning diamond necklace to help with the war effort. Forty-two diamonds, most of them larger than a sixpence. I went to the auction at Christie's, just to be able to see the necklace again. It's been wonderful how the newspapers have been describing it, all mysterious and generous.

I hope the funds help keep you all well.

Stay safe.

B xxx

THE AUCTION HOUSE

$\mathcal{A}$voiding the grand porticoed entrance at No. 8, King Street, St. James', the illustrious address of one of the world's oldest and highest profile auctioneers, Christie's International, an ordinary-looking man in his late twenties, with dark hair and pale eyes, walked past a series of elaborate window displays, showing furniture and *objets d'art* up for auction, the panes allowing tantalising glimpses of a surreal Dali hung inside, waiting for its auction.

He swiped his access card and slipped through a set of oak doors concealed from the red awning-covered frontage. This side entrance was for staff, marked by a discreet brass plaque engraved with one word, 'Christie's'. The door led to a sparse corridor and a pair of lifts. A far cry from the stark white walls in the ground floor reception, bathed in light and supporting stepped columns, leading the way across the limestone floor to a grand staircase, itself wide enough for six people to ascend side by side up to the main salerooms.

The lift took him up two floors to another unremarkable corridor, and to his office–a small, windowless room, decorated with tapestries recording various biblical scenes and studies of flora and fauna. None of the traditional Georgian features of the building remained in the offices of the minor staff, including that of Andrew Harvard, Senior Specialist — Costumes and Textiles, Christie's. A graduate from Oxford University with a degree in Fine Arts, they had offered him an internship at Christie's before he'd even completed his Masters. The only male in his class to specialise in linen and textile history, he was an anomaly in the industry.

Frustrated, he sat in front of his computer, tapping his desk with long fingers and gazing at the blown-up image on his screen of the sampler emailed to him by Sarah Lester.

'It must be a fake' he mused aloud, as he clicked through to the next image, and to the next. The colours were too bright, the fabric too perfect, marred only by four minute holes from being tacked onto a frame. He was regretting his quick reply to Sarah.

Why couldn't she reply with her address, or just courier the sampler? He needed to see it in person. The photos she'd sent through weren't high enough resolution for adequate enlargement for him to study. It was true, Christie's had at least three people on their books who collected these. He'd been hasty in contacting them and should've waited until she'd consigned the sampler to Christie's before he'd contacted any potential purchasers. *A novice's mistake*, he thought.

That was his problem. If the small cogs muck up, that affected the larger cogs, and now his supervisor wanted to see the sampler because one of the potential clients had bypassed Andrew, contacting his manager, making a pre-auction offer for it.

In vain, Andrew Harvard sat waiting for the mysterious Sarah Lester to reply to his email. 'Should have been politer,' Andrew muttered as he butted his head against the top of his computer monitor.

'Andrew?' a voice interrupted.

He looked up to see Hamish Brooke in the doorway. A pale, heavy man, dressed in the dark suit of an undertaker, whose main claim to fame, apart from his Masters in Art History, was that he was the great-grandson of a famous war hero. He was, without doubt, Andrew's closest friend at Christie's.

'Hi, Hamish, what's up?' replied Andrew.

It wouldn't do to show any hint of a problem, even to his oldest ally. Problems were not welcome at Christie's, and people who caused them never lasted long.

Hamish, not one to waste words, began:

'Don wants to see you about that Indian knife thing. They're excited. Even made Hannah head down to the archives to look through old catalogues. You know how she hates that. Nothing like it through here for years. He wanted to see you as soon as you arrived.'

Hamish waved farewell and hurried away. Sedate walking around No. 8, King Street was not the done thing.

The *katar* was of no interest to Andrew, but even he'd recognised it as a rare item. He knew little about Indian antiquities, so expected someone else in the firm to manage the acquisition. Christie's had always done well with such artefacts. Their founder, James Christie, had offered 'Four fine India pictures painted on glass' in the catalogue of his first recorded sale on the 5th of December 1766, and they'd offered prime Indian pieces for auction ever since. Andrew had forwarded Sarah's email to the Indian and South-East Asian Art Department, thinking nothing more of it, waiting instead in anticipation for the sampler to arrive.

He logged out and jogged up the internal stairs to the fourth floor; to the office of Don Claire, Senior Partner. With a deep breath, Andrew knocked on the polished wooden door. The only other time he'd stepped foot upstairs was when they'd offered him a full-time position and then it had been a short meeting. Don Claire was an imposing man; a champion diver in his youth, he towered over his employees. He'd been a policeman in the early days, specialising in investigating stolen artefacts. It was through this avenue Christie's employed him, twenty-five years earlier.

Jay Khosla opened the door, Senior Manager of the Indian Art group, a growth area of the business which had resulted in Christie's preparing to open a branch in Mumbai. The imminent Indian launch was an exciting time for the firm, winning the race against their main competitors to the newly affluent India market.

'Come in, Andrew,' said Jay in his singsong Indian accent, gesturing to the suite of Eames chairs placed in the office. Andrew lowered himself into a lounger and waited for Don Claire, who was murmuring into the telephone.

Jay and Andrew sat in silence. Spread over Don's desk were printouts of the pictures of the *katar* he'd forwarded to the Indian department earlier. When a potential seller emailed the auction house with photos of goods they wished to consign for auction, Christie's instructed them to bring it in or courier it using one of a handful of trusted courier companies. The senior management team never got involved, unless it was a glamour consignment, like Elizabeth Taylor's jewels or Wallace Simpson's estate, so it perplexed Andrew why two senior managers were so interested in a solitary Indian knife.

As the phone call ended, Don fixed his penetrating eyes on Andrew.

'Andrew, thank you for coming. We're just waiting on Hannah to return from Archives before we can get started, so while we do so, please share with us what you know.'

He steepled his fingers on the burr walnut desk and waited for Andrew's response.

Andrew flushed, cleared his throat, and considered what he could add to the conversation. The contact from Sarah Lester had been brief, with no details other than her name and email. He'd no idea why she'd chosen to mail him out of the addresses on the Christie's website.

'Well, sir, I received an email late yesterday afternoon from someone called Sarah Lester, about an embroidered sampler she was interested in selling.

'Then, an hour later, after I'd left for the day, a second email arrived from Miss Lester, this time with several photos of what appeared to be an Indian *katar* attached, which I forwarded to the Indian Art Department, via my phone, and... er... that's it.

'I replied to her first email regarding the sampler this morning, after I had contacted our key collectors to assess their level of interest.

In the email, I asked her to supply her address so we could send a courier to uplift it, but I hadn't thought to respond to her second email. I'd assumed someone from Indian Art would respond; it's not my area of expertise.'

Jay spoke up in his musical accent, the sort given by the gods to famous Bollywood actors:

'The *katar*, Andrew, is one of the rarest of its kind — immensely valuable. Many years ago, we auctioned an identical knife for what was a record amount. Hannah is trying to find the catalogue or a photo, and the sale and purchase records. As you know, they aren't all digitised, so it may be awhile before we have the precise details of the piece and the auction. This is an *exciting* moment. We are being entrusted to sell it again, which bodes well for us as a company and we *must* have it for our Indian Artefacts sale this spring. It will be the lynchpin of that sale, imagine the photograph on the front of our catalogue!'

As if by design, Hannah Gardner slipped into the room, a slim buff manila folder in her hands. She slid it onto Don's desk, and took a seat next to Jay, folding her ankles beneath her as she sat.

Don smiled at her, and caressed the top of the folder, but making no move to open it.

For clarification he asked, 'Had you ever had any other dealings with Miss Lester before her email?'

Andrew shook his head and Don continued:

'Apart from the one reply you sent, where you offered to dispatch one of our specialists to "uplift the sampler which will avoid any more stress on the threads and the fabric itself, due to incorrect handling"?

'How do you think Miss Lester may have felt, receiving that email from Christie's? For all we know, she may have a degree like yours, *Mr Harvard*. This is *not* how we respond to prospective clients. I am grateful that you replied *after* she'd emailed about the *katar* as I, for one, would never have entrusted a treasure such as this to someone who responded with such disregard for a client's potential intellect. One must *never* judge a book by its cover, Andrew.'

Andrew, who was still trying to recover from the fact that the company had been accessing his emails, sat on the chair; numb from the criticism he'd just received from the senior-most manager in London, he was at a loss for words.

Don sat silent for several moments after delivering his lecture, flicking the engraved lid of a sterling silver vesta case open and closed, open and closed, mesmerising Andrew with its regular cadence.

'What do you suppose our next course of action should be?'

Andrew had pondered this since Hamish had first told him they wanted him upstairs.

'Sir, I want to apologise for my poorly worded email to Miss Lester. I accept full responsibility, should she choose not to continue her relationship with us…'

Don interrupted, waving his hand at Andrew to stop him from going any further.

'Andrew, you misunderstood our position. Should she choose not to sell the dagger through us, your time with us will be over. We will not lose a sale such as this one.'

Andrew fell silent once more, his humiliation complete. The possibility of losing his dream job because of his excitement over the sampler had never entered his head.

'Sir, I will visit Miss Lester, wherever she is, and I will uplift the *katar*. I'm very sorry… please… just one more chance. If I send another email, to make up for my original response and, from there, I will get the piece for you.'

Andrew looked miserable. Don nodded to Jay, at which the other stood and opened the solid office door.

'Email me once you hear from the mysterious Miss Lester. I authorise you to use company funds to uplift the *katar* and your sampler. Jay will sign off on your email before you send it. Thank you, Andrew.'

Andrew made his way back to his office, sinking into his ergonomic work chair the way an alcoholic downs a bottle of vodka at the end of a long day. After firing up his computer, he drafted a response to Sarah, conscious of Jay leaning over his shoulder, smelling like rosewater and cardamom, praying he hadn't lost the sale of the century, nor the job of a lifetime.

POSTCARD #7

16/9/40

Dear Phil,

It is with some excitement I'm going to tell you what happened last night when we went to dinner at the Savoy. We'd barely begun eating when hundreds of people invaded the place. The mayhem was unbelievable, and then the air raid siren went off! You've never seen such confusion. The staff just didn't know what to do with themselves, or the uninvited guests. Before we'd even got to the shelter, the 'All clear' went. I've no idea how they got all those people out in the end, but it's a sight I shan't forget! You would have laughed! The Cabinet Ministers dining next to us certainly weren't!

Stay safe.

B xxx

THE SAVOY

With her head exploding in telltale pain, Sarah doubled over, clutching her knees for balance. The sudden sharp ear-piercing blast of a whistle frightened her so much she toppled over the trunk in a flurry of petticoats, gloves, hat and boots.

Several people rushed to her side, helping her to her feet, avoiding any impropriety.

Her head aching more than a bear's paw in a gin trap, Sarah tried to acclimatise to her sudden change in location - a train station. Not the dirty, graffiti-covered stations she was used to, devoid of staff, and full of travellers drenched in body odour, noses thrust in their electronic devices. This one was full of glossy painted benches with polished brass arms, and smart porters in uniforms ferrying suitcases and trunks, and brown packages tied with twine. Children in hats and shiny black-buttoned boots followed their mothers through the crowds.

'Are you all right, miss?' asked a moustached porter, brass buttons flashing brighter than the sun on his pressed black uniform, the red piping of his coat seams matching the prominent veins on his nose.

'I'm not feeling well,' Sarah answered, her hands fluttering up to her head, the pain flirting behind her eyes.

'It's best if we move you inside to rest,' suggested the porter, offering her his arm. The crowd of onlookers moved apart as he escorted her to the Station Master's Office.

Sarah felt as confused as Alice when she fell through the rabbit hole, especially after catching sight of a pair of long-haired mermaids, their tails entwined, Sarah surmised she was at London's Victoria Station. Still in London, but not *her* London. At least getting her bearings would be easier than when she'd woken in Betsy's kitchen.

From her seat just inside the doorway of the office, she could see another porter gathering up her belongings, including a blue travelling trunk, with shiny brass corners, and a padlock holding the lid closed.

Sarah laughed, imagining that if the same accident had occurred at Victoria Station in the twenty-first century, none of her luggage would have made it back to her, and she'd still be sitting on the floor, being moved on by a crass employee of British Rail, with soup stains on a belly straining to escape from his ill-fitting uniform.

After enquiring about her wellbeing, the stationmaster handed her a solid porcelain cup and saucer, emblazoned with the logo of the London Brighton and South Coast Railway Company, and filled with steaming sugary tea. Nothing had changed; every Englishman believed a cup of tea had that magical ability to solve every problem in the world. Why didn't psychiatrists just prescribe English Breakfast Tea to their clients? The stationmaster turned sideways behind his desk and pulled a tiny hip flask from inside his jacket, and poured a wee drop of something to his own cup. *Ah, that explains the Tube map of crisscrossed red veins on his face,* Sarah thought. She considered asking him for a splash of whatever it was inside his flask, but presumed that a 'lady' did not do such things. She wanted his hip flask-one of the most asked for items in her shop, and so hard to get. They sipped their drinks in silence and, after asking after her health again, he left her alone to compose herself.

With her luggage stowed in the corner, and her tea in her hand, Sarah relaxed enough to take stock of her situation. She knew where she was, and from where she was sitting, she could see the stunning façade of Grosvenor House, which was nowadays a hotel.

The stationmaster reappeared.

'Miss, shall we arrange a carriage for you?'

Sarah looked at him, so he repeated his question.

'Would you like us to arrange a carriage to the Savoy for you? I can send a porter with you to make sure you arrive. They are expecting you, miss, and will be worrying.'

Sarah, understood at once that having a lady on her own in his office was perturbing to the LB and SCR official.

He escorted her outside where there were a carriage and driver waiting. He helped her in and, with her luggage, the carriage clattered over the blue-grey cobblestones the short distance to the impressive Savoy Hotel. Assisted by another uniformed porter, she smoothed her peacock-blue taffeta skirt with a practised hand, despite her having rarely worn skirts, long or otherwise, and entered the lavish lobby.

Awed by an opulent glory, Sarah marvelled at the gold leaf detailing covering everything, and the pristine condition of the hotel.

'Excuse me, Miss Williams, may I help you with your luggage?' a uniformed bellboy hovered in front of her.

Sarah's eyes widened in surprise. *Miss Williams?*

In a bizarre twist, she'd morphed from being Sarah Lester, an antique dealer, to Betsy, kitchenmaid, and now to Miss Williams, a guest at the renowned Savoy.

Sarah followed the bellboy through an archway to a small lift. He closed the grille after her, and they rose two floors. She noted a small purse dangling from her slender wrist. How hadn't she noticed it in the mêlée at the station?

She slipped her hand inside and, to her relief, felt the tumble of coins between her fingers. She presumed that bellboys in Victorian times liked to be as well-tipped as their modern counterparts, and hoped that the coins weren't all gold sovereigns, as even in her confused state, she couldn't tip a bellboy with a solid gold sovereign or even a half-sovereign. Her father had a stash of gold sovereigns; his 'rainy day money' he called it. She hadn't sold them, hoping her father would come back to claim them; back into her life, his huge jangle of keys in his hand, a carton of 'treasure' in his arms, and his jeans smeared with dirt and oil.

The bellboy opened a polished wooden door to a heavenly room. She stepped through, agape at the heavy gold brocade curtains and exquisite furniture — the likes of which she never handled in her shop, and only ever saw in catalogues from the finest auction houses. Sarah opened her bag, withdrew two shillings, and handed them to the bellboy, his beaming face providing confirmation she'd tipped well.

'Could you bring tea up to my room?' she asked, assuming that her two shillings would encourage superb service from the bellboy, and aware that the other staff would hear of her generosity within minutes of him leaving her, through the infallible communication system that occurs in hotels around the globe. *Spy agencies could learn from the magical way information travelled between staff in these massive establishments,* she mused.

Alone for the first time since she'd lifted the travelling trunk's lid, Sarah sat on the bed and caught her reflection in the mirror. In a trance, she stood in front of the reflective glass. She looked the same; hazel eyes, thick brown hair, but... her clothes, and the diamonds in her ears. *Oh my!* The pearl choker around her neck caught her attention. Prettier than anything she'd ever seen. Pearls the size of macadamia nuts, with a lustre that only came from being genuine. In the centre was a brilliant green stone. A real emerald, given the quality of the pearls? Her fingers danced over the choker, finding the clasp at the back. She undid it, laying the piece out on the dressing table. She could just make out tiny inclusions in the jewel. If only she had her eye piece, she could read the maker's mark on the clasp.

A knock at the door interrupted her wonderings. The room attendant wheeled in an ornate wooden trolley on ceramic castors. Covered with an Irish linen cloth, it held a silver tea set, steam curling out of the spout of the teapot. This was a different staff member, so Sarah fished out another shilling and placed it in his palm. He grinned at the generous tip and left the room.

The heaviness of the teapot surprised her as she poured the fragrant tea into a fine porcelain cup. The kitchen had provided a sliver of cake, which she devoured, the tartness of lemon icing filling her mouth.

She emptied the purse onto the bed. She needed to know how much she was carrying. There were some half-sovereigns, but in a separate tiny brown leather pouch, each coin nestled in its own little sleeve. She had six half-sovereigns, twelve William IV silver shillings, fourteen crowns and a few sixpences. *I should have used* those *for tips*, she thought to herself, calculating the worth two shillings now. After counting the coins, she slipped them back into her purse, together with a crisp white handkerchief.

Next she turned her attention to her luggage, comprising a Caroline Reboux hat box, a leather valise, and the locked blue travelling trunk, although Sarah had found a key in her purse that might fit. Despite fashion not being her forte, she opened the hat box first.

She recognised the name Reboux from a Marlene Dietrich exhibition in Paris. Reboux the milliner, a celebrity in the fashion world. Sarah tried the hat on for size. Made from the softest grey felt, and crowned with a profusion of coloured feathers, it looked unworn, as if just delivered to the real Miss Williams, perhaps for her to wear with an outfit still hidden in the trunk.

Sarah admired her image in the mirror, disappointed there was no one here to see. She thought of Lord Grey and his laughing eyes-the only man she'd found attractive since she'd taken over the shop. She had little interest in dating since every man she'd encountered recently was old and crusty, or dodgy, or dying-which covered all the men in the antiques industry.

In a jubilant mood, despite her circumstances, Sarah tried her luck with the contents of the valise; a supple leather in a rich brown — and unlocked. She opened the top, half-expecting to end up back to her shop but, no, she remained ensconced in her room at the Savoy. At the forefront of her mind was the absolute possibility that her parents were here somewhere and, once she'd gone through her luggage to figure out who she was, she'd think of a way to find them.

At the top of the valise was a folded fur wrap, there for easy access if she took cold during her journey. But a journey from where? Underneath this was a plain brown paper package, held together with string. She put this to one side. Next was a beautiful wooden vanity case; complete, every item held in its purpose-made place.

She carried it over to the dressing table, setting it on the burnished wood to admire it better. Why didn't she ever get complete sets at the shop? There was always at least one piece missing its sterling silver top, or a glass bottle broken, or the mirror cracked. More commonly, over half the pieces were missing. This one was perfect. The glass bottles had sterling silver lids monogrammed with the initials G.W. There was a matching tortoiseshell container held in place with a firm leather strap with the word 'Pins' on its lid in silver italics. She slipped it out of its strap, opening it. Her breath caught-it was full of stunning diamanté hair-slides sparkling in the plain electric light.

Sarah picked one up, admiring it in the lamplight.

'Oh' she exclaimed, realising they were *real* diamonds, not paste as she'd thought.

Sarah took off the hat, pushing the slide into her wavy hair, just as someone rapped on the door. She opened it to find the bellboy back.

'Miss Williams, your father has arrived, and has asked you to meet him in the dining room at one o'clock for luncheon?'

Panicking, Sarah's words stumbled over each other.

'Oh, I'm not ready. What do I wear? I must look a sight. What should I do?'

The bellboy's eyes widened at her outburst. They stood together in the doorway. Distracted, she noted a gentleman in full Arab finery walking along the corridor. He caught her eye, and paused, inclining his head towards her.

'May I escort you to luncheon, Miss Williams? Your father and I have business later today, and I want to see him beforehand, in a more congenial environment than the Law Courts.'

His voice had the softness of silk, his words dripping like honey off a spoon. As he stood waiting, his hands clasped in front of him, Sarah fussed with her hair.

'I shall wait here while you gather your things,' he continued, his eyes laughing as he spoke.

The bellboy slipped away unnoticed. Sarah turned back to her room for her handbag. With a touch of vanity, she left the diamond clip in her hair. After picking up her purse, she surveyed her reflection. Should she change? Was that the done thing? With the unusual gentleman waiting outside her door, she decided her current attire would do just fine. She took a deep breath.

She dreamed of dining with her *real* father, talking with him again was her greatest wish. The questions she'd ask. Was he proud of her? Did he approve of the changes she'd made at the shop? Thinking of her missing parents brought the threat of tears. She blinked them back and left her room.

'Miss Williams,' the Arab tilted his head, his eyes sombre. 'Are you fine to dine with your father, or shall I tell him you are unwell?' he asked.

Sarah averted her eyes to hide her unspent tears. Her father's disappearance was still so raw she was unprepared to meet this stranger even if he was her father in this time.

The Arab gestured down the hall, and together they walked towards the lift. The first hotel in England to have an electric one installed, the Savoy's was the epitome of elegance, with intricate wrought iron, plush carpet, twinkling electric lights and its own operator, who closed the doors and delivered them in silence to the ground floor.

Once the gates opened, the Arab gestured towards the doors of the dining room. The opulent floor covering muffled their footsteps. The only sounds were that of silver Christofle cutlery clinking against bone china plates, mingled with the bejewelled tones of the guests, adding to the surreal quality of the scene. Sarah looked at as many faces of the diners as possible, searching for her parents. Distracted by her efforts, she walked right into the Arab, who had paused beside two gentlemen seated nearby.

'Mr Sullivan, Mr Gilbert, may I say your most recent production is by far your best to date. I shall enjoy attending it again tonight.'

He bowed his head towards the men and continued through the room, before Sarah even realised he'd moved on, leaving her standing alone at the table of the esteemed composers of comic opera.

'Uh... good evening, Mr Gilbert. *H.M.S. Pinafore* is my absolute favourite show...' she trailed off as the two men gazed at her.

'Thank you, Miss Williams, we hope to see you again soon. You must come to our current performance at the Savoy.'

Sarah nodded, and hurried off after the Arab, who had drawn out a chair at a table where, she presumed, her 'father' sat. Sliding into the proffered seat, she smiled her thanks, and murmured an apology before she looked into the eyes of a father she'd never known.

THE FATHER

Sarah raised her eyes and gasped in shock. The man whose eyes she met could have been her real father; bright blue eyes, framed by the salt and pepper hair of a solid man in his late fifties. Eyes lined by years in the sun, he didn't fit the sumptuous surroundings, although he behaved as if it were his natural environment. An air of quiet confidence radiated from him as it had *her* father.

He laid a rough hand over her ungloved one and gave it a brief affectionate squeeze before returning to his glass. Sarah expected to read him, but she was so adrift it was all she could do to not sob aloud. Instead, silent tears trickled down her face.

The Arab summoned a waiter to ask for a calming tea for Miss Williams. The father passed her a handkerchief. Once again, she'd forgotten about the small purse hanging from her wrist, which contained an embroidered handkerchief of her own, with the initials G.W. on it.

The tea arrived, steaming and fragrant. The British tradition of serving tea to solve the woes of the world continued at the Savoy. Their waiter poured the tea into the most delicate Royal Worcester cup, adding the milk next, then enquiring whether she needed sugar.

Sarah declined, using the proffered handkerchief to dry her tears. It was only after the waiter had left the table that her father addressed her.

'Grace, I shall overlook your lack of gloves–I assume your accident flustered you–but I *cannot* abide crying in public. You know this. I shall let it pass this one time, but please refrain from embarrassing yourself in public again!' he scolded.

'How did you know about my accident?'

The Arab laughed, 'Miss Williams, your father hears more of what occurs in London than the Queen!'

He continued chuckling as he considered his statement.

Meanwhile, he was looking at her with concern.

'I should have called for the doctor to come and examine you after your mishap. That was remiss of me. You may have had more of a fall than they told me as it has affected your speech.'

Sarah's hand flew to her mouth. How on earth *was* she meant to speak? She opened and closed her mouth as she tried composing a reply. The best she could muster was to parrot a clipped BBC voice.

'I am feeling faint, which may be what happened at the station, but I do not think I need the doctor. Just something to eat?' she tried.

He nodded. The pretentious accent enough to allay his fears. Those Trinity College elocution lessons he'd forced her to take at school were paying off.

He called for the waiter, ordering lunch for each of them, with no discussion. The dish set in front of her was the last meal she'd ever have ordered. *Suprêmes de Volaille Favorite*, chicken served on tossed slices of *foie gras*, with fragrant slivers of truffle presented on each breast, and served with a heap of asparagus heads covered in glistening butter. Next to her plate, the waiter placed a sauce-boat filled with a buttery meat glaze. Her stomach roiled in protest. She'd always hated asparagus; it had been a huge in-joke, with her always being offered it at family gatherings.

Plus, while she wasn't a vegetarian by any stretch of the imagination, she had an issue with animal cruelty, and the force-feeding of geese to provide a 'delicacy' was right at the top of her 'refuse to buy on principle at the supermarket as a protest' list.

Oblivious to the disgust on her face, he tucked into his meal of quails' eggs whipped into fluffy omelettes, spiced with slivers of peppers and herbs, and accompanied by giant field mushrooms.

She pushed food around her plate as the men talked in low tones of imports and exports, and business in India. Sarah forced herself to eat two of the smaller asparagus heads, to not upset her... well... *my father*, she thought, as she recalled her own father teasing her at their last Christmas dinner together. She tried to follow the threads of their conversation but became confused until they turned to the impending appearance at the Old Bailey that afternoon.

'Court?' Sarah interrupted.

They turned to look at her, reminded that she was present and surprised that she was listening to their conversation.

'Yes, Grace, court. It's no concern of yours. It is a minor matter of the classification of goods from India; nothing for you to concern yourself,' her father answered.

Not being raised under the strict Victorian conventions of the day, Sarah blundered on.

'But why are you involved? What goods in India? What are we talking about?' she blurted out.

Her father, incredulous that she'd questioned him further, replied in a measured and precise tone.

'I have explained to you, Grace, that my business interests with Mr Kurdi are of no concern. I ask that you stop interrupting, and that you give no more thought to this conversation. In fact, your aunt will be here soon to take you out; I presume you will need time to change and liberate your gloves from wherever you left them.'

He summoned the waiter to order a whisky for himself and honey-sweetened tea for Kurdi, signalling an end to the conversation.

As Sarah judged, she was being dismissed. But, before she had taken her leave, a gentleman with the finest white moustache she'd ever seen approached their table.

'Escoffier,' Robert Williams said.

'Mr Williams, what a delight to see you again. Mr Kurdi, Miss Williams,' said the famed King of Chefs, in a lilting French accent.

'It is, as always, a pleasure to be here in your restaurant, my dear friend,' Williams replied.

'Grace was just leaving,' he stated, allowing no room for misinterpretation as to his expectations.

'Such a shame. Perhaps tomorrow evening I may tempt you to try my *Pêche Melba?*' Escoffier offered.

Every child of London had heard of the dessert, Escoffier's most famous culinary invention; peaches resting on an icy bed of vanilla ice cream, topped with raspberry sauce and spun sugar. She wanted to say she had time to try it, but her father cleared his throat, signalling that this was not the right time. Sarah smiled apologetically at Escoffier, stood up, and bade them farewell.

Escoffier moved on to greet diners at another table, and the men retook their seats.

'Your daughter is brighter than I had expected, Robert. She will give you trouble, that one,' mused the Arab.

Williams snorted.

'She has always been trouble. Far too headstrong and being in London is making it worse. But, as my only child, she needs to be here for us to select a suitable husband for her and for my fortune.'

'She is a delight though, Robert. You don't give her any credit for her brain. Is it time to recognise that you have no sons, and that your daughter may be a worthy successor to your businesses?' Samer suggested.

Williams laughed, too loudly for the genteel nature of the restaurant, causing several heads to turn in their direction.

'Ah, my friend, at this moment, my sister is escorting her to the home of Lord Grey. It's time she married and produced a grandson for me to leave my fortune. There is no doubt her dowry will make her a fine catch for a destitute lord, despite her rash nature,' Robert continued, chuckling into his smoky whisky.

THE ARAB

*S*amer Kurdi, Arab businessman, entrepreneur and speculator, watched his business partner's daughter walk through the Savoy's restaurant. Her inquisitive mind a refreshing change from the vapid women flung his way on his sojourns to London. His money had made life easy, but *easy* didn't nourish the soul.

After Grace left, he observed Williams. They had a close relationship, despite their cultural differences. It saddened him that his friend was blind to her intellect. She would make someone an excellent wife, not for her fortune, but for her vitality and approach to life. He wanted to take it up further, but lost his chance when Robert started discussing the plan of attack for their court appearance, where they were being charged for evading Customs duties at the border. A complete farce; a trumped-up charge brought against them to swell the Government coffers, in his opinion. Robert was an astute businessman, so, when faced with a choice of classification for the goods they imported from India, they chose the lower tariff. They'd started out shipping goods back to England for officers stationed in the sub-continent. It wasn't long before the romantic idea of India bewitched London society and they could not keep up with the insatiable appetite for India's decorative wares. Now they sourced directly from the artisans themselves. Profiting from the favourable tariff, they were being scrutinised for their business decisions.

The Queen's Empire was unravelling, and the civil service tasked with increasing revenue collection. The nation's love of India did not extend to those who profited from it. And Robert had fallen foul of an arrogant and vindictive Customs Preventive Officer-Clifford Meredith, a career man who had clawed his way up through the ranks by ingratiating himself with senior officers. With a magical ability to avoid any blame for failure, by passing the onus onto his colleagues, Meredith took every slight personally. In one particular instance, his prejudices were heightened when, during a routine Customs inspection, Samer, an *Arab*, dared question Meredith's classification of the freight. Henceforward, every shipment Kurdi and Williams imported was subjected to the most rigorous of inspections, until Meredith felt he had enough evidence to prove they were defrauding the Crown.

'The court will accept our position? Such a shame old Lord Grey is no longer with us. He'd never have let this matter get this far. A jumped-up clerk, that's what Meredith is. And now we're letting it happen in India. As soon as someone marries Grace, I'm leaving this place. You should do the same, Samer. Take one of those brides your family is offering and leave this country. I weep for our country.'

Samer nodded, sipping his tea.

'Robert, my home is the world. Contentment follows wherever I find happiness. That may be in England, the spicy shores of India or the heat of my homeland. I am a seed on the wind, blown wherever Allah wills it.'

Taking a breath, he was about to broach the subject of Grace, when Robert stood up announcing it was time to go, leaving no room for further discussion. Together the men left the Savoy, and made their way to the highest court in the land, to plead their innocence, the immediacy of their predicament taking precedence over everything else.

THE AUNT

*C*onscious of their eyes on her back, Sarah strolled through the dining room, without looking around. She avoided the eyes of Mr Gilbert and Mr Sullivan as she passed their table, despite wanting to beg for tickets to their show, certain that wasn't the 'done' thing. She found herself wandering aimlessly in the lobby.

The bellboy sidled up to her, giving her a fright.

'Shall I call the lift for you, miss?' he asked.

'Yes, yes please,' she replied.

Back in her room, Sarah flung her purse away and collapsed onto her bed, landing on top of a wrapped parcel which hadn't been there earlier. Intrigued, she untied the silk ribbon. The wrapping fell open, revealing a black leather box with a tiny brass clasp at the front.

She raised the lid. Printed inside was the manufacturer's name, 'R and S Garrard & Co.'–the Crown Jewellers, most famous for re-cutting the *Koh-i-Noor* diamond. Nestled in a custom-made velvet bed was the most exquisite pair of sterling silver inkwells.

A stiff white card peeked out of the wrapping, upon which, written in cursive script, were the words:

In honour of your intellect, and to ensure that the well may never run dry of your words.

Isn't that the most beautiful sentiment ever written? she thought. But unsigned? Sarah wondered if the real Grace Williams would have known the identity of the sender. *Another mystery to add to the list.* Living in luxury, a father with business interests in India, mysterious Arabs, expecting an aunt she'd never met. And now, a secret admirer?

A gentle knock at the door saw Sarah stuffing the card into the box and closing the lid. She didn't want to explain the gift so thrust it into the top of her trunk. Behind the door was an upright-looking woman - angular and slender, from her nose to her long, gloved fingers, there was no softness to her.

'Grace!' the woman said. 'I have been waiting in the lobby for over five minutes. Although I bumped into one of my distant cousins, and his son, Phillip. It is fascinating the people who dine here, just when you think they have exhausted their funds. Such a shame the son is unsuitable. They were *such* a nice family. Imagine, he married an *Indian* girl, without his parents' permission, while they were over there. The scandal! Thank goodness they found out and had it annulled, but not before ruining his reputation. We don't know if the divorce is legal or otherwise; things in India are never clear-cut. Come, tardiness is not attractive. How your father *ever* imagines I'll be able to secure you a husband, given your timekeeping, is beyond me. We may have to settle for the Seymour boy if your daydreaming becomes common knowledge. Imagine that!'

This must be the aunt, thought Sarah. The notion '*Poor Phillip Seymour*' flitted through her mind as her aunt elaborated more on the scandal.

'I only wish your mother were alive. But the past is gone, and we make do with what God has given us. Now, let's go; your wardrobe needs refreshing. Country clothes will *not* do for town. Your father may not see the difference between a country seamstress and a city dressmaker, but the mothers of the suitable young men in London can. Put on your hat, I have a carriage waiting.'

Sarah, who'd still to say anything, mumbled 'Yes, Aunt', curious what her aunt said about her to others, given how she'd just heard the inadequacies of the unfortunate Master Seymour.

Together, they left the room, Sarah's hat on, purse on her wrist.

Her aunt's purse was as slender as she was, it didn't contain actual money, Sarah opined. The only part of her aunt *not* stick thin was the emerald solitaire on her hand. But her aunt carried it off, despite her arms looking too frail to withstand the weight of such a stone. *It must be two carats at least,* Sarah observed, as she admired it on the sly as they pulled on their gloves, while descending to the lobby.

Her aunt marched ahead through to a waiting carriage and together they rode in the afternoon sunshine through a London Sarah had only ever read about. The buildings looked movie-set perfect, so shiny and unsullied by the exhaust pipes of millions of cars. Sarah imitated a modern-day tourist on one of the open-top buses swivelling their heads trying to take in the famous sites: St. Paul's Cathedral; the Houses of Parliament; Westminster Abbey; and Big Ben, the simple monument to the Great Fire of London, her particular favourite. As a child, she'd kept the quaint certificate you received after climbing the three hundred and eleven steps.

Thus began an afternoon of visits to a dressmaker, complete with fittings and fabric selections, then off to the milliner, the glover. An endless parade of measuring tapes and fussy hands. Then the carriage stopped outside a smart address near Hyde Park.

'We shall be at least two hours, driver,' announced her aunt, as they alighted before she marched up the steps. The door opened before her aunt could knock, a young girl dressed head to toe in a *classic* maid's outfit-frilly cap, white lace apron. If Sarah hadn't known better, she'd have sworn they'd just arrived at a fancy-dress party, or a high-end Gentlemen's Club.

'Miss Williams, and Miss Williams, Lady Grey are expecting you. Come in,' said the familiar-looking maid.

It clicked. She'd been here before. She'd stood in this exact entrance way, or, more precisely, she'd lain in a heap at the bottom of the stairs. This was the home of Lord Grey and his family. And the maid? No wonder she looked familiar; it was Adelaide.

If guests considered the Savoy opulent, they would have declared the hotel a poor cousin in comparison with the grand décor inside the home of the Lord and his mother, Dowager Lady Laura Grey. From her previous 'visit', Sarah remembered too well how hard it was keeping a grand home looking so immaculate. Did the original incarnation of Betsy still work here, or had she disappeared when Sarah herself returned to present-day London. How did that work? Another mystery.

Remembering the mammoth hit to the head she'd given Benjamin Grey in the study, she stopped short on the front step with a gasp.

Her aunt turned to look at her. Vexed, she hissed, 'Grace, we must not keep Lady Grey waiting. What is wrong with you?'

Without waiting for a reply, she swept into the house, expecting her niece to follow.

The merest chance she may find her way home again, and acquire the matching *katar*, hit her. Oh, the possibilities!

She had one *katar* back in London. This might be her only opportunity to reunite the pair. She must get the second one, then sit on the Chippendale parlour chair. Perfect, the coup of a generation amongst antique dealers. Discussed not only in the blogs of antique enthusiasts everywhere, but on the front page of newspapers around the world. It might even trump last year's sales record for the antique carved rhinoceros horn.

With a deep breath, Sarah followed her aunt. Mutely, she appealed to Adelaide, trying to convey her queries regarding Betsy and Benjamin Grey, without uttering a single word. Adelaide did not understand what on earth she was trying to do, until Sarah whispered, 'Betsy?'.

Adelaide's eyes widened.

'Och nay, Miss Williams, she took ill and Lord Grey has confined her to her room.'

Her accent broadened as she whispered, 'He's afraid she caught a terrible illness from someone who came back from India with him.'

Blushing at her lapse in decorum, Adelaide bobbed a curtsey and scurried away. Sarah was desperate to visit Betsy upstairs in her pokey little room with the rag rug, to see her for real. Did they look similar? She'd never seen her reflection while she acted the part of Betsy. Was that why Adelaide did not appear startled by her appearance?

86

With her aunt seated on the couch, and Sarah viewed the remaining chairs with trepidation. There was the fateful Chippendale that had catapulted her back to her London apartment. She could return to her normal life if she sat on that same chair. Or did she want to follow through with this current life, one which was more luxurious than her last and more adventurous than her own twenty-first century existence, and lead to her parents, somewhere. Decisions, decisions, and avoiding the 'transference' chair with a wide berth, she perched next to her aunt, where they sat silently, waiting for her Ladyship.

In an 'alternative reality' way, Sarah considered her options. This was an important interview. She was here for vetting as a potential mate for Lady Grey's son; the same way they display cattle to bidders in the stockyards at auction time. Although she didn't expect Lady Grey to inspect her teeth, or slap her rump, the process was comparable, albeit in a more salubrious environment, with no stink of effluent and work boots.

The door swung open and in swept her Ladyship with a flurry of skirts and lavender scent. Giant strands of luminous pearls jostled for space around her neck, her fingers engulfed by rubies the size of marbles.

'Jessica, how lovely to see you, and your niece, Grace. How wonderful to meet you.'

Lady Grey's presence filled the whole room. Her stillness, the way she held her delicate hands with no superfluous movements, was angel-like. Her pale skin, flawless. If this was the modern times, Sarah would have wondered who her plastic surgeon was. As it was, she presumed superior breeding banished the wrinkles. If this was how a titled lady of leisure looked in the late nineteenth century, Sarah decided that staying here might be the better choice.

Lady Grey rang a small handbell, and settled herself opposite, casting an appraising eye over Sarah. It was at that point that Sarah felt like a prime piece of beef on the auction block.

'Although your aunt and I have known each other for years, I find I know little about you, given that your father has kept you hidden away. So, please, tell me, how do you find living in the countryside, away from this vibrant city, when your father spends so much time here,' Lady Grey directed.

Sarah cleared her throat but, as she prepared to fudge an answer that was half *Pride and Prejudice* and half *Oliver Twist*, the door flew open. There, steadying himself on the frame, was young Benjamin Grey.

'Mother,' he slurred, and lurched towards the only unoccupied couch, leaving a waft of alcohol behind him before depositing himself on a chair. He nodded toward Sarah, who recoiled in shock.

'So she's the country bumpkin you hope to marry my illustrious brother to, to save the family's name and the roof over our heads?'

Sarah was unaware of the extent that the late Lord Grey had destroyed the vast reaches of their historic title and wealth through his drinking and gambling. Marriage between Grace Williams and Lord Edward Grey was a match made in banking heaven. Youth, beauty and pounds, where before there were only age, alcoholism and pennies.

A guttural laugh escaped his lips. Lady Grey sat frozen in mortification, her hand at her mouth; whether to stifle a scream or to prevent any inappropriate comments, Sarah was unsure, but surmised that it was a mixture of both.

Within a heartbeat, the Dowager's breeding took control, and, with that very British skill, she elected to ignore her youngest son's behaviour, even his comments.

'Ladies, may I introduce my youngest son, Benjamin. He and Edward have returned from India, but Benjamin has been unwell since then. Benjamin, Miss Jessica Williams, and her niece, Miss Grace Williams. I think you might retire to your room, and I shall have your supper sent up to you. You shouldn't be out of bed,' she said with steel in her voice.

Sarah watched in fascination as Benjamin shrugged his rumpled shoulders and heaved himself from the couch.

'As you wish, Mother. Ladies, it has been a pleasure.'

As he made his way out, he kissed his mother on her silken cheek, then took Jessica's hand, planting a chaste kiss on the back of her gloved hand, before moving onto Sarah. As he took *her* hand, he whispered into her ear.

'And if my brother won't have you, I'll have my way with you.'

Sarah snatched back her hand, her skin crawling at his touch and at the memory of their last meeting, as he laughed and staggered away.

Adelaide arriving with the tea trolley broke the uncomfortable silence. As Adelaide busied herself serving tea and cake, Sarah observed Lady Grey, her hands fluttering over the tea things, her title no protection from the sins of her son. She was trying her utmost to entertain Sarah's aunt, to allay her fears.

The maid served up delicate slices of cake, paying no attention to the strained conversation between Lady Laura Grey and Jessica Williams. The former regaling them with stories of her time in India, and the adventures her sons had been having in the Army, before their sudden return to England due to Benjamin's illness. There was a reference to her late husband's fondness for India, and his family's standing with a maharaja or two.

Unbeknownst to Sarah, and despite appearances to the contrary, Jessica was now having serious doubts about marrying Grace into Lord Grey's family. Yet their marriage *would* give her family a social cachet they were lacking. The Williams family had money, but no title. Nor did they have any real link to nobility, other than by virtue of having more money than most.

Jessica mulled this over as she sipped the finest Ceylon tea brought back to London by Edward Grey after he had returned his disgraced younger brother to his mother's bosom.

Her Ladyship was spared any additional anxiety as the problems Benjamin Grey had caused in India had not yet passed through her own information network. The Army had done a remarkable job of hushing up a very embarrassing incident.

Now, his Lordship's mother was clutching at conversational straws, her composure still rocked by her wayward son's rudeness, but continued.

'Grace, Jessica says you travelled through France with your father. Tell me your opinions on the French. They *despise* us so much. Did you come across any animosity from them?'

Casting her mind to her O Level French lessons, and one bawdy hens' party across the English Channel to Calais, Sarah prepared to respond, before being interrupted by her aunt.

'Laura, I'm sorry, but I have a headache developing. Would you mind if we returned to the Savoy? You could join us for tea there later this week?'

With protestations of concern, and calls for the carriage, Sarah and her aunt rushed out of the house without having once laid eyes on the young Lord Grey.

The gentleman in question was, however, viewing the proceedings from a vantage point at the top of the stairs. Although against having a marriage arranged for him like a grocer selecting apples for his customers, he had to admit that Miss Grace Williams had a peculiar charm, and a familiar air he had difficulty placing.

As Sarah stepped into the carriage, she turned to wave farewell, and caught sight of someone at the window. Her wave faltered as she recognised the face. Jessica Grey chivvied her inside, and off they rumbled. Sarah twisted in her seat to look through the rear window, to stare at Lord Grey, immune to her aunt's muttering about inbreeding, and the evils of alcohol.

Jessica's monologue subsided in the face of Sarah's lack of response and they sat in silence; Jessica worrying about the Grey family becoming trustees of her brother's fortune, while Sarah mulled over her current predicament once more. Her *futures*: the immediate one here in Victorian London; and her life in her little shop. And the omnipresent issue of her real parents, and where on earth they might be.

She slapped her hand against her forehead in frustration, startling her aunt, who announced, 'We shall say nothing of what happened to your father, Grace. He has entrusted me with your betrothal and, despite the brother's unprepossessing state, it was a momentary aberration. I think he may be sick from his time in India.'

Thoughts of the suitability of the family disconcerted Jessica, something wasn't right. She presumed it was the behaviour of the brother that had unnerved her, but there was something else simmering beneath the veneer of civility that made her hesitate.

The clattering wheels rolled to a stop outside the Savoy. The liveried porter greeted Sarah fondly as he assisted her from the carriage. All she did in London was be assisted in and out of carriages, and drink tea. Where were the parties and the excitement she'd imagined moneyed young ladies enjoyed during this era? She ventured a question.

'Aunt Jessica, will we have time to attend the theatre before I return home?'

Her aunt looked at her oddly, taking her arm as they walked into the hotel.

'Our seats are there, as always. What an *odd* question. Your father invited *the Arab* to join us tonight. I am not sure that was appropriate, but we are to entertain him, now that their business is so entwined. It wouldn't have surprised me if your father had even considered marrying you off to him, to cement their business partnership. It's lucky I am here to avoid such a disastrous social *faux pas!*'

With an unexpected giggle for such a prim matron, her aunt laughed as the porter ushered them into the lift.

POSTCARD #8

28/4/41

Dear Phil
I've been invited to a costume party. This is the most exciting thing to happen to
me all year! Life is so dreary without you. After seeing the newsreel at the cinema
this week, I've decided to go as a maharani, *the wife of an Indian* maharaja.
The Indian officers in the news look so dashing, that I'm sure their princesses are
just as beautiful. I shall drape myself in jewels and beautiful silks. I wish you
could see me. I doubt that anyone will be taking photographs, but if they are I
shall send you one.
Stay safe.
B xxx

THE NECKLACE

S arah's aunt delivered her to her suite and advised her to be ready for the theatre by eight p.m. Jessica Williams then hurried to her own room - Room 361- the room favoured by Oscar Wilde. It was fortunate that the prim and proper Miss Williams was ignorant that the lascivious playwright preferred that room at the Savoy above all others. Her puritan heart would not have coped with that nugget of information.

Sarah closed the door and walked over to the trunk. What on earth did one wear to the theatre?

'Right, *Miss Williams*, you must have something for me to wear.'

The trunk was empty.

Sarah scrambled around and spied her toiletries laid out on the dressing table, it became clear, the staff had unpacked her belongings, putting everything away in its allocated spot.

Opening the doors of the wardrobe akin to what an archivist at the V & A might see. The smell of the fabrics enveloped her, the touch of the silk on her hands softer than a duckling's down and the intricacy of a lace collar on one dress announced that it was Honiton lace, made famous since it adorned Queen Victoria's wedding dress. The most stunning gown in the wardrobe a wine-red silk satin, cut with velvet in a stripe and leaf pattern. Layer upon layer of fabric including a bodice, and an underskirt with a bustle. Clouds of tulle and silk satin bows at the cuffs finished it. A work of art, living on a coat hanger. Sarah laid it flat across the bed. A discreet tag sewn into the neck proclaiming it a garment made by the magical hands of the *House of Worth* in Paris.

Figuring she'd need a Physics degree to get undressed out of her taffeta and into the red silk, Sarah procrastinated; sitting at the dressing table to examine the jewellery she might wear with the gown.

She opened the vanity case, noting the fine ivory inlay around the edges, and the elegant turned-horn feet, which marked it as a treasure from the Vizagapatam region in India. Inside was the tortoiseshell pin box, the one where she'd found the diamond hair clips. But now she was looking for a necklace to wear. She opened one of the concealed drawers, and like a reclining courtesan, sat a rope of heavy rubies, each stone divided by tiny rectangular golden beads. The *perfect* partner for the dress, like Fred Astaire and Ginger Rogers, or Antony and Cleopatra.

With the fire of the rubies in her eyes, she stroked the stones, half expecting to burn herself with their intensity. But, instead of burning her hand, a familiar shooting pain hit her with such force she sunk into oblivion.

THE COLLECTOR

Sarah awoke lain across the open travelling trunk, the diamond hair-slide glinting in her hair. She sobbed in frustration. She should have spent her time looking for her parents. Instead of living as Grace Williams. Sarah assumed that, by touching the antiques from the Williams' estate, she was living the life of their former owner. But that didn't explain how she'd become Betsy, who would never have reached the lofty heights in which Grace Williams lived. Being a maid at the Savoy, the closest Betsy could have dreamed; but never as a guest.

She tried to ignore her terrible headache as she noted once again that her clothes weren't her own - they were the clothes she'd worn at the Savoy. Historical artefacts in their own right, in mint condition, fresh from the seamstress' treadle machine.

Her hands flew to her neck. The ruby necklace! But she had never put it on. It had remained at the Savoy.

She swore, smacking herself on the forehead with the heel of her hand, knocking off the delicate hat.

A loud banging on the front door startled her, and she struggled to stand up, awash in petticoats and whalebone stays. The knocking became more insistent. Conscious of her peculiar clothes, it was tempting not to answer the door, but whoever stood outside would see any movement she made through the opaque glass.

So, steeling herself for another onslaught from Patricia, she walked over the door being hammered upon by someone with no patience.

'Stop it, Patricia, I'm coming!' Sarah yelled, fighting with the lock. As the door swung inwards, Sarah found a tall man in a dark three-piece suit in the doorway. He looked just as surprised when his eyes fell upon her, travelling from the tips of her boots, up her taffeta skirts, past her exposed neck, flitting over the diamonds in her hair-clip, before resting on her eyes.

'Miss Lester?' he said in a polished public school voice.

'Yes?' she replied, standing in the doorway of her shop, obscuring the view of behind her, although at well over six feet tall, her visitor had no trouble seeing over her head. Despite his height, he showed no interest in the shop's inside and, disconcertingly, held eye contact.

'Miss Lester, my name is Richard Grey, and I have been waiting outside your premises for the better part of an hour. Your published hours of business state you open at ten. It is eleven o'clock. I *am* surprised that a small enterprise such as yours can afford to treat your customers in this fashion.'

His supercilious voice, brusque manner, his choice of words, and his name, made Sarah's skin crawl, a warning he was trouble. *A Grey?* He exuded Benjamin Grey's abhorrent qualities. *What were the chances?*

'I understand you have an Indian *katar* you wish to sell? My client has sent me to buy the article. Shall we go inside to complete the transaction?'

His peremptory tone invited no dissension as he moved towards the door.

She replied. 'I'm sorry, Mr Grey. You've had a wasted journey. It's my intention to put the knife up for auction. It's not for sale. I don't know why you thought it was okay to turn up and demand to buy it?'

He silenced her with a wave of his bony fingers.

'Miss Lester, you will find my, ah, client's offer very generous. From our research, we took you to be a dealer of sensibility, although your fancy dress suggests otherwise. Let's go inside where we can complete this and I can leave you to play out your dress up fantasies alone.'

With that, Sarah tried slamming the door in his face. His rudeness was the last straw in a very confusing day. The door came to sudden stop inches from the doorframe, with Grey's foot wedged between the two.

Through clenched teeth, Sarah snarled, 'Mr Grey, I suggest you remove your foot before I call the police and have you removed from my premises.'

He held up his hand, silencing her.

'Miss Lester, I can assure you we will have the knife, either today, or soon. Here is my card. Good day.'

Grey withdrew his foot, his lip curling at her face, before stepping from the doorway and walking towards a waiting black cab.

Sarah closed the door, sliding the bolt home with a satisfying thud. It looked unlikely she'd open at all today. And leaving Grey's card on the counter, she scrawled a note and taped it to the window:

"Due to unforeseen circumstances,
the shop will not be open today."

'Right, I have to write this down, it's all too confusing,' she mumbled, unbuttoning the tiny mother-of-pearl buttons on the fitted silk bodice as she made her way upstairs, to change, again. Before she undressed, she peeked through the curtains to see Richard Grey, statue-still next to the cab, staring at her window.

Twitching the curtain back into place, she drew the more substantial drapes, shivering at Grey's threat. She finished undressing, the sensation of being watched never quite leaving her. While folding the taffeta skirt, the shirt, her petticoats and undergarments, she considered how much these would sell for at the Vintage Textile Fair she exhibited at once a year. Hundreds of pounds, no doubt.

The best thing was to wrap them up and hand them to Patricia, claiming they'd come from the estate sale. Which was technically true, but bothering Patricia with the strange details of the last few days was unnecessary. She'd march her off to the nearest hospital for assessment, citing potential blood clots or a mini-stroke.

Sarah decided to keep the Reboux hat, and perched it on an old wooden hat block, before nodding at it, and dressing instead in a sensible pair of jeans and a T-shirt.

She looked out the window and once satisfied Grey had gone, she checked inside the atlas, half expecting the sampler to have vanished. But it remained tucked inside a map of the Congo, and a quick check of the freezer showed the antique *katar* in situ.

How dare someone from one of the auction houses come to her house and threaten her? And how did they know her address when she'd used her personal email, not her work one? She hadn't typed her address or phone number in the correspondence so how did Grey know about the knife?

She'd had no involvement with the big auction houses before. Her most valuable sale to date had been a pair of Royal Staffordshire dog figurines she'd bought from an unwitting seller at a car boot sale for four pounds. She'd sold them for a thousand pounds — her most exciting find until this week. Now the prospect of making thousands from just two items overwhelmed her.

She opened her laptop to see a second email from Christie's.

Dear Miss Lester,

Sorry if my original email seemed presumptuous.

After viewing the photographs, my team and I were excited. It is rare we see such a fine example coming onto the market. It was wrong for me to contact our private clients about your sampler before hearing from you. Please accept my apologies.

I understand if you have reconsidered offering this piece to us. But if you want to continue please let me know and I will come to you.

Andrew Harvard

Senior Specialist Costumes and Textiles

Sarah sat back. Grey wasn't an emissary from Christie's. Perhaps he was from Bonham's, then? An Internet search could have turned up her name, linking her to the shop, and any simpleton could have connected the dots. A connection, or an assumption, and she had confirmed it. Damn. Why hadn't she thought harder about her responses to the peculiar Mr Grey? She'd all but told him where to find the knife and may as well have taken him by the hand and led him upstairs and served him the knife on a silver platter. So *stupid*.

She hadn't heard from Bonham's-it had been over twenty-four hours since she had emailed them, so the knife and sampler would go to Christie's. She needed an injection of funds, so flicked off a reply to Andrew Harvard;

Dear Mr Harvard,
   Apology accepted.
   Please pick up the sampler as soon as possible. And the katar.
   Kind regards,
   Sarah Lester

This time she included her address and mobile number

While making a coffee in her little kitchen, she gave a start as she caught her reflection in the window — the diamond hair-slide glinted in the light.

'Oh!' she exclaimed, her heart racing.

The value of the hair-slide alone covering her council rates for a year. Regardless of her unusual circumstances, she wouldn't look a gift-horse in the mouth. She had to sell it. Yes, it was magnificent, but valuable. In a rare moment of vanity, she slid it more securely into her hair, its mere proximity lifting her spirits. Carrying her coffee downstairs, she tried the front door — still locked, and settled behind the counter to price up her stock. Half expecting to disappear any minute, she approached every item with trepidation, and with a smidgeon of excitement...

~

Two hours later, her stomach rumbling and her hands filthy, the air felt heavy with disappointment. She had unearthed nothing worthy of excitement. She'd touched as many items as possible. Nothing. Even rifling through the old blue travelling trunk had elicited nothing more exciting than a broken fingernail.

Wedged down the side was a sheaf of old papers in a buff manila folder, stuffed full of fading facsimiles, old photos, and legal documents, Sarah put it on the counter to look through later. She was pleased with the assortment of shoe lasts at the bottom of the trunk, but most of the old clothes were moth-eaten, and the white trims were discoloured and fraying. Maybe Patricia had the magic to restore them to their former glory. Otherwise, off to a specialist vintage clothing fair, but she wouldn't be able to retire on what she could get for them there.

Flour sifters, lidded butter dishes, everyday dinner plates, preserving jars without their lids, and other assorted household items cluttered the counter. Sarah closed her eyes and prayed to Odo, the patron saint of antique dealers, that the other cartons were full of sterling silver and Royal Doulton.

Four cartons left, but she needed sustenance, and more than just a sticky bun. Sarah washed her hands, watching as dust from decades past swirled down the plughole, unlocked the door, then stepped out, securing the shop behind her. She walked to her favourite café, ordered her usual — runny eggs Benedict with hollandaise on the side, and found a table complete with an abandoned newspaper-crumpled and coffee-stained, but complete; and today's edition.

The headlines were the usual dross of modern society. Doom and gloom. Rapes, murders, fraud, heroin overdoses; and that was just the politicians. A tiny story on page five caught her eye;

"Salisbury. Someone has made a two million pound bequest to the Royal Artillery Charitable Fund. The funds solicitor stated that the donor died without heirs, and that these funds had become available after the sale of the donor's house, and that they had wished to remain anonymous. The only information available was that the endowment was in honour of a relative who served in the artillery of the British East India Company. It quotes the donor's executor as saying, 'Even I am perplexed about the historical relationship between my client and this officer.'."

Sarah mulled over the salient points for a few moments. Elizabeth Williams' house would have brought in two million pounds, given its extensive grounds. An investor could have purchased it for a housing development. There was plenty of land for at least two dozen houses. She wondered if the money was from Elizabeth Williams. No heirs. Sadly common, and it was the depressing road she herself was travelling. Still, she *was* young, but at this rate she'd end up married to an old antique dealer with poor hygiene who was more interested in the contents of her shop than the contents of her underwear.

With nothing further of interest in the paper, she grabbed a takeaway coffee and walked to the local market, held at the school every weekend. She'd never made it before because she was open on Saturday mornings, so this was a rare treat for which she had the uncomfortable Mr Grey to thank. If he hadn't turned up, she would have the door open, pricing up the new stock and helping customers find the "one Crown Derby plate they needed for their collection", or to locate a matching saucer to the set "their grandmother had left them that their child had broken during a game of cricket". Her usual customers.

She wandered around in happy solitude. Pots of basil, bunches of summer blooms, scrappy second-hand books. Something for everyone. For her, there were even a few bric-à-brac tables. These were the most interesting of all. Sometimes treasures lay waiting for the right person, and today that was her. Lo-and-behold, an old ink pot with a sterling silver rim, priced at only three pounds! Score. The seller didn't know it was sterling silver, the marks were so obscured by years of grime, but they were there: the lion passant; a leopard's head; a worn letter; and the Queen's head, visible on the rim. The maker's mark wasn't as worn, and she could make out WHW. Sarah wasn't familiar with that mark, she'd have to look it up in her book of London Makers' Marks.

Regardless, she had a piece of old sterling silver, priced as if it were scrappy tin. She didn't even haggle, just handed over the three quid and received a newspaper-wrapped piece of history and future profit. Perfect. The memory of a pair of pristine ink pots still rankled.

The next table had an assortment of salt and pepper shakers, none with their mate. It amazed Sarah that people were so careless as to lose one half of their cruet sets. It reminded her of the conundrum of the washing machine; if you put two matching socks in, only one emerged. Yet she was sure if you put a pair of salt and pepper shakers in the pantry, the pantry didn't swallow one. She carried on, but finding nothing as exciting as her silver ink pot, she moved onto Tesco to refill her fridge with something edible for the next couple of days.

Laden with groceries, she returned to her shop. As she passed Patricia's boutique, she saw half a dozen women rummaging through the racks, and her neighbour at the counter. Sarah extricated her hand from her bags to wave out.

Still with the 'Closed' sign on the door, Sarah priced the stock. She needed to finish up the old man's pile; the last things left were the box of costume jewellery, and his bundle of postcards and paperwork. Sarah settled down, her unnerving meeting with Grey hidden away.

A Service Record from WWII was at the top of the pile. She assumed it was his. Sarah hoped his medals were in there too as the combination would increase the value. Next was a ration book, half-used. These were collectable. A school report; stained, though. Six little pocket calendars that shops used to give out in the 1950s. *They'd look nice framed together*, she thought, and put them to one side. And now some postcards. These were genuine black-and-white photo postcards, so more valuable than the usual tourist ones. Dating from the war and featuring photos of navy ships. Even better. She had a collector who would buy these straight away. Sarah made a mental note to call Euan, her regular collector of everything military.

With everything priced up, and filed in the correct box, shelf or towering pile, she turned back to the group of shipping postcards. One showed the HMIS Cornwallis; that was unusual, a postcard of an Indian ship. And another; this one of HMIS Hindustan. She'd price these at a premium. There were five real photo postcards of Indian war ships.

Sarah flipped one; HMIS Cauvery. The old-fashioned spidery fountain pen writing hard to read, so she pulled out her magnifying glass to decipher the flowery script:

1st Nov '43

Dearest Iris, this is the ship I'm on at the moment.

I can't tell you what we are doing, but our ship is brand new, so everything is great. The rest of the crew is great, and some lads from training are with me. We've been fortunate with the weather.

Thinking of you.

Love Always,

Pat

The date puts them right in the middle of WWII. The address for Iris had her living at 2 Gothic Court, Harlington. Sarah knew it as a former quaint village, now merged with London. Ruined by clogged motorways and dirty overpasses. At the back of her mind, she put together a crazy plan for tomorrow; a nosy drive to Harlington. She wished she'd spoken more to the gentleman who'd sold her the postcards. Sometimes she didn't have time for the life histories of her customers.

Only just last week a middle-aged woman had sold her a silver christening mug, engraved with the name 'Lani'.

She'd asked 'Is Lani your name?'

The woman responded 'No, it was my daughter's. She died of cancer last year, and now we are ready to clear out her things.'

Heartbreaking, and embarrassing for Sarah, but one reason she was now so gun-shy with discussing the histories of goods she purchased.

In her own private world, she shot out her skin at a sharp knocking on the door, before catching sight of a familiar face.

Startled out of her daydream she laughed when she saw who had appeared.

'Hello, Manus,' she smiled as she unlocked the door.

'Hello, Sarah!' boomed a man's voice.

A middle-aged man, with long, dark hair, shot with a liberal helping of grey, tied at the nape of his neck. A large tiger's tooth, capped in gold, hung from his earlobe, and another round his neck on a hulking great gold chain. He walked into the shop with a limp, his gold chain jingling with the lucky medallions he wore on the end. To the untrained eye, his unruly hair, thick beard and uneven gait casting him in the role of a sixteenth century pirate. His unusual personal dress sense might scare little children, but he was the preeminent expert on Polynesian pottery, and she was lucky that he included her shop on his weekly sojourns around the antique shops, markets and auction rooms which filled London.

'What's new with you, Sarah?' he asked in his lilting European accent, one Sarah had yet to identify.

'Not much, Manus, an estate, some postcards. Nothing in your line yet. Have you found any treasures?' she asked.

This conversation is the most predictable thing about the week so far, she thought, as if someone scripted it for them both, and, unless she had something he collected, he would spend five minutes in her shop, then leave.

But, this time, he *had* found something of interest, sticking out of one box she hadn't sorted.

'What are you wanting for this, Sarah?' Manus asked.

He held up a dull green wedge. It looked like a triangular doorstop, two inches by six inches.

Sarah shook her head.

'I've no idea, Manus. You tell me what you think it's worth.'

It must be something important, Sarah pondered, for him to want to buy it. She had to pretend she knew what it was, so put on her game face and waited for Manus to answer.

'I'll give you ninety pounds. It's a nice New Zealand greenstone adze — more modern than I like, but it's OK'.

'A greenstone adze... well then, a hundred and twenty sounds nicer, Manus.'

'OK, I give you a hundred pounds. A good deal, yes?'

He turned away, smiling, to continue rummaging through the boxes stacked in the narrow aisle.

Sarah picked up the piece of greenstone, surprised at its weight and relative warmth. Milliseconds after touching it, a crippling headache struck.

Before losing consciousness, her last thought was of how far away New Zealand was...

THE BUSH

'*R*un!' the man's voice screamed before slumping to the ground. 'Run, goddamn it, woman.'

Sarah stumbled away, her long skirts tangling her unresponsive legs. She didn't understand why she was running, or from whom. She didn't see the tattooed warrior slip away, his revenge extracted for the theft of his gold. The retreating woman didn't interest him.

As the forest returned to its peaceful state, and birdsong surrounded the dying man, two grimy miners made their way towards the man's prone body. The younger man turned his attention to a small suitcase and was rifling through its contents. With the swiftness of the sly, the older man loomed over the injured man, searching his pockets, with no consideration to his injuries. As the victim succumbed to his wounds, he managed one last word, 'Run.'

Sarah fled through the native brush, so fast she missed the concealed riverbank, and slipped down a muddied slope into a fast-flowing river, strewn with rocks the size of cannonballs, and just as dangerous.

Heavy skirts dragged Sarah under the water, the boots laced around her ankles compounded her problems. Lungs wheezing with lack of oxygen, she struggled against the waterlogged cotton.

Mouthfuls of crystalline water competed with the air every time she surfaced. Through sheer good luck, she battled her way to the river's edge, hauling her way out of the arctic water. Shivering on the bank for what seemed like hours, Sarah struggled out of her heavy skirts, aware that the greater risk to her right now was succumbing to hyperthermia. With just her undergarments and her leather boots on, she crawled further up the riverbank, the cutty grass biting into her hands, leaving thin lines of blood on her palms, into the virgin undergrowth, where she collapsed among the roots of the nearest tree. Exhaustion stole away her fear and sleep crept in.

Blood-curdling screams echoed off the neighbouring trees. Curled into a ball, her face pressed sideways into the dirt, fear paralysed her. The screams sounded worse than a nightclub brawl. Inhaling the smell of sweet pungent earth, she lifted her head with trepidation. She found herself in a natural depression at the base of a giant tree, in a forest full of other such huge behemoths, that imagined she must have shrunk. The shouts of angry men surrounded her.

From her prone position under the tree, she couldn't see anyone, so sat up. Someone clamped a rough hand over her mouth, and struggling against her assailant's grip, Sarah's eyes widened in panic. Her heart rate rising, she struck out.

A second pair of hands pressed her arms against her sides, and a voice whispered, 'Keep her bloody still or those savages will have us.'

'If you hadn't bloody stolen their gold, we wouldn't be in this bastard of a mess. What the hell were you thinking, Isaac? They're bloody savages but they aren't stupid, they know the value of gold. Now we've lost our sluice, our picks, and they will cut our bloody heads off and eat us. And now we've got this damn woman screaming the whole damn forest down. I hate these shitty trees. Not a single oak on this whole shit hole of an island, just these *kauris*-and they're only good for ships' masts. What use is a tree that doesn't grow fruit or nuts?'

Isaac continued holding his hand over Sarah's mouth. She'd stopped struggling when she'd heard the word "savages". That word conjuring images from children's storybooks of cannibals with bones in their hair, brandishing clubs, cooking people in enormous cast-iron pots. But this wasn't story-time-the men were flesh and blood. She trembled under the pressure of Isaac's calloused hands.

The silent threesome sat under the tree for so long that melodious birdsong returned, and the rustling in the bushes became nothing more than local wildlife practising their millennium-old habit of foraging for food in their ancient forest.

The sounds of angry men had faded.

'You think they're gone, Seth?' Isaac whispered.

His lilting Welsh accent was more pronounced, now that fear had left his face.

'Yeah, they're gone. Let's see what we've got.'

With that, Isaac took his hands off Sarah's mouth, and Seth grabbed her chin, tilting her head.

'What are you doing here, trying to steal our gold? You and your husband in cahoots with the savages?'

'Let go of me!' hissed Sarah, as she whipped her head out of Seth's rough hands. She rubbed her face, wiping away the sweat and the dirt from the forest floor. 'Don't touch me again. I wasn't spying on you and being here wasn't my idea and I want nothing to do with you or your gold. Which I guess you don't have, seeing as you were stealing from those other men,' she retorted.

Isaac grimaced, 'From the natives, you mean. They're not *men*. You're lucky they didn't find you, lady. They'd have fun with you, that's for sure. It was *our* gold. We'd only gone into town to get supplies and those heathens stole our claim. We were retaking our patch, there's gold there, we already found a nugget...'

'You shut your mouth!' growled Seth, backhanding Isaac in his attempt to stop him from saying anything more.

'And if your husband hadn't made so much bloody noise, those filthy natives would have never even known we were there. It was his own fault he died. And now look where you are; up shit creek without a husband. I don't know whether leaving you alive is a good idea. You may be worth something to us. I'll think on it.'

Sarah tried steadying herself. So it was her *husband* who'd told her to run, and she'd done nothing to protect him. She'd run like the fox runs from the hounds, like a *coward*.

'I'm not interested in your gold. Just tell me where I am and point me towards the nearest town, and I'll leave you both to get your heads chopped off,' said Sarah, concerned more about the mental health of her captors than the 'natives'

Seth was the first to reply.

'I wouldn't push it, lady. I said I'd think on it, but you're not making me like you very much with that mouth on you. You must know where you are? You're just outside of Bruce Bay. It'll take you hours to get into town, if you avoid the savages. But if any of the other diggers see you, I guarantee you won't make it. You must be the only single woman within a hundred miles.'

He laughed; a bitter laugh; a laugh only men with nothing know.

'Which direction? Tell me, please,' Sarah begged.

'Come on, Seth, we'll take her. The Reverend will take her. He'll put her on the next boat, I guess,' said Isaac.

'We won't be looking for anymore gold here, will we, Isaac? We must move on to somewhere where none of their bloody tribe will recognise us. They'll kill us for sure for trying to muscle in on their claim. What bloody savages want with gold is a mystery,' muttered Seth.

'We'll take you, lady, but if you speak one word about the gold, you'd better hope there's a place in heaven for you, 'cause that's where you'll be.'

The men got up and Isaac offered a hand to Sarah, who stumbled clumsily. Isaac caught her, and for the first time he looked at her. He pushed her away from him, but held her by her shoulders as his eyes raked her, taking in the odd nuances of her undergarments. Blushing, Sarah struggled in his strong grip.

'I've never seen a lady in her underthings before,' he uttered, raising an eyebrow in surprise. 'What happened to your clothes?'

Despite being covered up by *her* time's relaxed standards, Sarah drew her arms across her front.

Fumbling for a more believable excuse than "I'm from the future", she replied,

'I lost them in the river, and I'm not sure what's happened to them now.'

Seth nodded; something indefinable flashed through his eyes.

'As the only lady here, best I have a closer look.'

He pushed past Isaac to examine Sarah in more detail. Nodding again, he appeared to reach a decision, and walked off, calling over his shoulder.

'Come on, we need to clear out. The priest will dress her. No point you worrying about her clothing. What are you now, a dandy?'

He chuckled to himself as he strode away through the giant trees. Isaac followed, motioning to Sarah to come.

Together, the three of them slogged their way through the forest, as tiny fantails danced in their wake, catching insects disturbed by their trek.

They'd been walking no longer than half an hour when, ahead of her, she saw Seth drop to the ground behind the trunk of another towering kauri. Isaac did the same, pulling Sarah with him. She had neither seen nor heard anything to alarm her, only birdsong, and the chirruping of summer crickets. She attempted to ask what was happening, but Isaac held his finger up to her lips, silencing her. Then, they heard something much larger than a bird in the forest ahead of them. No, not *something*; the sound clearer now- 'someone'. Through thick undergrowth, Sarah saw half a dozen Englishmen milling about. Although Seth and Isaac didn't want to interact with them, Sarah strained to see if any of them were her father, though she'd reached the conclusion that the likelihood of stumbling across him was remote. He could be anywhere, in any time.

After an inordinate length of time, the militia moved away. Sarah's companions didn't move, hiding behind trees second nature to them, unfazed by the discomfort of the forest floor. It was, however, digging into Sarah's twenty-first century body; one more accustomed to surfing the Internet than to getting up close and personal with centipedes and curious birds. She shifted her limbs, frightening off the ones who had been inching closer to her.

Isaac cupped his hands together and cooed out to Seth, in a fair imitation of a wood pigeon. Seth shuffled back towards them.

'We'll pitch further in there tonight, make our way to town tomorrow. Too many of them militia for my liking and you never know when they might turn against their own kind.'

He spat out the last sentence, leaving no uncertainty as to his opinion of the militia.

The men pushed deeper into the undergrowth, the canopy of silvery ferns embracing them in the dusk. Sarah had two options; stay behind to fend for herself, or follow them. Her choice was easy.

Seth and Isaac were pulling fronds from the surrounding plants, crossing them to form a springy bed. The men were comfortable sleeping rough under the stars with no tent or blankets. The weather was mild and Sarah crossed her fingers, hoping it would stay dry, as she had no other layers to wear.

Her stomach rumbled, expressing its displeasure at being empty. Sarah tried to stifle it with her hands. Neither man had mentioned eating as they carried on creating little fern cocoons to sleep in, and she'd given up on having any food until they made it to Bruce Bay.

Seth laughed.

'Hungry, are you? Well, there's more than enough out there waiting for you to catch it, and then you can eat it.'

Cackling, he pulled off his boots, plonking them upside down on two small sticks he'd dug into the ground. He wiggled his toes, and the odour that assailed Sarah's nose did much to abate her hunger.

Isaac dug his friend in the ribs.

'She's hungry, Seth. Give her something to eat.'

'We ain't lighting a fire with those army boys wandering around. They'd sniff it out in minutes. She can eat *huhu's*. Eat them or starve.'

'I'll eat whatever is going,' she replied, channelling her inner *Fear Factor* contestant bravado.

With his sock-clad foot, Seth rolled a piece of broken-off log towards her.

'Your dinner is in there.'

He busied himself with a pocket knife and a piece of wood, whittling away at some whimsy, ignoring her confusion.

She was at a complete loss what to do with the hunk of rotting wood resting at her feet. Isaac left off his ministrations with fern fronds and peeled back the bark. Sarah choked back the vomit in her mouth-dozens of white *huhu* grubs wriggled in the bowels of the log, each grub about three inches long. Isaac picked one up, held Sarah's eyes, then popped it into his mouth, savouring the richness of the grub. Revolted but starving, Sarah selected the smallest one she could find and placing it in her mouth, she tried chewing without gagging. Seth was laughing so hard at her reaction, tears rolled down his unshaven face.

She plucked out another squirming grub, and, pinching her nose shut with her other hand, shoved the whole grub into her mouth, chewing furiously, lest she taste what she was eating. Her body revolted against her efforts and kept trying to purge itself. Despite heaving, she swallowed after chewing the grub to death.

Deciding she wasn't hungry anymore, she turned away from the two laughing men, and, following their lead, attempted to make a fern mattress too. Isaac carried on eating the grubs, causing Seth to continue laughing at the humour of the situation.

The light dimmed as the sun found its way back to London. Sarah imagined it rising and directing its light onto her little shop and she wondered what was happening there. Through the canopy of trees, tiny lights distracted her from her thoughts as one by one, stars appeared. The thousands of stars in the heavens reminded her she was a tiny soul in the spectrum of light. And, regardless of where she was, stars would continue to sparkle and the sun would set.

As she tossed and turned to find a comfortable sleeping position, tiny pinpricks of light surrounded her. It was as if baby stars had fallen from the sky, caught as they fell into the arms of the surrounding trees. Fascinated, she reached out to touch one. The light flickered out. Sarah waited, and moments later reappeared. She tried touching it again, and again it vanished, the glow-worms playing a never-ending game of hide and seek. They comforted Sarah in her bush-clad bed and she closed her eyes, never expecting sleep to come, fully prepared for nightmares about savages, and wild militia, and marauding animals. Half-asleep she called out.

'Isaac, are there wild animals here?'

'No, only birds, bats, and beetles. You're safe.'

With his words, and her tiny night lights, she fell into the sleep of the exhausted.

THE CHURCH

*I*saac shook her awake as the sun struggled to reach the horizon. She saw him holding a finger to his lips, and nodded in understanding, amazed at how quickly she'd accepted a life sneaking around the countryside with two strangers.

He sent her towards Seth, crouching behind the base of a tree. Squeezing into the space behind him, she peered round the ancient trunk. She couldn't see anything to arouse her suspicion. *A fine bushranger I'd make,* she thought.

They waited for the best part of an hour, and, with the sun visible over the treetops, Seth uttered two words.

'Come on.'

With no explanation for the enforced silence that morning, they walked on without speaking, Sarah swivelling her head with every step, checking for any hidden dangers.

Before long, she could have sworn she smelt the ocean. There was more bird life, including seagulls, visible through trees which were thinning out. Sarah begged for a rest on the sawn-off stump of a giant of the forest; the diameter was wider than she was tall. Isaac sat next to her, whittling a piece of wood into an uncanny replica of the fantails which followed them through the bush.

'What's your name, lady?'

She hesitated, before accepting that these men had kept her alive; 'Sarah.'

'I make these for my brothers. They'd love to see the birds here; not so many where they and me mam live. One day I'll send them home. Just can't get the face right. That's why I keep making new ones.'

Sarah leaned over to admire his work. It looked perfect to her.

'It's perfect, Isaac. Just send it to them.'

Isaac blushed at the unfamiliar compliment. Few people had ever given him any form of encouragement. Seth reappeared, shoving them from the trunk with a muttered curse. The moment of simple pleasure between the two lost.

After a couple more hours, they reached a sprawling wooden settlement next to the most exquisite bay in the world, just as the sun had passed its highest point in the blue sky.

Bruce Bay, with a harbour dotted with the bobbing hulls of a dozen small boats, surrounded on one side by a thousand different hues of green — tall wooden sentinels, which would one day fall to the axes of progress. Along the high tide mark were cairns, pancaked rocks in tottering pyramids; placed by locals and travellers waiting for a boat. Canvas tents crowded the banks of the river-flotsam and jetsam washed onto a beach after a storm–a shantytown of hope, and misery.

'Welcome to Bruce Bay. The arse end of the world. Home to bastards, the sons of bastards, us, and now you.'

Seth gave Sarah an elaborate theatrical bow.

The two disparate views — the stunning scenery and the dismal shantytown — assailed Sarah's senses. Several wooden buildings squatted beyond the tents. Puffs of smoke were everywhere, carrying smells of cooking on the offshore breeze. So unlike the London she knew, this hodgepodge of squalor was like nothing she had ever seen.

Her companions made their way through the outskirts of the settlement. Sarah followed.

'Bruce Bay. "Where everything that glitters is gold", is what they told us,' mumbled Isaac.

'Not true, is it?' retorted Seth.

'But you said you'd found a nugget...'

Seth whirled around grabbing her arm.

'You forget you ever heard mention of our gold, lady! It's none of your business. I warned you to *never* speak of it, to anyone. People get killed round here just for the chance they may have gold. Rumours have wings and nowhere do they fly faster than on a goldfield. Don't think for one second that killing a lady would worry me? Watch your step.'

He let go of her arm and carried on towards a small church under construction up a hill, away from the detritus of the canvas ocean.

Two men were standing in front of the bones of the church, its half-finished steeple prodding the sky. One a man of the cloth, the other a head taller than the minister, with the shoulders of an Olympic rower, clad in moleskin trousers, and a blue plaid shirt. From behind, he looked powerful, this image reinforced by the rifle slung over his shoulder.

'It's that bastard Price,' Seth muttered to Isaac, slowing his approach. 'Remember, lady, you say nothing about what happened, nothing.'

'Good day, Reverend Young. Warden Price,' called out Isaac.

Seth muttered something similar, although inaudible, including words not meant for polite conversation.

'Seth, Isaac. I've had the natives by today complaining about you trying to muscle in on their claim? Take it easy, boys, you don't want to upset them. Come winter, they may be the only ones keeping us alive in this godforsaken bay. No offence, Father,' he added.

Warden William Price. Keeper of the peace at Bruce Bay. The Governments intermediary between the natives — the Māori — and the fools trying their hand at making their fortune. An Englishman by birth, he'd travelled to Australia as a warden on one of the convict ships, and carried on to New Zealand on board the vessel *The British Empire*. Like many single men of the day, he thought to make his fortune in the goldfields discovered at the bottom of the world.

His natural leadership had, instead, seen him appointed as Warden by the local government, who recognised his previous employment, his peacemaking skills, and his prowess with a rifle. After mulling over their offer, and realising that the life of a digger was back-breaking toil with no reward, William Price had accepted the position.

In a time when 'nutrition' wasn't in the dictionary, this man looked like a god. His clothes were rough linen, but clean. His facial hair cropped short, unlike the priest with his unruly pepper beard, and long hair. Price's was shoulder length, but caught back in a simple leather tie. His eyes haunted her. Long black lashes, with pupils so dark he seemed able to look into her soul.

'Madam,' Price doffed his hat.

He looked at Seth and Isaac, his eyes seeming to ask, *Who is this?*

Spying the half-finished church, Sarah responded. 'I'm Sarah, Sarah Bell, from London. I... a widow now, and I'm just trying to get to a city where I might catch a ship back to England.'

She glanced towards Seth, who was staring at her.

She hoped they would not question her any further, as she was unsure how well she could create an imaginary life, without it sounding like an episode of *Little House on the Prairie*.

'Pleased to meet you, Mrs Bell,' responded Reverend Young. 'So sorry about your husband. If I can, ah... your... mode of dress is most... ah, well, the camp residents may view it as, ah, inappropriate and..., revealing...' he tailed off, embarrassed at his visual assessment of Sarah's wardrobe.

'I fell into the river, and this is what I had left...' started Sarah.

'That's all the natives left her after slaughtering her husband. We found her after they'd killed him. Bloody mess it was. The militia needs to deal with them. Menace they are,' interrupted Seth.

'We were hoping Mrs Young might... cover her up,' Isaac suggested.

'Oh, yes, er,' stammered the Reverend. 'An excellent idea. Yes, better than undergarments.'

Sarah squirmed at the penetrating gaze from Warden Price. He of the smouldering eyes, and the long, strong fingers he was tapping against his polished rifle butt.

KIRSTEN MCKENZIE

Price bent to pick up a burlap-wrapped package at his feet, before announcing, 'Right, Reverend, I'll look after the candlesticks from Canon Newton, make sure they're kept safe from any unsavoury characters.'

He looked at Seth and Isaac.

'Mrs Bell, it was a pleasure meeting you. No doubt we'll see you at the service on Sunday, more suitably attired.'

For the first time, Warden Price smiled. A smile as rare as the gold the miners searched for, and as bright.

Sarah smiled back.

Reverend Young took her arm and led her towards a large wooden house, wrapped with a fine veranda. *At least it isn't a tent*, thought Sarah. She barely had time to realise that Price had gone off in the other direction before Isaac called out 'goodbye'.

Sarah stopped walking, feeling peculiar that she was leaving the relative familiarity of Seth and Isaac's company, to stay with a minister and his wife in a town where the only other person she knew was a dashing soldier in homespun trousers, with an English accent, unsullied by American sitcoms, and lazy comprehensive schools. She waved 'goodbye', calling out her thanks. Seth had turned away, walking off towards an old-fashioned general store.

Isaac lingered.

'Mrs Bell, I'm happy we could help you. I'm real sorry about your husband, it was never... well, it was hard luck you were there when they was looking for us, but it's done now, and I'm sure Seth wanted no one to get hurt and all... but, I'm sorry.'

With a shy smile, he shoved the wooden fantail into her hands, and hurried to follow Seth, the same way a seaside donkey follows the only path they have ever known.

Sarah blinked away her tears, taken aback by Isaac's sudden display of humility, and allowed the Reverend to guide her into the house.

THE GENERAL STORE

*I*saac hurried after Seth, turning to watch Sarah, until the Reverend's house swallowed her. Isaac felt a keen sense of loss. He didn't know her, but she'd shown a rare kindness to him. She'd conversed with him.

In the normal course of his life, the conversations he had were one-way orders from Seth, sneers from the other prospectors, and suspicious glances from the shopkeepers in town, due to the bad reputation that Seth had made for himself, well before Isaac came on the scene.

Isaac caught up with Seth. The older man looked thoughtful as they entered the General Store. He gathered up a few items before leaning on the rough-hewn counter.

'So, what's new in town, Toomer?' he asked.

The store owner, Grant Toomer, stopped unpacking a batch of prospecting pans, and glanced over.

'Ah, Seth Brown, welcome back. Nothing much. The natives are getting restless. They gave some men digging further up the coast a hiding; something about prospecting on *tapu* land. What the hell is *tapu* land, anyway? How's things with you?'

'We've had a dry spell but ran into a woman in the middle of the bush. Found her husband too, stuck like a pig in the gut. Stone cold dead. Guess that makes her a widow now. The Reverend took her in, but *we* brought her to safety. Think I should try calling upon her family for some reward money. Might help if a man like yourself, someone friendly with the Reverend, could drop in a few words 'bout how I rescued her,' Seth winked at Grant.

Isaac, alarmed at the talk of Sarah, abandoned his new pick and shovel, interrupting the conversation. In his mind, Sarah was his friend, and the thought of Grant Toomer or Seth getting too close to her appalled him.

'Seth, Mrs Bell won't stay long. She'll be on the first boat to the city, I reckon,' he managed.

Seth ignored him, and carried on, 'Yes, sir, girls who look like her always come from well-off families.'

'What?' asked Grant.

'Said she escaped with just the clothes on her back. But that is a lie. The family will want to hear from me. That's what I'll do, 'cept my letters aren't any good, can't make head nor tail of the damn things. So I'd be much obliged if you'd write it for me, Toomer. I'll get her details out of the Reverend, and we'll take it from there. There'll be something in it for you, I give you my word.'

Toomer agreed, and after exchanging more gossip, Isaac and Seth left, leaving Toomer pondering whether he should stock up on ammunition if the natives were more than "unsettled".

'How d'you know she was lying?' Isaac asked Seth as they made their way through the triangular tents to their dirt-grey apology for one. Swiped by Seth from a dead man's claim while he was being buried at the graveyard, Isaac thought stealing it had kicked off their run of bad luck. The tent was no palace, small with several rips, and, regardless of how they pitched it, the roof always sloped lower on the left-hand side, the side Seth made Isaac sleep on. Their campsite looked just the way it had before they'd gone on their ill-fated incursion into the natives' land looking for the mother-lode of gold nuggets.

'How'd I know she was lying?'

Seth spun to face Isaac, and thrust his hand into his trouser pocket, pulling out a gleaming diamond hair-slide.

'This, Isaac, this is how. She said she escaped with the clothes on her back. So how come she had this?'

The diamond hair-clip looked obscene in Seth's calloused hands.

Isaac reached out to touch it. Seth's hand clamped shut over the small treasure, putting it back into his pocket.

'This is how, and it means her family has enough money to pay me a reward for rescuing her. Between this bauble and the gold we found, and the money you got from her old man's suitcase, we're almost set. A couple more runs at that claim after the natives have gone, and a fat, juicy reward, and that's it, I'm done, back to Australia.'

Seth crawled into the tent, pausing only to remove his boots at the flap, before falling into the deep sleep granted only to those devoid of morals. Isaac sat outside and loosened his boots. It was still daytime; it wasn't time for sleep — unless Isaac wanted to head out tonight. With resignation, he crawled into his bed space and tried to rest. Thoughts of Sarah in trouble plagued his dreams, so it was not the restful sleep of the pure of mind, or the sleep of a social miscreant.

THE MINISTER'S HOUSE

*T*he Reverend ushered Sarah into the white-painted home, bellowing, 'Christine! Where are you, woman?'

The house was immaculate, as any house of the clergy should be, and Christine Young appeared clean-cut and predictable as any vicar's wife should be — a bustling tornado of curves, curls, and smiles who whirled into the room, and came to a sudden halt with an exclamation of surprise.

'Oh, John, you never... well, I never... well, well, hello, young lady. I'm the Reverend's wife, Christine, and I don't believe we've met before?' she chirped, looking to the Reverend for explanation.

'Ah, Christine, this is Sarah Bell, recently widowed, God rest his soul, and in her haste to escape, she could only, um... rescue, ah, the wardrobe she is wearing. I suggest that, um, you might... ah, perhaps outfit...' he tapered off, blushing.

To her credit, Christine laughed. A bawdy laugh, more at home in a bar than a reverend's front room.

'You silly man! Come with me, Mrs Bell, we'll get you out of those, into something that won't embarrass my dear husband.'

Sarah followed her down a dim hall, through to a room dominated by a double bed, a dressing table that would fetch thousands of pounds at an auction in modern day New Zealand, and a matching mottled kauri wardrobe.

Christine flung open its doors and pulled out a fine woollen frock, with as much shape as a flour sack, and a bonnet.

'This will do. It is not one of my best frocks, and as long as this husband doesn't die on me like the last one, I won't need it for some time.'

Sarah warmed to Christine more every minute.

'Your last husband?' she queried.

'Oh yes. Died on the ship coming here, first week of the voyage. Only good thing he ever did, stupid man. But it meant I had the best time on board. Laughing and singing, and we even danced on the decks once. He would have had me whipped if I'd sung anywhere other than the church. No, the best thing was him dying, of seasickness. Weak.'

'Met the Reverend in Lyttelton, of all places. He'd placed an advertisement for a housekeeper in the paper, after he knew the church was posting him here, and, one thing led to another, and I never did do much housekeeping.'

She laughed her bawdy barmaid laugh.

'You'll stay with us while you get things sorted?' asked Christine.

'There's not much to do. I'd prefer to go to the nearest town and go back to London,' said Sarah.

'That'll be Dunedin. But London, why would you want to go back? Here, without a husband, you can be anything you desire. Although, having a husband does occasionally have its positives.'

Christine winked.

'We'll have a proper dinner to welcome you to town. The ladies would love to hear of your adventures. If it's not too painful for you,' she added. 'We almost never get visitors of note. Warden Price will come and Mr Toomer from the store, and whichever officers are in town. John will know. Now, you get dressed, and I'll meet you in the kitchen. We're about to have supper, so you tidy yourself up and you can tell me all about your family.'

As Christine left the room, Sarah summoned up the courage to ask about her parents, just on the off chance, hope in her voice. 'Do you know the Lesters?'

'Sorry, no, I haven't been here that long, and haven't left Bruce Bay since I arrived! I know no one other than those who live in town.'

Christine left her visitor alone to get changed.

Sarah trailed her hand across the smocked bedspread. Why this was happening was for the gods to answer, but what an adventure! She wondered what had happened to Manus at the shop. Had her disappearance left him frozen in time waiting to pay for his greenstone adze? Or was he looking for her? Had she collapsed behind the counter and all this was a dream, *à la Dallas* and who shot JR?.

Sarah slipped out of her cotton underthings, changing into Christine's stark but serviceable dress. She was about to make her way to the kitchen when she remembered the diamond hair-slide she'd left in her hair in London. But with a sinking heart, she realised it was probably at the bottom of the river where she'd had her impromptu swim.

'Christ!' she exclaimed, a tad too loud inside the house of a minister of God. Tears prickled. Here she was, a modern woman, and yet all she did was cry or threaten to cry. A poor example to womankind. Why couldn't she be strong and purposeful, like Margaret Thatcher or Mother Teresa?

She heaved herself off the floor, and found the kitchen, sniffing and wiping her eyes. No gleaming Formica benches here, just plain wooden counters, scarred by knife marks. Huge iron pots and a copper kettle dominated the décor, and a colonial hutch dresser took centre stage against one entire wall, filled with a Royal Doulton dinner service, its pattern unfaded by frequent dishwasher use. It surprised Sarah that people put old dinner services in dishwashers and microwaves.

Sarah found Christine having an animated conversation with a shorter, rounder woman, covered in a fine film of flour.

'Ah, Mrs Bell, there you are. Cook has made supper for us, and tomorrow we will drop into Mr Toomer's store to order supplies for our dinner party. It is not like Regent Street here. Oh no, it's just the one shop for everything, except ale, that you can get that from a dozen places. Three months I've been here now. Time flies but soon we'll celebrate the completion of our church. You'll stay for that? There are so few women here. It will be delicious to have someone appropriate to take tea with. Most other 'ladies' here aren't so much the ones who enjoy luncheon, but more *ladies of the night...* I can save their souls. I just can't have them round for tea!'

Christine laughed her infectious laugh at her little joke and Sarah and Cook followed. Cook had thrown together a hearty supper, which Sarah devoured. It had been a long time since she had eaten anything more substantial than the eggs Benedict, back in London before Manus arrived.

The Reverend, his wife, and Sarah ate in the dining room, tucking into slices of roast pork and a sweet potato she had never tasted before.

'This is *kumara* from the natives. They grow it,' the Reverend said in response to the look on her face as she inspected the orange vegetable on her fork.

'Delicious,' Sarah replied, enjoying its sweetness.

The conversation was eclectic and amusing, the Reverend full of amusing anecdotes of miners and their misdemeanours; of finding love after giving up hope; and life in an antipodean gold mining town. Sarah's sides were sore from laughing.

Christine didn't hold back either. She told a delicious tale of a ferryman who had dallied with one of the native women and, when her family had found out, forced him at spear point to 'turn native', as Christine so eloquently relayed it.

After the meal and a cup of tea, for it would seem that the British tradition of a cure-all cup of tea had reached the colonies, Sarah excused herself, and retired to bed. She slipped into the softest feather bed she'd ever slept in. Christine had rustled up more clothes for her, including a nightdress and a jacket. Sleep came swiftly, devoid of dreams.

After breakfast the next morning, Christine plonked the bonnet onto Sarah's head, and arm in arm they headed out, walking the short distance down the muddy horse hoof-worn road to a substantial wooden building. 'Toomer's Goods', proclaimed a large, hand-painted sign. Through the open barn-like doors, Sarah could see dozens of barrels and crates; stacks of pans, axes, and wooden-handled picks. Huge drawers labelled 'Flour', 'Oats', 'Rice', and 'Sugar' lined one wall.

Sarah gazed at them in awe, remembering how sought after these old-fashioned kitchen storage bins were, condition irrelevant, and here was a whole wall, brand new, filled to the brim with raw ingredients. She laughed, wondering how much it would cost to get them home! She was daydreaming about shipping them back to London and putting them into very, very, long-term storage when Christine introduced her to Toomer, explaining her recent widowhood and arrival. Sarah swore she saw a gleam in his little piggy eyes after Christine mentioned she was a widow. Ugh. The last thing she wanted was a jowly middle-aged shopkeeper leering after her. She had enough of that in her own time. After Christine had placed her order with the obese Mr Toomer, she invited him to come to dinner later that week, which he accepted a little too much enthusiasm.

'I'm sorry about your loss, Mrs Bell. It was fortunate that Seth and Isaac found you when they did,' he fished.

Sarah nodded, 'Right place, right time.'

'How exciting it was them who found you!' Christine exclaimed.

Her knowledge of Seth's nature coloured by what the Reverend had told her on previous occasions.

'Do you think I need to invite them to dinner too?'

Toomer spat his chewing tobacco with precise aim into the nearby spittoon.

'I don't think we need to have them at our dinner, Mrs Young. No need to lower the tone, baking would suffice, I'd think,' he offered.

'Yes, that's for the best. How brilliant of you to think of that, Mr Toomer. Lovely.' Christine beamed.

As the two women left, Christine pointed out the key landmarks in Bruce Bay: the wharf; the bar; the unfinished church; and native settlement — '… they call it a *marae*, you know…' — past the hill where the church was being built.

Everywhere they walked, men stopped to greet Christine with obvious respect, and Sarah with unconcealed interest. A respectable single woman in town was almost as exciting as a gold strike. The women they passed greeted Christine cheerfully enough, but gave Sarah only the tiniest of nods. Another woman might reduce their revenue and, until they were sure she was no threat, friendship wasn't an option.

Sarah tried to ignore the stares, and to be pleasant, but it was a tiring undertaking. She felt that, once again, she was being paraded in front of potential mates, none of whom held a candle to the suitability of Lord Grey. As they walked, the West Coast weather, known to the locals for being fickle, threatened to strike. Dark clouds rolled in like treacle spilling down the sides of a jar, filling every nook and cranny with thick, misty clouds.

Christine bustled her inside the Reverend's house, moaning how bad the weather was in this part of the world.

'Rain, rain, rain, that's all we ever get. The Reverend only sees the good, but I pray for a week of sunshine. This rain makes everything I own mouldy and damp and I can't tell you how miserable it makes the men. I'm surprised they aren't near the end of their tethers, to be honest.'

THE NATIVES

The morning dawned misty, with drizzle dancing through the trees, giving an ethereal quality. Sarah leaned her forehead against the window and imagined being alone in this land, at one with the earth. She dressed herself in the one black dress she now owned, adding her worn leather boots to her ensemble, like an Amish matron.

A thousand thoughts flew through her mind. The dinner party was tonight, with Warden Price. What she wouldn't give for a long shower and her trusty concealer, and hair straighteners. She blushed when she realised she'd been thinking of Price. Such a foolish idea! He was from a different country, and century.

Sarah made her way along the dim hall to the front room where she could hear movement. A fire had been lit to ward off the chill chased inside by the rain. Christine was working at a lady's Davenport; the writing desk and her dainty script incongruous in this manly room. There was little sign that a woman lived here, apart from the desk. Māori weapons adorned the walls-long staffs trimmed with feathers she didn't recognise, greenstone adzes, huge clubs — wooden ones and others made from greenstone, each carved with intricate patterns of swirls and whorls.

Sarah greeted Christine, and examined the amazing collection on the walls-a collection probably in a museum now, hidden behind glass, where the warmth of the stone couldn't escape; where the breeze couldn't ruffle the luminous feathers, making them move as if still attached to the bird from whence they came.

Imagine getting one of these to auction off with her jewelled *katar*. She would be the talk of the antiquities world, her father's contemporaries flummoxed by her good fortune.

Christine looked up from her writing.

'Good morning, Sarah. Today I will take you on a *proper* tour of town, and to visit the natives. Our shipment of bibles has arrived from Dunedin, and my husband has tasked me with delivering them to the Māori. Will you come with me if that isn't too painful? I'm sure it wasn't our locals who killed your husband. We've always been on such good terms with them.'

'It's fine, Christine.'

She was curious about the rest of the settlement. After everything she'd learnt, she fancied a new focus at work, if she ever returned. A focus on things Pacifica, which entail a trip to modern New Zealand. *How magical would that be?* What would become of Christine and Reverend Young? Did they follow the gold rush around New Zealand, or die from illnesses no longer in society? Did they have children? *Imagine meeting their descendants*, she mused. She tried not to think of her life in London, of Patricia, or Manus fumbling around in her shop. Or any of the things that preoccupied her in 'normal' times. The biggest question now was how could she return to London? A question she hid away in her mind, closing the door on it.

Christine tidied away her ink and paper, explaining that she was writing to her parents, reassuring them she was alive and well, and her new husband was still treating her well.

'I try to write at least once a month. After my first husband died, they wanted me to return to England, but I couldn't do that. That life is behind me. The people here are honest, and I have a peace I never experienced in England. Living with nature fills my soul every day, it's heaven on earth and I shall never leave.

'Now, enough grand words from me, let's go see parts of this town that *aren't* related to heaven; they are closer to Hell, but, oh so entertaining!'

Christine laughed, tossing her curls.

Sarah pulled her borrowed jacket tighter over her shoulders as they walked the road toward a hundred plumes of smoke. The cold an insidious lover caressing her neck. She shivered in the half light illuminating the scene before her. Gaunt men huddled around campfires, eyes blazing with a religious fervour. Here, it was devotion to gold, and gold alone, that kept these men alive. They called out greetings to Mrs Young; the wife of their Reverend the closest thing to their own wife or mother they had here. Most appraised Sarah the way a horse trader might a mare at the annual Hanoverian Verband horse auctions. Sarah felt their looks, as she and Christine traversed the canvas settlement, to the waterfront. Dozens of eyes raked her, questioning whether she was for sale, available, or forcible. Sarah avoided their eyes as she walked across the uneven ground, pitted with the heel impressions of hundreds of hungry, lonely men.

They found themselves at the small jetty, referred to as a 'wharf' by Christine. It wasn't a wharf to rival those in Newcastle or London, but it *was* busy with small wooden boats tied to the jetty – the workhorses of the larger trading sailboats littering the mouth of the harbour, unloading provisions for the prospectors. Some were pushing off, carrying passengers clutching their meagre belongings-those who had given up, forced out by the unrelenting ruthlessness of life.

Christine strode up to a clean-shaven heavy-set man, who doffed his tatty cap, showing a balding head. He motioned to a scrawny young lad, to pick up a bulky package on the jetty. It was *far* too heavy for the boy who struggled under its weight, but a sharp clip to the back of the head forced him to wrestle the package over to Christine and Sarah, where he could get a proper grip.

Christine seemed oblivious to the abuse of the boy.

'Mrs Bell, may I introduce Mr Bryce Sinclair. He has sailed up from Dunedin to deliver my husband's bibles. His son Samuel will carry them for us. Mr Sinclair, let me introduce Sarah Bell, a widow, and staying with us. We are having a small dinner tonight to welcome her. Will you be able to attend?'

Sinclair's weasel eyes brightened at the mention of Sarah's widowhood.

'Why, yes, I am here for the night.'

He looked toward the harbour, caressed by a gentle breeze, waves licking the beach.

'I *had* planned to leave for Nelson tonight, but the tides are not in our favour. So, yes, I accept your invitation.'

Christine glowed. Party planning agreed with her and the guest list was scaring Sarah, as she imagined being married off to a sailor, a shopkeeper or a soldier by the Reverend and his wife at the end of the meal.

As they left, Sarah felt Sinclair's salacious look painfully as a rose thorn in the palm. She didn't look back as they moved off, followed by Sinclair's diminutive son and his package of bibles. There was something about him that pulled at her soul. She had seen the cruelty in his eyes before, but as she tried to grasp at those strands of her memory, they slipped away, thread uncoiling from a cotton reel.

They made their way to the brow of the hill; a hard slog in long skirts and cumbersome leather shoes. As they crested it, Sarah saw a dozen naked children running barefoot around the settlement. The children were laughing, carefree, unburdened by the concerns of adults — so unlike the boy they had with them. A group of women squatted around a campfire, at ease with their land and life. On seeing Christine and Sarah, one woman rose to greet them. Sarah had to stifle a small shriek-her reaction to the woman's tattooed face-her chin covered with fine green filigree, the lines and whorls identical to the carvings on the weapons in Christine's front room. Her lips tattooed so dark, giving her face an otherworldly quality.

The women pressed their noses together, with Sarah shuffling uncomfortably behind her friend, as the Māori woman stepped forward to greet her the same way.

With the formalities complete, Christine beckoned Samuel

forward. The package was so heavy, and he was so terrified, he tripped and dropped it, scattering leather-bound bibles at the feet of the women. The Māori *wahine*, woman, didn't flinch, but looked at Christine with contempt. Christine was oblivious, she was too busy helping Samuel pick up the precious books before the damp spoiled the pages. The gift of bibles was not what the native woman had been expecting and Sarah tried drawing Christine's attention to the changing atmosphere, which had grown as cold as the breeze from the ocean.

Christine stood up with arms full, her smile fading as she saw the woman disappear into a wooden building, guarded by two columns carved with terrifying creatures, their eyes glinting in the light.

'Come, Christine, we should leave before we make things worse. Samuel, gather up those books. Make sure we leave none behind. Pass me some, I'll help you,' Sarah commanded, looking over her shoulder.

Christine stared at the empty ground, even the children had disappeared, the women abandoning their cooking station.

'Christine, we need to leave. They do not want your bibles, come on!' Sarah tugged on her arm.

Christine turned away and squared her shoulders.

'He'll think I did not try. That was Sophia. Though she does not speak English, we always understood each other, I thought she was open to the word of God...' Christine trailed off, chastened by her failure.

'We'll give them to the miners, Christine. The Reverend will approve. They cannot miss what they have never had, and handing them Bibles they don't want isn't worth losing your head,' Sarah said, remembering Seth and Isaac's stories of the natives decapitating their enemies.

Christine shook herself out of her fugue.

'Yes, the miners have much more need for God's guiding words, and with the church so near completion. Let's deliver these, then we should go home. Samuel, you will eat with us before you return to your father. You need more meat on those bones.'

Sarah looked back towards the *marae*. Standing outside the triangular building were several men, their faces fully tattooed, muscular torsos bare in the chilly wind, watching them leave. Warriors, every one, and their inscrutable faces scared her more than Seth and Isaac and the miners put together.

THE DINNER

*A*fter accompanying Christine and Samuel through the miner's tents, where she spied Seth and Isaac on the extreme edge of the camp, and surviving ribald suggestions about what she could do with her spare time that evening, Sarah returned home with them.

She'd handed a Bible to Isaac, thanking him for his help. Seth had scoffed when she attempted the same with him.

'God doesn't live here, Mrs Bell. The only use for that book is as firewood.'

The weak sunlight made them both look ill and thinner than the last time she'd seen them, but their wellbeing was not her concern, and, after spending a few moments at their campfire, she moved on. They'd told her that the other miners were considering leaving, as news of lucrative gold finds further north had reached them. It had been weeks since any decent weights of gold had come from the rivulets and streams flowing into Bruce Bay from the rugged hills surrounding them, and the place was restless. Idle hands spread idle rumours, and rumours turned uglier the further they spread.

As they returned home, most of the bibles gone, Sarah asked if she might keep one. Christine agreed, overjoyed at Sarah's piety.

'Oh, sweet lady you must have one! I forgot that you have no belongings. It will comfort you in your grief.'

Except for Isaac's carved bird, the bible was Sarah's first real possession in this brave new world. Christine insisted on writing an inscription inside to her new friend; she did not understand how very apt it was.

Dearest Sarah

    It is with the greatest love I gift this to you.

    May the word of God fill your soul, and this country.

    May God bless your footsteps through His land, from this day on, and

for all your days, wherever those steps may take you.

    The fondest regards,

    Christine Young

    15 March 1864

They ate luncheon in the pale light of the dining room. Even in colonial New Zealand, class standards were strong. They sent Samuel to eat in the kitchen with Cook, which made his day. Unbeknownst to the Reverend and his wife, the poor boy hadn't had a proper meal since his mother had abandoned him to his abusive father several years ago, and Sinclair had taken her betrayal out on the boy. Withholding food from his son was a favourite punishment for the most minor misdemeanour. Samuel needed only to look askance at his father to receive a beating; his behaviour, good or bad, not an accurate gauge if his father might thrash him that day. Bryce Sinclair enjoyed violence, and took a perverse pleasure in disciplining his son, and no one could stop him; not the Warden, the military or the Church.

The Reverend joined the ladies, overjoyed that they had given the Bibles to the miners. That they had not gone to the Maori settlement didn't concern him; he viewed life from the same rose-tinted glasses as his wife.

They talked of the characters he had seen during his time on the

West Coast of New Zealand, discussing whether gold was plentiful, or more just a fanciful notion. The Reverend showed Sarah a small nugget he'd found himself in the very early days of the gold rush. He'd had it fashioned into a pendant for his wife, which she refused to wear, for fear that someone may take it from her while in the grip of drink, which was more plentiful in the town than gold was in the rivers. For anyone not paid by the church, they would have sold it. But Reverend Young had the luxury of being able to keep gold for jewellery.

Christine and Sarah both retired to their rooms for the afternoon. Sarah could hear Cook directing Samuel to bring in more coal and wood for the stove, and to take the slops outside to the pigs. *At least that skinny boy ate this afternoon* thought Sarah as she drifted off to sleep. An afternoon nap was a luxury with which she was unfamiliar. Not since her university days had she lain in bed in the daytime.

A gentle knock woke her from her slumber. The change in the light showed at least two hours had passed since she'd fallen asleep. Christine opened the door with an armful of clothes.

'I've pulled these out of my travelling trunks. Not this year's style in London, or even in Dunedin, but one of them may do. Pick one to wear for dinner tonight. They'll be here within the hour. So much fun!'

She clapped her hands with glee.

Sarah got up and splashed water over her face from the china jug as Christine bustled around her, laying beautiful taffetas across the bed. Reds and golds, resplendent autumn colours, followed by various greens, sapphire blues and a dove grey that spoke of moonlight and the shadows of stars.

The two women played dress-ups and a riot of colour filled the drab room, bringing daylight into the room. Christine explained that her family had business ties on the Indian continent, and her father had bolts of the finest cloth set aside for her and her sisters to have made into gowns, taking the view that if they looked wealthy and elegant, they would marry the most eligible men.

After an hour of battling with whalebone stays and buttons the size of her fingernails, Sarah settled for rich emerald green, trimmed with a velvet ribbon. Jet buttons completed the outfit. The inbuilt stays made her waist tiny and shunted her breasts higher, breasts concealed behind layers of organza — treasure obscured behind a veil. Christine wore a russet gown, shimmering with shots of gold as she moved in and out of the candlelight. A magical sight.

Christine helped with her hair. Hundreds of pins held her wavy locks high on her head, exposing her slender neck. The other woman's curls confined under a tiny swatch of matching fabric, and pinned in place with tiny clips adorned with citrines, which caught the light of the candles, making her golden curls appear angelic. The sound of voices from the front room, coupled with tobacco smoke, curled into the bedroom.

'Shall we go?' asked Christine, raising a cheeky eyebrow at Sarah.

That one eyebrow told Sarah what she needed to know. This dinner was not a mere gathering of friends; it was about survival of the species. Finding her a mate, a husband. Death so prevalent in this time that normal grieving was a forbidden luxury. She was a widow, a widow with good looks and of childbearing age, so must marry.

Christine gave Sarah a gentle push towards the door, and together they walked into the front room, now transformed by candles standing in gleaming silver candlesticks. Cut crystal glasses sat on the sideboard. No teetotallers here. While they adhered to many social norms from England, it was too hard to abide by others, so they gave the ladies glasses filled with amber liquid, and introductions made.

Even in candlelight, the rugged good looks of Warden Price were unmistakable. Sarah's heart quickened. His eyes shielded by his long black lashes, his skin unblemished. He nodded at her.

'Mrs Bell.'

In complete contrast, the shopkeeper, Mr Toomer, accompanied by his daughter Felicity, was doughy. His jowls swung, and the sweat on his pock-marked face shone in the flickering light. He pumped her hand, sliding his thumb across her palm bizarrely, a caress? She wiped her hand on her skirt in disgust.

The man from the wharf had arrived - Bryce Sinclair. His head devoid of hair, ears torn from back alley fights, with the nose of a pugilist; his nature was clear. Poor Samuel; it was obvious to Sarah that Sinclair used his fists more than his brain. How the Reverend and his wife couldn't see his cruelty was beyond her. They only saw the good in everyone. The candlelight did nothing to improve Sinclair's demeanour; it enhanced the callousness of his nature. His familiarity niggled, but she told those thoughts not to intrude on the night. It was no wonder she was feeling flustered, the continual backwards and forwards in time, with no warning or logic, would puzzle Albert Einstein and Stephen Hawking, let alone a young woman from middle-class London.

Christine introduced her to another couple, Frederick Sweeney and his wife, Margaret; a young woman with a worn face, and pregnant. She smiled at Sarah and greeted her as a sister. Sarah liked her at once. Sweeney, a successful businessman, owned the largest tavern in town. He proved to be an entertaining dinner guest, keeping the conversation light and full of laughter. He and the Reverend had a great relationship, despite ministering to men at different ends of the spectrum. Between the two, they told tales of foolish men, failed gold claims, scams the prospectors tried, myths of the prowess of the natives, and fanciful stories of huge gold deposits waiting for discovery.

Over dinner, Sarah could have spent the whole meal staring at Warden Price. But they had seated her between Toomer and Sinclair, who competed for her attention throughout dinner. Neither asked about her family, or her dead husband; instead regaling her with stories of their strength, wit and fortunes. It was exhausting.

Price had been listening to those conversations, his brow furrowing when one tale sounded too farcical to be true. After finishing his main course, he laid his cutlery on his plate and, interrupting one of Toomer's tales of trading with the natives, asked, 'So, Mrs Bell, what are your plans from here? Will you be staying with us, or returning to your family?'

Sarah turned to Price and wanted to say she'd stay wherever he was but, full of nerves, said it was her intention to travel to the nearest city, Dunedin, which had been Christine's suggestion, and from there she'd sail to England.

'But first I must write to my family for funds for my passage home.'

A loud pummelling on the front door interrupted her.

They could hear raised voices outside, and chairs scraped across the floor as the men stood. The Reverend was moving down the hall, followed by Price, with Sinclair not far behind them. Sarah noted he was smiling as he hurried toward the noise. Toomer stayed seated, his meal more important than whatever was happening. Margaret had one hand on her swollen belly, the other on the arm of her husband.

The uproar outside had changed from outrage to a mixture of panic and anger. Sweeney kissed his pregnant wife on the forehead, and gently lifted her hand from his arm, and followed the other men. Toomer was still oblivious to the fracas and as Sarah stood up, his hand shot out, pinning hers to the table.

'It's not a problem for women to concern themselves. Go tell that cook to bring more food. I'm hungry.'

His piggy eyes drilled into her. Did she have more to fear from the obese shopkeeper than from the fists of the sailor? She wrenched her hand back, and pushed her chair away from the table, to make her way to the kitchen. Out of sight of Toomer, she turned back to see what was happening at the front door.

The gentlemen were standing on the whitewashed porch, surrounded by a crowd of men carrying kerosene lanterns, gesturing towards the crest of the hill, towards the native settlement. She saw at least three with their arms in crude slings, soaked with blood. There were plenty of rifles in sight, and tensions were rising. The men shouted that they wanted to see the Warden, not the Reverend, who stood wringing his hands in consternation. Sinclair was arguing with Price, encouraging him to take an armed party to the native settlement. Sarah could only hear snippets of the various conversations:

'Deal with them...'

'It's not right, them having their painted faces, and getting away with murder that lot...'

'They'd as soon as kill us in our beds, Reverend. You've no right...'

'You stupid woman, I told you to get more food from the kitchen, not eavesdrop!' Toomer bellowed as he came through the doorway and caught sight of Sarah in the hall. He grabbed her wrist, twisting her towards the kitchen. His girth blocked most of the light from the dining room.

At the sound of the shopkeeper's raised voice, Price turned and his eyes sought hers and in that instant, Sarah lost her heart to this colonial man.

His eyes widened when he saw her assailant twisting her wrist as he masticated the food in his mouth. Toomer was so intent on inflicting pain, he did not see Price striding down the hall until an almighty fist thumped into his ample stomach. He doubled over, choking on the food in his mouth. Sarah massaged her wrist, released at the moment of impact.

Price's dark eyes probed her face, satisfied he turned back, removing his coat from the Kauri hall stand, and strode outside, barking orders to various men. Instead of marching to the Maori settlement on the hill, he turned toward the miners canvas city.

Sarah skirted past Toomer, doubled over in the doorway, pausing long enough to hiss, 'You are a disgusting pig, and no woman in her right mind would ever touch you with a bargepole. If you have any testicles, I hope they shrivel up from lack of use, tosser!'

She raced outside, but before stepping off the porch, Reverend Young placed a restraining hand on her arm.

'Mrs Bell, this is not the place for a woman.'

'What's happening? Why are the men here?' Sarah asked, wide-eyed at the sight in front of her.

Half the miners in Bruce Bay had massed in the middle of town, with more men joining them. Candles and lanterns transformed the slovenly town into a wonderland of dancing light and undulating shadows. The Reverend responded, resigned to being surrounded by headstrong women.

'There have been accusations of claim jumping, and the miners tried to take a claim being worked by the natives, and some Māori died in the fracas. This will end badly. We must get back inside and prepare to defend ourselves if that happens.'

He looked past his unfinished church towards the Maori settlement, the fear in his eyes magnified by the lamplight.

Sarah stood on the porch, looking for Price, but only lanterns bobbing through the tents were visible. More lanterns were being lit as the camp came alive like a swarm of disturbed fireflies.

Toomer stumbled out. Reverend Young moved in front of Sarah.

'Mr Toomer, I am sorry but we must call an end to tonight's festivities. You'll leave Miss Felicity here with us tonight, given the unrest in town?'

The Reverend's statement left no room for Toomer to decline, and, after throwing Sarah a vicious look, he lurched from the porch, clutching his belly. He made his way to his shop, ready to defend it from the drunken miners, the fierce natives, or to profit from both sides. *Profit the most likely option*, thought Sarah.

She followed the Reverend inside to find the women had moved to the front room where Christine had a large Bible open on her lap and was reading aloud. Young Samuel sat on the floor by Christine's feet. Better he was here than with his father in the escalating mêlée.

Sarah excused herself. If trouble was coming, she'd prefer to be wearing something more appropriate than a green silk gown, if she had to flee for her life. She changed into the black dress and had no choice in the footwear department as she only had the black leather boots-they were old friends now. Her only other belongings were the Bible and Isaac's carved wooden fantail. She slid them into the bottom drawer of the wardrobe. Not religious, she kissed the cover of the book before making her way back to the other women.

A miner had summoned the Reverend while Sarah was getting changed. They needed him to minister to dying men. Margaret had paled at the news and gripped Felicity's hand so hard the girl winced in pain. Felicity had a much better sense of propriety than her father, for she never once complained, instead stoically allowed Margaret to continue holding her hand.

A massive volley of shots sounded right outside the house. Shouts and cries of pain made their way into the front room. A thud against the front door rattled the house so violently that a greenstone-tipped spear fell from its place on the wall. Sarah picked it up and stood holding it in her clammy hands. Any weapon far better than no weapon.

THE RIOT

The front door burst open.

'Out, out!' screamed the Reverend, shooing the women out like chickens. A line of men holding torches and rifles broke the night, surrounding Sweeney's tavern to protect it from the rioting miners. Almost five hundred men fought in and around town.

The Reverend tried ushering the ladies towards the tavern, surrounded by muzzle flashes, and the ear-splitting sound of rifle fire. Margaret was screaming and Christine pulled her towards Sweeney's, no hint of fear on her cherubic features. Felicity had tears streaming down her face and stumbled over the rough ground. The Reverend was ahead of them, concentrating on his wife and the pregnant Margaret. Sarah bent to help Felicity, who had curled into a near foetal position, hands clasped against her ears, the way a child hides from the sound of fireworks.

As Sarah hauled her up, someone knocked them over from behind — a pair of miners fleeing from the fight, tripping over themselves. As they regained their feet, a single shot rang out, taking out the taller one. He fell on Felicity, pinning her down with his dead weight. Sarah tried pulling Felicity up and the second man, realising Sarah was defenceless, grabbed her, wrestling her toward a row of tents.

She struggled to break free, his grip around her vice-like. Sarah screamed, and a hand slapped her.

'You'll be my ticket out of here,' he huffed, weaving his way through the tents, half of which had come down. Guy ropes and loose pegs made their passage through the tent city treacherous. Sarah struggled against her abductor, fearful of what was to become of her. As they rounded the side of the furthest tent, another miner tackled them, flinging Sarah to safety. The men tussled, rolling over and over, grunting as punches landed. Wrestling, they made it to their feet, and full body blows rained. A knife slashed a silver arc in the dim light, thrust into the stomach of her abductor. It didn't slow him as he threw punch after punch into the other man before grabbing in by the throat and throwing him to the ground.

The moon emerged and shone on the young face of Isaac as he fell next to her. Young eyes full of fear and helplessness.

'Mrs Bell,' he rasped, his throat crushed. 'Help me.' His left hand reached towards her.

'Isaac, oh, Isaac.'

Sarah inched over to him, sweeping the hair from his face. His body was lying at such an angle that his ribs had lost their shape. Tears traced lines in the blood on his bludgeoned face.

'Stay with me, Mrs Bell. I don't want to die alone.'

He coughed, and blood speckled the dirt.

'In my pocket is a letter for my mamma, and a nugget. I wanted to cash it in and go home but Seth wanted more. We stole this one that's true; from the Māori and they found out. That's what started this. Please send it to my mam. My family needs it more than Seth. Please...'

Her abductor, ignoring his knife wound, tried dragging Sarah to her feet. She struggled against him, screaming. Despite his injuries, Isaac rolled to one side, the knife still in his hand and with a desperate stabbing motion, he sliced the Achilles tendon of the miner's ankle. Agonised screams followed as the man released Sarah and toppled backwards to the ground. Sarah fell against Isaac, who coughed again, blood dribbling from his lips, mingling with the earth from the newest nation on earth.

'Mrs Bell, my mam's letter...,' Isaac whispered.

Sarah reached into his pocket, finding the letter and a small stone, which she assumed was the nugget. She shoved them unseen into her skirt pocket.

'You stay with me, Isaac. You saved me, so you stay right here. We'll get you to a doctor. Stay with me.'

She held him as he died. This young man had given his life for her; for someone who shouldn't be here, in this time or town. She sat there, rocking him, Isaac's slowing heartbeat mingled with her own, creating a colonial soundtrack, with night insects and birds providing the backing vocals. The newest star in heaven tonight.

'You bloody bitch!'

Her abductor limped towards her, a trail of blood behind him, Isaac's knife in his hand.

Sarah sat paralysed with fear, Isaac's unresponsive body across her lap.

An explosion ripped through the air. Warden Price strode out of the blackness, a rifle in his hands. Scurrying behind was young Samuel. He must have followed her from the house, seen what happened and fetched Price.

Price lifted Isaac from Sarah's lap, laying him on his side. In one sweep, he had Sarah in his arms, and was striding away from Isaac's body before she knew what was happening.

Moving back through town, the fighting had ended, leaving crumpled bodies in the dirt. Men hobbled towards their tents, helped by friends equally damaged. She assumed she was being conveyed back to the Reverend's house but, instead, Price carried her to Sweeney's store where the ladies panicked, mistaking Isaac's blood for hers.

Price stood aside, his dark eyes searching her face, assessing if they hurt her. After reassuring himself that she was well, he asked her to relay what had happened. But she hadn't managed a word before a grubby face appeared in the doorway.

'Warden, you're needed now!'

He pulled his eyes away from Sarah and donning his hat, he slipped out, leaving her staring at his retreat. A woman attended her with a damp cloth, dabbing at her cheeks and grazed arms.

Men came and went, the injured brought to Sweeney's, where the women pitched in to tend to their injuries as best they could. Even Sarah, with her minimal schoolgirl first aid training cleaned wounds, and applied tourniquets, rinsing bloody cloths, and sitting with men scared of their mortality.

Sarah was so caught up in the frenetic happenings she didn't notice the inkiness of night gave way to the fingers of dawn. In England, one might enjoy the dawn chorus of common garden sparrows, but here a cacophony of native parrots, darting fantails, and a hundred other species welcomed the dawn.

A hand settled on her shoulder but it wasn't until she heard her name repeated twice that she turned away from the young miner she'd been tending. There was Price, his hand still on her shoulder. With his other, he helped her stand. She half expected him to kiss her, but he pulled her to the door. This was not a *Mills and Boon* moment, it was life. Outside were the other ladies, in a similar dishevelled state. Dirt and rusty blood covered them head to toe, streaking their faces.

The Reverend announced, 'Time for home, ladies. It is safe now. There will be no more fighting. The boys have seen off the troublemakers. And the Warden settled things with the Māori. Go home and rest. We will arrange our own breakfast, no need for you to wait on us this morning.'

In the early light, mist rising from the forest floor and the shoreline obscured Sarah's vision, creating a dreamlike scene of shadowy figures frozen in the half light.

Christine and Sarah made their farewells to Margaret and Felicity, and picked their way up the road, stepping past discarded hats and lone leather boots. As they approached the front porch of the Reverend's house, Sinclair met them. His rifle gleamed a dull grey in his hands. Propped against the stairs behind him was Seth, wrists bound, head hanging on his chest.

At his feet, a burlap bag lay half open on the ground. The dawn light caught the contents: glittering silver candlesticks, the sort that grace the altars of the great cathedrals in Europe. It was the same burlap sack Sarah had seen Warden Price holding when she'd first seen him with the Reverend on the hill a million days ago.

'Caught this one running away with these during the commotion. Reckon he's stolen them from someone. Had me some trouble with him, so gave him a clip round the head.' Sinclair laughed, gesturing towards Seth with his rifle.

Sarah looked at Seth, and at the lake-like pool of blood next to him. She bent to wake him and recoiled in horror, falling backwards, half landing on the burlap bag. Something had obliterated the side of Seth's head. Sinclair's 'clip round the head' had been a point-blank rifle shot.

Christine spun on her heels, running to the tavern as fast as her skirts allowed.

Sinclair's voice cut through the still air.

'You get off that sack, lady. Those candle holders don't belong to you, either. They're mine now. They'll sell well in Wellington. I may just sell them back to their original owners.'

Stunned, Sarah didn't move as time slowed and sandflies swarmed in the sunlight around Sinclair's head, muffling the sounds of the settlement. The intricate engraving on the silver candlesticks was familiar. Where had she seen it? At the meeting on the hill? Before she'd ended up on the West Coast of New Zealand? When her father had disappeared? In the glory days of her youth, when her time was her own to wander around museum exhibits, and leaf through glossy photographic books?

Like wading through quicksand, Sarah reached for the candlesticks. Sinclair, afraid that Sarah would grab them, reached out to snatch up his loot.

Sarah and Sinclair's hands touched the gleaming silver candelabra at the same time.

And they both disappeared.

THE BIBLE

*C*hristine arrived breathless at Sweeney's, seeking her husband and Warden Price among the men drowning their pain in drink.

She found them at the back of the tavern, each with a drink in hand, analysing the events of the night. If it surprised the Reverend to see his wife again so soon, he didn't show it.

'You must come! Sinclair caught Seth trying to steal the candlesticks.'

Her voice caught in her throat.

'I think he's shot him.'

Chairs scraped across the rough-sawn floor, as the men abandoned their drinks, making their way to the Reverend's house. Christine followed as fast as her long blood-encrusted skirts allowed.

Of Sarah and Bryce Sinclair, there was no sign. Price got to Seth's side first, where it was obvious someone had shot him in the head, his death instantaneous.

'Where is Mrs Bell?'

'She was right here, with Sinclair, checking to see how... how Seth was. And she was next to him, right where you are now,' Christine replied, panting, struggling to catch her breath. 'The candlesticks were next to Seth, in a bag... and now the bag has gone too.'

'Where has he taken her then?' asked the Reverend, his arm around his wife's shoulders. 'And the candelabra. They were a gift for the church.'

'He's taken her and the candlesticks. I never understood why you trusted him, Reverend. You have a good heart, but of all God's creatures, he didn't deserve God's love. They'll be at the wharf. Mrs Young, it's best you stay inside. I'll send someone to...'

His hands motioned towards Seth's body in the dirt.

Christine paled.

'Yes. I'll sort out breakfast for when she returns. Right, best you hurry. They can't have gone far on foot.'

She scuttled up the steps of the porch as the men took off towards the harbour. She watched the morning mist swallow them before going inside.

Days passed and they found no sign of Sinclair, or Sarah. Sinclair's boat remained tied to the wharf, with Samuel huddling miserably on its deck waiting for his father's return. Reverend Young had invited him to tea every other day, with the Sweeney's feeding him the other days.

Word of gold being discovered in Thames found its way to Bruce Bay and a mass exodus began; miners streamed out using any means possible, including commandeering Sinclair's boat — leaving Samuel on the wharf, his eyes once again blackened; this time for standing in the way of the miners stealing his father's boat.

Price ranged further and further afield, looking for any word of Sinclair and Sarah, each time returning to Bruce Bay more despondent. He found Samuel on the wharf, bruised and bloodied, and boat-less. He took him up to the manse and delivered him into the capable hands of Christine. The Warden and Reverend discussed the shrinking town and the mystery of Sinclair's disappearance.

'There's no sign of them and with the miners leaving for the North Island, any trace they may have left has gone.'

'What of the Māori — do they know?'

'They claim not to know anything and they've nothing to gain by lying,' Price answered, blaming himself for Sarah's disappearance.

Every day he chastised himself for not escorting Sarah and Christine back to the Reverend's house. If only. But 'if only' didn't change the past, so he carried on.

Christine bustled into the room, waving a letter in her hand.

'I've had word from friends in Dunedin that they know of a Mrs Lester there, from England. Shall I write to them to ask if it's any relation to Sarah? Perhaps she's gone there?'

'In Dunedin, you say? She mentioned Dunedin. Yes, write to your friends and ask them, Mrs Young. In the meantime, I'll make my way there. There's not much more for me to do here now. Would you say we'd lost about four hundred men to Thames, Reverend?'

Reverend Young thought for a moment.

'That's on the low side, Warden. We've only just completed the church, and now there'll be no one left here to use it. We'll stay on though, God willing.'

He stood and shook Price's hand.

'You go find her, Warden. And Sinclair. I don't care what you do with him, God forgive me, but make sure she's safe, and tell her we miss her.'

Christine gave Price an almighty hug, pressing upon him sliced ham and bread for his journey. Samuel watched from the doorway as another male role model in his life left him.

The Reverend had Samuel go with him on his visits to members of the parish. He keenly missed Warden Price's company, although trouble hadn't followed his absence, since most of the miners had left for greener fields. Samuel kept him focussed on his role, and their outings together filled the Reverend with a new vigour for life.

With her husband out with their new ward, Christine wandered through the house. She'd had such grand plans to fill it with babies, but that hadn't been God's plan to date. For a short period, Sarah filled with her light. But that too had vanished, and God had given her Samuel and she loved him as if he were her own. The sins of the father should never be visited upon the son, he was their ward now, and she would give him the home he deserved. As she tidied Samuel's room, Sarah's old bedroom, she discovered the wooden fantail and Bible in the wardrobe's drawer. Christine had forgotten she'd given one to Sarah and turned it over in her hands, rereading the inscription she'd signed.

Her mind made up, she took it to the front room where she wrapped it in brown paper, and wrote an address on the front, before putting on her hat and taking it to Toomer's store for the post to Dunedin.

THE BASEMENT

*S*arah raised her head. Her body was bent at an unusual angle, tangled in long skirts and sacking. Crammed into a tiny, dark space, silence surrounded her. Frightened and disorientated, she stifled a small sob. Slowly, she unfolded her frame, disentangling herself as reality formed around her.

She found herself squeezed between towers of crates stacked upon one another. Old stock from before her father's disappearance, unlabelled and precariously balanced, left in the long aisles of the basement storeroom. Sarah had never sorted through the boxes mouldering down here. She rarely came to the basement unless she needed to access the bubblewrap, a light bulb, or the archaic fuse box.

In the darkness, Sarah stood up, wincing from the random bruises, and reaching to support herself, she stepped forward, stumbled, and fell over a shapeless form on the ground - a burlap sack.

The metallic sound of silver candelabras crashing into each other stung the silence of the gloomy room. Sarah knew where the switch was, but only from the top of the stairs, not from the back of a storeroom she'd never explored.

With the sack in one hand, she felt her way, taking care not to dislodge any of the tottering piles. Sensing she'd come to the bottom of the staircase, Sarah nudged forward with her toe until she reached the bottom stair tread. She flicked the Bakelite switch, and the glow of the dusty lightbulb banished her irrational fear of the dark.

Rubbing her bruised backside, she hefted the bag over her shoulder and, like an old Hollywood portrayal of bank robbers with their swag, climbed the staircase, not bothering to turn around. If she had, she might have seen a pair of boots next to a large mound of boxes covered in a decade of dust. The boots — and the legs in them — were free of dust, yet speckled with the unmistakable marks of sand and fresh blood.

THE CANDELABRA

*S*arah emerged at the top of the staircase, and the burlap snagged against the brass umbrella stand filled with wooden golf clubs, well past their use by date. As she heaved at the sack with frustration, it ripped, spilling its contents into the aisle. The torn burlap was the final straw. Sarah sat on the floor and burst into tears.

Manus poked his head above a cabinet he'd been fossicking through.

'Ah, there you are. I, ah… was wondering where you'd got to…' he trailed off. 'Are you all right, Sarah?' he asked in his lilting European accent. 'I was looking at the plates, and when I'd finished, you'd disappeared. I looked around…'

Sarah looked up at him in amazement.

'How long have you been waiting?'

'A few minutes. I thought you'd gone to the bathroom. I like this new work outfit! Are you going to dress for different eras here at the shop? Is this a thing now? Not sure what your father would say!' he joked.

Sarah wiped her eyes, stuffing the candlesticks back into the sack. Manus showed no interest in the sterling silver, but she couldn't be sure she'd be able to answer any questions if he asked, but he'd made his way back to the counter and was pulling cash out of his wallet.

'Now, can I pay for the adze? There's an auction on today and they have three pieces of pottery I want, but I need to be there for the whole auction or the others will suspect I'm there for one thing. It's a game of poker sometimes and not as easy to win the quality pieces.'

Sarah brushed herself off and stood up, nudging the sack of silver out of sight with her foot.

'Sorry for the delay. I thought I'd try out my new costume on the regular customers first!' she improvised.

As Sarah slipped behind the counter, she recoiled when she saw the greenstone adze laying where she'd last seen it.

'Do you need me to wrap it Manus?' she ventured.

In response, he picked up the adze, and slipped it into one of the vast pockets of his leather vest.

She smiled as she took his proffered cash.

'Thank you, Manus. I may give up on this period dress idea, it's not that comfortable.'

Manus laughed, patted his pocket, and replied, 'You may want to send your costumes out to the dry cleaners. There is a strange aroma here. Your father was never one for cleaning, but perhaps it is time for a rethink!'

With his laughter booming through the shop as he left, and after she'd locked the door behind him, Sarah retrieved the candelabras from the floor, plonking them on the scratched counter.

She sat on her battered shop stool and attempted to untangle the mysterious strands of her recent life. Putting aside the incomprehensible possibility that any person could traverse time, not just once, but several times, Sarah wondered why she'd ended up in the times and places the artefacts had sent her.

She'd woken up in London and was a 'below stairs' girl. Next, she'd appeared in a train station, dressed in the height of late Victorian fashion, complete with a purse full of sovereigns. Within the blink of an eye, or rather with the flash of greenstone, Seth had attacked her on the West Coast of New Zealand. No matter how she wove the threads of information, the strands refused to connect.

With a sudden gasp, Sarah's hand flew to her mouth.

'What if I've changed the fate of Margaret and Christine?'

The deaths of Seth and Isaac hit her with the subtlety of a head-on collision. So, too, did the loss of Warden Price, a man she barely knew, an acquaintance of less than a week, but his impact on her life was immense. She'd had no one special before, apart from her family, and although her feelings for Price were foreign, they were welcome.

In circumstances of the heart, a girl only needs three things - her best friend, chocolate and wine. Given Patricia could only have part of the story - because otherwise they'd cart her off to the nearest psychiatrist - she'd need all three crutches to get through it.

Sarah rang Patricia's mobile.

'Hi, it's me... do you want to get an Indian tonight and a couple of bottles of wine and a movie?... excellent... can I come to yours?... I've got something I need your advice with... heart stuff... no, not heart problems, you idiot, love heart stuff!... yeah, it's not something I've ever asked you before... no, I will not tell you over the phone... no, you can just wait till tonight! See you at six... no! I'll tell you tonight! Patience is a virtue — now go sell your hideously overpriced clothes... yep, see you then.'

She hung up, grinning at her friend's enthusiasm for the possibility that Sarah had found someone she liked. Although explaining Price to Patricia would be a tricky undertaking, she was sure.

To fill in time before her much needed therapy, she cleaned the candelabra, for something brand new, they'd accumulated a fair amount of grime. Sarah buffed the hallmarks with a silver cloth, clearing away the dirt, revealing a stunning lustre, and the most marvellous engraving. Her fingers danced along it, tracing vivid imagery of lions, and the sharp ridges made by the lions' claws on the four edges of each candelabra. The imagery reminded her somewhat of the work of London's most famous silversmith, Paul de Lamerie. She'd seen examples of his work at an exhibition at the Metropolitan

Museum of Art in New York on a brief visit to her cousins who lived there.

Never suspecting that the silver marks she'd uncovered *were* those of de Lamerie, she fumbled around her messy shelves to unearth her hallmarks book. With one candelabra clenched between her thighs she pulled out her jeweller's loop and peered at the marks. Definitely London, with the rampant lion, 1747. Wait. What? Sarah rubbed her eyes and refocused. The date stamp was 1747, and the maker's mark... the unmistakable *P* and *L* of Paul de Lamerie.

Sarah sat back and, as if she were holding a slumbering serpent, placed the candelabra onto the counter. She moved the other objects away from the vicinity, making room on the counter for the second candelabra. The twin of the first. This made her experiences on the hostile West Coast all the more worthwhile. No wonder she'd recognised the patterns in the sunlight.

How was it possible a pair of de Lamerie candelabra had wound up in New Zealand, in the hands of the church? The master silversmith had done commissions, but usually for gentry so perhaps this was a one-off, lost to history? She couldn't even comprehend the worth of a pair of these on the open market. They'd need authenticating first, but the sale would be enough to pay her taxes for the foreseeable future.

She carried the candelabra upstairs, and grabbing her camera, took special care to document the hallmarks. After uploading them to her laptop, she paused for a moment. Nodding to herself, she addressed an email to her only contact at Christie's, Andrew Harvard.

Dear Andrew,

Sorry to trouble you again. The sampler is still here waiting for you, but I've just received this pair of candelabra, and I was hoping you could refer these images to the right person at Christie's.

I want to auction them off. I believe them to be by Paul de Lamerie, and (they told me) their provenance is that someone commissioned them for the church, and then sent them to New Zealand. Please reply as soon as possible and let me know when I might expect you?

Thank you,

Sarah Lester

Not realising the trouble she was about to cause, she pressed 'Send'. And, in a small office at Christie's, the email addressed to Andrew Harvard was being read by someone other than the intended recipient.

Her sense of smell confirmed that Manus was right, *she* was the source of the earthy scent. Sarah decided a bath was a priority when she noticed the dirt festering under her fingernails. She laughed as she considered what the Ministry of Agriculture inspectors might say about her illegal importation of foreign dirt into England. Closing her laptop, she carefully wrapped the candelabra in an old tablecloth and hid it behind the couch, next to a stack of boxes which had migrated from downstairs. She was as bad as her father.

She heard her mobile phone ringing downstairs. In a decision she'd later regret, she elected not to answer it; a bath far more urgent than answering a call from someone selling their Franklin Mint plate collection, and she needed to get ready for her girls' night in with Patricia.

After knocking back a bottle of cheap Chilean wine and spending at least three hours trying to persuade Patricia that the spicy curry and the heavy red wine would mend her broken heart, Sarah returned to her flat above the shop, and fell into the sleep of the dead.

Sarah's filthy clothes lay in a heap on the floor at the foot of her bed, and the battery on her phone ran flat until its feeble light shone no more.

And deep in the city, Andrew Harvard willed her to answer her phone. The pictures of the candelabra, coupled with the sampler and the *katar* had started an avalanche of queries, and now the Art Loss Register was making enquiries with the auction house as to the provenance of the items.

THE SCHOLAR

*D*espite the number of times Harvard tried ringing Sarah, he'd had no luck. And she hadn't responded to any of his emails. Only one way remained now: he had her details, he would turn up at her shop. Whilst no one at the auction house had her address, he assumed they were still reading his emails, worried he may lose them the consignment. He couldn't believe after the first email about the sampler, she'd sent two more, with finds of the century for him to auction for her. He'd estimated his percentage take from these auctions could give him enough for a decent deposit on a flat.

If he didn't drive out to her shop now, they'd send someone else, and then it'd be their name on the contract. It had to be him.

He'd grab a work car tomorrow and, in anticipation, he packed up his case with everything he might need to examine the candelabra, the knife, and the sampler. Before he agreed to take any of the objects, he'd have to inspect them, to complete the auction contract. While not his forte, he had enough experience to know his sterling silver from his silver plate. But determining if it was by the famous silversmith de Lamerie was not his responsibility. The Silver and Objects of Vertu Department had that responsibility. As for the *katar*, he'd photograph it, measure it, and write up a description for the sales

163

contract. Verifying the age and provenance of the sampler might be more difficult, but it fell within his area of expertise, and he would treat the sampler as if it were the treasure he suspected it was.

His mother had despaired of his love of fabrics and sewing, predicting that he may be gay. He'd scoffed at her deduction, although realising that his hobby *was* unusual for a boy. He'd been strong enough to ignore the taunts from those in his senior years at secondary school.

University had been heaven - studying famous tapestries, runners, wall hangings, and historically important clothes. He'd excelled, and, together with his fellow students, had one of the highest scoring classes in the course's history. Christie's offered him an internship when he was only halfway through his study. So he'd had the last laugh, especially now they paid him tens of thousands of pounds to "play with dolls' clothes", as the boys at school termed it, while those same boys were applying for banking jobs during the world's greatest economic downturn since the Great Depression.

Stepping out of the Tube, he arrived at work. Christie's was closed on a Sunday, but it never *really* shut. Several appraisers were always there, catching up on a backlog of consigned goods. They had their own art conservation department, the conservators more dedicated than anyone he knew. Most of them had no life outside their temperature-controlled labs. They lived for oil paint on stretched canvas. All too often, when a marriage soured, the wife took a kitchen knife to her husband's priceless pieces of art, resulting in a never-ending stream of delicate repair and general restoration work. Naturally, guards worked on Sundays too; the value of articles consigned to Christie's worth more than the GDP of many of the lesser nations.

Even though he'd only gone into the building to get keys to the pool car, several staff members who'd heard of the dagger and candelabra, wanted the inside word, delaying his departure.

He located the pool vehicle in the cavernous underground car park. Once inside, he sat clutching the steering wheel, staring out the window, the events of the last two days replaying in his head.

'Right, right,' he muttered.

He tried Sarah's phone one last time; her voicemail clicked on, so, after the tone, he recorded yet another message.

'Hello, Miss Lester. Andrew Harvard from Christie's here, again. Just to let you know I'm leaving for your shop. Given the traffic I should be there in forty minutes. See you soon.'

He hoped Sarah Lester would not turn out to be a 'Trapper', a phrase coined by Philip Mould, co-presenter of the BBC's show *Fake or Fortune?*, to describe a dealer who dishonestly suggests a piece of art may be by a famous artist, knowing it to be a fake. It was becoming more of a problem in the industry. Fakes turned up at auction all the time - copies of famous paintings no longer in vogue now that anyone could Google whether the genuine painting was hanging in a gallery or private collection. But a 'Trapper' would claim a sketch or an unknown painting *was* by a renowned artist, with an elaborate provenance to match; for example, that the artist had given the sketch to the grandmother of the seller etcetera.

In his heart, he felt that Sarah was genuine. Her emails were too fantastical to be anything else. He started the engine and drove off to find *The Old Curiosity Shop*.

POSTCARD #9

1/7/43

Dear Phil,
You know churches aren't normally my thing, but today we visited the most
divine little parish church. I can't remember the name of the village, but we had
lunch under the most magnificent trees in the churchyard. It was so wonderful
getting out of the city. So peaceful. It was almost as if the war hadn't touched
this part of London. We'd actually gone to visit Alexandra at Dawley Court, but
she was indisposed and we hadn't received her card in time telling us not to come.
You'd love this town. Perhaps we'll picnic here when you get back.
Stay safe.
B xxx

THE ROAD TRIP

*W*hile Harvard was at Christie's, Sarah stirred in bed, stretching in the half-light of dawn; when the day starts with every possibility your dreams suggested.

When she woke, she rewound and replayed recent events. Was it possible that in one instant she'd fallen in love and then had been the reason two men had lost their lives? Her breath caught in her throat. She couldn't think of Seth and Isaac, of Price.

Feeling a headache coming on, brought on by stress and too much red wine, she eased herself out of bed and into the kitchen where there was a life-saving packet of aspirin waiting for her. Dry swallowing two tablets, she chased them down with a piece of toast and a cup of sweet tea. Together they helped reestablish her equilibrium. Her reflection in the bathroom mirror shocked her. Red-eyed, with shadows reminiscent of London fog, death warmed up. She reviewed her sleeping and eating habits of the last few days - abnormal and lacking in substance. No wonder she looked like a shadow of her former self.

Another long, hot bath took care of most of her physical woes, but not the lingering dark memories. She tried stifling those as she brushed the knots out of her hair. Today she would concentrate on

preparing everything for auction and hopefully she'd have another
email from Andrew Harvard. As she dressed, she nudged her dirty
clothes towards the laundry hamper with her toe, the effort of picking
them up too much. She forgot about the nugget of gold and Isaac's
letter, still in the skirt's pocket.

She made her way downstairs. Today was Sunday, not a day her
father had ever had the shop open. Now it was just her, she
tried opening as often as practical. Every sale was a tiny step closer to
solvency. The last couple of days were still a blur. She'd thought the
time with Patricia would have helped, but in a fit of impulse she
grabbed her keys and left the shop, locking it behind her. She ducked
next door to Patricia's and hammered on the door.

'Patricia!' she yelled through the letter plate. 'Patricia!'

Patricia's head popped out from the back of the showroom. Her
face spilt into a smile when she saw it was Sarah. She hurried over to
unlock the door.

'Hey you, how are you this morning?' queried Patricia.

Sarah yawned.

Laughing, Patricia motioned her inside, 'Come on, we'll talk more
inside and I'll make you a cup of tea and you can tell me more about
your man.'

Patricia hustled Sarah into her shop. They made their way into the
back room, kitted out with a couch, an armchair and a design desk
strewn with fabric samples, sketches, swatches and loose zippers
filling every conceivable space.

A retro Goblin Teasmade sat on a scarred sideboard, but it was the
battered old kettle and the trusty Twining's tea bags Patricia reached
for. As her friend fussed with the tea, Sarah closed her eyes, and
leaned back on the couch.

'Patricia, what would you say if I said I want to visit New Zealand?'
she asked.

'Pah! Forget New Zealand, I told you last week we should book
that Greek Islands cruise. Remember my friend Annabel? She did it
last month. Her cruise ship had enough alcohol for the entire
population of New Zealand! Come on, book it with me. We'll go after

my birthday; that way I can ask my parents for some cash towards it as my present! New Zealand is so far away, and it's only got sheep. Greece is *Greece*. Come on!'

Patricia danced a small dance around the couch, spilling hot tea on Sarah's legs and jolting her out of her reverie.

'Patricia!' squealed Sarah.

'Oops, sorry.'

Patricia lowered herself onto the armchair in an unnaturally flexible position and stared at Sarah and with dancing eyes demanded to hear more of the man Sarah had told her about over dinner.

Sarah groaned.

'Leave it, Patricia, I'll never see him again. I doubt I even left enough of an impression on him for him to remember me. It's impossible. I need time away from the shop. I was planning a trip out to Hounslow later today, and I'd love it if you came with me. It's to do with some stuff I got in the shop. A silly idea, but I need a break from being cooped up in here. I think I'm going crazy!'

Patricia clapped her hands.

'Oh, a road trip! Yes, let me close up and we'll grab snacks on the way. I never go out that way unless I'm going to Heathrow, and even then I don't think I've ever driven there. I always go on the Tube.'

Patricia disappeared to lock up the shop.

They ducked out the back door to Sarah's van, parked next to the brick wall in the alley. Each shop had one parking space allocated. Patricia didn't have a car, choosing to live her life out of taxis, the Underground and favours from friends. They buckled themselves in and, after plotting the Harlington address of Iris into Patricia's phone, they headed into the traffic.

On the drive along Harlington High Street, the two friends noted the abundance of pubs on every corner. Gothic Court turned out to be a small strip of terraced houses, built around the end of World War II. *Nothing historic.* Dejected, Sarah slumped into her seat. She'd had no plan before she and Patricia had set out on this errand, and no idea what she would have done if they had found a beautiful historic home with a polished brass door plate.

Patricia looked at her.

'Pub?'

Sarah nodded.

They parked the van and walked into The Red Lion. For a late Sunday morning, there were a handful of people already drinking their first pint of the day. *Here for an early lunch*, Sarah thought. They each ordered a shandy and a Ploughman's; just the thing for a sunny day.

A century ago, the pub had a lovely view of fields and farmhouses, and the quaint church nestled between towering oaks further along the road, but now it abutted a filthy arterial road, and a flyover loomed over the grounds of both buildings.

Sarah asked the publican for information on the flats across the road. He knew nothing other than what he knew from a series of black and white framed photographs on the walls, showing local scenes from the past century. Sarah and Patricia pored over them, to the amusement of the barman. Patricia was admiring the outfits worn by the people in the photos while Sarah was trying to find a photo showing the opposite corner.

Patricia gave a squeal.

'There, Sarah, your building! See, the pub, and there's the church steeple, so that grand house must be the house. It has to be.'

Sarah leaned in for a closer look at the photo screwed to the wall, to deter any thieves. She couldn't take the photo off the wall, so traced the house behind the glass with her finger. Yes, it was a photo of the house, before its demolition to make way for the drab set of terraced houses. Even in the photo, the house looked abandoned. Nobody posed in front, the trees and bushes, long since gone. Sarah snapped a picture with Patricia's iPhone, asking her to message it to her later. They walked out to the beer garden with their drinks. They would not waste a rare fine day in London sitting inside a stagnant pub.

Neither woman noticed another car pull in behind the van. Two men jumped out and tried the vans handles. One produced a kit, the size of a woman's manicure set, from which he drew a small pick. With deft hands, he sprang the lock and the smaller man vaulted into the back and rummaged through it, turning up nothing but old copies of *National Geographic* and woollen packaging blankets. After closing the rear door, the two conferred, looked at the pub, then climbed into their car and drove away. Their assumption the van was carrying the valuable cargo was incorrect.

Sarah and Patricia remained oblivious of the break-in, tucked out of sight in the sunlit garden, pretending to ignore the roar of arterial traffic.

After a fortifying lunch at the pub, the girls were ready to drive back to London. Patricia eager for more information about the mystery man, having spent the entire meal grilling her friend, but Sarah wasn't spilling any more on him.

As Sarah climbed into the van, she felt an odd sensation, as if there were someone else with them. Shaking it off, she turned the key in the ignition and drove home.

THE HUSTLER

*A*s Sarah and Patricia motored back down the M4 from Harlington, Bryce Sinclair woke in the darkness of Sarah Lester's storeroom with a crushing headache, with no idea where he was or how he got there. His only thought was that the bitch had stolen his silver, and he was going to kill her.

He flexed his booted feet, then his legs and eased himself up. He pulled out an old tinderbox and striking a flint against the char cloth, a wavering light illuminated the room. *They've locked me up,* he thought to himself as he scouted around. It looked much like a basement from the nineteenth century and it wasn't until he went upstairs that the true conundrum of his predicament presented itself.

Antique shops existed in the 1850s — Sinclair himself entered some of them to sell off his ill-gotten gains before he fled to the colonies, avoiding the law, but this one was full of items not invented during his lifetime: rotary dial telephones; mass-produced picnic sets in their cosy mock cane baskets; assorted Lloyds and Barclays money boxes, resplendent in their plastic glory. He touched a framed black-and-white photograph of a pair of uniformed men standing in front of a squadron of RAF Spitfires parked on a runway. *What is this magic?*

Sinclair made a circuit around the shop, his fingers trailing over the dusty spines of Korean War books, comics depicting Spiderman and Wonder Woman, before he stumbled over Sarah's vacuum cleaner. He backed away from the foreign object, bumping into the glass-topped counter. He turned, and spied the old shell casing behind it, holding an array of old bayonets, officer's swords, and ceremonial daggers. His eyes lit up, something he recognised, and understood. Sinclair tried several blades out for balance before selecting a Scottish silver dirk, with an ornate knot-work leather handle, topped with what looked like a giant topaz, but was a gold foil-backed piece of glass. The hilt was ringed with silver bands engraved with Celtic symbols. The dirk disappeared into his rugged jacket.

It didn't take him long to figure out that depressing the key with the pound symbol opened the cash drawer of the old 1915 National cash register. The notes looked different from any money he'd ever handled before, but he wouldn't look a gift horse in the mouth, and he scooped up the small bundle of five-pound notes before pushing the drawer shut.

He stuffed the money into his pocket and made his way to the front door. Twisting the lock, he tugged it, and the door opened inwards, revealing a whole new world to the antipodean hustler. Stepping across the threshold, he pulled the door shut behind him, automatically engaging the lock. He sucked in the sights around him as he walked out into the streets of London.

THE PHONE CALL

*R*ichard Grey could barely contain his anger as he listened to the caller at the other end of the phone.

'You'll just have to search the shop then, won't you... no, arrange a distraction... that's what I'm paying you for... yes, I'm sure she still has it. My source inside Christie's says it isn't in their possession yet... there is no mistake, it is the matching *katar* to the one my family owns. Someone stole this from us many years ago... no. For the last time, you're paid to retrieve something which belongs to me. We will not allow it to fall into anyone else's hands on the open market... right, I'll hear from you tomorrow, then.'

He stabbed at the 'End' button as he strode through his apartment lounge and over to a bank of windows. Ones with commanding views over the city of London. *How hard can it be to get one knife from a girl?* he thought, his hands clenched, in a manner much like his father, and his great-grandfather, Benjamin Grey.

Richard Grey didn't have problems getting things he desired whether women or objects — which were much the same thing. But nothing obsessed him more than reclaiming the antiquities from an inheritance denied to his great-grandfather. It was the *bête noire* of his existence, and his father's before him, and his grandmother's, who'd grown up listening to increasingly bitter tales from Benjamin Grey about his stolen inheritance, details of the treasures taken from him through his brother's poisonous marriage.

Grey had religiously tracked down several items from the estate; items over the years to defray costs, or to contribute to the 'war effort'. *Who donates diamond necklaces for the war effort?* That last one had blown him away. Someone sold his great-great-grandmother's necklace to *contribute* to the war fund.

It had been an anonymous donation, but his family spent *years* cultivating relationships with the larger auction houses specifically to find their belongings and so it wasn't hard to trace the whereabouts of such an exquisite piece, especially knowing how much Christie's courted the press, even in the Forties. And it hadn't taken long to get his contact within Christie's to locate the Sale and Purchase records, which proved that his cousin's family had sold the jewels.

It still rankled; the memory of going to the old lady's house. No, not a house, a mansion. One bought using the proceeds of an estate, half of which should have been his, or his family's. She'd shown him the door, refusing to answer his questions about the diamond necklace. He'd only gone there to ask her what right she'd had to dispose of a family heirloom that way. Who gave her permission to sell it? The sale had achieved nothing. It had saved no lives. It was going to cost hundreds of thousands of pounds to retrieve it from the new owners — or it would have, if he'd paid for it, which he hadn't. Now it was safe in the family vault, his father would be so proud, his great-grandfather even more so.

Grey turned to his left and nodded to the fine gilt-framed oil painting hanging on the wall.

'Not long now, Grandmother,' he promised the serious-faced woman in the portrait.

THE VANITY CASE

*B*ack at the shop, Sarah hesitantly said goodbye but Patricia was oblivious to her friend's hesitation as she took her leave, with designs for her next collection filling her head after their trip to the pub. Patricia always behaved this way when she was embarking upon a new collection. She had one thing, and one thing only, on her mind - her designs. Sarah would be lucky if she saw her again in the next month.

For a Sunday afternoon, no one was around. The bakery wasn't open, and nor were the tailor and greengrocer. Sarah didn't want to be the only one open. She didn't like being alone, but she was, with no family and no boyfriend. At least she had her work which mostly kept her happy. Unlocking the back door, she entered the lonely environment of home.

Dust motes danced across the breadth of the shop, disturbed by the opening door. Sarah breathed in the familiar scent. She'd often heard customers make snide comments behind their hands about the smell. *It's not a rubbish dump*, she thought to herself. It smelt old and dusty because it was full of old and dusty things. She had a saying, which she trotted out when anyone asked if she ever dusted: she'd say she dusted everything twice - once on the way in and again on the way out. Except for at Christmas when she was so busy selling there wasn't time to dust or polish things as she wrapped them. That was the downside of being a sole trader. *Everything* was her job. But she loved the dusty, musty scent. It smelled like home.

What to do on a late Sunday afternoon?

One look at the looming pile of unpriced stock provided the answer. The first carton contained blue and white chinaware, including lots of Booths' Real Old Willow, a popular pattern, especially the old stuff, now that Royal Doulton had taken over production. No one wanted *that*, just the Booths. Two nice pieces of Blue Danube rounded out the contents. She didn't understand why people liked this stuff; the blue looked sickly to her. The first box passed in a blur. She cleaned it, gave it a stock number, entering it into the new stock control programme she'd invested in when she took over the business, and then created a reasonable price. The hardest part was finding a suitable home somewhere on the cluttered shelves.

Sarah wandered around the shop, a large blue and white water jug in her hands, past cabinets full of other people's forgotten treasures. After doing a complete lap, and still not finding an empty spot, she walked to the window. She'd planned to have a shop outfitter redo the display, but that was off the priority list now, especially after the price they'd quoted. So it remained the same as it had for decades - glass shelves crammed full to overflowing with faded price stickers and desiccated insect carcasses.

She pulled out a pair of turquoise-coloured vases adorned with cherubs and plonked the jug in their place. These beauties would go in the next box lot she sent off to her local auction house. They got all her old and damaged stock - the odd cups, the modern dinner sets, and loose cutlery and the tourist tat she ended up with from estate lots. The sheer number of her fellow citizens who must have travelled to Venice and bought identical ceramic masks from the same street hawker went beyond any amazing feat mentioned in the *Guinness Book of Records*. Even in the few short years she'd run the shop, she must have seen at least thirty of the same Venetian souvenirs.

Thankfully she had a good relationship with the local auctioneers -

Trotters, and they were happy with what she gave them. She made sure every box contained at least one good thing - a nice undamaged cup and saucer, or a Victorian vase. That way, they didn't mind taking her damaged stuff. They had dedicated clientele who bought damaged chinaware for mosaics and obscure art installations. Others bought lightly damaged stuff at auction to sell it at the weekly flea markets or car boot sales for a meagre profit.

Sarah wrapped a sheet of newsprint around the vases, noted the stock number in the back of her sales register, and put them in another box. She turned to the next carton from the Elizabeth Williams estate. What would this have in it? It was a lucky dip. She wished she'd boxed up the whole estate, but the solicitor had been adamant she could only be on-site with the staff from their office, for one day, to remove everything - a condition of them accepting her offer.

A layer of bubble wrap sat on the top of the carton. Shock settled in as Sarah lifted the packaging - nestled in more protective wrapping sat the *exact* vanity case she'd last seen on her dressing table at the Savoy. Its polished gleam had faded over the past century. Did it still have its contents? Sarah closed her eyes and crossed her fingers as she imagined the glorious rope of rubies still in there. She muttered another silent prayer to Saint Odo.

With her eyes superstitiously shut, she reached in, feeling for the smooth sides of the box. But, instead of lifting the fitted lid, her head exploded with crushing pain, just as Harvard pulled into a parking space across the road from *The Old Curiosity Shop*.

POSTCARD #10

2/6/41

Dear Phil

The Germans are treating London as a giant ribbon-wrapped gift, using the
Thames to get their bombs here. Apparently they fly up the estuary and follow
the river to the city. I've not been to see any of the damage, but it's unlikely I'll be
spending any time on the river this summer.
When you get back we'll hire one of the boats and take a cruise.
Stay safe.
B xxx

THE BOAT TRIP

*W*ith a sinking feeling, Sarah knew that when her eyes opened, she wouldn't be at work. Frozen, she strained to use her senses.

Thoughts of her location disappeared as an overpowering sense of nausea swept her in its arms and squeezed. Her stomach heaved, wanting to vomit, but having nothing left to purge, overwhelmed her and she struggled to sit up, a sweaty sheet impeding her every inch. Abandoning that idea, she twisted to the side as her body involuntarily removed the bile from her stomach.

The whole room swayed, and not in the gentle manner a parent rocks their baby to sleep. The room violently swayed from side to side, then twisted on its axis, and the motion changed direction. Sarah vaguely realised she wasn't alone as she could hear the anguished retching of another person in the room.

A pale shaft of light fell as the narrow door opened. A sturdy woman entered, carrying a lantern and balancing a jug on a tray.

With the door open, the surrounding sounds amplified: groans of wood protesting at the manner in which it was being treated; in the distance men yelling out instructions. She feared the wind would steal those instructions, and the men issuing them, for it sounded like a tornado had them in its bosom. Every gust threatened to break open the tiny round window, which Sarah now realised was a porthole, and, through that realisation, she knew she must be on a ship. On a ship, in a storm. She retched again, the swaying interminable.

The woman stumbled across the moving floor, wiping Sarah's mouth and face with a damp cloth, rinsing it in the wash bowl, and returning the cloth to Sarah's clammy forehead. Next she moved to the other bed and repeated the exercise.

A wail came from the bed as the woman bathed the other girl.

'I'm dying. Let me die in peace. I will die an old maid on this ship. Please just let me die, Elaine.'

Her cries interspersed with the sound of vomiting.

'Hush, child. You're seasick, not dying. The captain assured us the storm will pass by morning. Then it's only two more days before we arrive in Calcutta. It'll be better in the warmth on shore, with solid earth under your feet. Now hush, you need to regain your strength.'

She bustled around the room, straightening bed covers, emptying bowls of bile, and tucking stray locks back into hair caps. For their comfort and her convenience, she'd left the door ajar, allowing a modicum of stale air to circulate through the cabin.

Sarah lay exhausted against her pillow. She caught calming wafts of lavender every time she moved her head, from the sprigs Elaine had tucked inside the pillowcase. Concentrating on the lavender forced the nausea to fade, but did nothing for the swaying in her head. Sarah positioned the damp cloth over her face, trying to decipher her predicament. She drifted off to sleep, her arm slipping coming to rest against the vanity case she'd uncovered at *The Old Curiosity Shop*.

Hazy sunlight forced its way into the cabin and Sarah opened her eyes. She was so parched, she expected someone had glued her mouth shut with a strong adhesive. As she surfaced, she breathed a sigh of relief that the violent rocking from the night before had subsided to an imperceptible sway.

'Good morning, Sarah,' mumbled a plain-looking girl from the other bed. She looked like she'd spent the night fighting a legion of octopuses. Her hair had escaped from her nightcap, her shift stained with what Sarah presumed was vomit, and her face as blotchy as a Jackson Pollock canvas.

Sarah forced her parched mouth open.

'You look like you had a rough night.'

The girl laughed.

'I had a rough night. When do you think Elaine will be back? I can't wait to get cleaned up, and I'm starving. Imagine if we ventured to the dining room looking this dreadful, we'd never find husbands! Word'll spread that we turn into Medusa at night and devour our lovers!'

Sarah joined her in laughter at the imagery of two women rampaging through the ship at night, cascades of writhing snakes around their faces. They were still laughing when Elaine returned to their cabin, much steadier on her feet now.

'You two are bright as buttons this morning. The smells from the galley are heavenly today. Given Calcutta is so close, the chefs used all the eggs and the last of the bacon. We'll be dining well today, unless you two lazybones don't get out of bed and dressed. Stop gabbing in bed like teenagers. Come now, Maria, Sarah, get up, and I'll help you both dress.'

Still laughing, Sarah and Maria scuttled out of their bedclothes and dressed for breakfast. This wasn't how Sarah imagined her Sunday panning out, but she was up for the adventure. India had always been on her bucket list.

THE FISHING FLEET

*T*he volume of conversation as loud in the dining room as the noise from the wind the previous night, as the passengers regaled their friends with tales of how sick they'd been, their stumbles, or, for those sporting bruises, how they'd injured themselves during the storm. As was now her habit, Sarah surveyed the room for the faces of her parents, but to no avail.

As Sarah, Maria and Elaine sat at their allocated table beside three other young women, they overheard a curly-haired girl bemoaning her night.

'Just look at my eye! No one will have me now. I may as well return to England as an *empty*. You'll nab the best lieutenants and, if I'm lucky, I'll be stuck with a fusty old Customs Collector from a horrid place in the middle of nowhere.'

She stabbed at her breakfast on branded P&O crockery as a pale, mousy girl patted her shoulder.

'It will fade, Margot. Once you are wearing your *topi*, we'll add a mosquito veil to hide it. Five days at the most you'll have to cover it. There will be plenty of parties, we're not all going to marry the minute we step off this boat. Except for Karen.'

The girls turned to face the most serene girl of the group, eating her scrambled eggs with a look on her face suggesting she knew she was triumphant in negotiating a betrothal aboard a Fishing Fleet boat.

For Sarah was on one of these. Known as the Fishing Fleet, it was a boat full of unmarried Englishwomen of good breeding stock. Lots of "fifth daughters of the vicar" girls, and girls born in India to British officers, sent to England for their education, and now returning to other officers or highly placed employees of the East India Company. There was a smattering of upper-class girls, who were plain of face, and hadn't secured a husband during several 'seasons' in London. If you didn't marry after three seasons, the only hope left was to sail off to India and, given the lack of competition from other girls, you'd score yourself a husband regardless of your looks.

Karen had achieved what many other girls had before her. She'd identified a suitable prospect on board, and they'd already announced their engagement. They were due to marry as soon as the ship docked. For, although the Fishing Fleet boats carried unmarried women to India (to make sure the Englishmen married none of the native women), they were also transporting returning officers, new graduates off to work for the Company, family members and adventurers. The chances of a young woman meeting her future spouse on the boat were high.

Karen Cuthbert was now the subject of envious glances from the other young ladies at the table. Sarah absorbed all this, while not contributing to the conversations, she filed away the information. The topic on everyone else's lips was the afternoon's scheduled activity of 'spar fighting' on deck. She could taste the testosterone as the men discussed who would win, and who they should place their wagers.

The conversation dwindled as diners finished breakfast and left to prepare for the day. Sarah sipped her fragrant tea, satisfied she understood this tradition, although she'd kill for a good coffee - even a Starbucks. Elaine fidgeted in her seat, consulting the elegant gold wristwatch on her wrist.

'Elaine, I'm not sure if I've asked this, but do you know the Lesters by any chance?' asked Sarah, relieved she now knew the names of those around her, and chancing that this woman had met her parents. Fate was a funny thing.

The absence of a wedding band on Elaine's finger was telling, given her age. Not here to find a husband, it was more likely she was on the ship as a chaperone — to make sure her charge, or charges, remained virtuous until delivered to their destination, and into the arms of a suitable spouse.

'Friends of your parents, are they? I'm not sure I know them. But if they are in Simla, we'll ask around when we get there. Have you finished your tea? Let's go, shall we?'

After several turns round the boat, the threesome made their way up top where the fighting was about to start. Crowded around the rails, with a tarpaulin strung under a long wooden spar, were handsome sailors dressed in gleaming white uniforms. Groups of ladies gathered on the opposite side, safely away from the crew. No woman planned to hitch their marital wagon to a sailor, so it was best to keep them at arm's length. Common sailors had wooed and ruined many a girl.

Sarah and her friends found a space at the edge just as two men climbed over the rail and in good humour straddled either end of the spar, holding pillow cases filled with grain and securely tied at the top. A huge roar went up from the crowd as the combatants inched towards each other. The taller of the two, a huge dark-haired gentleman with a fine moustache, swung first, missing his opponent. His chalky red-haired opponent mimed a small jig to entertain the onlookers. The ladies laughed and cheered at his cheekiness, momentarily distracting him as he mock saluted them, and allowing the giant a second opportunity to swing his sack. This time, it connected with the other man's abdomen, unseating him, and he fell from his perch, landing safely onto the stretched tarpaulin underneath. Catcalls and whistles filled the deck. The sailors stomped their polished boots and cheered the champion. Caught up in the excitement, Sarah was oblivious to the lingering looks she was receiving from a man leaning against the wall, filling his pipe. He'd been casting glances her way since they'd arrived at the fight.

A second man had climbed over the railing and was slithering his way along the spar to the encouraging cheers of the crowd, the ladies leaning out, joining in with calls of encouragement.

Both men hefted their sacks and swung them over their heads in the style of a lasso thrower. The sacks collided with each other, but both men held their seats. Sarah could see the furious exchange of money across the pit as young men placed wagers on the new fighter.

More ladies joined them to watch the match, jostling Sarah in their eagerness to see. Both fighters were the younger sons of titled families, sent to India by their frustrated relatives to limit their philandering and prolific spending of their parents' money. The fight was good-natured, but the boys competitive and wealthy, making them attractive to the ladies. So far on the voyage, neither man had been captivated by any of the offerings on board, but that hadn't dampened the women's perpetual optimism they could change that, if only the men would notice them.

As the fighting continued, with both men landing good blows, the crowd jostled Sarah as more girls sought a front row position. She turned to tell the girl behind her to stop pushing but, as she did so, a rogue wave caught the bow of the ship. It tilted the ship a few degrees, enough to catch Sarah unawares as the change in the deck's angle pushed her up against the railings. Sarah grabbed Maria's arm for balance, before they both tumbled over at the exact moment the men fell from the spar, surprised by the sudden lurch to the left.

The tarpaulin wasn't designed to take the sudden weight of four people, health and safety considerations not a high priority. and the cloth gave way with a great rending sound that filled the air, competing with the screams of the women.

Men clambered over the railings, reaching to the women and the spar fighters clinging to the remnants of the tarpaulin. Too terrified to scream, Sarah held onto an edge with a death grip. There was no way she planned on dying on board this ship, with no family or friends by her side.

The P&O ship's narrow beam was renowned for rolling badly, and that caused the accident Sarah was now part of. The fighters, epitomising their fine breeding, were trying to help the ladies before themselves. Maria flailing around so much her foot collided with the brow of one. He lost his grip and with an anguished cry that wrenched at Sarah's heart, he slipped through the growing tear, plummeting to the lower deck. The sharp crack of his neck breaking brought a crushing silence to the onlookers.

The pipe-smoking gentleman tied himself to another spar and was being lowered down to her where he grabbed her roughly by the wrists before gesturing to the men to pull them both up. Another sailor had done the same and was rescuing the inconsolable Maria, who knew within her heart she'd caused the young man's death. The remaining spar fighter, Gary Dundonald, son of the Earl of Dundonald, hoisted himself up, reaching for the willing hands waiting for him. As he tried to lever himself, his foot caught the ripped material, and the force of his weight finally rent it in two, just as the crowd pulled Maria and Dundonald to safety.

Elaine took both women under her wing and hustled them below deck. Maria refused to set foot on the deck again until their ship berthed in Calcutta. In all the hurly burly there hadn't been a chance for Sarah to say 'thank you' to the man who'd rescued her. With this preying on her mind, she ventured out of the room alone while Maria and Elaine were sleeping.

A death on board did far more to lower morale than the weather or terrible food, and most people had taken to their rooms to complete their packing before the ship berthed, leaving the hallways deserted. In the dining room, Sarah found a group drinking more than a fortifying tea, her rescuer not among them. She climbed up to the deck where the sultry sun shone, blind to her feelings. There, gazing at the distant shore, was the man with the pipe — her rescuer.

'Excuse me?' Sarah started.

He turned, pipe clamped in his mouth, tiny puffs of smoke competing with those from Calcutta on the horizon.

'Miss Williams, how are you fairing this afternoon?'

The gravel in his voice reminiscent of her father's, courtesy of years of heavy smoking.

Her reply caught in her throat.

'I'm fine, thank you. I wanted to thank you for saving me.'

He inclined his head, saying nothing in response.

She carried on.

'If you hadn't climbed down, I'm sure that both Maria and I would have fallen, and, well, thank you, again.'

He nodded, turning back to the horizon.

Sensing her dismissal, Sarah turned away. As she was leaving, he called out to her.

'I'll always be there to save you, Miss Williams.'

She turned around, but he wasn't looking at her. Was it possible she'd just imagined his cryptic response? She opened her mouth to query him, when he turned towards her, the light of the setting sun catching him in profile.

'Always,' he repeated, before tipping his hat to her and walking away in the opposite direction, leaving her standing open-mouthed on the now-empty deck.

THE PORT

*T*he madness of their arrival into port made more so by last-
minute clinches in corridors between lovers and
suitors, aware they'd left their run too late. For most of the girls,
vigilant chaperones or families were waiting for them at the dock, and
it was now too late to announce their love and become betrothed to
anyone on the ship.

From here, the Fishing Fleet girls could pick from thousands of
suitable men; men deemed suitable by their protectors, and not the
girls themselves. Women lined the railings of the ship, straining
for their first glimpse of exotic India. Even Margot made it up to
the deck, her unfortunate black eye forgotten in the excitement.
Maria remained in her room, adamant she wouldn't step foot on
deck apart from the steps she'd need to take to get off the 'cursed
ship'.

Sarah allowed the tide of happiness sweeping the ship to carry her
away and she tried finding the pipe-smoking man among those
gathered on deck, but he was gone. The passengers disembarked and
laughing women jostled for space on the gangways. Sarah found Maria
ready to leave, hat on her head, her white-knuckled hand clutching her
portmanteau.

Elaine was chiding Sarah, 'Hurry, we have to meet the driver. What have you been *doing*? You should have packed hours ago.'

Sarah hadn't packed her bag, because she didn't know what was hers, or what belonged to Maria. If she left it long enough, Maria would have packed her things, leaving everything that was Sarah's.

'Sorry, Elaine, the sight of Calcutta distracted me. So many people. It was mesmerising!'

As Sarah replied, she threw her things into a brown leather case, black monogrammed letters impressed into the top, an 'S' and a 'W'.

Voices rang out through the halls as they made their way to the gangway amidst soldiers in their uniforms, and women in their best travelling frocks and bonnets. The morning sun already punishing them for their tardiness, the heat unbearable. Sarah could not believe women covered themselves in so many layers of fabric in this heat. Surely once she arrived, wherever she was going, the dress code would be less English and more Indian? She hoped so.

She trotted behind Elaine and Maria, fearful that if she lost either of them, she'd be stranded. There'd been no convenient purse full of gold coins or priceless jewellery on *this* adventure, unlike her travel back to the Savoy, which was a lifetime ago. Or was it?

Elaine was talking to the Indian driver of a horse-drawn carriage. Maria had climbed straight in, claiming the back corner, wasting no time in closing her eyes and feigning sleep. Sarah looked to Elaine for direction, but she was in a heated discussion with the driver, the conversation punctuated with words as foreign to Sarah as the country itself. She stood by the carriage, one foot on the running board, surveying the mass of people gathered at the port. The likelihood of finding her parents here was as remote as seeing another white face.

'Miss Williams,' came a gravelly voice behind her.

She stilled. Recognising the voice, she responded, 'Hello.'

Elaine interrupted the moment.

'Ah, Major Brooke, thank goodness you're here. This man refuses to listen when I explain where we are going. He insists on talking to my husband. How this country operates is a mystery. A *husband*. As if I'd need a husband,' she muttered to herself.

193

'I can deal with this for you, Miss Barker,' Major Warren Brooke murmured back.

Elaine nodded, still muttering about women not being allowed to be in control of their own destinies.

This was not Elaine Barker's first trip to India, it was her fourth — the last three in her capacity as a professional chaperone. The first had been as an unsuccessful member of the Fishing Fleet where she'd returned to England unmarried but in love with India. Elaine had set about trying to find a way back — no easy task with no family behind her. The local minister came to the rescue — his daughter was off to India and needed a companion. His wife had come from money, so there were sufficient funds available to recompense Elaine for escorting their daughter to join her eldest sister who'd gone out there with her husband. From that point, she had secured her occupation as a chaperone which now provided a comfortable income appropriate to someone of her station. The work wasn't arduous, and her charges had been well-behaved young women, intent on achieving their goal of marrying well, and not returning to England as a spinster.

On this trip, she was being paid double to escort two girls to Simla. She'd never been there, but word of its beauty had entranced her, and she hoped she might find a permanent position, as the long sailings were taking a toll on her health. She'd given up any idea of marrying, realising that she had control of her own life. No father or husband to instruct her. No family to frown upon her choices. This was freedom, and because as a woman she had so little, she clung to hers.

Still, occasionally, a man *was* useful, and she was not above utilising the skills of those around her to deal with recalcitrant carriage drivers. She thanked Major Brooke, and climbed into the carriage, settling herself in for the long journey to the Simla hill station. At the rear, their trunks had appeared and were being strapped down by a pair of wiry Indian men. The Major completed his conversation with the driver, and appeared at Sarah's side, offering her his hand. She looked at his hand, devoid of any rings, before meeting his eyes. Clean and blue, they stared into her soul. *Does he know I'm from the future?*

'Miss Williams,' he stated.

She allowed him to help her into the carriage, the not-unpleasant scent of tobacco following her. He didn't join them inside, instead leaping up to sit with their driver.

All around them, families greeted their loved ones, catching up on the news from home, comparing stories of the trip, climbing into their own carriages or rickshaws, depending on the distances they needed to travel. For Sarah's group, there would be no rest before they left — their journey to Simla adding another two weeks to the trip. The driver called to the horses, and they set off, leaving the buzz of Calcutta's busy port behind them.

They pushed through the heaving throngs of humanity — more people than Sarah had ever seen. They represented every permutation of life and beautiful gemlike colours adorned every woman she saw through the window as she drank in the sounds and scents of one of the greatest cities on earth. Sacred cows decorated like courtesans walked in concert with them through the streets.

Later, the competing scents gave way to lush fields, replacing the hectic city sounds with the tranquil trills of bird life and farm animals. The change of scene did nothing to budge Sarah from her position by the window, absorbing the culture in front of her. Elaine and Maria had both drifted off to places where dreams were true, and real life was the fantasy. Major Brooke conversed with their driver — their voices adding to the hypnotic feel of the ride. Sarah settled deeper into her corner, and before long, the motion carried her away into dreams which were neither truth nor lie.

THE AMBUSH

*T*heir days travelling the Grand Trunk Road passed enjoyably enough. Elaine entertained the girls with stories of balls and banquets, polo and parties. Major Brooke occasionally sat with them, not contributing much to the conversation but it was pleasant having him there. Sarah found his pipe-filling ritual fascinating and soothing in equal measures and the more than a thousand miles they needed to travel would give ample time to study him without seeming too curious.

Their trip was uneventful and the weather comfortable. The season was changing from late summer to autumn, which brought the daytime temperatures down so much that by nightfall the women added a shawl to their ensemble. At Kanpur, they stayed for three days in the P&O hotel, built to break up the long trip. There, Elaine announced another couple would join them for the stretch between Kanpur and Delhi, before they carried onto Simla.

Their new companions were Reverend and Mrs Montgomery, an older couple, well-versed in the vagaries of India and her people. They enthralled them with tales of Indian gods and goddesses, anecdotes of accidental encounters with bandits and beggars, and sweeping saga-like tales of love in the colonies, punctuated with cautions about rampant disease in this beautiful country. They were en route to Delhi to take up a post in a missionary school there, having already established a school in Kanpur. The locals had been less than pleased with the thought of Christianity being preached to their children, albeit through the mask of a British education. They'd left a young Christian woman in charge of the fledgling school as they moved on to their next challenge.

'You left a woman running the school?' queried Elaine.

'Why yes,' replied the Reverend. 'Who better to teach the way of our Lord than an educated woman, who has chosen the path of a teacher instead of as a mother?'

Elaine settled back into the cushioned seats, a whole new world opening to her.

'What did her family say about her teaching at the missionary school?' she probed, although with no immediate kin to concern themselves with her decisions, the question was more than rhetorical.

'The poor girl has no family left, Miss Barker, so it was a good fit for the Church and for her. We will keep in touch with her, and will act as her guardians should any issue arise. As always, when travellers such as yourselves pass through Kanpur, we encourage you to visit the school, and Miss Morley. She'll not want for English company, I can assure you,' the Reverend submitted in a satisfied tone, his wife nodding next to him.

Maria, who'd feigned sleep for much of the journey, stirred in the corner.

'She doesn't have to marry, and everyone is fine with that?'

Her voice trembled, whether through lack of use or the after-effects of the incident on the boat, no one could tell.

The Reverend Montgomery pondered her query for some time before replying.

'With no family to guide her, child, or to make the introductions and arrangements, she made the honourable decision to serve God instead. Whilst marriage is a sacred covenant, she is doing God's work.'

Mrs Montgomery and Elaine nodded in unison to this last statement.

'Amen,' said Mrs Montgomery, her large brown eyes raised to the heavens, as if Jesus himself were listening to their conversation in the carriage.

'Amen,' echoed Elaine, her tired face radiant at the idea of a new career.

The Reverend had just started on a new story detailing the extravagance of the local Maharaja's and their courts, when the carriage tipped to the right, flinging Elaine and Sarah into the laps of their companions. Major Brooke and the driver were shouting outside, their voices muddied and inseparable.

Sarah's arm was jammed between the wall of the carriage and the shoulder of Elaine, who herself was pressed so hard against Mrs Montgomery, that the Reverend's wife was in danger of falling out should the lock on the door give way. The carriage slowed and halted after turning at such a speed that the driver could have been challenging Charlton Heston in *Ben Hur*. Now at a standstill, the occupants untangled themselves, laughing at the twisted muddle of arms, legs and luggage they found themselves in. Sarah reached over to open the door, bracing herself so she didn't tumble out.

Despite this, she all but fell from the carriage, jarring her ankles as she landed on the uneven ground, her feet bound in unforgivingly laced leather boots. As she reached up to assist Elaine and Maria, she felt the cold bite of metal against her cheek, and froze. Her eyes took in the look of horror on Elaine's face — enough to tell her that the person applying the knife to her cheek was not the sort you struggled with, nor one you turned to face.

THE MAJOR

*M*ajor Brooke called out.

'Stay still Miss Williams! Do not move, and you won't come to any harm. Miss Barker and Miss Scott, please climb out carefully, we are on a slope here. We have to avoid moving the carriage in case it slips any further.'

Sarah could not tell where he was calling from, but something strained his voice, as if he was holding back his words.

Maria and Elaine eased themselves out, moving to the side of the carriage. The Reverend and Mrs Montgomery followed. Sarah still hadn't budged, the hard metal forming a perfect imprint of the blade against the softness of her cheek. Once the passengers were out, someone shoved her towards the rest of her group. Elaine caught and hugged her before Sarah turned to face the unknown.

The body of the driver lay sprawled on the gravel, his head at an unnatural angle. Standing next to the body was Major Brooke, his arms at his side, his rifle now in the hands of a dirty, barefoot Indian man, dressed in nothing more than rags. He was, however, holding the rifle like he'd been born with it in his hands, and it was pointed at Major Brooke.

It was an Enfield rifle, and, as the rifle of a British Army officer, it was especially accurate — and deadly. Sarah counted another five men, all dressed the same. Two had taken the time to cover their faces, although to Sarah they looked indistinguishable in their filthy clothes, and road-hardened feet. She looked to Major Brooke with a mute appeal in her eyes. He shook his head. They could do nothing apart from agree to whatever the bandits demanded.

The men talked in their native tongue, focussing on the tower of luggage strapped to the carriage. The most impressive trunk belonged to Maria; burgundy leather and polished brass corners. Their smaller bags were still inside, and one bandit was throwing them out as if his life depended upon just how fast he could empty the carriage. His malnourished body disguised an extraordinary strength as he threw the bags a gold medal distance.

The carriage rocked wildly as it was being emptied, and Sarah backed away, drawing a curt yell from one man. He appeared unarmed, so Sarah ignored him and carried on moving, dragging Maria with her. The man yelled at them, and although his language was incomprehensible, his tone was clear, and the women froze.

They unhitched the horses and led them away. Without their stabilising weight, the carriage had nothing to hold it steady, and it slipped on the stony ground, imperceptibly at first, but the bandits movement inside increased the angle, and gravity kicked in.

'Elaine!' Sarah yelled as the rear of the carriage followed the earth's gravitational pull and swung around.

Elaine, realising what was happening, pushed Mrs Montgomery away, just before the carriage collided with her and the Reverend, sending them all tumbling down the bank. A trail of clothing lost from the pillaged trunks marked their path.

Major Brooke tried sprinting to the carriage, but the bandit swung the substantial wooden stock of the rifle against his head, felling him like a giant oak. The raider, dressed in filthy pyjama bottoms, face obscured by a piece of cloth, carried on striking the Major as he lay on the ground. He hit him again and again. They could hear the sickening crunch of cartilage through the screams of the women until he tired of his sport. The bandits left Brooke bleeding onto the stones.

Elaine lay unmoving amongst the detritus of the ditch. The carriage rolling over her pelvis before carrying on its destructive path down the hillside. Of the bandit inside, there was no sign. Elaine looked as if she were sleeping, but the spokes of the wheel had caught the Reverend as the carriage lurched to its side, pinning him underneath the heavy steel carcass as it slid down the hill, caving in his head, leaving his arms and legs unrecognisable as limbs.

Maria and Alice sunk to the ground, holding each other, their cries tearing at the air. The bandits were collecting up the last of the luggage strewn on the ground, paying no attention to the women. Sarah stood in the mêlée, her heart breaking at the thought Elaine, the closest thing she had to a friend in this time, was dead. Then Elaine stirred.

THE RESCUE

'Elaine!' Sarah yelled, running towards her friend. Maria and Alice stirred and rushed after her.

'She's alive,' Sarah stated, as Elaine opened her eyes, and tried unsuccessfully to sit up. She fell back to the ground, whimpering in pain. Sarah probed her hip.

'You've broken your pelvis, I think. It's OK, Elaine, you'll be OK. If we can just get you to a doctor, you'll be up and dancing in no time. Alice, we need to keep her warm, can you find something to cover her up, Alice?'

Looking around, Sarah saw Alice walking towards the mangled body of her husband.

'Alice, come back!' Sarah called out.

She jumped up from Elaine's side and, stepping over the rocks littering the hillside, she grabbed Alice's arm, pulling her away from the grisly sight of flies settling on the sticky blood covering the remains of the Reverend's face.

'Leave him, Alice, there is nothing we can do for him now.'

Sarah only just managed not to retch at the sight of his mangled body. Death scenes in the movies were always so much cleaner, more clinical. She'd no idea that death smelled so vile.

She pulled on Alice's scrawny arm.

'Come on, Alice, we have to look after Elaine and the Major. Come on.'

Pulling her arm again, Sarah all but dragged the bereaved woman up to the hilltop where she found the bandits had disappeared, taking with them the horses and their luggage. The Major was motionless on the ground, his chest moving up and down. So, alive but no use. There wasn't another person around, the shrouded hills the only witnesses to their predicament.

Sarah shrugged off the feelings of panic. Her companions were as useless as newborn babes with their sheltered lives and lack of education. Needlepoint wouldn't help them. She snorted as she realised her public schooling and first aid courses had given her more knowledge than all these women put together.

'Alice, stand on the road and try to find someone to help us. We have to get Elaine to a doctor,' she instructed, grabbing the nearest item of clothing strewn on the ground.

It happened to be one of the Reverend's spare cassocks. Sarah paused. The black cotton scrunched in her hands, Alice's porcelain face turned an even paler shade of white. Unapologetically, Sarah threw it over Elaine. Reducing the effects of shock was more imperative than protecting the sensibilities of the widow.

'The road, Alice, the road. *You* need to stand on it.'

Alice nodded at Sarah's repeated instruction, rearranging her face into an unreadable mask. *It takes a special woman to rise above her own grief,* Sarah thought. She called out to Maria.

'Maria, can you check on the Major? You may need to turn him onto his side, to make sure he can breathe properly.'

She fussed over Elaine, trying to make her as comfortable as the hillside would allow. Being on an incline was not ideal, but Sarah didn't think she had the strength to move the woman on her own. She'd have to wait until help arrived.

The sun pulsed down, baking the ground and the women on it. Sarah wiped sweat from her brow, thankful for the first time that her voluminous outfit protected her from the rays. At some stage, Elaine had lost her bonnet; her skin was turning pink in the heat. Sarah sat so her shadow provided a modicum of protection.

'I'll bet your face hasn't seen this much sun in your whole life,' she joked, bringing a faint smile to Elaine's face.

'The last time I spent days in the sun was when a group of us girls went to Ibiza for a Bank Holiday weekend. You'd love it there — you wouldn't understand it, but you'd love it,' Sarah carried on, knowing Elaine was in too much pain to comprehend anything she was rabbiting on about. 'I had this new bikini, and the catch at the back kept coming undone; *so* embarrassing. One of the girls had to put a safety pin in it, just so it would stay up between the towel and the water.' She prattled on, saying anything just to keep Elaine awake.

The sun set, and with it the temperature fell, chilling them all to the bone. Sarah and Alice dragged the unconscious Major down to Elaine, and together they huddled under the stars, the injured woman drifting in and out of consciousness.

Maria advocated moving down to the broken carriage.

'It'll be warmer, and we could use the seats as cushions. It's better than staying here in the open. We can carry Elaine between us, and come back for the Major,' she whined.

Alice didn't respond, staring at the heavens above her, lost in memories of her husband.

Sarah replied, 'No, Maria, we won't be moving Elaine because we don't know how bad her injuries are, unless you have a medical degree we don't know about? We'll stay here with her. We've done the best we can for Major Brooke, but we're safer here, just off the crest of the hill for now. It's better to stay together to avoid any risk of exposure.'

She lowered her voice.

'Think of Alice, and the Reverend. We won't be going any further down the hill.'

At the sound of a wild animal howling in the distance, Sarah added, 'We're safer together.'

The night passed, each of them finding no comfort in the countryside's openness, the sounds of nature creeping closer and closer. Sarah felt Elaine's brow, hot to the touch, her breathing shallow. They were all parched, in part dreading sunrise, but impatient for the sun to crest in the hope a new day would bring salvation along the road. Sarah sent Alice back up to keep a lookout for travellers. Maria sat sulking further up the hill, glowering at Sarah, blaming Sarah for her sleepless night, and the stone bruises adorning her body.

Sarah dozed next to Elaine, dreaming of pork dumplings served in broth, when Alice shouted from her position by the road.

'A carriage, with British soldiers!'

Sarah and Maria scrambled up the bank, joining her at the roadside. There were a dozen or so mounted soldiers escorting another carriage coming their way. The women waved at the red-coated Englishmen, and two of the outriders urged their mounts on towards them.

The lead rider pulled up in front.

'Ladies, what the devil are you doing on the side of the road? These are dangerous times to be out without an escort. The Sepoys are rioting in other parts of the country. Where are your menfolk?' He looked around.

Sarah stepped forward.

'They attacked us — locals, I think. Our companions are injured, and one is... one is dead. We need your help.'

At her account of being attacked, the second rider wheeled his horse around and cantered back to the carriage, shouting instructions as he went.

The first rider dismounted.

'These are uncertain times. You are fortunate they didn't kill you. Women and children are being slaughtered in other places where the troubles have erupted. We can escort you to Delhi, but we are en route to Simla and we mustn't delay any further. We'll see what we can do for your injured companions, to make them comfortable for the journey. I am Colonel Scarborough and...'

Sarah had been about to interrupt him when another shout took her words away. Two of the riders had found Major Brooke, and were hauling him up the hill, still unconscious.

'Sir, it's Major Brooke.'

The Colonel abandoned his conversation with Sarah and rushed over to the Major.

'Jesus, what happened to you?'

The Major stirred, his eyes still closed, not yet back in the world of the living.

'You know each other?' Sarah asked, as she joined them.

She couldn't help feel protective of the man who'd saved her life, and who had risked his life to help Elaine and the Reverend. The new carriage had now arrived, and the soldiers mobilised to transfer Elaine and to recover the Reverend's body.

Alice was in her element, directing them the way a choreographer produces a cabaret, her grief submerged under her efficiency. *Perhaps she'd been hasty in dismissing the abilities of her friends,* Sarah thought. Alice was proof that everyone can rise to the occasion. Maria, however, had climbed into the carriage, and lapsed back into her default position of curling into the corner, shutting the world out by closing her eyes.

The Colonel replied, 'We trained together in England, a long time ago now. He was coming out to join the regiment here. We need all the good men we can get at the moment. The problem with the Sepoys is getting out of hand. Poor decisions by others led to this, and now, attacking English travellers on the roads, bloody unacceptable.'

He caught himself swearing.

'Excuse me, ma'am, it's rare I'm in the company of ladies at present. My manners are rusty. Please, ride in the carriage. I'm sure his Lordship won't resent the intrusion, given the circumstances. We'll send a telegram to Headquarters, advising them of the attack, but that's low priority at present. We're all being deployed to quell what some are calling a rebellion. All over some damn shell casings. Stupid decisions, poor leaders, that's what caused this.'

He looked abashed at his coarse language again.

'I'm sorry. It's been a long time. Let me help you.'

'Thank you, Colonel, I'd rather Elaine, and the Major had the comfort of the carriage. I can ride upfront. That'll give them more room.'

'I'd not be comfortable with a lady riding up front, ma'am. We can make room, I'm sure.'

The Colonel looked unhappy.

Sarah looked inside the carriage. Alice sat in one corner with Elaine stretched out along the rest of the seat, her head in Alice's lap. Maria slouched in the opposite corner, eyes closed, deep shadows etched on her face, with the Major propped up facing Alice, and Lord Napier in the middle, putting on a stoic face at the influx of passengers into his conveyance.

'No, I think I'll sit up front.'

Ignoring his protestations, she clambered up and sat herself next to the young driver. The Colonel could do nothing more than shake his head, his sense of propriety wounded. He remounted his gelding, and the troops carried on their way.

From her perch on top, Sarah surveyed the countryside. It all seemed so innocent. She tried not to think about the body of the Reverend, strapped to the back like a piece of luggage. If she ignored the soldiers, the body, and her damaged friends, she could make believe she was on holiday, that all was well, that after the tour she'd return to London, to her bills, her shop, and her friends.

THE BROTHER

A light breeze moved the hair around her face. The scents carried on the wind were exotic and heady, intoxicating in their heaviness.

The sounds of melodious voices came to her in waves. Her whole body cocooned in a thousand different fragrances. Gentle laughs mingled with tinkling bells, and the breeze wove the scents of a thousand flowers into her hair.

When she opened her eyes, she found herself in bed, in a room with vases filled with fantastical blooms. Flowers she'd never seen before, arranged as if they were the subjects of a still-life painting in the Louvre.

From the window there was an endless expanse of blue sky, a deeper blue than she could have imagined, uninterrupted by clouds. She padded over to the window, the immense blue so bright it assaulted her senses, and shading her eyes, she leaned out of the window. People thronged the street beyond, but there wasn't a pale English face visible, just a sea of Indian faces, covering the spectrum of brown, from rich coffee through to a delicate caramel. A snow-sprinkled mountain range framed the whole picture, reminding her that this was not home.

Sarah sank to the floor, leaning her head against the wall. The events of the past weeks came back to her. The boat trip, the ambush on the highway, the jostled ride to Delhi, Elaine's painful moans, and the Major's bruises, which blossomed on the journey.

They buried the Reverend in Delhi - one more Englishman in an Indian cemetery, forever claiming that patch of India as England. Alice elected to stay in Delhi as planned - God's work would not stop. And after delivering Elaine into the hands of the doctors in Delhi, and reassuring Elaine that Colonel Scarborough would look after Sarah and her virtue, the remaining group carried on to Simla, without Maria. Only Elaine's pleas from her hospital bed had moved the Colonel into agreeing that Sarah could go with them. Elaine had a contract to deliver Sarah to Simla, and a broken pelvis wouldn't stop her from delivering on that agreement.

Maria had roused herself during the trip to Delhi once she realised an actual *lord* was with them in the carriage. There was no better match than a lord. She'd been sparkling and witty, engaging her feminine wiles. Lord Napier had to quell rebellion and had no time to flirt, regardless how charming the girl was. Sarah presumed Maria was too lowborn for him - Maria was a girl a gentleman dallied with, but not the sort they'd marry. Little did she know that after leaving her friend in Delhi, Maria, a well-trained *Fishing Fleet* girl, would reel in Napier and, after an indecently short courtship, they would marry.

Sarah wondered if she'd ever see Elaine again. The chaperone had been adamant the Colonel deliver Sarah into her brother's arms. Sarah had never had a brother, so having one in India delighted her no end, and she'd put the terrifying ambush aside, concentrating on the prospect of being part of a family. The journey to Simla from Delhi passed without incident. This time, the Colonel had placed her inside the carriage, and refused to change his decision despite her protestations. After the burial of Reverend Montgomery, they'd only stayed long enough to procure emergency clothing for Sarah, and she wondered what had been in the trunk she'd lost to the bandits. They'd found her vanity case abandoned on the side of the road - the only one of her belongings the bandits had dropped. She'd never recover her other belongings, not now that there was a full-blown rebellion in the region.

Sarah's arrival in Simla was a crushing disappointment. In the failing light, they'd arrived at her brother's silent house, the Colonel too busy to do anything more than escort her to the door, with Major Brooke doing nothing more than doff his hat to her.

'Good luck with your brother, Miss Williams,' his parting words.

Odd, thought Sarah. *Why on earth would I need luck dealing with my brother?*

No lights nor fulsome embraces from her brother greeted her. No one welcomed her other than a small array of wide-eyed Indian servants, who did nothing other than show her to her room. Of her brother, there was no sign.

That had been a week ago. To date she still hadn't met her elusive brother. The servants tiptoed round her like she was a porcelain doll. With a limited wardrobe, and no social contacts, Sarah amused herself by taking strolls in the garden, and took her meals alone. The silence was killing her. Her only visitor had been the tailor, sent by her brother to replace her lost clothing. Sarah had a ball choosing fabrics she adored but could never in a million years wear on the denim-clad streets of London.

'Can I fetch you anything, memsahib?' asked a girl crouching by the door, gazing at her with the largest brown eyes. 'Memsahib?' the girl repeated.

Sarah took a deep breath.

'A glass of water?'

Noticing that she was only wearing a thin white shift, Sarah hurried back to bed, and clambered in, which was preferable to being on board the boat, but the emotions of the past week had caught up with her and she was so tired, and lonely. Her Indian servant her only companion, and yet they didn't speak, save for mealtimes and in the mornings when she dressed.

The girl disappeared, reappearing moments later carrying a lacquered tray with a glass and a carafe of water. She set it on the bedside table, casting glances at Sarah, huddling under the covers, only her pale face visible with her eyes closed against the light, and India.

When she heard water being poured into the glass, Sarah opened her eyes and reached for the glass. She took a large gulp of water and pulled the covers up further. Sir William Jones, a scholar of ancient India, had once written that India had "fallen into England's lap while she was sleeping". Sarah had fallen through Alice's rabbit hole while *she* was sleeping.

With no warning, a red-coated soldier strode into her room. A very British soldier; polished boots, bristling moustache, with the posture of a man born to be behind a rifle, the silver sword hanging at his side a giveaway he was an officer.

Unbuckling the sword belt, he flung the lot onto Sarah's bed.

'Christ!' he muttered as he strode across the room.

'You know what that Viceroy wants now? He wants us to apologise to the bloody Darbar's for daring to move their damn bazaar. Goad is furious. It burnt to the ground and they're making out as if we set it on fire with our own hands. It's a mess. They still have a bazaar, Goad's just building it further away from us here in Station Ward now. The sooner we leave this hole, the better. I have never wanted a decent English fog more than I do today.'

After finishing his rant, he realised Sarah was shrinking away in horror — his sword belt narrowly missing her when he'd flung it onto the bed. Sarah's scared eyes followed him around the room.

'You're still in bed? I was expecting you to be ready by now. Get up and get dressed unless you're dying; more than likely in this heathen country. We have this damned soirée Sir John is hosting tonight for us, to show how contrite we are about their bloody bazaar. It's those clerks their Government bring here in the summer — they're the only ones upset about it being further away. Hell, it just means a longer ride with one of their mates in a litter? Everybody wins? The coolies make money, the clerks spend more time out of the office. It's not as if they spend much time in their offices. Bloody lazy, the lot.'

He noticed the servant, clad in an elegant garnet coloured sari, waiting by the door.

'That includes you, lazy, every one of you. Get your memsahib up and dressed for Sir John's party tonight. She's not sick, so there's no excuse for her to stay in bed.'

'Stupid lazy girl,' he added under his breath.

Turning back to his 'sister' he barked, 'Get up, Sarah!' before storming out of the room, scooping up his sword belt on the way.

'Can I help?' whispered Nirmala, the young girl assigned to the lady of Firgrove Estate, one of the finest homes in Simla.

The town, once described as a 'make-believe British haven' and the permanent home of Army Headquarters, was quintessentially British India. With the influx of British soldiers, officers, their wives, children, clerks, and associates, Simla had become a bustling metropolis which required all the trappings of modern-day life. For it to run efficiently, it required coolies, clerks, servants, stewards, and shopkeepers. From there, the bazaars had developed.

As the number of high-ranked officers and members of the East India Company moving to Simla increased, the minor Indian royalty followed them. It became a place where the British and the 'British Indians' socialised, romanced and debauched together. Rudyard Kipling described Simla as having a reputation for "frivolity, gossip, and intrigue". Which was true. The clerks were the worst — nothing their masters did or wrote was ever a secret.

When the Viceroy of India, Sir John Lawrence moved the offices of the Army Headquarters from Calcutta to Simla permanently, the Government followed suit. Every summer there was a major exodus from Calcutta to the more temperate climate in the north-west, and the rounds of parties and polo began for the season, and numerous love affairs, keeping the solicitors busy for years, dealing with the fallout.

The proportion of women to men was low, and to avoid their employees marrying the local women, the British Army arranged the passage of socialite women from England, on husband-hunting 'scholarships'. It was against this backdrop of eligible British bachelors, Army officers, marriage-hungry women, theatre, adultery, banquets, and bullies that Simla evolved and prospered. This was the town Sarah was in with no back story to help her, no prior knowledge to draw upon.

'Memsahib?' Nirmala repeated.

Jolted out of her daze, Sarah turned towards her.

'Yes?' she replied.

'The Sahib said you were to change. What will you want to wear?'

Nirmala's voice was musical and calmed Sarah as she placed the decision in someone else's lap.

'I don't know. Will you choose for me?'

The maid didn't look surprised, and disappeared behind a screen, re-emerging moments later, her arms laden with frothy lace and frills. She laid it out on the bed, smoothing the rampant puffs of lace. Sarah stared at it aghast.

'You're dressing me as a giant meringue?'

Nirmala laughed.

'Oh, I know, memsahib, but since you arrived without your clothing, we will have to make do with the Sahib's wife's clothes. He does not want you looking desirable tonight; you are to be plain. The Sahib might be angry if you looked too beautiful…' she said, tapering off.

Sarah slipped out of the covers and ran her fingers over the fine lace. She could not bring herself to look like a bride in a gypsy wedding extravaganza.

'No, I can't wear that. What will everyone else be wearing?' she asked, looking for guidance.

Nirmala looked at her, trying to fathom what type of Englishwoman the Sahib's sister was.

'You could wear your new dress — it arrived this morning. I did not think they'd make it in time, but Sanjay has a cousin, Amit, who works for Ramsay & Co. He told Sanjay that Mr Ramsay made your dress before the others because you had chosen the superior fabric, and that Mr Ramsay said it showed you had better taste than the other women here.'

The maid had been nodding during this long speech, showing that everything Amit had relayed back to Sanjay, who had relayed it to

Nirmala, was a fact, and that she agreed with Mr Ramsay's opinion of her mistress.

Sarah, asked to see the new dress and Nirmala scurried behind the screen adorned with a dozen birds resting on it. Examining it closer, Sarah could see the three panels were hand painted with the birds in relief constructed from real feathers, the oak frame carved with a profusion of native fruits and berries, replicating the diet of the birds. She wanted to stroke the tail feathers of the proud peacock perched on the nearest panel but, as she was reaching out, Nirmala returned from the room hidden by the screen, her arms full of more fabric.

Together, they laid out the gown on the rumpled bedclothes. *Patricia would be in Heaven*, Sarah thought, as Nirmala revealed the true beauty of the dress.

'Memsahib will be the most elegant woman there,' whispered the girl as Sarah stroked the silk. The dress was the same blue to the sapphire of the peacock feathers.

'This is perfect.'

Regardless of her situation or her station, she would at least *look* fabulous. Nirmala vanished, and returned with a team of young girls, who gushed over the garment before helping Sarah wash and change, with the maid fussing over them like a dictator.

The girls were twittering about the ball tonight, their voices as musical as a flock of nightingales. Like young girls anywhere in the world, they had a network of friends in the other grand houses, and they shared tit-bits on who was wearing what, and whom their ladies liked. Sarah received a crash course on the other ladies in town as the girls chatted amongst themselves. Sarah stored the information away, hoping it may save her from any unfortunate social *faux pas*.

In no time, they dressed her and her hair, slipping her feet into embroidered dancing shoes. There was no mention of jewellery, so Sarah assumed the bandits stole those too.

'Nirmala, how will I get to this party tonight?'

She didn't know where she was in relation to the rest of the town.

Her night ride through Simla with the Colonel, without street lights or neon advertising signs, had shown little of her surroundings.

'Your brother has gone on without you. He did not want to wait for you to dress.' Nirmala said, brightening as she added, 'But Mrs Abbott has sent word she will come with her palanquin to take you to Kennedy House, where Mr Williams will meet you. He will fall in love with your dress, and you will find a husband, and, oh, how wonderful,' she said, clapping her hands.

They exasperated Sarah. No matter where she was, someone was always trying to marry her off to a suitable man.

'Fine, let's go.'

If she hadn't known she was in India, she would have suspected she was in a Tudor manor house, owned by someone with an interest in the Orient. It was English in everything but its location. With walls adorned with awe-inspiring landscapes of the surrounding Himalayas, majestic in their coats of snow. The furniture had an English slant, but made from woods with unusual grains and hues. Not an expert, she could only recognise the rosewood and mahogany pieces, but mixed in amongst those superior pieces were small pieces done in red cedar, satinwood, and rhododendron. Sarah recognised some woods were now on the endangered species list *because* of the rampant felling of trees to make furniture such as this.

She followed Nirmala to the ornate front door where a young Indian lad opened the door for her.

At the base of the steps, four Indian men, wearing the finest white outfits, waited by their poles next to a palanquin, resplendent in deep mahogany and golden tones. Someone drew back the curtains as Sarah walked down the steps.

THE MATRIARCH

'Sarah Williams, what a delight to meet you. May I say, it was well worth the wait, look at you. You'll be turning every head there tonight. A week you've been here, and you've not had one visitor, nor have I have even seen you in town. There's not even been a delicious flutter behind a door to gossip about! We were all despairing! Your brother locking you away from us is hardly the done thing! Now hop in and let's get better acquainted,' a clipped English voice boomed out.

Naomi Abbott's bejewelled hand waved Sarah imperiously into the palanquin.

Mrs Naomi Abbott's loyal staff alerted her to Sarah's arrival in Simla, staff who fed her lust for gossip. The news that Simeon Williams had a sister, and that she was coming to town after the sudden death of their parents, had given Naomi such a thrill.

The young ladies sent to India to snare a husband, considered Naomi Abbott the best matchmaker in the business. And for Naomi, the excitement of Sarah's arrival was bolstered by the information she was an heiress in her own right — her parents bequeathing her half their estate, with the proviso being she could not inherit until she married, and that until that time, her widowed brother would manage the estate on her behalf. Finding Sarah the perfect husband would be the jewel in Naomi's matchmaking crown.

But since Sarah's arrival, no one had seen her. She'd attended no performances at the Gaiety Theatre, nor any of the parties which whirled through the town. Naomi and the other ladies called on her, but were rebuffed by Simeon who claimed Sarah was too fragile for visitors after her ordeal on the road to Delhi.

He is an unusual man, Naomi mused. Prone to violent outbursts, according to her husband, who'd also told her that the only reason they still tolerated him in India was due to rebellions brewing around the country. The siblings' father, Arthur, had been a hero during the First Sikh War in the 1840s, and officers who'd served with him were now Simeon's superiors. It was in deference to his father that he remained in the regiment. Naomi pondered whether Arthur's death would cause the ignominious return to England of Simeon, although the troubles in India made it unlikely.

Despite being a young man with an inheritance and no luggage other than a conveniently deceased wife and an attractive sister of marriageable age, there were no circumstances where Naomi Abbott would send any eligible young women his way for a potential betrothal. Distasteful was the most polite word she could think of to describe Simeon Williams — distasteful and disturbing.

THE BALL

*T*he palanquin jostled its way along the road up through The
Mall. As they passed the Ridge, the majestic Christ Church
appeared, its yellow hue reflecting the early evening light, while
candlelight from within illuminated the arched stained-glass windows.
Mrs Abbott kept up a patter of information about the guests expected
at the Viceroy's party. Names and titles bandied about, the same way
gossip magazines nowadays talk of Hollywood starlets.

'I hear Major Brooke will be there tonight. It's wonderful to have
him back, *so* dashing, *and* unattached. To think you spent so
much time with him on the journey! You are the envy of every lady
here.'

The 'matchmaker' smiled at Sarah, who'd turned to look out the
window, causing Naomi to frown in frustration.

'You survived a dastardly experience with bandits, and we are on
our way to the most important party of the season, yet you are
showing no discernible interest. I just don't understand.'

Sarah turned back to her.

'Sorry, the scenery is so *breathtaking*. The size of those mountains is
humbling, and although I've never felt more alive than I do now, I'm
still somewhat lost.'

While Sarah's small speech described her feelings perfectly, Naomi misinterpreted them.

'Oh, child! I can understand your feelings. India does that to you. Nothing is like home here. Not having any other family makes it *so* much harder., if only your brother weren't so difficult. He's not doing himself any favours with the other officers, keeping you tucked away at home. Oh, I've tried talking to him. Tonight he will have to change his ways. The Viceroy all but commanded him to bring you. Your inheritance must be why he doesn't want you to find a husband. Is that why he's kept you cooped up inside that big house?'

Naomi studied at Sarah, who'd been nodding through this prattle, trying to make sense of everything.

'Although Major Brooke doesn't need your money; his family have plenty of their own. It's quarries they own, back in England, or so I'm told.'

Naomi carried on, extolling the virtues of every single man who'd be in attendance tonight, whether young or old. The primary area of interest lay in whether they were unattached *and* suitable, for not all single men *were* suitable for a woman of Sarah's breeding, and future fortune. Sarah could not get a word in edgeways although she was dying to ask if Naomi knew the Lesters. She seemed to know everyone else.

Their conveyance turned into a sweeping driveway, leading up to the graceful Viceregal Lodge. The British were the masters of grand architecture in the nineteenth century — the Viceregal Lodge stood three storeys high with a turret, its Gothic archways spilling onto a manicured lawn, dotted with guests socialising in the mild air.

As the men lowered the palanquin to the ground, Mrs Abbott took Sarah's arm and together they entered the grand lobby Sarah gazed in wonder at the intricate intersecting circles decorating the ceiling. Done entirely in walnut, it was a masterpiece of carving. A majestic staircase dominated the end of the entrance foyer, a symphony of teak and walnut. Uniformed staff ushered them into a reception room, where turbaned waiters in snow-white uniforms offered them crystal flutes filled with honey-coloured liquid, Naomi greeting the other guests as bosom buddies as they progressed towards the relative cool of the open veranda doors.

Sarah could have sworn she saw Major Brooke before the crowd swallowed him. She felt oddly close to her fellow-traveller and missed his solid presence. Hurrying behind Naomi, who sliced through the crowd the way an Antarctic icebreaker moves through the ice floes, Sarah knew she'd meet the Major later, as her new companion would make sure the couple spent quality time together tonight, under her matchmaking eye.

And of the Lesters, there was no sign.

THE FIGHT

*S*imeon swore, drawing Christopher Dickens' attention. Christopher followed Williams' line of sight and whistled.

'Your sister? I wouldn't mind having her on my arm!'

He jostled Simeon's arm good-naturedly.

Simeon scowled. The sight of his sister in that inappropriate gown had done nothing for his foul mood. Her dress wasn't one he'd approved, and shaking off Christopher's hand, he strode over to Sarah, who was standing next to that bloody busybody Naomi Abbott. *If Campbell Abbott spent more time with his wife and less time with whores, she wouldn't have time to interfere in other people's lives.*

He grabbed Sarah by the wrist, dragging her from earshot of Naomi, and hissed, 'What on *earth* are you wearing? Are you trying to embarrass me in front of the Viceroy? You'll make me the laughingstock of the regiment, dressed like a harlot!'

Taken aback by his vitriol, she stood there, gaping. The pressure round her arm was growing more painful by the second as Simeon squeezed.

She snapped, and wrenching her arm from his grasp, she hissed back at him.

'I am not dressed *like* a harlot, and I am not someone you can order around, I am not a servant. I'll damn well wear whatever I choose. Now leave me alone and go bully someone your own size.'

After giving him a withering look, she returned to Naomi, who'd watched the whole scene, filing it away to share later.

'Oh my! He wasn't expecting that now, was he. Delightful to know a young lady so confident!' she exclaimed, linking her arm through Sarah's.

She steered her towards another reception room, well away from Simeon. She could hardly believe Sarah Williams had stood up to her obnoxious brother. The telling of this would be *so* delicious at the next gathering of the Gaiety Theatre Committee.

Naomi was not the only person to witness the altercation. Christopher, who'd been standing nearby, stepped toward the arguing pair, but held back from interceding just as Sarah pulled away from her brother. She'd brushed past Christopher without giving him the slightest glance. He spun to follow her when a bony finger dug into his ribs and he was not at all surprised to see it was Simeon.

'That's my sister you are ogling. If you value your health, you'll refrain from any more glances in her direction. She's not for you, nor is she for anyone else here. You understand? She's *my* property, and shall stay that way.'

Simeon's eyes were glassy, like an opium addict.

Christopher laughed it off.

'You have a fine way with words, Simeon. I apologise if I caused offence. I was merely enjoying the lovely view, nothing more.'

Throwing his hands up in mock submission, Christopher was laughing so much that he did not see the violent punch that landed dead centre into his stomach. He doubled over, gasping for air. Simeon landed a second blow to his kidneys, sending him crashing to the ground. Christopher Dickens was blind to his fellow officers entering the fray, pulling his attacker off him, and helping him to his feet. They manhandled Simeon outside, as he yelled insults about the purity of Dickens' mother, among other more creative invectives. Christopher spat a mouthful of blood onto the intricate parquet flooring.

Attracted by the noise and commotion, Sarah and Naomi rushed back in time to hear Simeon's rant, and to see him hauled out the lawn. Without realising what she was doing, Sarah ran to the man on the ground.

'What happened?' she asked the nearest officer.

'Who knows! That lunatic Williams tore into old Dickens here. This'll be the final nail in Williams' coffin, I bet,' he replied, not realising that he was talking to Simeon's sister.

Sarah helped Christopher stand and Naomi handed her a starched white handkerchief embroidered with tiny red poppies, which Sarah pressed into his hand. Christopher used it to wipe his mouth, turning the handkerchief into a literal field of blood-red flowers. He turned to thank his benefactress.

'Ah, it's you. Not sure I should use this, given what your brother did for just looking at you. Using your handkerchief might be a hanging offence in his book.'

Even in his pained state, he joked amiably, as was his well-bred nature.

Sarah grinned.

'First, it's not my handkerchief, and second, there's nothing you need to fear from my brother. He needs a lesson in manners. I'd apologise on his behalf, but I'm coming to the quick conclusion that living with my brother isn't that enjoyable, especially when he treats my friends this way.'

'Friends?' queried Christopher, grimacing as he straightened.

'Yes, friends,' replied Sarah.

The crowd of onlookers thinned now the entertainment was over, and Sarah and Naomi supported Christopher to a wicker cane sofa. A uniformed servant boy hurried over with a silver tray bearing a large pitcher of water and chilled crystal glasses. Sarah poured one each for them.

They sat watching the milling guests while Christopher recovered his breath. Naomi had withdrawn, hoping that without her there, it would force Sarah to mingle with the other guests, and she could think of no one more suitable for mingling with, than Christopher Dickens.

They both spoke at the same time, their words tumbling over one another. Sarah laughed and gestured that he should speak first.

'How are you finding India, Miss Williams?'

Sarah sipped her iced water, tiny droplets making their crazy path down the side of the glass.

How am I meant to answer this? How do I like India?

She'd had more adventures in India than she'd had in her entire life, but if she told him that, he'd think her deranged, and no wonder her brother kept her locked away. She snorted with laughter into her water as she thought about his reaction to the truth.

'To be honest, this past week has been the most exciting of my life!'

Christopher glowed at her answer and bravely, she continued.

'I'd love to see more of the countryside. I'm missing out on getting to know the true India.'

Christopher grinned.

'Miss Williams, let me call on you tomorrow and I can show you the countryside? Mrs Abbott will undoubtedly agree to be our escort for the day.'

With Naomi's return, the three of them discussed the plan for the next day, oblivious to the glowering glances from Simeon who was outside in the moonlight, taking in the scene of Sarah on the couch with another man, enjoying herself at his expense.

The group of three didn't notice Major Brooke, half concealed by the window, his eyes resting on Sarah. He had no quarrel with Dickens, and no opinion of Williams — apart from the solid truth that one day he would have the pleasure of killing him.

THE PICNIC

*T*he next day dawned clear; perfect for meandering trips into the countryside.

Stretching in bed, Sarah mulled over the events of the evening. She'd not seen Simeon again, and she'd come home with Naomi after a wonderful night of laughing and dancing. Her feet felt like they'd danced with half the regiment last night. In reality, it was less than that, but her feet disagreed. Bugger the Savoy and the oblique luxury there, nothing she'd experienced in her life had matched the joyful fun she'd had last night.

With a tentative knock, Nirmala entered, a radiant smile on her face.

'Memsahib, you must get up, we must make you beautiful for Sahib Dickens.'

'How do you know about that?'

Nirmala responded with a giggle.

'We know *everything*, Memsahib. You danced and danced. We are now deciding how long it will be before someone marries you. He is a wonderful choice.'

Her face fell as she continued.

'I know that Sahib Williams will be unhappy.'

Sarah threw back her covers and leapt out of bed, bundling Nirmala into a giant hug, squeezing the air out of the poor girl's lungs.

'Don't you worry, I'll sort out my brother. Today is too glorious for worrying and too short for unhappiness. Let's have breakfast and then we can go through my wardrobe together. There must be something spectacular I can wear in this house.'

The household bustled around Sarah and her desires. Her breakfast tray a riot of silver and the finest bone china, piled with exotic fruit, complete with an aromatic tea. A tiny part of Sarah railed against the contentment, whispering she should try to return to her real life. Sarah quashed her internal voice, pouring her tea with a shaking hand.

The most jarring note of this whole adventure had been Simeon. As an only child, she'd longed for a sibling, a brother. She couldn't say why that appealed more than a sister, but just that a brother was her dream. Through the hand of fate, here she was in India with a brother. *He* wasn't perfect, but then what sibling relationship in the world's history was?

Sarah threw herself into choosing an outfit for her next experience. This time, she accompanied Nirmala into the vast closet housing the wardrobe of Simeon's wife. It was akin to walking through the wardrobe department of *Gone With The Wind* with rack after rack of exquisite dresses, hats, and drawers full of undergarments. Each piece handmade. Although Simeon's wife hadn't socialised outside of the house in any real sense, it was clear she hadn't let her wardrobe suffer despite a lack of social engagements.

Nirmala was busy shaking out a sweet buttercup yellow dress, trimmed with a high neck of lace. It wasn't a shade Sarah considered attractive, on her or anyone else, so she took the hanger out of the girl's hands and returned it to the rack, tutting under her breath about how she wasn't geriatric yet.

She ran her hands along the hangers, wishing Patricia were here to experience this moment. Her eyes glittered over a cornflower-blue sundress. Still too heavy to be truly comfortable in the heat, but it was the lightest out of the couple of dozen choices. She turned to

Nirmala, holding the dress up under her chin. The maid reached up and selected a nondescript box containing a matching bonnet trimmed with royal blue ribbons.

'That will be perfect, Nirmala.'

Sarah grinned, trying the hat on for size while striking several poses, reminiscent of a contestant in *America's Next Top Model*. Nirmala giggled. She was unused to having such fun and frivolity in the house. Her former mistress had been as timid as a mouse. Too frightened to leave the house for fear of the Sahib's reaction. He permitted her visits to the tailor and begrudgingly allowed her to call on Mrs Abbott. Her death due to tuberculosis had been swift. Simeon didn't appear to miss his wife, and there had been no mourning period for her.

The staff had hoped his sister's arrival would lead to a happier household. But the troubles that had occurred en route to Simla from Calcutta had put Simeon in the foulest mood possible. The last thing he needed was his sister consorting with officers, without her chaperone. He blamed Elaine for the incident, and would brook no further discussion on the matter. He'd even deducted part of Elaine's final salary to account for her remaining in Delhi to convalesce, instead of escorting his sister through to Simla. Of this, Sarah knew nothing. The staff, though, *had* seen the correspondence between Elaine and Simeon.

But today Memsahib was going out, with a gentleman and Mrs Abbott, and so Nirmala hummed to herself a gentle Indian melody, and not one of the dreary Protestant hymns they'd taught her at the local Missionary School.

Another young servant, engaged by Simeon to attend his wife, and now his sister, was Kalakanya, whose Sanskrit name meant 'Daughter of Time'. Her slender body was resplendent in the palest pink sari, earlobes decorated with tiny golden hoops, and her long, black hair twisted into an intricate plait, covered with a light scarf. She had been assisting with Sarah's wardrobe, and pausing in her work, she cocked her head to one side.

'They are here, Memsahib.'

'How do I look?'

She stood up and performed an impressive twirl for the girls, an ice dancer's pirouette. The two girls clapped in appreciation.

Kalakanya was to accompany her on the hunt, so together they walked the tiled hallway to the front door. She adjusted Sarah's bonnet, twitched her headscarf over her own head, and ordered the boy to open the door.

Blinding sunshine flooded in, filling the hallway with a glow and infusing the tiles with such warmth it made Sarah feel as though she were walking on a Roman hypocaust.

Outside the house, stood a myriad of servants, ladies festooned in lace and frippery, a dozen young Englishmen, attired *de rigueur* in hunting khakis and conical pith hats, shotguns slung over their broad shoulders. The hesitation she felt was due to the six lumbering elephants, festooned with ornate bridles and the carriages perched precariously atop the pachyderms.

Kalakanya gave Sarah a discreet nudge, forcing her onto the veranda. There, on the lead elephant, was Christopher Dickens, waving at her. He shouted instructions to the mahout leading the giant animal, and in an unintelligible tongue the keeper bade his charge kneel, for Sarah to climb into the basket tied to its back.

Other guests already filled the baskets of the other beasts — laughing young ladies and confident officers and employees of the East India Company — men, sure of their invincibility and their right to rule this ancient country. A country with customs and a history far older than their own. Full of their own importance, most of these men viewed India as a country to rule with an iron fist, and to indulge themselves with a lifestyle to which they were not so entitled in England.

Many did not come from moneyed families, or were from impoverished noble houses without the funds to support polo matches or hunts, balls and lavish picnics. But in India, the world was their oyster, and they mixed and mingled with minor Indian royalty draped in more riches and jewels than Queen Victoria held in her strongroom.

The Raja of Nahan was accompanying them today — a man known

for his astute business dealings and extensive land holdings around Simla. His retinue, equalling the number of men in the British contingent, waited at the rear of the party, laden with the equipment the party needed for their day trekking through the forest, hunting tigers. The assembled group was in a jubilant mood; the mahouts announcing someone had spotted a tiger near to Simla.

What they didn't say was that the same villager had also reported that the tiger had snatched a local child, killing it and dragging it away. The local hierarchy of the Company saw no need to spread alarm by telling the residents of Simla of the tiger's taste for blood, especially as their younger officers had planned a hunt, anyway. The British Army's prowess with the shotgun eliminating any potential risk. And advising the ladies they were hunting a 'man-eater' was not good for morale. No one wanted to frighten off the already-scarce ladies in Simla by telling them tales of ferocious cats with a taste for human flesh.

Sarah took her place in the rattan basket next to Christopher. It contained another couple, who introduced themselves as Abe Garland and Sally Brass. He was more than cordial and effusive in his welcome, while she reluctantly made space for Sarah, viewing her as a competitor in the hotly contested husband market. After welcoming her coolly, Sally turned away to converse with another friend on a neighbouring elephant.

With the party now complete, the procession lumbered away into the vegetation surrounding Simla under the hot sun. Cheery calls rang between the various baskets, and there was a natural air of gaiety among the group. Turbaned mahouts walked barefoot alongside the elephants. Behind these, Mrs Abbott and another stalwart of Simla-Loretta Smith, were in their respective palanquins, chatting through protective net curtains, well aware they were there to preserve the propriety of the young ladies. At least a dozen men sat astride striking horses, nostrils flaring at the cacophony of noises and scents around them.

The servants followed, trudging barefoot; loaded with picnic baskets, umbrellas, chairs and rugs, unconcerned by the heat of the day. With all these accoutrements, there were more servants than guests.

'Isn't this grand?' chatted Christopher, gesturing to the sweeping hills in the distance, drinking in the majesty of the Himalayas, so solid and permanent on the horizon. The rolling gait on the elephant was lulling Sarah into a somnolent state as she leaned on the edge of the basket. Sally hadn't deigned to speak to her, apart from the frosty hello, choosing instead to simper at every utterance of the two men, so Sarah had turned away, spending the trip gazing in wonder at the lush vegetation and a view worthy of a hundred masterpieces.

At the front, the Raja called a halt, declaring they would take lunch in the sheltered clearing they'd just entered. It was the length and width of a football field, surrounded by rhododendron bushes. Lush rosewood and cedar trees provided leafy canopies for shelter, and the servants hurried to spread out blankets and embroidered cushions for the comfort of the party. The shouts of the mahouts as they encouraged their charges to kneel so the passengers could disembark mingled with the chattering calls of the macaque monkeys, their pinched faces watching for any opportunity to help themselves to the delicious food concealed in the plethora of picnic baskets being unpacked by the uncomplaining servants.

Throughout the glade, gentlemen were assisting ladies out of the baskets atop the kneeling elephants, causing Sarah to laugh. Christopher looked at her.

'Why do you laugh?'

'My entire life comprises being helped into or out of carriages. I just find it amusing. I don't think this ever happened at home!'

Once again laughing, she took Christopher's proffered hand as he helped her from the basket and passed her to the waiting servant-climbing down from the back of the elephant was not the easiest thing to do, confined as she was by lace and petticoats, bonnets and pearls.

Together they walked to where Naomi sat with Loretta.

'Ladies, I will return, the men are having a short chat about the plan for the hunt after lunch.'

He gave a small nod and strode to where the Raja of Nahan held court with the other men. The profusion of rifles made it look like a war party rather than a simple hunting expedition. Christopher joined the group, standing near the back, hand resting on the shoulder of one of the other men. She could see the other man lean into him, whispering into his ear. Both men laughed, and Christopher's arm slipped to the man's waist, where it stayed momentarily before he joined in on the group's now raucous conversation.

Sarah put the odd tableau to one side as her thoughts drifted to the hunting.

'I'd love to see those rifles,' she murmured, more to herself than to the other ladies.

She'd been rifle shooting many times in her younger years, and was more than proficient, obtaining her marksman badge, and an impressive third placing in the Ffennell Commonwealth Shooting Competition in her late teens. Sally, who'd sat with them, and had been preening herself in a sterling silver mirror, smiled.

'You should go over there. I'm sure the men would *love* to show you how they work,' she tittered.

The other young women round her joined in-humiliating their female rivals was as much of a sport as finding a husband, and it was gloves off between her and Sally.

Sarah, with a *robust* education care of her local comprehensive school, could tell the ringleader of a group of bullies a mile off, and Sally Brass had the makings of such. Sarah may not have been born in the 1800s, but she knew there were things a lady did not do. If she knew she was staying in this life, she'd have stayed with the other women, sipping tea from porcelain cups, nibbling on rectangular slices of loaf. But there was no guarantee she'd remain in India any longer than this moment. So, seizing the chance, and to Sally's astonishment, she clambered up, and strolled over to where the men were checking their rifles.

Silence descended upon the group as she cleared her throat, addressing Christopher.

'Could I borrow a rifle, I didn't bring one, and I would love to have a shot, too.'

Jaws tightened with sharp intakes of breath as she crossed an unmarked social boundary. The poor woman whose life she'd possessed could never live this one down. But from what Sarah could see, and had heard, the real Sarah Williams needed a decisive kick up the butt to take control of her own destiny, and not leave it in the hands of her resentful brother.

Christopher took Sarah by the shoulders and tried to steer her back towards the women. She shrugged him off and restated her request.

'I very much want to try shooting with your rifle. Or perhaps I could ask the Raja?'

Christopher's resistance fled. He did not understand why Simeon had told his colleagues his sister was as plain as a teapot and as dumb as a kettle. From what he'd seen so far, she had a strength and intelligence absent in every other woman in Simla. She was the wife he should have. With her in his home he could almost, *almost*, ignore the urges he had, the ones he hid in his night-time thoughts. His eyes drifted to the group of men, seeking a familiar figure. No, he couldn't cheat her out of a husband who would be true to her in life, and love.

'Tell you what, I'll let you have a turn later, when none of the others are watching. It's best to leave it till then. I'll pass it to you when we're on the hunt,' he whispered.

It was the best he could do.

Sarah smiled, satisfied at his concession. As she turned to leave, the Raja called out to Christopher.

'Major Dickens, please introduce us to this inquisitive lady?'

Christopher smiled in response, relieved that Sarah's unusual request was being viewed favourably by the local royalty. The men from the East India Company rarely socialised with them, but on occasions like this hunt, it made it that much more realistic having the locals involved, with their additional pomp and ceremony. They had the best trackers and, more importantly, the elephants were theirs.

Escorting Sarah, he introduced her to the Raja.

'Your Highness, may I introduce Miss Sarah Williams, recently arrived from London to stay with her brother Captain Simeon Williams, after the death of their parents.'

Sarah bobbed a small curtsey and raised her eyes to look at the Raja seated on his own rosewood chair. He met her gaze with rugged good looks and a regal moustache and beard, befitting the strong lines of his face. A turban rested high on his forehead, adding an extra foot of height, although it wasn't until he stood up that she truly appreciated how tall he was.

Lithe and broad-shouldered, compared to the other Indian men serving him, the Raja was a *giant*. He took Sarah's hand and, in the European fashion, kissed the back. In a voice that revealed his English education, he announced, 'Whilst the death of your parents is tragic, their wings have brought you here to us, and for that we are grateful.'

He waved his hand towards the space next to him, and another chair appeared. Smaller and lower than his and carved just as strikingly. Designed as a pair of 'his and hers' chairs. The Raja motioned to the empty seat.

'Please sit.'

As she seated herself in the proffered chair, servants rushed forward with damp towels, rinsing her hands, and those of the Raja. Someone had laid a veritable feast out on the low table before her.

'Tell me more of your family. I do not believe I have met your brother. And what do you make of our beautiful India?'

Sarah wanted to ask why they needed a vase of fresh flowers on a tiger hunt, having just watched a servant fussing over a spray of flowers in a brass rose bowl, but instead she answered with more tact.

'India is surreal, as if artificially enhanced a hundred times to capture its colours. It has a majesty about it, some magical quality that words can't describe. I want to hold it all in my hands and then hide it away so I don't have to share it with anyone else. I know that sounds deranged, but I can't think of any other way to describe what I have experienced.'

The Raja steepled his fingers, gazing at her, deep in thought. Sarah squirmed under his deep scrutiny. She sat on her hands to avoid plucking at the embroidery on her dress.

'And your brother?' the Raja continued at length.

Sarah frowned.

'I have spent little time with him since I arrived, so I'm not sure how much I can tell you,' she replied.

She knew *nothing* of him, other than what she'd seen at the Viceroy's ball, and snippets from the servants and Naomi. The rest she could only guess at. Honesty, as far as she could take it, was the best policy.

'Is he not here escorting you today?'

The Raja surveyed the surrounding men, most now seated beside young ladies on the picnic blankets dotted around the clearing, enjoying their luncheon. Naomi and Loretta were the only other people seated on chairs as befitted their age. Their height made them the *de facto* guardians of virtue for the unmarried ladies surrounding them.

Sarah took a sip from the glass on the table in front of her, allowing her time to gather her thoughts. The heat and the shimmering colours were competing, making her somewhat lightheaded.

'No, he didn't come. I don't know why because I didn't see him this morning. I presume he was working.'

The Raja digested her words.

'Good, it has allowed us to talk unheeded. Your description of my country has uplifted my spirits. It is rare that an Englishwoman can feel India in her heart as you can. Please, eat. We have an exciting afternoon ahead of us.'

And with that, he began eating from the silver plate proffered by his manservant.

THE HUNT

There was little time for more small talk before the servants packed away the picnic, and the mahouts loaded their mounts. The Raja stood up and reached down to assist Sarah up from the throne-like seat. He bowed his head and remarked, 'It has been a pleasure, Miss Williams. I hope very much to see more of you during your time in Simla.'

He nodded and strode away to his mount, waiting patiently in the shade of a grove of trees.

Christopher reappeared, having decorously left her in the company of the higher-ranked man. He'd dined with Naomi, regaling her and the others with tales of foolish officers and inept servants at the barracks. In good spirits, he loaded Sarah back onto their elephant, into their basket, which was empty. Sarah shaded her eyes with her hand, but could see no sign of Sally nor Abe. Christopher bounded on board, and she turned to question him, just as the mahout gave the beast an almighty whack on its rear to get it moving.

'Where are Sally and Abe?' she asked.

'Oh, I imagine they took another ride. They'll be fine. I, for one, am enjoying the company much better now that it is just the two of us. And it gives me a chance to show you how to use the rifle, with old Simpering Sally not here to judge you for misbehaving. That silly girl has tried to lure every eligible bachelor in Simla since she landed here last summer. Word has it she's being sent back to London as an 'empty'; that's why she's clinging to Abe. He's had no luck in the wife stakes, so they'll make each other miserable, I'll wager, but they will marry. Anyway, enough of the womanly prattle; I sound as bad as Mrs Abbott. Come, let me present the Enfield P53.'

He demonstrated the loading and correct handling of the weapon, and handed it to Sarah. She braced her feet against the side of the swaying basket, leaning into a corner to counteract the elephant's lumbering gait. Choosing *not* to aim the rifle toward the head of their mahout who was sitting cross-legged behind the elephant's gaily decorated ears, she instead pointed it out the side, peering through the adjustable ladder rear sight.

Christopher murmured appreciative noises as he took in her stance, her left arm extended. Her right had the wooden butt firmly tucked into her shoulder, to reduce any potential damage from the recoil. Left eye closed she sighted a fork in the lush branches of a nearby pine tree. With her right index finger resting alongside the trigger, so there was no risk of accidentally firing, she lowered the rifle, keeping the muzzle well away from Christopher, the mahout and herself.

'I'd love an opportunity to try firing it,' she said, twiddling with the dull metal sights, correcting them almost by instinct.

Her companion laughed, the booming sound making several of the ladies craning around in their baskets to look, curious to see who was entertaining the quiet Major Dickens — whom none of them had yet snared, despite their best efforts. The tittering between the women started anew and Sarah bit her lip.

What sort of life will the real Miss Williams have after I've left? Will they shun her as a deranged unstable spinster after this is over?

Then an unearthly scream ruptured the air.

THE TIGER

Spinning around in the basket, Sarah and Christopher tried to pinpoint the origin. Several of the ladies were calling out, making it hard to find who was screaming. The panic escalated, making the animals skittish, and the mahouts slipped from the backs of their charges, taking hold of their trunks or guide ropes, though what hope a tiny Indian man had of controlling a panicked beast was beyond Sarah's comprehension.

Trumpeting elephants joined the cacophony of hysterical voices. The shrieking was coming from the rear, and Sarah strained to see through the group behind them. The profusion of running servants, men on horseback, and baskets filled with frightened women made it impossible to see anything.

Sally's screams reached fever pitch, as she dashed between two of the elephants, running for her life. Her immaculate dress smeared with broad strokes of red, her shoes missing and her hair flying in the breeze, framing a face awash with terror.

Christopher slid down the side of their elephant and approached the inconsolable Sally, holding his arms out in front of him, trying to placate her. Another officer had done the same.

Sally was beyond being calmed. A woman possessed, she grabbed

237

the arms of the nearest man, looking over her shoulder to the stand of trees untouched by the subtle breeze. Long grass, depressed in places by the picnic mere minutes ago. Sally's cries were incomprehensible, and Sarah recoiled in shock as Christopher slapped the other woman's face. The resounding crack of his hand against the English rose complexion brought immediate silence. Then, the whimpering of one of the younger women was the only sound Sarah could hear.

A group of rowdy men gathered, their voices making everyone uneasy. The mahouts cooed to their elephants, Mrs Abbott claimed Sally and, after assessing that none of the blood was hers, eased the distraught girl into her palanquin. Sarah was eager to know what was happening, but knew her input would not be welcome. She was one of the few women still atop her elephant; the others huddled in groups, waiting for the men to tell them what to do.

With no man to speak for her, Sarah knew her lofty position provided the best protection from whatever had scared Sally witless. From her basket, she saw the Raja dismount his bejewelled elephant, and was in deep conversation with one of his men before he walked away from his entourage until a stand of satinwood trees concealed him — so he could relieve himself unseen she presumed. Embarrassed that she'd caught him in a private moment, Sarah surveyed the surrounding vista.

An abrupt yell, cut off before it finished, caused Sarah to spin round to locate the source, certain it was where the Raja had been. The men congregating in the clearing's centre were trying to identify the yell, too. The Raja's man was waving his arms wildly, pointing to the thicket where his master had gone, but in his panic reverted to his native tongue, incomprehensible to the British officers. Tears streaming down his weathered face, he tried to tell them that the shout had been from his Highness.

Sarah yelled out to them.

'The Raja has been attacked!'

To the men, she was a hysterical woman, and they ignored her as one ignores an irritating fly. Around her, men prepared their rifles, confident that whoever was attacking their party would show themselves, and that by mere dint of them being British, they would prevail.

Sarah peered into the trees as the Raja barrelled from the undergrowth, his *sherwani* — his glorious gold brocade coat — stained a deep crimson. His turban gone, revealing jet black hair. Of the dozens of strands of luminous pearls that had graced his elegant neck, there was no sign — lost to the jungle.

Sarah shouted out to Christopher

'Christopher, the Raja!'

Christopher followed her frantic gesturing and, with a shout, summoned the men. The Raja faltered, and Sarah was not the only one to watch him sink to his knees. As he fell, a silent figure followed him out of the brush; a streak of orange and black. Faster than any of the men there, and more menacing than the shadows that haunt you at night.

As the group caught sight of the big cat, the women panicked, running away, parasols and bonnets abandoned. The tiger was unfazed, intent on finishing the job it had started. Like a domestic cat playing with a cornered mouse, the tiger batted at the body of the Raja, barely visible above the swaying grass. Sarah imagined she could smell his blood; that the iron-filled scent was in the wind.

The men were barking orders, preparing to encircle the beast. Some fumbled with their rifles, their fear overriding their training. Sarah looked at her hands. Here she was, with a direct view of the Raja and his attacker, and in her hands a loaded rifle. With a quick, clean motion, she brought the rifle up to her eye and hard into her shoulder. She slowed her breathing, even as she heard more shots go off as men fired blindly, going well wide of the Raja's position, and the tiger.

She adjusted her stance and trained the rifle on the tiger's torso. With a silent apology to the World Wildlife Fund, she squeezed the trigger.

Boom. The sound of the shot reverberated through her eardrums. The rifle's powerful kick stunned her for a moment, before she slung the rifle over her shoulder, smoke still curling from the muzzle.

Clambering over the basket, she yelled to the mahout. He rushed over in time to catch her leap from the elephant. Picking up her long skirts, she sprinted towards the grass where she'd shot the tiger. Where she was sure she'd hit the tiger. The men yelled at her, but she paid them no heed.

'Come on!' she urged them.

She didn't know how injured the Raja was, but she wouldn't let another man bleed to death because she was a woman and it wasn't seemly for her to run or to fire a gun.

She could see the tiger laying on its side, panting, a spreading lake of blood pooling underneath its striped fur. It raised its head as she approached, its eyes sorrowful. Killing such a magnificent animal was not something she ever imagined doing. She thrust those thoughts away to think on later. With the tiger in her line of sight, she knelt by the head of the Raja. He, too, was still breathing, but his eyes didn't open at her touch.

By now, the men had arrived and Christopher approached the tiger with his handgun drawn, firing a single bullet into the beast's head. It was only then that Sarah saw blood staining the tiger's mouth. She checked the Raja for wounds, his manservant wailing in protest. Ignoring him, Sarah addressed the nearest soldier.

'Get one of those litters, we'll put him on there. He needs to get to a doctor.'

Her fingers came away sticky after heaving him onto his side. She'd located the source of the blood, a series of lacerations on his thigh and his back. His breathing was stable, but not ragged, so it was unlikely there was any damage to his internal organs. To her surprise, the soldiers moved in unison to carry out her instructions.

Naomi bustled over to them, in the most ladylike way possible, given the circumstances.

'Sally just told us what happened! She'd gone walking with Major Quilp, and a tiger... a tiger attacked them, and, oh my...' she trailed off as the long grass revealed its prey. 'Oh, oh dear, is he dead?' she queried, her hand to her mouth.

'No, no he's not dead. Stay with Sally while these boys try to locate poor Abe. I don't think he will be as lucky as the Raja. I'll stay with his Highness until we can find a doctor.'

Sarah pushed Naomi away from the bloodied body of the prince, back towards the palanquin where Sally sat, gazing away from the bloody tableau. It would be a long time before she spoke again, and she'd end up leaving Simla on the next ship back to England as soon as there was a berth available — an 'empty' returning to a life on the shelf.

Christopher walked over to Sarah.

'Let me hold that for you,' he suggested, removing the rifle from over her shoulder.

'Oh, I'd forgotten I was still holding it,' she faltered, as a creeping flush of red advanced over her cheeks; the realisation that she'd been the one to shoot the tiger dawning, as shock took hold.

Christopher watched her, unsure how to respond to someone who behaved so unpredictably as this woman.

'Well, you said you wanted to shoot the rifle. But it's best if I look after it from here. I will have the devil of a time explaining to the Viceroy a woman saved the Raja. You go on ahead with his Highness and I'll stay with the men to find Quilp.'

Sarah turned away.

He called after her 'And, Miss Williams, thank you!'

THE GIFT

The first sign that the Raja had recovered well enough to recall his attack and his rescue was when one of his servants arrived at the house and was announced as a representative from his Highness. Sarah and her brother, who were eating silently at the breakfast table, both rose. Simeon's eyebrows raised in a caricature of surprise.

'Well, show him into the study then, we'll not receive him here.'

Sarah followed, curious to meet the Raja's envoy.

'Yes?' demanded Simeon in an imperious voice.

'Sir, the Raja of Nahan has sent me to reward Miss Williams for her bravery the other day. It would honour him if she accepted this gift from his Highness.'

With that the man presented a black leather case, the size of a large shoebox.

Since none of his regiment talked to him, and because his servants avoided him, Simeon knew nothing of the adventures of his sister.

'What on earth are you talking about? My sister has not met your master. Now please leave, you are mistaken.'

He made to usher the man out.

'But, sir, your sister saved the Raja's life on the tiger hunt. She shot the beast, she is a hero,' replied the manservant who'd adroitly avoided Simeon's attempts to escort him from the room. The manservant pressed the gift into Sarah's hands.

Simeon snatched it from her.

'I've asked you to leave. You have made your delivery, now go.'

Sarah stood slack-jawed at his rudeness. The reverberating crash of a door closing told her Simeon had ejected the Raja's servant from the house. Simeon marched back into the room, slamming the door behind him — a man better versed in door slamming than in social niceties.

'What *exactly* did you do?' Simeon asked through pursed lips, his rage at being shamed in front of a servant, an Indian servant, threatening to boil over with every word he uttered.

Sarah lifted her head high.

'I attended the hunt with Naomi and Major Dickens. When I was carrying the Major's rifle, I saw the tiger attack the Raja. I had a clear line of sight, so I shot it, but didn't kill it,' she added, thinking that if she downplayed her role, it might mollify Simeon.

He said nothing, but opened the leather case. There, nestled in the custom-made box, were the twin *katars* Sarah had last seen in London, their vibrancy beyond description, the stones saturating the room with prisms of colour.

'Oh, they are beautiful!'

Sarah reached out to take the box from him.

Simeon shut it, the click of the latch loud in the study.

'You want it?' he asked. 'You want this *gift*?'

Sarah looked at him quizzically.

'Of course I do, the Raja gave them to me,' she replied, reaching for the carton in his hand.

With no warning, Simeon whipped the box up, connecting with the side of Sarah's temple. She crumpled to the ground, blood pulsing through her fingers as she held them to her head.

'I know you "want it" you whore. Now I'll be the laughingstock of the regiment. My own sister fornicating with the *natives*. I said you weren't to leave the house without my permission. You disobeyed me and I will not tolerate it again. They will not make me a fool. You shall behave as a devout Christian woman.'

He went on, brandishing the *katars*, 'Any gifts that come to you, rightly belong to me, as your guardian. So no, they are *not* yours and they will *never* be yours. Now, get off the floor and clean yourself up before the servants find you.'

After tucking the leather box under his arm, he left.

After several minutes, Sarah stumbled back to her room. Once there, she sunk onto her bed, which is where Nirmala found her.

Fussing over her like a mother hen, the maid mumbled to herself.

'The Sahib did this? I knew he was a bad man when I met him, and I told my mother I didn't want to be in this house. The energy is evil. But my uncle, he makes the decisions, he said it was good for the family and that, even though the Sahib's wife had died, perhaps the Sahib's sister would take me with her when she married. And now this.'

She prattled on, shaking her head, gently dabbing the split skin on Sarah's forehead. Her ministrations transforming the bowl of water beside her mistress to colourful swirls of rust. Sarah placed her finger in the bowl. The concentric circles were her life and everything she touched affected someone else. Her finger moved in a circle, round and round, mixing her blood with the Indian water. Blood was thicker than water, but her brother had forsaken any right to have her as his family, as his possession.

How will the real Sarah Williams cope after I leave? If I ever leave?

Nirmala left her to sleep. Sarah could hear the murmurings between the maids as they discussed Simeon's treatment of their mistress, their voices fading as they disappeared to wherever it was they went when not with her. Sarah's mind drifted back to London. Not being in the shop had concerned her, but with the excitement and adrenaline rush of the boat crossing, the ambush, and now the hunt, it had faded, and she had almost settled for this life. But living with Simeon would kill her. She hadn't grown up as a Victorian lady, subservient and compliant, so would never fit into this life. She slipped into a disturbed sleep, her dreams punctuated with visions of trying to find a way home by touching every antique in the place — but everything she touched turned into Simeon and, before long, hundreds of Simeon clones surrounded her, coming closer and closer, sneering at her, mocking her futile attempts to escape.

THE GAMBLER

Simeon Williams believed he was as godly as the next man, and a damn sight more so than some. Superior in breeding and beliefs, there was nothing he wouldn't do to ensure his family's good name remained just that. A man's reputation was as effective as armour in war. He would not tolerate unseemly behaviour from his family and, by God, he would punish Sarah if she continued to defy him.

However Simeon was not as perfect as he liked to portray. Simeon Williams was a sycophantic and sadistic officer who used his position to cow others to his will. Abusing his rank, he had an unhealthy obsession with demeaning the locals and destroying the careers of any who crossed him. He was prone to using tirades against 'the heathens', to strip them of their possessions, things he coveted. He was above paying for such things. What could heathens need such riches for apart from to worship their false gods? Better that he held onto them. He had a good transport company, an *English* company, more than prepared to ship his treasures home for a fair price.

Simeon Williams, like most bullies, enjoyed the rush of power he felt from denigrating those around him, especially when it resulted in seizing antiquities without having to pay a penny. It was his forte; that and gambling.

Gambling was where many of his ill-gotten gains ended up, but only the sacrilegious pieces, Simeon reasoned, as he examined the pair of *katars*. He hadn't seen a more ungodly item than these hideous knives. The heathen's script marring the hilt, those cursed words he couldn't read, an affront to civilised mankind, only good enough to be used as collateral tonight at Lord Grey's table. *You needed big stakes to play his table, and the gems in these will do the trick.* It paid to have a little in reserve for a big hand.

Simeon strode through the house, calling for his horse as he marched through the well-appointed rooms. He'd always considered that this was the life he should live in England, surrounded by servants to cater to his every need. God dictated that every person had their place on earth, and *his* place was at the top. His father forcing him to join the army, swearing there wouldn't be a penny of inheritance until he had proven himself a man. So he'd sailed to India, and waited for his father to summon him back to take over his interests, but that hadn't happened, and now the old man was dead, the man as spiteful in death as he had been in life, leaving his inheritance split between Simeon and Sarah. But, as long as his sister stayed unmarried, the entire inheritance would be his, and as God was his witness, he would make sure she died a spinster, as a punishment for the shame his father had wrought upon him.

Now it was time to bolster his coffers, using the heathens' knives. He expected Lord Grey to be in his cups by the time he arrived, adding liquid luck to Simeon's hand. He packed the *katars* and enough gold to buy his seat at Lord Grey's table, and left the house, full of the glory and righteousness of God.

Several army officers filled Lord Grey's house, clouded in the fug of cigar smoke. Whisky abounded and, with no women in attendance, the men unbuttoned their collars and relaxed their morals. Simeon entered unhindered. He may not have been able to count any of the other attendees as friends, but his money was still welcome at the table.

God was not on his side, and his anger at his sister clouded his judgement. He was not well-liked by other officers in the regiment, so no one stepped forward to stop him when, in a fit of frustration at his losing streak, he placed his remaining gold, and the *katars*, as his stake.

His fellow officers were educated enough to know the value of the pieces, not just for their gemstones, but as historical artefacts. Simeon was the only one too blind to see his folly — the blindness of faith, a fate suffered by millions around the world.

And that blindness saw him bet everything on a hand that would never win. Simeon laid out his cards.

'Four of a kind,' he said, eyeballing the other players.

Lord Henry Grey, who hadn't been drinking as much as normal, on account of his bad gout, which would speed up his return to England on the grounds of ill-health, spread his own cards out on the felt-covered table.

'Royal flush.'

THE VICEROY

𝒶 new day arrived. Sarah watched the dawn sun push its way over the top of the Himalayas as if it had crawled out of an icy crevasse, its rays cleansed by a glacial stream. She stretched in bed, the slight discomfort of her forehead the only jarring reminder of the nightmare from the day before. The blue skies promised her infinite opportunities.

Nirmala appeared at her bedside.

'Memsahib, will you be up for breakfast this morning? They have called the Sahib to the regiment, so he won't be here...'

Sarah understood the hint; breakfast in the dining room, without Simeon's glowering countenance watching her.

'Yes, Nirmala, I will. Then we'll call on Mrs Abbott, to ask how she is after the other day.'

The girl hurried out, calling to Kalakanya to follow.

'Memsahib wants to go out after breakfast. Run and tell Amit that he must get a palanquin for Memsahib, she should not be walking with her injury. Then send word to Memsahib Abbott that I will call on her.'

Kalakanya, her eyes wide that Sarah would disobey the Sahib again, scampered away. In minutes, the whole of Simla would know. The servant grapevine was already abuzz with what Sarah had achieved with the rifle, and the punishment meted out by Simeon.

Breakfast in India, in a vast dining room with servants; it's a far cry from two slices of toast and instant coffee in a flat above a shop in London, Sarah thought as she sipped another cup of fragrant tea. The aroma of the dosa, a crêpe, mingled with the heady spices of the chutney and tamarind sambar accompanying her breakfast. The temperature outside was rising as she ate her food. Fascinated, she watched winged insects dance above the table, enraptured by their impossible machinations. The maids kept up a delicious, and futile, charade of trying to shoo them away.

Scraping her chair backwards, she admired the room's high ceiling, and how the glass doors leading onto the veranda dominated the room, framing the lush gardens outside. Another wall held an ornate fireplace, empty for the present; but Nirmala had told her that any day now, they expected the temperature to dip with winter's arrival. In reality, winter in Simla far surpassed any summer in London. The dining table featured an ormolu trim inset into the rim, with sideboard to match. Graceful blue and white lamps with opaque glass chimneys balanced the tableau on the sideboard. Matching jardinières filled the room, floral blooms tumbling over themselves trying to rejoin the fragrant garden outside, and framing the fireplace were two fine portraits of Indian nobility, glittering with finely applied gold.

Sarah frowned at the portraits and wished she knew why Simeon had hung them here when he had little regard for the people of India. Filing away the thought for later, she examined the exquisite bronze statue in the mantelpiece's centre. Sarah could not help wonder where the money was coming from to keep her brother in this lifestyle. A question for later.

'That's Parvati. A fine piece. It surprised me your brother had the funds to purchase it. But then, your brother has always had the ability to surprise us,' interrupted a male voice behind her.

Sarah stared at an unknown English gentleman, dressed impeccably, with the bearing of the upper class, someone whose world had always delivered whatever they desired. He dipped his head, and walked over to admire the striking bronze of the half-naked woman, his hands clasped behind his back.

'The Hindu Goddess of Love and Devotion, Simeon would do well to visit one of her temples to pray for guidance.'

With that his gaze travelled over the bandage on her forehead.

Sarah offered her hand to the stranger.

'Sarah Williams, and you are?'

At that point, Christopher Dickens stepped forward from the doorway.

'Miss Williams, may I introduce His Excellency, Viceroy, Sir John Lawrence.'

'Oh...' faltered Sarah, unsure whether she should curtsey or continue with the handshake. The Viceroy, sensing her confusion, gently shook her hand.

'I am honoured to make your acquaintance. I missed you at the ball, entirely my oversight, I apologise. You have had some adventures since your arrival in India. I trust they have not put you off our beautiful country?' he asked, as he released her.

Finding her manners at last, Sarah gestured to the table, still groaning under the weight of breakfast dishes.

'May I invite you to join me for tea?'

Sarah chastised Nirmala. Where *was* that girl? She'd been her virtual shadow, and, now, she was missing, and with the highest ranked Englishman in the country in her home.

'Splendid, Miss Williams! It is rare I am invited to take tea. It is one drawback of the position. More often than not, I dare not spend the time with those whose company I most prefer, for fear of upsetting people, or causing animosity amongst other members of society. Under these circumstances, taking tea with you is a privilege.'

Perplexed, Sarah rang the tiny silver bell on the table. While awaiting fresh tea she asked, 'Sir, may I enquire as to the reason for your visit? My brother has gone for the day, and I don't know where he is.'

'It is not your brother I am here to see, but yourself. News of your bravery has reached me through Major Dickens, and I wanted to thank you. Times are fraught in India at present. So, although it was a tiger who attacked the Raja, and not British soldiers, if he had perished, word would have spread that we had caused his death. There is trouble in the provinces, so we must do what we can to keep the peace, or a veneer...'

The tea arrived on a heavy silver tray that dwarfed the young boy who carried it effortlessly. Another servant was on hand to pour, and to clear the breakfast dishes. Nirmala finally appeared, eyes widening as she saw who their guests were. Sarah glared at her. The girl scooted over to the corner, averting her eyes. Her mistress instructed her to open the doors and, as she did so, the scents of India didn't just seep into the room, they swept through, taking Sarah on an olfactory journey through lush forests, heady gardens, plantations, spice markets, and every other unmistakable scent of the exotic sub-continent.

While sipping her tea, Sarah commented she hadn't heard the gentlemen arrive, otherwise she would have prepared refreshments for them.

'Your manservant answered the door and welcomed us. I presumed your staff had noted our arrival and had informed you.'

'No' Sarah replied, glaring at Nirmala, surmising that the manservant may have had other thoughts on his mind when answering the door.

'Well, no harm done.'

They spent a comfortable half hour discussing Simla, the weather, the theatre, and home, before the Viceroy took his leave.

'Your hospitality has been much appreciated. Now we must leave; my duties call me back to my office. Please take care, Miss Williams. These are uncertain times. Thank you once again for your hospitality.'

With that, her visitors stood up but, before leaving, the Viceroy paused at the doorway to reach into his jacket pocket, and withdrew an elegant box, handing it to Sarah.

'I almost forgot. This is in appreciation of your contribution to peace in the British Raj. I understand from Mr Hamilton, of Hamilton & Co., the pre-eminent jeweller here in Simla, that it is a Mughal piece. We would very much like you to have it as a token of appreciation from the Empire for your service.'

With that, he left the room, leaving Sarah still in shock, before she recovered enough to accompany them to the impressive front door, the box unopened in her hands. A magnificent horse-drawn carriage awaited the Viceroy outside Firgrove House, and he climbed in, his duty completed.

Christopher paused on the steps.

'Miss Williams, our first outing came to a rather abrupt ending. Perhaps I might have the honour of escorting you to the Gaiety Theatre tonight? A group of us are attending, and your company would greatly improve the evening.'

Sarah smiled and agreed that he could escort her to the theatre. He grinned and, after placing his cap firmly on his head, mounted the horse waiting behind the Viceroy's carriage.

With Nirmala close behind, Sarah returned inside to prepare for her visit to Naomi, leaving the box on her dressing table for later. Despite what the Viceroy had said, she doubted it was anything more than a tourist bauble touted as a genuine Mughal piece, and she'd seen plenty of those come through the shop.

Sarah spent the day in carefree abandonment at Naomi's; where they gossiped about the goings-on in town, the potential love interests of the eligible bachelors, and the paramours of the married men. They drank tea, and ate cakes, and in the late afternoon they moved to the veranda to enjoy the sight of the sun falling to its knees. Sarah took her leave before it was truly dark, returning to Firgrove House with Nirmala to dress for her evening at the most famed theatre in Simla, a gothic architectural masterpiece. The maid delighted in reporting that the play tonight was *Time Will Tell*. The title couldn't have been any more appropriate.

POSTCARD #11

12/5/41

Dear Phil

The damn Germans, they bombed the Queen's Hall the other night, during an Elgar concert. We were to go there for the Proms, but now we can't. I've heard that they'll relocate them to the Albert Hall, but it won't be the same. Nothing is the same.

Do you remember the last time we went together? How glorious the music was? I pray every night that you have music where you are. It lifts the soul more than we realise.

Stay safe.

B xxx

THE THEATRE

he trip to the theatre with Christopher, Naomi, and most of British Simla had been enjoyable, free from any trauma, except for one actor who'd refused to shave off his moustache to play the female lead, so a hirsute heroine entertained the audience, and the crowd was raucous in their appreciation of the amateur theatrics, making the actors take bow after bow at the end of the performance to a standing ovation.

The audience seemed untroubled by the reports of Sepoys continuing to revolt in other parts of India, with laughter ringing out through the impressive premises. Officers attending in their immaculate dress uniforms, didn't speak of the troubles, although Naomi mentioned there were fewer in attendance than normal, as evidenced by the abundance of women there without a male escort.

Servants offered glasses of punch from silver trays to the guests after the performance. Christopher took two, one each for Sarah and Naomi. Naomi chugged a good portion of hers back straight away, lifting another one from a passing tray and replacing it seamlessly with the emptied glass at the same time. Sarah sipped hers. Gin; gin and a massive quantity of quinine. She screwed her face at the unexpected aftertaste.

'Best thing to keep the mosquitos away, I'm told,' Naomi advised her.

'Drink up. Malaria will kill more of the people in this room over the next year than any Indian soldier unhappy about beef-greased cartridges. I say, have another glass. To the Queen!' she continued, raising her crystal tumbler above her head before taking a large sip of her drink.

Sarah looked at her quizzically, 'Beef-greased what?'

'Mrs Abbott, now is not the time to bore Miss Williams with stories. We were here to enjoy the finest theatre in all of India, not to discuss the troubles.'

'I think I should know about any troubles now I'm living here,' Sarah parried, her eyebrows lifting.

Christopher shrugged.

'The rumour is that the Sepoys thought someone had greased their rifle cartridges with beef dripping. As you recall from the other day at the hunt, you bite the end off the cartridge to load it into the rifle. Well, the Indian soldiers, the Sepoys, take issue with putting something tainted with beef oil in their mouths. I for one would kill for a nice piece of roast beef, drowned in gravy, with lashings of potatoes, and beans with butter, but that's not the done thing here in India. You can't eat beef. They think the beasts are sacred. Heaven forbid if you accidentally shoot one. Anyway, I've no idea if it's true, about beef fat on the cartridges, but it's caused a flare up in the other regions. It's nothing to concern yourself, Major Brooke has it under control — he and Colonel Scarborough.'

Christopher turned away to converse with another officer, his dark hair foppishly covering one eye. He was the gentleman from the hunt, Sarah realised, although no one introduced him. Immersed in their own conversation and men didn't seem to encourage any company.

The press of the crowd swamped her, filling her ears with conversations and her nose with the competing smells of scent and sweat. Vague classroom memories sprang to mind and she could visualise the old history lessons on the blackboard, the story of the Indian revolt, the Sepoys rising against the British. There was a massacre, Englishwomen and children mutilated, pulled from a fort where they had taken refuge. Butchered. Uncensored photos of the scene in black and white in their textbooks.

She felt light-headed, and Naomi declared it was time to retire for the night. They joined the throng of other theatregoers leaving, calling out fond farewells, despite knowing they'd see each other again on the morrow. Separating from his friend after briefly clasping arms, Christopher took Sarah's hand and placed it on his own. The night drew to a close, with her companions escorting her home, Christopher gaily reciting the funnier lines from the show and keeping the little group in high spirits.

Firgrove House was silent, apart from the heartbeat of the Georgian grandfather clock gracing the hallway. Its Englishness out of place in a home adorned with so many Arabian and Indian decorative pieces.

Simeon was still out, with no word of his whereabouts. "Away with the army" the servants said. The cut on her forehead had scabbed over although it still throbbed when she leant down. She'd received several sympathetic glances from the other women at the theatre, but no one had asked her how she'd received the injury. *They knew*. At least she'd made two lovely friends in Naomi and Christopher. She had her suspicions he might only ever be a *friend*; despite his obvious overtures to her, his true nature betrayed him.

Sarah settled into bed, clothing flung haphazardly on the ottoman by the window. Her refuge from life, she pulled the starched sheets up to her neck and drifted off, trying to count the infinite stars luminous in the sky.

With no real plans, Sarah approached each day as a one to treasure and as an opportunity to play explorer. As always, her morning started with Nirmala waking her. Today, Nirmala brought with her a small silver salver, upon which lay a note sealed with red wax, impressed with a monogram. Smiling, the girl withdrew to the dressing room to choose clothes for her mistress.

Intrigued, Sarah opened the note, sliding her nail under the sealed flap. Ornate script danced across the page. It was from the Raja, inviting her to attend an afternoon tea in her honour. She called out to Nirmala, despite the maid already knowing the contents from the porter who had delivered the note. There were no secrets in Simla.

An unfamiliar warmth spread through Sarah as she recalled the Raja's regal bearing, and the interest he took in her, before the tiger attacked him. Nirmala returned from behind the peacock screen, a smile on her face.

'Nirmala, can we send a reply, saying I'd love to attend?' Sarah asked, rereading the crisp note.

Nirmala smiled.

'Of course, Memsahib. I'll fetch your writing slope.'

Sarah grinned. This was a life she could get used to!

'What should I wear, Nirmala?'

This didn't differ from going out with Patricia; both getting ready for the night, giggling over what to wear. Like dating, but much more exciting. An Indian prince had invited *her*, a simple girl from London, to afternoon tea!

Nirmala reappeared with a rosewood writing box, edges protected by gleaming brass corners, a key protruding from the lock. She placed it on the bed and returned to the wardrobe.

She and Kalakanya had spent hours discussing Sarah since she first arrived at Firgrove House. Both girls hated working for Sahib Williams — more so since his wife had died, but the news that his sister was coming to live with them had encouraged them to stay; that, and that their uncle had placed them there.

'Everyone in the family must contribute,' he had said, when they complained about how Sahib Williams treated them.

It was their lot in life that their master was as sly as a fox, with a temper like a mongoose and the arrival of Miss Williams had been an anticlimax. The Sahib ordered his sister wasn't to go out. She was to keep to herself. The same instructions his wife had to abide by.

Simeon's wife had contracted consumption or White Fever, and died alone in her bedroom, now Sarah's room, ignored by her husband, who considered her illness a slight against him. He paid scant attention to her when she was alive, and even less while she was dying. She'd failed to provide him any children, which he believed contributed to his vindictive father splitting the inheritance.

There was no way on God's earth he would allow her to get her hands on *his* money. This was why he'd had her shipped out to India, where he could keep a proper eye on her. Left alone in London, who knew what sort of gold-digger would seek her out, sweeping her off her feet. No, she was better here with him. Also, with no wife to control the servants, he needed her here to make sure the thieving locals kept their hands off the treasures he'd accumulated over the years.

Now Sarah had emerged butterfly like, her wings open, and Nirmala, Kalakanya and the rest of the servants were enjoying her metamorphosis.

Sarah opened the writing box, the deep green leather undamaged by silverfish or other little pests that enjoyed nibbling on such items. Back in the antiques shop, Sarah had always sworn at the damage they caused to such beautifully made pieces. This one looked brand new, fresh from the workshop. Several pieces of thick, monogrammed paper were in the slope. She had a choice of blue or black ink, and two different pens: one a sterling silver telescopic pen; the other a delicate mother-of-pearl-handled dip pen with a gold nib.

Sarah drafted a response to the Raja. Her writing left lots to be desired. It wasn't the flowery script expected from ladies, but more the hasty scribble of a busy emergency room doctor, but she was satisfied with her wording and hoped that the Raja would look beyond her poorly formed scrawl.

She passed the note to Kalakanya, who sprinkled a fine layer of sand over the ink, to avoid any smudges, before folding it and slipping it into a matching envelope.

'You can send this off to the Raja now, Kalakanya. Imagine what his house must look like! I'll be like a kid in a candy shop.'

Sarah clapped her hands in excitement, oblivious to the confused glances her maids exchanged at the words 'candy shop'. Their new mistress came out with strangest of sayings, but they were getting used to it now.

Kalakanya vanished with the note in hand. She couldn't read, but the Raja's man could. He was waiting on the back porch for the memsahib's reply, and he'd tell her what it said.

Meanwhile, Nirmala helped Sarah into a long-sleeved, printed silk chiffon dress. Its white cotton trim was a stark contrast against the red patterned dress. They cinched her waist with a wide silk taffeta belt, and a straw boater, gloves and small brown leather handbag completed the outfit. The maid pinned a large shell cameo, set in a heavy rose gold mount, at her throat. Sarah touched it. The cameo had two faces in profile, one male and one female, a rare pairing, expertly worked.

'Whose is it?' she asked, stroking the shell intaglio.

'That was the Memsahib's. She told me that someone had made it for her in Italy as a wedding gift from the Sahib. He disposed of most of her jewellery, but this one he forgot. She had fine jewellery from her family. Not as exquisite as the diamond necklace they gave you though, Memsahib.'

Nirmala chatted, listing the items Simeon had sold after the death of his wife.

'There was a smart pearl brooch, the Memsahib's favourite; very large and looked like a flower. She had many strings of pearls — they are popular here in Simla. I think some are still in her jewellery box. I can find them for you, and—'

Sarah interrupted her.

'What do you mean, "not as exquisite as the diamond necklace they gave me", what necklace?'

'The one the Viceroy gave you yesterday when he called on you.'

'Oh my God, that's what was in there?' Sarah cried.

'And to think I didn't even open it in front of him. How stupid could I have been? What an idiot! Show me the necklace, Nirmala. I must send him a thank you before I go out,' she said, as she dashed back to the writing box, still open on her bed.

Nirmala ducked behind the screen to the dressing room, returning moments later with the black box. Like a magician, she flicked the catch with her index finger and opened it with a flourish, presenting it to Sarah. The necklace inside drew in the light to reflect the grandeur of India, the history and romance of the Mughals. A rope of diamonds, cut in the traditional style.

Sarah sucked in her breath at the magnificence of the piece. She couldn't believe she'd received such a precious gift from the Queen's representative here in India.

The girl was still holding out the box, waiting for her mistress to take it.

'It's beautiful, Nirmala, but please hide it away for now. We mustn't let Simeon see it,' she said, touching the scab on her forehead.

Sarah itched to hold the necklace, but couldn't have pushed herself any further away from the stones. She was going to afternoon tea with a prince, and all the diamonds in the world wouldn't stop her from enjoying the moment.

Nirmala nodded, closing the lid with a snap.

THE RAJA

They conveyed her to the Raja's home by a decorated palanquin. The sun cast its glow on the lofty Himalayas, making the town picture postcard perfect in the lengthening shadows of the afternoon. A smattering of ladies walked through the mall, like extras in a costume drama.

The Raja's summer palace was a comparable size to her own, but that was where any similarity ended. This was a *mansion*, built and maintained with an infinite amount of money. Liveried servants waited on the steps to greet her, their turbans impossibly white, oiled moustaches as grand as the house they represented.

The entrance hall was larger than her London flat, well-lit and airy, designed to maximise any breeze that entered the house. Sunlight filtered through latticed windows, giving a geometric display on every surface. The floor tiles had a Moroccan feel; a profusion of bright reds, vivid blues and greens, laid in complicated repeating geometric patterns. The servants divested her of gloves, hat and bag, and motioned that she follow her guide. Of the Raja there was no sign, but with his injuries, she presumed they compromised his mobility and he was resting.

She followed the manservant through the regal rooms: a reception room; the dining room; and finally, through to a less formal sitting room, where she found the Raja.

He was reclining on a day-bed beside the open patio doors. From somewhere in the house came the melodious notes of a lute, or the Indian equivalent, creating the faint aura of an opulent film set. He was resplendent in pantaloons festooned with gold thread, his injured leg raised on a pile of tasselled cushions. His jacket was a symphony of gold brocade embroidered with tiny pearls, and his moustache immaculately groomed, his beard gleaming with scented oil. Giant pearls adorned his ears, and ropes of matching pearls worn artistically around his neck, resting on his muscular chest.

'You must forgive me for not rising to greet you,' the Raja purred.

Sarah swallowed. He exuded a sexuality she'd never encountered before. The combination of his title, his wealth and his presence was overwhelming.

'Please sit,' the Raja said, waving to a large leather armchair placed next to the divan on which he stretched out. Separated by a brass tray resting on ornate wooden legs, the two pieces of furniture seemed absurdly close in the large room.

Sarah sat, folding her hands in her lap, having no idea what to do with them otherwise.

'Thank you for inviting me to tea. It is an honour to be here...' Sarah started, before the Raja waved at her to stop.

'Miss Williams, the honour is all *mine*. How can one match the price of having their life saved with a mere offer of tea? I am indebted to you, and I shall be for the rest of my life. My descendants, too, can never repay this debt. Your courage is no trifling matter and remains at the forefront of my mind every waking moment. Let us have tea as a start, and an infinitesimal measure of my gratitude will be delivered.'

With that, the Raja rang for tea.

A manservant appeared and presented Sarah a domed silver platter. He lifted the lid with a flourish, revealing a plate of sliced glossy tomatoes mixed with green onions and brilliant hued mint leaves. The aroma of the lemon juice dressing was mouth-watering.

'*Tamatar salat*,' the Raja gestured towards the salad. 'To start.'

265

The servant ladled the food onto her plate, and then the Raja's. Sarah dipped her silver fork into the salad and a tart taste exploded in her mouth. Another servant appeared with two tumblers containing a thick fruit juice before retiring to leave the two of them making small talk. The Raja proved to have a perfect grasp of English humour, and the afternoon passed in a blur of small dishes, refreshing juices and laughter.

She ate warm flat bread coated in luscious eggplant dip; *baingan bharta,* the Raja had called it. A meal so different from the benign butter chicken she was used to at her local curry house in London. There had been a plate of *palak bhaji*, spicy fried spinach. Who knew adding turmeric, cumin, coriander, chilli and ginger could transform food into heaven for the taste buds? They served Tandoori chicken next, covered with fragrant onions, a servant squeezing a segment of lemon over the spicy chicken as he placed it on her plate.

Laughing, she asked the Raja, 'How many more courses are you serving today?'

His eyes crinkled.

'If I could feed you every day, I would still never have repaid my debt to you, Miss Williams. Do you enjoy the food of Mother India?' he asked.

'It has been divine, but as my brother prefers to have 'English' food served at home, I have had little opportunity to try the local food. This is a rare luxury, thank you.'

She smiled at the Raja, falling into his liquid eyes. She turned away, sipping her juice.

Delivery of another tray interrupted them — a dessert this time; a tray of *gulab jamun*, fried milk balls in a sweet syrup flavoured with green cardamom, rosewater and saffron.

'Leave us now. I shall summon you when we have need of you,' the Raja directed his servant.

The man bowed and left the room. While they were being served dessert, other servants lit candles around the room, and the sounds of bird life replaced the sounds of man-made music, creating a magical atmosphere...

The Raja selected one of the sugary balls and, leaning over to Sarah, said, 'Let me…'

He placed the delicacy into her mouth. Sarah's eyes widened. This was not *normal* Victorian behaviour.

The setting sun, caged songbirds, the sugar, and the intoxicating presence of the Raja drew all caution from her, and she copied the Raja's actions, placing a sweet into his mouth, holding his eyes with hers. He caught her hand, licking the sweet syrup from her fingers. Time stood still. Although, for Sarah, time was a peculiar thing, hard to grasp and harder to understand.

The *gulab jamun* forgotten, the Raja reached out to Sarah's face, caressing her with his honeyed eyes and hands. Lost in the moment, she allowed him to pull her from her chair onto his divan.

He pulled her face to his, and their syrupy lips met. Sarah abandoned herself to his arms. The warmth of the room, his body, their breath, took her on another journey. His caresses were more than just kind, his movements as smooth as silk, as he released her buttons, and shed his tunic. Sarah leaned forward to kiss on his chest, his bronzed torso smooth and muscular. Her buttons undone, he pushed her dress from her shoulders. She shrugged it off, and he drew her onto him. The thrill of their naked chests warmed her more than a hundred fires.

His caresses grew more urgent, and Sarah removed his pantaloons, conscious of his leg, still heavily bandaged. She stood up, and pulled off her undergarments, revealing her naked body. Was there any light more flattering to the naked body than candlelight? She straddled the Raja and lowered herself onto him. This time, *his* eyes widened in surprise at her.

THE TROUBLES

*T*hey lay entwined on the divan, the pale and the dark, the yin and the yang, watching the last vestiges of light fade from the day. The aroma of the Raja's hair oil mingled with the heady scents carried from the garden into the room by the evening breeze.

'You are more magnificent than I dreamt, my little tigress,' murmured the Raja as he stroked her hair. 'This is not how I imagined showing my gratitude,' he laughed.

Sarah smiled. For the first time since her adventure had begun she felt safe; safe and loved as she pictured this life being her own. She stroked his face and shivered as the breeze dipped in temperature.

'I anticipated giving this to you after tea. And as this is indeed after tea, it is fitting you wear it now. Perhaps the stones will give you extra warmth?'

The Raja reached underneath the divan, and pulled out a fabulous string of rubies, draping it around Sarah's neck as one flings a scarf around one's neck in winter.

Sarah gasped. The necklace was identical to the one she'd seen in her room at the Savoy in London. She wanted to stroke the gleaming rubies but being catapulted back to England, to a life far less vivid than this, terrified her. A life which didn't include the loving arms of the Raja. She'd already lost Warden William Price, and she didn't think her heart could bear another loss.

The last time she'd touched the rubies, they'd launched her back to the present day. *Do I want to go home?* Sarah pondered, looking at the Raja. Then this life, all of it, would vanish.

Sarah struggled with her emotions.

In a stark analysis, she could gather everything of value, pop it into a suitcase, touch the necklace, and be home, setting her up for life. The necklace, the sampler, the katars and the candlesticks — from the brink of insolvency to a life of luxury. But what was life without love, without family?

'My little tigress, these rubies shall always remind you of the life you saved. You prevented my life blood from feeding the earth. For that, you will always have my love.'

He kissed her again, his coffee-coloured hands caressing her.

A perfect moment cannot last forever, and theirs ended with an urgent knocking at the door. Pulling the throw over Sarah and himself, he called out.

'Come in.'

His manservant entered. If it surprised him to see Sarah and the Raja on the divan together, he gave no sign. And standing just inside the doorway, he addressed the Raja.

'Your Highness, there is a disturbance across town. Perhaps it would be best if we returned Miss Williams to her home before night falls?'

'Thank you, Layak. Please summon the driver and see Miss Williams home. She will be ready soon.'

Layak bowed and left, closing the door behind him, pointedly oblivious to Sarah's naked state beside his Raja.

'I am sorry, tigress, but we must part, but only until tomorrow. Then we shall continue with my attempts to show you my gratitude for my life.'

He pushed her wayward hair behind her ears, kissing each earlobe as he did so.

'And these ears need jewels, they are too beautiful to be naked. I

269

shall rectify that tomorrow, but now we must dress and my driver will deliver you home.'

Sarah nodded.

'I wish I could stay with you tonight.'

'But then there would be nothing to look forward to tomorrow. Tigers prefer coming out in the dusk, they conserve their energy for then, and that is what you must do, my tigress!'

Sarah stood up, gathering her discarded wardrobe. The Raja helped her with her buttons and after the last button was closed, and her skirts smoothed flat, she stood uncertainly in front of him. He coiled his luscious hair back underneath his turban and returned to his immaculate self — any trace of their former ardour hidden under the veneer of civilisation.

'Till tomorrow,' he said, placing the rubies at her throat.

'Till tomorrow,' Sarah replied, placing her fingers on her lips, and then on his.

He rang the bell, and the tinkling hadn't yet faded before Layak opened the door.

'Miss Williams, please come with me.'

She followed him out of the house to a waiting litter.

'Saptanshu will deliver you home, Miss Williams. Safe travels.'

The driver and his partner lifted the wooden handles of the litter, and with no warning, took off. Sarah swivelled in her seat, looking for any sign of the Raja. He stood at the window, back lit by lamp light, his silhouette filling the ornate arabesque frame, one hand raised in farewell.

THE FIRE

The Raja's coolies scurried along the dirt road, uncluttered compared to previous days. Sarah sat back in the tottering litter, holding onto the sides. There was no obvious reason for the streets to be empty. She frowned in puzzlement. Every other time she'd ventured out, they had been teeming with people, even on her way to the Raja's earlier. Then, Indian and British residents sauntered in the Indian sunshine, taking in the air. Tonight, the only people moving anywhere were low caste Indians carrying out their duties. Even the omnipresent soldiers were absent from the fading watercolour scenes of the mock Tudor town.

She'd tried talking to Saptanshu, but whether he didn't speak English, or was pretending not to understand, she wasn't sure.

After travelling at a brisk pace, Sarah noted the horizon shimmering with a fiery glow. Red shadows bounced off the hills surrounding the township, creating an alternative Northern Lights experience.

'Driver, what is on fire?' she asked Saptanshu.

He ignored her, his breathing growing laboured as he struggled up one of Simla's many verdant hills.

'The fire, what is on fire?' Sarah repeated.

Frustrated at his lack of English, she tapped his shoulder and gestured towards the red glow illuminating the town.

Three riderless horses galloping past them. Bridled and covered in sweat, they raced away from an unseen foe. The coolie stopped, his skinny turbaned head pivoting to follow the horses' unchecked trail, and ignoring Sarah, he turned to the other coolie at the back of the litter, yammering in their guttural native tongue, their discussion rising in volume with every word.

'What's going on, I don't understand?' Sarah queried, looking at the agitated men.

Saptanshu dropped the handles of the litter, pitching Sarah forward in her seat. He came round to the side and, and pulled her from her seat, shouting at her now. No matter how hard she pulled back, his starved frame was still stronger than her, and she fell forward into the road.

'The Raja will not like this!' Sarah yelled at him. 'Get back here. You can't leave me here. Saptanshu, come back!'

They abandoned her in the road and took off with the litter, as if Kali, goddess of time, change, and war, was after them.

Stunned and winded, Sarah sat on the road, gloves despoiled, her hat awry, and her ankle twisted underneath her. Ugly sounds of rifle fire echoed around her, followed by shouts carried on the acrid smoke blanketing the town. She stood up, and limped off the road, into the shadow of the nearest building. The cobblestones grabbed at her twisted ankle with every painful step.

The vivid red sky gave off enough light for Sarah to consider retracing her journey back to the Raja's house, but that would send her towards the fire. It would be best to carry on to her house where Nirmala would know what was happening. Leaning on the buildings for support, she walked home.

The sound of booted feet running on the cobbles saw Sarah shrink back into the shadows. She had no way of knowing whether the running feet were friend or foe. In addition, she didn't know what the conflagration was. Her mind puzzled over the possible explanations for the driver's fear, the riderless horses, and the fire. She crouched behind a large planter in front of one of the Elizabethan-style shops — one advertising wares for gentlemen, its window a profusion of pipes, cigarette cases, and glossy walking sticks topped with carved ivory heads.

The design of the street funnelled the noise of the fire, so the street crackled with energy, the sound of running feet dissipating as they moved further away. Sarah stumbled home on her sprained ankle, looking fretfully over her shoulder, fire reflected on her face.

The light didn't reach further than the centre of town and, away from the main street, the roads were dark and abandoned, windows of the buildings shuttered, as if the mere presence of a piece of wood would protect the occupants from whatever terror was approaching. Although Sarah didn't know the residents in these homes, it was prudent to avoid them and concentrate on making her way back to her own house.

After leaving the relative protection of the buildings, she felt exposed on the open road. Although she was travelling away from the fire and the noise, the riderless horses had unnerved her more than she wanted to admit. The sooner she got home the better. With daggers piercing her ankle every time she placed any weight on it, the going was slow. Soon the large façade of her home loomed ahead of her, its silhouette giving her more comfort than a down-filled duvet. Even her home was devoid of light when before there'd always been a glimmer of light leaking from the windows. She hobbled up the wooden stairs onto the painted veranda. In the dark, the vibrant colours of the flowers filling the garden had vanished.

Sarah hammered against the polished wood of the locked door with both hands, coughing from the effects of the smoke slinking through Simla.

'Nirmala, let me in!' she yelled in between hacking coughs.

Silence.

'Nirmala!' Sarah yelled again.

Nothing.

Rifle shots nearby broke the silence of the night. Panicking now, Sarah limped around the boards, trying the patio door — all locked and the drapes drawn, making the house feel abandoned. Sarah slipped down the back steps and limped to the servants' entrance. It was ajar, the open doorway ominous in the dark; her desire to get inside hampered by a sudden fear. Bile rose in her throat. Why was *this* door open when the other doors weren't? Had they left it open for her, knowing she'd be back soon? Why hadn't anyone warned her about what was happening on the other side of town? With a jolt, she realised the army barracks were there, far away from the homes of the senior members of the Company, nowhere near the Indian aristocracy, and far enough from the palatial lodgings of the Viceroy that the troop movements and practices wouldn't disturb him.

Was this the uprising they'd learnt about in school? If it was, Sarah knew the threat was real and the haunting images from her textbooks crowded her mind.

Putting those thoughts to one side, Sarah decided that being inside was preferable to being outside, so approached the open doorway, her ears straining for any sound. She couldn't surprise anyone inside, with all the yelling and hammering she'd done at the front of the house. She cursed her stupidity — she should have come straight to this door after finding the front one locked.

Two steps led inside, and favouring her twisted ankle, Sarah made her way down the steps and into the kitchen. Empty. Sarah closed the door behind her, plunging the room into absolute darkness. She wedged a chair under the handle, hoping it would hold it shut should anyone try to enter the house that way, and using her hands as guides, she made her way through the kitchen, down a short narrow corridor, and into the entranceway.

Here, the moonlight made its way into the house via the intricate stained glass around the front door. Sarah stumbled along the hall towards her room, leaning heavily on the panelled walls. Sweat from her palms marked her path, her gloves abandoned somewhere on the road between town and the house. Ruined beyond repair. She would love to tell Patricia about her disastrous relationship with gloves. A useless item of clothing she'd decided, like men's ties. Gloves should only be worn in winter or when skiing, she'd concluded.

She pushed open her bedroom door, shading her eyes against the sudden flood of light. Nirmala was sitting on the bed, holding Kalakanya silently. Perplexed, Sarah started into the room, using the wall for support.

The door slammed behind her, revealing Simeon, his uniform encrusted with soot, black smears across his stubbled cheeks, and his normally impeccable black hair in chaos. His filthy hands gripped the ornate hilt of his officer's sword as its honed silver blade sliced through the air pendulum-like. Slow and steady. Simeon's consistent rhythm more terrifying than the fire and gunshots she'd just escaped.

'Simeon, what is going on? There's a fire and gunshots. Shouldn't we be moving somewhere safer?' Sarah asked, looking from Nirmala back to her brother.

Her heart thumped in her chest, so loudly she fancied everyone could hear it. She realised it didn't matter what she asked him; she had to keep him talking, but it didn't look good. His eyes had no soul.

The sword paused mid-swing.

'What is going on? Sarah, I believe that has an answer only *you* can give. When young women cavort with the local heathens, can there be but one outcome? You have disrupted the natural balance of God's law. Hundreds of Englishmen will die tonight because you could not obey your brother and stay in the house. You have been whoring yourself out. With how many men, I know not. Your maids have told me of your behaviour. And it shall not go unpunished.'

Simeon drew himself up and raised the point of his sword until its tip was resting in the flushed hollow of Sarah's throat.

She shuffled backwards until she hit the door.

'I think you are very mistaken, Simeon. The Raja invited me for afternoon tea, and now I have returned home. Remove your sword right now.'

'Afternoon tea!' he sneered. 'Do *all* your afternoon teas result in gifts of ruby necklaces?'

His sword danced over the rubies at her neck. Sarah flinched.

'You are a whore, and I'll treat you as one.'

Simeon stepped forward and slapped her before she knew what had even happened.

'It is just as well our parents will never know of this shame.'

Simeon reached forward and wrenched the necklace from Sarah's neck. A hammering at the front door interrupted his tirade. His red face, twisted with hatred, turned towards the sound. Sarah skittered past him, grabbing the hands of Nirmala and Kalakanya, pulling them up off the bed and towards the shuttered veranda doors at the end of the room.

'Help me with this, Nirmala!' Sarah instructed as she fumbled with the catch on the shutters.

'I don't think so,' Simeon growled, dragging her away from the doors. She slipped on the light matting by the door and fell against the ottoman.

Nirmala released the latch, and flung the doors open, with Kalakanya catching hold of Sarah's other hand and pulling her from the Sahib.

Torn between answering the incessant knocking at the door and punishing his sister, he didn't have to decide when a squad of red-coated soldiers appeared at the open veranda door.

THE SOLDIERS

'Williams, what the blasted hell are you doing *here*? The bloody Sepoys have gone berserk, and your Company is missing its bloody commanding officer. Get out of there, we've got a bloody mutiny on our hands! Half of us must be Captain bloody Bligh. For Christ's sake, hurry up!'

Sarah looked up from the floor.

'Major Brooke!' she exclaimed.

Simeon was so stunned by the unexpected guests filling the room he released Sarah's hand. Lanterns carried by the soldiers, lent a menacing air to the proceedings.

Major Brooke's face registered shock.

'My apologies, I did not see you there on the floor,' he said, reaching to help her up. 'We need to move you to safety. You're not safe here; the Sepoys are rebelling, thanks in no small part to this man,' he spat, gesturing towards Simeon.

'You are an insult to your country, Brooke. Mollycoddling these heathens. They should shoot with what we issue them. Worshipping cows and gods with elephant heads — it's unnatural. Exodus gives us the Second Commandment which states *"Thou shalt have no other gods before me".'*

'You're mad!' Major Brooke stated. 'And you'll be dead if you stay here. You'll get to meet *your* god then. Now, get your rifle and rejoin your Company, or it won't be the Indians that kill you, it'll be me!' Turning to Sarah, he softened his voice, 'Come, Miss Williams, my men will escort you to the Lodge.'

Sarah limped from the room, supported by Nirmala and Kalakanya, ignoring Simeon.

As the lanterns retreated with the soldiers, Simeon bent to scoop up the ruby necklace, the gems warming his hand. *There will be no whore's necklace here when she gets back*, Simeon determined. He'd see to that, and feeling his way in the dark, he passed through the empty house to his room, to prepare for war.

THE LODGE

The soldiers delivered Sarah and the girls to the Viceroy's Lodge, their hurried march in the starry night, flanked by silent soldiers, a surreal event. Although Major Brooke walked beside Sarah, who was leaning heavily on Kalakanya for support for her sprained ankle, he paid her as much attention as one would a stranger on a bus. Their only interaction when he placed his hand in the small of her back when she appeared to be flagging.

She found his touch reassuring, not in the exotic heart-thumping way she had when the Raja touched her, but comforting, safe. Her time with the Raja a lifetime ago. *Whose* lifetime, though? Her free hand worried at her naked neck. *The Raja's rubies — gone.* It was not fate's plan that she'd *ever* get to enjoy those precious stones, not in this lifetime, nor in any other.

The Lodge was ringed with riflemen, with canons positioned on the gravel drive and men rushing around — a far cry from the revelry at the Lodge the last time Sarah had been here. At the grand entrance Sarah turned to the Major.

'Thank you. I never realised my brother was such an arse.'

If the Major thought her language uncouth for a lady, there was no sign.

He inclined his head.

'Perhaps when this is over, you should return to England. I'm not sure India agrees with you, Miss Williams. Conflict follows you.'

Sarah took immediate offence.

'Conflict does not follow me, Major Brooke, it follows you. First the boat, then the carriage and now this. Men die wherever you are. I am just a woman, and I've learnt that this means I am of no consequence, so thanks for your help, but no doubt I can find someone else to look after us here. I'm sure you are needed elsewhere.'

As Sarah entered the Lodge, she thought she heard the Major speak.

'You are of every consequence.'

Before she could process his words, he'd wheeled away to join his men. Sarah stood stock-still, jostled by a stream of Englishwomen coming inside, in varying states of dress, showing many had been asleep when they'd woken and rushed to the assumed safety of the Lodge. The female chattering inside was worse than the rifle shots outside, and Nirmala took Sarah by the arm to pull her inside, to safety.

THE MEETING

*A*ndrew hammered at the door of *The Old Curiosity Shop* for twenty minutes though it could have been longer.

Frustrated, he ran his fingers through his hair before cupping his hands around his face and leaning into the window to see if he could see any movement inside. He slumped to the worn orange and black tiles in the doorway — the last original relic from the 1920s and hung his head in despair. What was he going to do? Sit here all day waiting for the mysterious Sarah Lester to return from wherever on earth she may be? Feeling hopeless, he waited, his leather briefcase clamped between his knees as the filth of a thousand diesel delivery vans transferred to his suit.

Patricia poked her head out her door, alerted by the constant knocking.

'Oi, what are you doing?' she called out from the safety of her doorway.

Andrew looked up in surprise.

'Miss Lester?' he asked, standing up and brushing the dirt from his trousers.

Patricia stepped out from the doorway.

'Sorry, no. Is she not in?' she answered.

'No, and I was hoping to speak with her about the items she wished to consign to us. I must get hold of her.'

Patricia pulled out her mobile. Andrew interrupted her as she was punching in Sarah's number.

'She isn't answering her mobile, either.'

Patricia put the phone up to her ear, ignoring Andrew's last comment. The call went straight through to Sarah's answerphone. She snapped her phone shut. She peered through the window of *The Old Curiosity Shop*, knocking on the glass.

'So you're the auction guy, then?'

'Yes.'

Patricia consulted her watch.

'She should be in.'

She called up to the window.

'Sarah? Sarah, open up!'

Still no response.

'I'll just get my keys. Wait here,' Patricia instructed.

She returned less than a minute later with a set of keys on an old hotel keyring — ironically a souvenir from the Savoy hotel. Slotting a key into the deadbolt, Patricia turned it and opened the door to the empty shop.

'Sarah, are you here?' Patricia called, walking past shelves crammed with brass bowls and copper vases.

Harvard followed behind her. As he rarely frequented shops like this, it astounded him they still existed, given the huge rise of Internet-based businesses. He couldn't remember the last time he'd been in a local second-hand shop.

In awe, he turned in a circle, taking in the fur coats hanging from the ceiling, the overflowing crates of rusty biscuit tins under the table, the bookcases and cabinets groaning under the sheer weight of their contents; layer upon layer of stock, each precariously balanced on top of one another. A cardboard carton labelled 'Linen' in blue felt tip caught his eye. You never knew what treasures could hide in a box like that. He moved towards it, momentarily forgetting he was waiting for

Sarah, but the glorious Reboux hat distracted him, sitting on top of the trunk where Sarah had left it.

As he reached for it, Patricia interrupted his treasure hunt when she popped back downstairs.

'That's odd, she's not here,' she told him, walking round the counter to check the diary propped up above the keys of the old cash register. 'Nope, nothing written here. Maybe she left for an appointment? I can't leave you in here so why don't you come back to my place and I can make you a coffee while you wait?' she offered.

'Sure,' he said. What other choice did he have? He couldn't demand the right to search for the *katar* without Sarah there, so he followed Patricia outside and into the sweet-smelling clothes shop next door, where racks of women's garments stood with military precision, devoid of any rust lurking in the corners; a complete contrast with *The Old Curiosity Shop*.

Patricia showed him through to her workroom where she set about fussing with a flash Italian espresso machine, the one so complicated she needed to refer to the manual to use it.

'Instant is fine,' Andrew volunteered, as he saw her reading a dog-eared copy.

Patricia laughed.

'One of these days I won't need the manual. Seriously, it's no problem. Think of it as good practice. Just bear with me a little longer.'

She carried on twisting the knobs and poking more buttons than an astronaut uses on the space shuttle.

Andrew perused the clothing on Patricia's workbench, fingering the swatches of lace and fabric littering the surface. His hand hesitated as it brushed a simple white shirt, half disassembled.

'This is an interesting shirt,' he called out over his shoulder.

'Which one?' she queried, staring at the liquid finally pouring forth from the nozzle, concentrating on catching it in the previously unused espresso cup — she preferred her coffee in a mug large enough to sustain her for hours, so the espresso cups were more for show; a bit like the machine.

'This one, dates from around 1880, or slightly later. You never see them in such pristine condition,' he said, more to himself than to Patricia.

She walked over to the bench, cups in hand.

'Ah that one. It's from Sarah, from an estate she bought the other day. Fits her too! I've got the skirt that came with it.'

She fumbled through a basket till she pulled out the heavy black skirt.

'And what about this one, then? *Mastermind* question for you: how old is this skirt?' she joked.

Andrew took it from her hands.

'Given the weight, and the dye used, the stitching around the hem and the quality of finish of the pockets, I'd also date this to around 1880 to 1890. It has had some wear.' Pointing to the hem, he carried on, 'You can see where the hem has been taken up at one point, suggesting it's had more than one owner.'

Andrew picked up the espresso cup and took a long sip.

'Perfect!' he announced, smiling at Patricia, who was standing open-mouthed at his near-faultless analysis of the skirt.

'Dare I ask how you know so much about women's fashion?' she asked, pushing a stool towards Andrew and perching on one herself.

'Let me introduce myself. Andrew Harvard, Senior Specialist, Costumes and Textiles at Christie's, graduated Oxford University with, and much to my mother's dismay, a degree in Fine Arts, specialising in Linen and Textile History. At your service.'

He bowed modestly towards her.

Patricia's smile above her coffee cup widened.

'A kindred spirit!' she exclaimed.

A loud knocking next door interrupted them, and Andrew looked to Patricia.

'That's someone else at Sarah's door and knocking a damn sight harder than you were. Come on,' Patricia responded.

She marched out of her shop, stopping outside of Sarah's, her diminutive Lancashire frame dwarfed by the towering form of Richard Grey. Unfazed, she stood with her hands on her hips.

'If you keep hammering on the door, you'll break it,' she remarked to his back.

Grey stopped knocking and turned to face her. His eyes narrowed as he appraised her eclectic clothing.

'I was trying to get the owner's attention. She never seems to be open, regardless of the business hours posted on her window. Not the way to do business, so I'm not surprised she's in financial difficulty.'

Leaning on the closed door, he crossed his arms, awaiting a reply.

Andrew, who'd followed Patricia, eyed Grey from behind her. His face looked familiar, and Andrew spent a few moments trying to place him before the penny dropped. *One of our more regular auction attendees.*

In the world of antiquities, there was a small but dedicated pool of buyers, who you could count on to be at almost every auction of note, and this man was one. Andrew moved closer to Patricia to listen to their conversation.

'Whether her business is doing any good is none of *your* business. She is not in, and the shop is shut. Can I suggest you come back another day?' Patricia said.

'If she spends more time closed than open, she won't have a business to come back to,' he threw back at her.

'You should leave now,' said Patricia, stepping towards Grey until they were toe to toe.

'I will return later to uplift my family's belongings. Good day.'

He bowed his head towards her and sauntered off down the road, oblivious to the glare she was directing at his back.

She and Andrew returned to the serenity of Blackpool Love, closing the door behind them.

They didn't notice the scruffy, skulking figure of Bryce Sinclair as he left the doorway he'd been leaning against across the road, and hurried after Grey.

POSTCARD #12

23/1/44

Dear Phil
Now don't panic, but I've had a small accident. I'm resting at home, and there is absolutely nothing to fret about. I tripped over one of those awful Indian brass planters you filled the house with!
I'm resting on the couch as my ankle is very swollen, but the doctor assures me it's not broken.
Don't think you'll get out of waiting on me when you get home. I'm sure it will still be somewhat painful when you return!
Stay safe.
B xxx

THE INJURED

*H*er maids guided Sarah to a low couch. Nirmala disappeared and Kalakanya removed Sarah's boot. As the pressure around her ankle released, she cried out in pain and Naomi appeared at her side.

'Oh my child, what a mess we are in now. To think it was just the other night we were here having such fun. What a *terrible* experience you are having in India. Wouldn't it be marvellous if we could turn back the clock and start again? Although I'd turn back time a little further; I miss the face I used to have!' she laughed, patting at the lines around her eyes. 'I might choose a different husband, slightly more racy — like the Raja...' she said, scrutinising Sarah's face for any reaction.

To Sarah's relief, Nirmala arrived with a bowl of ice chips and a bottle of liniment.

'Thank you, Nirmala,' she muttered through clenched teeth, as they wrapped the cold compress around her swollen ankle.

She leaned back on the couch, closing her eyes, the warmth of the room and the undercurrent of voices lulling her to sleep. Even the distant pops of rifle fire contributed to her somnolent state. The maids curled up at the end of the couch, each trying to find a patch of comfort in the crowded room.

Sarah woke with a start at the sound of shouting, and forgetting her ankle, she tried standing up, before falling back. She caught sight of Christopher being carried into the foyer, blood visible on his uniform.

'Nirmala, quick, help me!' she yelled.

All around her, the women became distressed, as word spread that injured soldiers were being brought into the Lodge.

With Nirmala and Kalakanya supporting Sarah, she hobbled over to the throng surrounding the Major and several other wounded men dumped on the ground. Sarah knelt by Christopher, who already had a doctor by his side, ripping Christopher's tunic open, exposing a ghastly wound in his side. The women rolled up their sleeves to help the harried doctor, and were calling out instructions to the servants hugging the walls in the grand foyer, dispatching them for blankets, sheets, water, and whisky.

Sarah, recoiling in shock at the gravity of his wound, smoothed back the hair from Christopher's face, trying to keep the fear from her eyes. Clammy to the touch, he shivered as she stroked his head. He groped for her hand, clutching it once he found it.

'Miss Williams, will you do something for me?' he whispered.

'Of course,' she replied.

'There is... my friend, can you tell him...'

He coughed, bloody-spittle leaking from the corner of his mouth.

'Please...'

'Shush,' Sarah replied, placing her fingers over his mouth. 'I'll tell him. I'll tell him you are thinking of him, and that will keep him going until you recover. Now, stop this silly talk and conserve your energy. You're one of my only friends here and I will not lose you.'

Christopher's eyes widened as Sarah spoke. 'You know?' he whispered.

'Yes, I could tell, but I doubt anyone else noticed — well, apart from Naomi, but nothing escapes her. I'll not tell anyone else. I'll keep your secret.'

Clasping his hand to her chest, she stroked his forehead, smoothing his furrowed brow as he closed his eyes. Sarah looked up as the doctor shook his head before moving onto another wounded man on the floor.

She stayed by Christopher's side until his grip on her hand faltered and his last breath left his mouth. Naomi pulled her sobbing body away.

'Come, child, let's leave the others to help the boys. We'll serve them better if we don't get in the way.'

Nirmala and Kalakanya, helped her to her feet, supporting her as they moved away from the carnage and into a quieter reception room. Here, a small cluster of women sat in a circle, listening to an elegant woman read from the Bible. The wives of the commanding officers — faces pale with shock — praying for their own husbands, barely gave Sarah a second glance as she entered the room. This one, like the others in the Lodge, had high decorative ceilings, full-length windows, now shuttered, their opulent curtains drawn. An abundance of house plants in decorative pots filled the nooks and crannies, settled atop of lace doilies.

The girls helped Sarah to a horsehide couch before taking their leave from the room.

The quiet reciting of Bible passages and murmured conversations numbed Sarah from the loss of her friend. In her *real* life, the only people she'd ever lost were her parents. She'd never even been to a funeral.

Since embarking on this unbelievable journey, she'd lost both Seth and Isaac, and Reverend Montgomery. Elaine confined to a wheelchair, and now Christopher was dead. Naomi placed a reassuring arm around her shoulders.

'Do you know the name of Christopher's friend?' Sarah whispered as she leant in to her heavily perfumed shoulder.

Naomi nodded, shushing Sarah as she did so.

'Leave that with me. This will be over soon, it won't take long. There's only a few hundred of them letting off their frustrations. I'm sure we'll be able to go home tomorrow. Tonight will be uncomfortable, but we'll be fine.'

Sarah looked at her hands, stained with Christopher's blood.

'But I want to go home now. Back to my flat, to my friends, to my shop. I can't handle more of this. Simeon is an absolute bastard. And if I can't go home, then I'll go back to the Raja's house. I can't stand this. I can't stand Simeon.'

Naomi looked at Sarah, perplexed.

'Your shop?' she laughed. 'You silly girl!'

Her face turned serious, and whispering she carried on, 'I wouldn't speak too loudly about your relationship with the Raja. Whilst we turn a blind eye to the casual intimate relationships the men have with the locals, trust me when I say that if these ladies catch a whiff of anything but a platonic friendship between the two of you, they will ostracise you. And no one recovers from that here. No, you're better off marrying quickly now, and Brooke is your best choice.'

'Brooke? Major Brooke?' Sarah interrupted. 'You've got to be joking! He won't even speak to me. No, Naomi, I need to go home. I need a way home...'

Sarah trailed off, her eyes tracking the deft movements of one woman working on a piece of embroidery. Sarah wondered about the sampler back in her flat. The *katar*. Of course! She sat up, knocking Naomi's glasses from her nose in her haste.

'Naomi, where are Nirmala and Kalakanya?'

The other woman shrugged. 'I presume they are with the other servants. They'll be back with refreshments, no doubt. Or you could ring the bell to summon someone if you need anything?' she offered.

'No, I need to ask them about the gifts from the Raja. What if someone steals them? I've got no idea where they are. Simeon had a massive tantrum over them and took them off me. Christ!' she exclaimed too loudly, as everyone spun round in shock.

Red infused her cheeks and Sarah stammered out an apology before stumbling to her stockinged feet, and, with Naomi protesting, she limped from the room into the corridor. There was respite anywhere, wounded men lay everywhere, with varying degrees of injuries. Half a dozen women, dresses soaked with blood, prioritised the men as they came in.

Sarah's ears were ringing with the shrieks and groans from around the building. She couldn't stand it any longer. She eased her way past soldiers on the floor and opened the door into a side room. Empty and quiet, once she closed the door, Sarah felt the stress and embarrassment slipping from her shoulders. An aroma of tobacco lingered in the air as if the occupant had finished a cigar before leaving the room. It reminded her of how the smell had clung to her father's belongings, leaving a part of him behind, even after he'd left for work in the mornings when she was little. Just as she slipped into the masculine armchair, her stress put aside, the door opened. The figure of a man appeared, back lit by the light from the hall.

'Sarah?' he asked softly.

THE ENGLISHMAN

*S*arah had the eerie feeling she recognised his lamplit profile.

'Sarah,' he repeated, raising his voice enough to carry through to the deepest recesses of her memories.

'Dad?'

Her face was incredulous as she moved towards him, her hands reaching for his face.

'Dad?' she whispered.

He nodded, grasping her hands in his and pulling her into a bear-like embrace, their sobs mingling in the humid Indian air.

Questions tumbled out of her mouth, words tangling themselves in her hurry to speak, to connect with the father she'd lost so long ago.

'Shush, shush now, we don't want to draw attention to ourselves. You won't understand this, but I need you to go back.'

'Go back?' Sarah asked in confusion. 'To the foyer?'

'No, sweetheart, back to London. You being here has changed too many things. Of all the places, this was the last place I expected to find you.'

He stroked her head, the pain in his voice clear.

'I can't go now, there is nothing for me there. And you're here so why would I leave you?' Sarah pleaded with her father.

'You have to, Sarah. I did not know that even the slightest change in circumstances could alter the course of history. I was wrong not to try coming back, but you would have thought I was mad if I'd tried to describe to you what had happened to me. And I thought I could find your mother that perhaps she was in India too. I knew you would be fine, but your mother was so reliant on me. She used to call me her rock. It's torn me apart that I haven't found her yet. I've never stopped looking. When I heard the rumours about Simeon's sister, I hoped it was your mother, not that I'm disappointed it's you,' he added.

'But she could be *anywhere*, Dad!' Sarah argued. 'I've been back in time, in London and New Zealand, and now here. So there's no knowing where she is. Please come home with me?'

Her father looked aghast.

'You mean this isn't your first journey?'

'No, it's not. I'm your daughter and I needed you, and now you're telling me to go away. But I won't, not without you. Mum could be anywhere and the only way you're likely to find her is if you figure out what it was she last touched. And seriously, Dad, after all this time, that's bloody unlikely, isn't it?'

Sarah flung herself onto the nearest chair.

'I didn't realise, I'm so sorry. All this time, I thought I would find Annabelle, that she was here somewhere, and I hadn't found her yet. But I don't understand how you got here. Surely you aren't working at the...' he petered off, realisation dawning in his eyes. 'Oh, my God, you *are* working in the shop. What happened to your degree? What a complete and utter waste of money. You should be at one of the big museums now.'

Lecturing her, he continued, 'I did not pay thousands of pounds for your education for you to waste it working in a bloody second-hand shop.'

His voice had been rising as he tried to disguise his heartbreak with anger.

Sarah sat in the chair, absorbing her father's words. She'd always imagined having this conversation when her father returned, and it was playing out *exactly* as she had imagined. *It's funny how people never change.* Just like when she was a teenager. The best way to manage him was to wait for him to run out of steam. Which he did.

'We're in the middle of a revolt, and you think now is a good time to discuss this? Shouldn't we be talking whether we stay or try to get home?' Sarah asked.

Her father sat behind a desk laden with unfinished paperwork, an overflowing ashtray, and military orders. He ran his fingers through his unkempt hair, a familiar nervous habit, he cleared his throat several times. He leafed through the papers on the desk, avoiding her gaze.

'I can't come back with you, Sarah, my life is here. There is no life left for me in London and it would complicate yours no end if I came back. I've invested too many years looking for your mother to just walk away.'

'But, Dad, this magic; this mysterious thing that's happened. I don't understand it, but just for a moment imagine our life with this special secret. You've no idea of the amazing things I've got at home. Oh, Dad, you should see these silver candelabras. They're English, but I found them in New Zealand. You'll want to keep them! And back at the house here, there's a ruby necklace — the rubies are huge! It's weird, but it's the second time I've seen it. We can go back to the house, get the necklace and then find a way home. It will be fine, Dad. It'll be painful having to come up with something to tell the police, but we'll sort through it...'

Sarah stopped talking as she registered her father's shocked face.

'You took things back? What do you mean you took stuff back? Do you know what this means, what the impact is?'

He got up from the desk, striding over to Sarah's seat. 'The only thing going back is *you*. How did you get back before?'

'I... I... once I sat on a chair. Another time I touched the candlesticks. I ended up here after touching the vanity case. Maybe if I open it again?'

'So touch something that's in the shop? Have a look around at everything, is *anything* familiar? If you have to touch something that's already at the shop, to take you back. Think. What's here that is also back home?'

He shook her by the shoulders.

'Dammit, Sarah, was there *anything* at Simeon's house you recognised?'

He walked over to the windows, pushing one open, allowing the sounds of battle to limp into the room.

'I never took things back on purpose. It just worked out that way. I never stole them. There was no intent...' Sarah retorted, but the rage left her the more she tried defending herself.

'Sarah, sweetheart, as soon as you took something home, you changed things irrevocably from here on in for everyone else. What were you thinking? It's done now. We must manage it as best as we can.'

Kneeling beside her, he continued.

'Can you think of anything you have seen here that is at the shop? There's not much time. I must get you back to Simeon's house. Was he there when you left?'

'He was there, but I don't want to go back if he's still in the house.'

Somewhat embarrassed, she asked a personal question.

'Dad, what about relationships? What if you like someone, and spent time with them, does that affect the future?'

Sarah couldn't meet her father's eyes, looking instead at the Persian rug on the floor, tracing the complex geometric patterns with her toes.

Her father brushed her concerns aside.

'No idea, so it's just as well you haven't been here long enough to do too much damage. Was it a clock? A pair of vases? It's too late for me, but I need to get you home.'

Sarah sat and considered everything she'd unpacked from the Elizabeth Williams estate, nothing stood out as familiar. She closed her eyes, running through the images the way you scroll through someone's Instagram account. Flashing through the pictures of old bottles, copper pans, pillowslips, and photo frames. She paused on the frames; the ornate scrollwork on one prickled at her memory. The picture wasn't Indian; it was a black-and-white photo of an RAF officer standing next to a Navy one, with planes behind them. But the frame... the frame was a heavy brass. Ornate scrollwork decorated the corners. And she'd seen that frame before — here in India.

'There is something... an old brass frame. I saw it at the house and I know it's at the shop. I haven't priced it up yet, but I remember it being at the top of a box...'

Sarah stood up, wincing as she put weight on her twisted ankle.

'I can't walk all the way back there, sorry, Dad.'

'It's fine, we'll just keep you out of the way here, and when the trouble subsides, we'll go back. Where was it? I could get someone to get it for us,' he theorised, looking through the windows into the dark expanse outside.

'It was on the mantelpiece, in the dining room. It had a picture of a woman in it. Simeon's wife, I guess,' Sarah replied, limping over to the window, leaning on her father's shoulder, absorbing his quiet strength like she used to when she was little.

POSTCARD #13

14/10/43

Dear Phil

We had our photographs taken today, and I can't begin to tell you how utterly tedious it was. You'd think it was the King's royal portrait, the length of time the photographer took. It was Cecil Beaton. Mama wanted him to take our photos after she saw the pictures he took of Maharani Devi from Jaipur.

Talking of photos, I absolutely loved the one of you and Duke with your Spitfires. It made all the papers. Simply glorious! You must bring him to visit when all this is over.

Stay safe.

B xxx

THE FAREWELL

While Sarah and her father spent an uncomfortable night snatching sleep in the wing-backed leather chairs, the dawn saw a winding down of the night's hostilities. The army regained control and rounded up the ringleaders of the revolt.

The Viceroy's aide-de-camp woke them.

'Mr Lester, His Excellency has been looking for you, sir. I was to prepare the study for him, er... if...'

The ADC looked uncomfortable, assuming that Sarah and Mr Lester had been intimate in the study.

Mr Lester brushed off the young officer's assumptions, as he extended his hand to Sarah, and pulled her up from her chair.

'Miss Williams, I trust that ankle is much improved this morning? Captain Doulton, can you locate Miss Williams' servants and arrange an escort to return them to her home? She'll be gathering her belongings before returning here, so the escort is to stay with her. It would be best for them to go inside with her, to be sure there are no deserters hiding indoors. It will be safer for her here while they dampen the troubles down. Can I leave that in your capable hands as I prepare for the Viceroy?'

'Yes, sir,' replied the ADC, giving Sarah a quick look before leaving the room. His curiosity left unsated but tempered by Mr Lester's curt instructions.

'What do you do for the Viceroy?' asked Sarah, who'd tested her ankle, then sunk back into the chair, massaging the bruising.

'No time for that now, Sarah. Suffice to say that due to my, ah, historical knowledge, I've been able to assist the Viceroy through some of the more tricky patches he could have gotten himself into.'

Sarah tried interrupting but her father held up his hand, stopping the words before they'd escaped.

'I knew the troubles were coming, but I could do nothing to stop it because they form such a part of India's history. Now, the best thing is to make sure you don't become part of that history. Do what you're told. Get a housemaid to grab the frame, and whatever else you need to make it look natural, and come straight back. I'll be with you when you go, but... I won't be coming with you. I'll stay here to help the real Sarah Williams assimilate back into her life. God help her, you will have made it very difficult for her. But I will do my best to minimise the impact your actions will have had.'

Sarah nodded and, trying to make light of things, she asked, 'So, no ruby necklace then?' she said, smiling.

Her father checked her face and saw the smile.

'No, Sarah, no ruby necklace.'

Pulling her into a giant embrace, he kissed the top of her head, as if she were still five years old, and left the room.

THE FRAME

*N*irmala and Kalakanya, together with Captain Doulton, followed the instructions of Albert Lester, escorting Sarah to Firgrove House. As they passed burnt-out buildings and the detritus of a running battle, Sarah's heart sank, as she worried they might have razed the house.

As the palanquin rounded the corner, the façade appeared unscathed. The gardens still stood as a testament to nature, untouched as they were by the problems of mankind.

Doulton, and the two men accompanying him, disappeared inside through the open front door, which was itself ominous, given Sarah couldn't use it the night before because someone had locked it. A soldier returned to help Sarah from the palanquin and into the hands of Nirmala and Kalakanya. The trio of women entered the house. Sarah's first thoughts that the house had escaped unscathed were premature.

'Jesus Christ!' she exclaimed, as she saw the devastation inside.

She stepped over upturned pot plants — their roots like dying hands reaching for salvation and navigated her way past paintings ripped from the walls and slashed with knives or bayonets. Walking through to the dining room, she found the table broken in half, its ormolu trim hanging from the damaged ends, and shards of blue and white pottery littered the ground.

The wanton destruction of such valuable pieces of art tore at Sarah's heart. She always considered it a tragedy when she unpacked something beautiful at the shop to find it cracked or chipped. But the dining room lamps had been rare examples of the early work of the Meissen factory. Sarah picked up a fragment of the base of one, the iconic crossed swords intact on this remnant. Worthless now, smashed to smithereens. She palmed the small fragment, a jagged edge biting into her soft flesh.

The frame had sat on the mantelpiece with the lamps.

'Nirmala, can you help me find the picture that was up there? The one in the brass frame? I need it,' she said, 'for the family.'

The soldiers had retired outside, taking a rare opportunity to smoke on the veranda, swatting away the mosquitoes assaulting them. Despite the winged kamikaze insects, this was a nice change from fighting with their Indian counterparts and they were more than content to babysit a group of women. Doulton peered in through the windows to see the women righting chairs and sweeping up broken pottery. He shook his head and returned to the men. They should be packing, but in typical female fashion, they were cleaning. He'd give them ten more minutes before he had to return to the Viceroy, whether they'd packed or not.

'It's not here, Memsahib!' called out Nirmala, wiping a fine coating of dirt from her hands with her sari, after sifting through the broken pieces of pottery littering the room.

'Nothing we can do about it now. Pack some clothes and things, and we'll head back to the Lodge.'

Entering her bedroom was like walking into a snowstorm of fabric. *Every* item of clothing shredded into nothing more than mattress ticking. Expensive silks and taffetas were unidentifiable, and a rainbow of colours swirled on the floor as the women walked through the room.

'This wasn't the work of rioting soldiers, was it?' Sarah surmised. 'Simeon did this,' she added redundantly, as that was exactly what

Nirmala and Kalakanya were thinking. 'I don't suppose there's a chance either of you know where that ruby necklace is, is there?'

Both girls shook their heads.

'Don't worry, I think I know where it is,' she said, walking from the room and down the hall, stepping over the broken landscapes littering the ground, stopping at the door to Simeon's room.

Nirmala pushed past her.

'I'll go in first, Memsahib,' she said, grasping the cool porcelain door knob in her childlike hand.

It turned smoothly, and she crossed the threshold into the undamaged masculine bedroom. It was as if a destructive whirlwind had torn apart the whole house except for this room. The one room where the only damaged item was Simeon himself.

THE BODY

Screaming, Nirmala backed out of the room as fast as her sari allowed and fleeing down the hall, her cries reverberated from the empty walls. Kalakanya stood motionless in the doorway, blocking Sarah's view.

'What is it?' Sarah asked, pushing past the diminutive girl.

'Oh!' she exclaimed.

Sarah swallowed the bile in her throat, and approached Simeon in a daze — the contents of his stomach pooling on the floor, his tangled intestines hanging like brocade tassels on a curtain tieback.

Captain Doulton ran into the room, after Nirmala nearly bowled him over in her haste to flee the house, falling to her knees and retching on the manicured lawn.

'Christ!'

He grabbed Sarah by the arm and pulled her away from the body. Sarah wrenched free of his grasp and stepped towards her brother. Not her *real* brother but the brother this life had given her. Regardless of how he'd treated her, his loss affected her, another death at her hands. At his feet was the brass photo frame she'd come to the house to collect. It seemed as if he'd been holding onto the only thing that had mattered to him when he was slit from his groin to his neck. The stench was overpowering forcing Sarah to hold her hand over her mouth and nose and, forgetting everything her father had told her, she leant down, and picked up the frame.

Her father knew best. As soon as she grasped the frame, her world dissolved, the cloying scent of Simeon's death replaced by the pollution-tainted smells of *The Old Curiosity Shop*. The sounds of bird calls morphing into the incessant whine of traffic and the impatience of car horns.

THE AGREEMENT

*S*inclair hurried to keep up with Grey as he walked down the street. He'd deduced that the man was no friend of Mrs Bell's, which meant that they had something in common, and he meant to find out why. Ducking his head, he entered the stone doorway of the George and Vulture. Such establishments littered London, and although many of them claimed to be older than New Zealand had settlers, this inn was.

Sinclair scanned the room, he could be back in 1860, given the decor. Established in 1600 and rebuilt after the Great Fire of London, the inn was where Dickens' Mr Pickwick lived until he retired to Dulwich. It is said that Dickens wrote *The Pickwick Papers* with the George and Vulture as his muse, and could often be found drinking in the very same premises.

After finding his prey in the dim light, Sinclair slipped into the wood-panelled alcove — designed to offer a modicum of privacy to the drinkers confined within. Drinking a fine draught of port was how Sinclair found Grey.

'Excuse me, mister.'

Grey drew back. His mistrust of strangers, and his need for excessive personal space, were two of his less peculiar attributes.

He sneered at the homespun roughness of Sinclair's clothes and his ragged ears, Grey replied.

'You mistake me for someone else,' he said before turning back to his port.

'No, sir, it is you who are mistaken. I'm here about Mrs Bell, who I understand you also know?' Sinclair replied, whilst simultaneously summoning the waiter.

'You are confused, I know no one by that name.'

'You do, you were knocking on her door for a good few minutes just before. I was watching you. Now, what's a man to eat here?'

Grey allowed himself to answer, his curiosity piqued by this stranger, from the colonies judging by the accent.

'They recommend the Welsh rarebit as the best dish here, despite being made with ale, or the steak and kidney pie is exceptional — my personal favourite.'

'Can't recall any Welshmen I actually liked, so I'll have the pie, with a strong ale,' ordered Sinclair from the plump waiter.

'*Mrs* Bell, you say? I heard she wasn't married. She goes by the name of Sarah Lester. How do you know differently?' Grey queried.

'Told us the Māori had slaughtered her husband, but I never believed her. The others did, but I thought something wasn't true. Guess I was right. 'Cause here we are, and she's got my silver candlesticks, and something of yours too...'

Sinclair laid his cards on the table.

'Undoubtedly a lie cast to acquire stock at a discounted price, reprehensible behaviour. Candlesticks, you say?' mused Grey. 'You mean to say that the de Lamerie candelabra are yours?' Grey asked, his face a mask of incredulity that this uncouth individual could claim ownership to those exquisite pieces of silver. Hannah, his mole at Christie's, had forwarded him the email Sarah had sent Christie's with the photos of the candelabra attached. Grey had paid no attention knowing his family had owned no such items by the London silversmith, but now he was interested.

'Well, I've no idea if they were by Lamery...' started Sinclair.

'*de Lamerie,*' Grey corrected. His obsessive need to be right, or to berate others, more of his 'celebrated' foibles.

Sinclair cleared his throat. His arrogance was on a par with that of Grey's, and being corrected did not sit well with him, but given his current predicament, he let it slide.

'Yeah, him. But it's the truth that Mrs Bell, or your Miss Lester, stole them from me, and I want them back. I think we can help each other.'

'I'm listening, Mr...?'

'Ah, Sinclair, Bryce Sinclair. I'm not from around here. Well, I was, till I shipped out to Australia, then I moved to New Zealand, but now I'm back. I haven't caught up with any of my, ah, former acquaintances, and I've yet to find a place of abode, so I thought you might help a fellow in need, especially when we have a common acquaintance? Joining together could be mutually beneficial.' Sinclair finished with a flourish, draining the pint placed in front of him by the waiter.

Grey tried ignoring the film of beer foam on Sinclair's unshaven face, as he took another sip of his own drink, savouring the age of the liquid tumbling over his tongue.

'I have an apartment you may use, and friends who have so far failed to retrieve my property from Miss Lester's shop. I shall put them in touch with you and leave it to them to assist you further. What is your mobile number?'

Grey pulled his phone out of his blazer pocket.

'Don't got me one of them yet,' Sinclair bluffed, with no notion of what a *mobile* was or what it did.

'Right, well, my associates will contact you at the apartment. Don't venture too far away until they make contact.'

Feeling queasy at the sight of his table companion attacking his pie, Grey stood to take his leave.

Sinclair looked up, a mouthful of flaky pastry and thick lumps of rump steak visible as he called out to Grey.

'I never got your name, mister?'

'And you are unlikely to,' Grey replied, throwing a handful of pounds onto the table top, together with a crisp square card with an address printed in bold type.

'This should cover your meal. It's been an experience making your acquaintance.'

He inclined his head towards Sinclair and slid out of the tavern.

Sinclair shrugged, and grabbed Grey's glass, draining the dregs. He patted his pocket where the cash from Sarah's register was hiding, before ordering another pint from the waiter.

THE ESTATE

*T*he original floral carpet, threadbare in places and of indeterminate age, was what Sarah saw when she woke up, lying with the floor at eye level; decades of accumulated dust under the counter, one stray clip-on earring gazing at her from its dusty crypt. She gulped back the pain in her ankle as she used it to leverage herself up. Looking down at her hand still clasping the brass frame, she cried out.

'No, no, no!'

With her heart suffering more than all her other pains combined, she leant into the counter, sobbing. She'd left her father behind. This was worse than him disappearing the first time. This time it was *her* fault.

A hammering at the door brought her heart to her mouth. Sarah swivelled to look through the window and recognised the lofty shadow of Richard Grey. She shrank back into the clammy glass counter, grateful that the back of the door heaved under an assortment of haphazardly hung army coats and airline bags, blocking the view of anyone outside, and ensuring no one could see her unlocking and opening the grand old safe next to the counter.

Sarah scuttled behind the counter, putting it between her and any line of sight the front window might give. She couldn't believe she was hiding in her own shop. She was a strong woman, unafraid of spiders or tigers, or madmen and monsters. *What on earth am I doing hiding?* The hammering continued, making the chinaware dance on the shelves. Dust leapt from porcelain vases, motes flinging themselves into the still air.

The sound of raised voices followed, the words indistinct. The knocking ceased and the voices and shadows receded from the brick building.

Her heart thumping, she clutched the frame to her chest in the faint hope that it would send her back to India, to her father. Sarah slapped her head as she realised that ironically that the frame was worth nothing. She should never have touched it, she knew that. He'd warned her what could happen. *Why didn't I get someone else to grab the stupid frame?*

Sarah staggered over to the stack of crates from the Elizabeth Williams estate. She could ignore the aching loss of Warden Price, given that she scarcely knew him, and she could put to one side the slight pang that she'd never get to know Lord Edward Grey. And in the cold light of reality, she knew her interlude with the Raja was a moment of madness brought on by the exotic headiness of India. But her father. Her heart broke over again and she yanked items from the top crate, searching for anything to send her back.

The matching brass frame, the one with the picture of the two servicemen, slipped from the top of the box, landing on top of a carton of linen, slipping out of sight. Oblivious, Sarah continued her frenetic search. Her hand fell upon an old cigar box. It rattled, so sitting back on her heels, wincing in the pain because of her ankle, she opened the lid.

'Curse it! Damn it, damn it, damn it!'

She flung the box, filled with medals and uniform hat badges, to the ground.

On an ordinary day, the militaria would have made her day. Medals were collectable, one of her best sellers. She never cleaned them like other dealers. Her father had drummed it into her that collectors preferred to buy medals, badges, and coins in their original condition. She had a velvet tray full of medals in the jewellery cabinet; a sad reflection on the descendants of the recipients. An eclectic mix of World War I and II medals, a couple from the Vietnam War, and a handful of assorted Eastern European and Russian ones. Those weren't so sought after, because the USSR gave them out like candy through both World Wars, and the Cold War.

If Sarah had taken a better look through the items in the box, she might have seen that they had once belonged to a pilot serving with No 92 (East India) Squadron during the Battle of Britain. The cobra, placed in the crest's middle of the lapel pin, was there to remind the pilots that the people of India funded their Spitfires; that 92 Squadron was a 'Gift' Squadron.

The piles around Sarah grew as she pulled out handfuls of items without a second glance, just touching each was enough. An old canteen, an officer's tiny compass in a brown leather case, a dog-eared War Office-issued copy of an Italian phrase book dated September 16th 1943, a pay book, and, in a small cardboard box, a set of foxed cardboard dog tags, with the name 'WILLIAMS, P. J.' stamped into them, and a service number.

The carton teetered on the edge of the pile before tipping off and falling open. The tags lay on the floor, leaving the distinctive blue and white diagonal stripes of the Distinguished Flying Cross ribbon just visible at the bottom.

Frustrated, Sarah stood up and kicked the empty box, sending it crashing into a precarious pile of meat platters underneath the table. The resounding sound of chinaware smashing as the stack toppled over, was loud enough to wake the dead.

THE FRIENDS

'What was that?'

Andrew leapt off his chair. Patricia was already ahead of him, scooping up her keys as she ran from the room.

'Wait for me!'

By the time Andrew made it to Patricia's side, she was fumbling with the keys, trying to get the right one into the lock. It finally slipped in, and they tumbled into the shop, stopping at the sight on the floor.

'Sarah?'

Broken crockery crunched as Patricia made her way to Sarah and crouched down.

'Are you OK?'

'I want my dad, but I can't find him.'

Her eyes swollen with tears, she didn't look up at her friend.

Patricia signalled Andrew to shut the door, and to come help her with Sarah. Together, they pulled her up and escorted her to the stairwell. At the first step, she sunk to her knees.

'I can't make it upstairs, sorry. I've buggered my ankle.'

'Just as well we are here to help. Come on, you silly goose, let's go.'

Patricia heaved Sarah up under the arm, and with Andrew awkwardly assisting on the opposite side, they manoeuvred themselves up the stairs like competitors in a three-legged race.

'I'll make a pot of tea,' Andrew announced, disappearing off to the kitchenette.

Patricia sat next to her friend, concern written all over her face. 'Where have you been? Didn't you hear that lunatic knocking on your door? How on earth did you get that bruise?'

Her finger traced the fading purple hue on Sarah's temple.

'You didn't have it yesterday. And I don't want it to seem like I'm only ever interested in what you're wearing, especially when you're hurt, but... well, you know me! So, tell me, what *are* you wearing?'

Sarah tried answering as Andrew emerged, awkwardly attempting to carry three mugs.

'Where shall I put these?'

Sarah pushed a pile of *Antique Collecting* magazines off the coffee table.

'Here, just put them straight down. Thank you, er...'

She looked at Patricia, confusion on her face.

'Oh yes you two haven't met. This is your auction man, Andrew, from Christie's.'

'Oh my God, I'm so sorry, I completely forgot about you. You're here to pick up the sampler.'

He nodded.

'I've had a hard time in recent days and haven't been thinking straight. Is it OK if we leave it a few days? I can drive it to Christie's, but now's not a good time...'

Andrew paled when Sarah suggested leaving the handover for "a few days", the words of Don Claire threatening his employment echoing loudly in his head.

'She's right, Andrew. Thanks for helping get her upstairs, and for your company this morning, but business is the last thing on her mind. I can show you out downstairs if you like?'

He drained his tea, trying not to gag. Tea wasn't his favourite drink, which always made him think he wasn't a proper Englishman.

But his mother had raised him to recognise that when a lady said no, she meant no. He stood.

'Yes, yes of course, sorry to have disturbed you, Miss Lester, I tried ringing your mobile, but it went to your answerphone, so I assumed that turning up was okay. I'm terribly sorry. I'll... er... I'll be off.'

Shoulders slumped, he walked to the staircase.

Patricia followed behind, trying to think of something to say to the only man she'd met who knew the difference between tulle and lace. Despite the curious behaviour of her friend, she wasn't going to let *this* fish back into the ocean.

'Um, thanks for your help back there. I've got no idea what's up with Sarah, but I can assure you she's normally much more... well, more *normal* than this. If you can give me your, ah...'

She blushed.

'... ah, your number, and I can ring tomorrow after Sarah has sorted herself out, and perhaps then we can have a coffee or a wine, and have a more sensible conversation about the stuff she's trying to sell you?'

As oblivious as most men, Andrew failed to notice Patricia's pretty blush, but the invitation for a drink he seized upon.

'Yes, a drink tomorrow would be perfect. To be honest, my boss is very keen for me to get Miss Lester's things back to the office, so I'd been hoping to pick them up today, but...'

Then he stammered out the next sentence, without taking a breath, afraid he'd lose his nerve.

'... but having a drink with you would be far more interesting than an old knife, and hopefully Sarah will have the sampler too. I'd love your opinion on that, and... well, I hope that... that we can spend more time together, when Miss Lester has recovered.'

Inside, Patricia was pumping her fist, but her calm exterior belied her excitement, and opening the door to the shop, she replied. 'Perfect, I'll ring you tomorrow and, once again, thanks. Cleaning up this mess is next on my list after I find out from Sarah precisely what the matter is. Thanks.'

She closed the door behind him, shot home the dead bolt, and turned back to the cluttered shop, grimacing at the pile of ruined platters, pieces of their decorated borders a kaleidoscope of colour on the worn carpet. Electing to ignore it, she skirted past it and loped upstairs, pausing on the landing to recover her breath. *I've got to exercise more, if I can't even run up a staircase* she mused, before entering the lounge.

'You have to re-paper this room; mismatched wallpaper is so 1970s!'

Patricia laughed, attempting to break the undercurrent of sadness, and plonked herself on the couch next to Sarah.

Sarah surveyed the walls — there had to be at least five different wallpapers gracing them. She'd always found it quirky, especially after her father had explained that her eccentric grandmother had decorated the room as part of a wedding present to her parents. Sarah's mother had, understandably, never appreciated the peculiar gift.

'I've never thought about it. I suppose I should soon,' Sarah said, spying curling edges under the old plaster cornices.

'What did you think of Andrew?' Patricia threw out.

Sarah's mind was still processing the interior décor of her home.

'Huh?'

'Andrew, the auction guy from Christie's. He had a degree in textiles — who even knew there was such a degree?'

Panicking, Sarah jerked up.

'From Christie's? Why didn't you tell me? He must have been here to pick up my stuff.'

'I told you, like, seriously, only two minutes ago. You said you'd deliver the stuff up to him in a few days. I've got his number if you want to ring him? Where's your phone?'

'Downstairs?'

Patricia ran downstairs again and, spying Sarah's phone on the counter, grabbed it and ran back up, panting at the top. *This exercise thing must be a priority next year.* She plugged it into the charger on the overflowing bookcase. After a few moments, the phone chirped with increasing frequency as the messages made their way into the in-box.

'His number is probably on one of those messages,' Patricia threw over her shoulder as she carried her tea into the kitchen, tipping it into the stainless steel sink.

In the lounge, she found Sarah cross-legged in front of the bookcase, a large atlas open on her lap.

'Ah, it's not that hard to find your way to Christie's that you'll need an atlas!' she laughed.

Sarah smiled up at her.

'This is what I wanted to show him; for him to auction for me.'

Her hands smoothed the edges of the sampler, nestled within the pages of the book.

Patricia bent to see.

'It's beautiful! Look at those stitches, I've never seen such tiny needlework before. Can I hold it?'

Sarah laid the sampler across Patricia's outstretched hands.

'How much is it worth?' Patricia asked, peering at the reverse side, as if trying to absorb the skill of the artist.

'I'm not sure. It's not something I've ever dealt in before. One of my customers, Vicky, may know, but last time I spoke with her she was leaving for a buying trip, to Melbourne of all places, so she won't be in for ages. She's the closest thing to an expert on old fabrics in the business. That's why I just went with an auction house.'

'I love it. Wish I could afford it but, given he drove all the way here for this, I guess I won't be bidding on it!'

'He's not just here for the sampler, Trish. I've found other things...'

Sarah chewed her lower lip.

'I'll show you, but tell no one else, until after I've handed them over to him because I can't exactly explain their provenance.'

Sarah tucked the sampler back into the atlas and put it away on one of the lower shelves. She limped into the kitchen and opened the freezer. Patricia, who'd followed her, stood frowning in the doorway.

'He's also here for this.'

She peeled the lid from the Tupperware container, the light from the bare bulb dancing off the jewels in the *katar*'s hilt.

'Oh, Sarah, it's magnificent. Reminds me of an ancient torture device, but it is stunning. What is it?'

'It's an Indian *katar*, or a tiger knife. It used to be part of a matching pair, but someone separated them a long time ago.'

'So this is the knife Andrew mentioned. Could you try tracking down the other one? Surely auctioning off a pair is better than selling one on its own?'

'I guess Christie's could try.'

Sarah replaced the lid, sliding it back between the pre-packaged chicken Kiev and the cheap frozen peas.

The girls retired to the couch where Sarah continued.

'And downstairs, I've got a pair of rare sterling silver candelabra, from New Zealand, valued at somewhere around the... oh, guessing somewhere in the vicinity of fourteen thousand pounds, give or take.'

Sarah shrugged at her friend's shocked expression.

'He didn't just drive here for the schoolgirl sampler.'

'Did they come from that big lot you bought up Salisbury way? The place where the clothes came from?'

'I'm losing my mind, Trish. Even if I told you where I'd found the stuff, you'd have me committed to the nearest psychiatric ward without blinking.'

'Try me,' Patricia demanded.

'India, and New Zealand, and the house of a Lord — an *actual* Lord, not some knighted celebrity. Yep, that covers it,' Sarah said, avoiding Patricia's gaze.

'Ri-ight.' Patricia drew out the vowel and enunciated every consonant. 'Given the whole thing about your parents going missing, perhaps now is the right time for some counselling—'

Sarah stuttered.

'No, no don't interrupt me. You've never spoken to anyone about your parents leaving you. So yes, you need counselling,' Patricia concluded.

'I've just *seen* my dad, Trish. He wanted me to come back here. But

Jesus! I should have stayed in India with him. And now I can't get back.'

Sarah lurched off the couch over to the window, twitching at the curtains like an actor in *Coronation Street*. With nothing but an empty street to stare at, she turned back to her friend, who'd been gazing at her back in consternation.

'Shouldn't you tell the police your dad is alive?' Patricia started, processing Sarah's words.

'What, that Dad's alive in India, right in the middle of the Indian Mutiny? Um, no.'

'You're not making any sense, Sarah. We ate a fine Indian curry last night, that's true, but not in India. Either you know *exactly* where your dad is, and you've been lying all these years, or you're making things up. So, what is it?'

Patricia couldn't disguise the hurt she felt that her friend had lied to her.

Sarah flung her arms around Patricia.

'I know it doesn't make any sense, but just know I'd never lie to you. It's impossible to believe, but please listen and I'll try to explain it as best as I can. Will you do that for me?'

Patricia nodded.

Sarah leaned back on the couch, staring at the ceiling as she tried to explain the bizarre experiences of travelling through time and finding her father in India. The way she'd taken the *katar* from Lord Grey. Benjamin Grey, Warden Price, the Raja. She omitted the glorious afternoon she'd spent with the prince; that was for her memory alone. Finally spent, she checked Patricia's reaction.

'Well?'

'That's one way to put it!' Patricia declared. 'Best we go downstairs and try to get you back to India.'

'You believe me?' shrieked Sarah, grabbing her friend by the arms.

Laughing, Patricia extricated herself from her exuberant grasp.

'What else could I do? Drive you to the loony bin? Then I'd be doing myself out of a muse. I've already designed most of my new collection based on the various outfits I keep finding you in — even this magnificent thing you're wearing now!

'Yes, I believe you. I don't know why, apart from what on earth do you have to gain from lying? You could have just sent everything off to auction and banked the proceeds and I'd be none the wiser. Or you could have stayed away and become another Missing Persons file featuring *The Old Curiosity Shop* — the police would *love* that.

'It must be the most wonderful feeling in the world knowing your mum and dad never left you intentionally. And if you end up profiting from it that's the icing on the cake! Come on, let's go downstairs and clean up the mess, and find your ticket back to India.'

THE INVALID

he commotion caused by Simeon's brutal murder would linger in the colony for weeks and months to come.

Captain Doulton pulled Sarah away from Simeon's mutilated body. She had paled more than he thought possible and stumbled into his arms. She looked up at him blankly. *Shock,* he guessed. He'd seen it affect his men in battle and in the hospital afterwards. Most recovered, a few didn't. The vacant look in their eyes haunting those around them. He drew her from the room.

He didn't notice the brass picture frame she'd stooped to grab was gone. It wasn't his nature to recognise such mundane nuances in his life and, with the only other person in the room eviscerated, there were no other witnesses to the photograph existing of Simeon's wife.

Doulton's men had each made the journey to view the body after their commander had escorted the women outside into the humid air. One soldier emptied the contents of his stomach on the lawn, mirroring Nirmala. And none of the others joked at his weakness. The captain, realising he couldn't care for Miss Williams any further here, ordered his men to transport her back to the Lodge, as she was in no fit state to travel under her own steam, and he was sure that there would be ladies aplenty there to tend to her. That was also where the good whiskey was, and he needed one tonight.

Doulton dispatched a soldier to tell the Viceroy of the murder, and he couldn't have left the scene any faster, urging his horse away with a swift jab to the beast's ribs with his solid boots.

Nirmala and Kalakanya huddled with their mistress on a wooden love-seat in the garden. The fragrant jasmine covering the archway above wrapped its cloying sweet scent around them. In years to come, none of the girls could ever stomach the floral bouquet of jasmine in any form.

A small contingent of weary soldiers appeared at the house, with an ornate palanquin following behind. Despite the heat, the three girls pulled the cotton throw up over their legs, the plush transport requisitioned by Naomi Abbott to pick up her friend.

Sarah had yet to utter any words. The maids exchanged worried glances across the bowed head of their memsahib.

'Memsahib Abbott will know what to do,' whispered Nirmala.

Kalakanya nodded.

Upon their arrival at the Lodge, Mrs Abbott did indeed know what to do, and abandoning the injured men she'd been comforting, she was the first outside as they lowered the palanquin in the grandiose entrance. She pushed past the Indian doorman staring open-mouthed at the sight of Nirmala and Kalakanya travelling in such a style.

'Get out of the way, you foolish man!' shrilled Naomi. 'Come now, girls, help Miss Williams inside, you take an arm and I shall hold the other. That's right, come now, Sarah, one foot in front of the other. Left foot, right foot, let's get you indoors.'

She waved at a hovering servant.

'You there, we need fresh tea for everyone, and a small sherry, too, I think. Stop dawdling, see to it. We shall be in the parlour.'

Waving her free hand at a random soldier viewing the proceedings, she instructed him to light a fire, and such was her presence, he rushed to obey, completely forgetting the errand his own superior officer had given him.

With a steaming tea and a snifter of sherry in front of her, Mrs Abbott cajoled Sarah into taking alternating sips of both beverages.

'Now, my dear, tell me everything. It's better to talk about these things than to bottle them up. Women need to share; it makes us stronger than the men, I've always thought.'

Sarah looked at her, the steam from the cup of tea rising in the still air.

'Please, where I am? I'm afraid I remember nothing since being awfully sick on the boat.'

Sarah Williams was a shadow of her former self. Withdrawn and uncommunicative, she showed no interest in talking with Naomi, or receiving any other visitors.

Nirmala and Kalakanya were beside themselves with worry. They'd tidied up the house as best as they could after the army had removed the body of Simeon. The girls had closed the door of his room, too scared of his damaged soul to enter.

The Raja had sent gift after gift, which piled up unopened in Sarah's room.

'Shock,' diagnosed Captain Doulton again in a heated discussion with Naomi and Major Brooke during one of the many held at the Lodge during the investigation into the murder of Simeon Williams, and the state of his sister.

'It has been a month now. The best thing is to send her back to London where she will receive much better care than she can in India,' Naomi Abbott agreed.

Albert Lester refilled his pipe, the ritual of tampering down the fragrant tobacco hiding his shaking hands.

When he'd first arrived, he'd slipped seamlessly into the East India Company, using his historical knowledge and a keen mind. Living the dream; living and breathing the antiques he'd loved his whole life. Every day he tripped across another treasure: an ivory statue; a bronze Hindu *Gajalakshmi* Altar-Piece Lamp. And only yesterday, he'd seen a watercolour of Maharao Ram Singh II of Kota. Everything was exquisite and pristine.

But his priority at present was young Sarah Williams. Not the daughter he'd spent a precious few hours with during the revolt, but the *real* Sarah Williams, a young woman only just holding it together. And *he* felt responsible.

'She should go back to England, but she needs someone with her she knows. Surely she came out to India with a chaperone?' he proffered.

Naomi stared at him.

'How on earth am *I* supposed to know? That brother of hers kept her locked up in that house, and if it wasn't for Major Dickens, she'd have had no social life. You must know, Major Brooke? You were on the boat with her?'

The Major weighed his words. The Sarah Williams he'd known had disappeared into a hermit shell, and he agreed that she should return to England, to a doctor who understood conditions such as hers, but privately, he wanted her to stay in Simla, sure that she would no doubt recover in time. His heart conversed with his mind, and they could not agree.

Finally he answered. 'She had a chaperone, Miss Elaine Barker, but she was grievously injured, and she remained in Delhi, recuperating.'

Albert removed his pipe from the safety of his mouth.

'Mrs Abbott, can you write to Miss Barker, detailing Miss Williams' condition, and advising that the Viceroy is more than prepared to arrange their passage back together. And given the service Miss Williams has done on behalf of the Empire, we will cover all costs, including a nurse if required. Will you ask?'

Major Doulton, who was there for no reason other than he was the one who had witnessed Miss Williams' descent into shock, commented that this was reasonable, and for the best. Major Brooke nodded his agreement.

It was such a sensible arrangement that Naomi had nothing left to contribute, other than offering to arrange the packing of Simeon's things — correction, Sarah's things — for shipping back to the family home in England.

The little group broke up, with Albert walking Naomi through the panelled lobby.

'What of the Raja, Mrs Abbott? I hear he is still sending gifts to Miss Williams.'

'She saved his life, Mr Lester.'

'Is it not more than that?' he probed.

'Mr Lester, I shall pretend that we never had this conversation. She had afternoon tea there that is all. Now if you could excuse me, I have your letters to write, and a young girl to send to London. I disagree with you, she should stay here, but what would I know? I am just a woman,' and she slid into the waiting palanquin.

Leaving Albert Lester to stare at its retreating rear.

Naomi wasted no time in writing to Elaine Barker. And, in what amounted to good time for India, the letter arrived at the Missionary School where she was convalescing with Alice Montgomery. Elaine had *no* intention of returning to England, regardless of who was paying her way. Her injuries had left her with a limp but no other permanent disability, and the school was fulfilling every need she'd ever had. To be useful, wanted, and valued. Such was her nature, though, that she wrote back suggesting that Sarah joined her in Delhi to recuperate away from any reminder of Simeon, and the troubles.

With very little ceremony, they loaded Sarah Williams into a carriage outside of her Indian home, with Nirmala, who was to go with her as far as Delhi. Naomi hugged and kissed the unresponsive girl, smoothing her hair under her bonnet.

'Don't you worry about anything. I shall have your belongings sent to England while you concentrate on getting well. After a time, it will seem like a dream, an adventure.'

'Thank you for everything. I'm so sorry if I've been such a bore. I just can't remember anything, and I have been feeling so unwell. Seeing Elaine again will be a relief,' Sarah mumbled.

'It's the shock, Sarah, it does funny things to people. Major Doulton assures me it will pass. He has seen it in soldiers, and he promises one morning you'll wake up and it will all be a horrible dream,' Naomi paraphrased.

'Does shock make you sick every morning?' Sarah queried, her face pale in the light.

'I... it might,' Naomi said, her mind racing to do the uncomplicated mental calculations, before smiling at Sarah, giving her a final kiss on the cheek.

'Good luck, sweet child. Please write, but I will understand if you don't.'

THE BABY

*N*aomi Abbot's calculations were correct; Sarah Williams was in the family way, but couldn't recall anything of the act that put her there.

Days after her arrival at the Anglican Mission School for the Society of the Propagation of the Gospel in Delhi, run by Alice Montgomery and assisted by Elaine, Sarah was so visibly unwell that the women immediately guessed her complaint.

Patient questioning led them no closer to the truth as to the identity of the father, so they assumed that it must be Sarah's deceased brother, and it was this abhorrent act which had destroyed her mind, and not the viewing of her brother's butchered body.

Between the three women, alone in the teeming city they devised a plan to preserve Sarah's name, and to ensure that a good family would raise a baby conceived in sin.

'No one will know it's your child, Sarah. They will believe it is Simeon's baby. Trust me. People will believe what we present them. If they have no other evidence for a different story, they will accept yours,' instructed Elaine.

Alice, raised only to speak only God's truth, was the least enthusiastic of the trio.

'You must not correspond with anyone from your time in Simla. The less you weave a web of lies, the less you will become entangled in it. The baby needs a good home and in England, with you, it will have that. It is the only way, without you being ruined.'

Sarah, still in a state of fugue, agreed to the plan. She was now the sole beneficiary of her parents' estate, and the Viceroy's solicitor had written to her in Delhi finalising Simeon's holdings, which were extensive. She was a wealthy woman. If she could live the lie she was telling the world, she would survive.

She remained at the Mission until the safe birth of her baby; a boy, Robert. So mild in colour, no one could say for sure whether the child's father was English or Indian. It never crossed the mind of Alice and Elaine that the father was anyone other than Simeon Williams. They had dispatched Nirmala back to Simla after delivering her mistress to Delhi. There was nobody else who knew Sarah or her background in Delhi. The women kept to themselves, concentrating only on teaching the boys of high level merchants sent to them for an education, boys who had no interest in the private lives of the Englishwomen who taught them.

Letters from Naomi Abbott went unanswered as did the few pieces of correspondence from Major Brooke. By the time Sarah left for England, it was as if she'd never existed in India at all.

And so it was that Sarah landed in England, a babe in her arms. The passenger manifest declared him to be Robert Williams — Simeon's son, Sarah's nephew, and ward. They baptised the child as Simeon's, and no one questioned her. His brutal murder had made the papers in England months after the fact, so time further muddied the waters.

Sarah's hacking cough was more of a concern to those around her than the baby she was raising. She died of consumption, several months after arriving back in England, her lie lost to history.

Her nearest relative, a cousin, Jonas Williams, adopted Robert Williams and, on his behalf, took possession of the belongings Naomi Abbott had packed up from Firgrove House, including all Simeon's stolen treasures, and the gifts from the Raja of Nahan. And it was thus that young Robert Williams started life with enough money to support his future endeavours.

THE OFFICIALS

'*G*em, have you seen this?' Ryan called out to his partner as he perused the latest media release by Christie's Auction House.

Though sparsely worded, it conveyed enough about the upcoming Indian Art auction to pluck at Ryan's photographic memory of missing art works on the internationally renowned Art Loss Register.

Although originally trained as a chef, Ryan Francis developed an appreciation for all things artistic after several years traversing the world on high-end cruise ships. He'd found it amazing the things people talked about within earshot of the invisible staff on board the mammoth cruise ships on which he'd served. Most serious collectors, those who operated both within and outside of the law, couldn't help bragging of their latest acquisitions to those in their circle of trust. And often those people travelled together.

He'd discovered early on that organisations paid for information that led to the recovery of stolen artworks, and found he could supplement his income by feeding snippets of intelligence to organisations such as Interpol, and to the better-funded Art Loss Register. He'd been too successful, and it wasn't long before the company let him go for breaching the privacy of their well-heeled customers, regardless of the fact that those clients had broken laws in several countries. That was immaterial to the profit-hungry and competitive cruise ship operators.

From his desk in an open plan office in Hatton Cross, he read media releases by galleries and auction houses from around the globe, even as far afield as New Zealand and the tiny Pacific nation of Fiji, for any evidence of stolen art emerging onto the market. But it was the latest Christie's release that caught his eye.

The diminutive Gemma Dance walked over to see what had excited her colleague. Puzzled, she read the announcement, noting nothing of interest.

'There's nothing there, Ryan. What's caught your eye?'

With fever in his eyes he replied, 'The *katar* they mention, don't you remember the meeting we had a few months ago with Mr Grey, where he mentioned that his family were missing one half of a pair of rare tiger knives, and that the family suspected a staff member had taken it?'

Racking her brain, Gemma had no memory of that conversation with the peculiar Richard Grey. He'd always made her feel uncomfortable, and it was a relief when Ryan joined the Register, and she could foist on him the huge file containing the relevant information about items Grey *claimed* were stolen from his family over the years. She believed Grey was a nutcase with a grandiose opinion of himself, but he was one of the firm's largest clients, and paid well for any piece they tracked down on his behalf.

Gemma shrugged and walked back to her desk to continue with her own investigative work, calling out to him as she sat down.

'Ask them to send you a photo. They'll love that!' she sniggered.

An enquiry from the Art Loss Register had the ability to reduce even the mightiest auctioneers to quivering wrecks, fearful they may be auctioning stolen artworks, losing both the article *and* the profit. A constant stream of plundered art and antiquities kept the auction world afloat, and most flew under the radar.

It's said that most antiques have been stolen at some point in their life. And it was the job of Ryan and Gemma, and their colleagues, to reunite stolen *objets d'art* with their grateful owners.

THE LETTER

*P*atricia helped clean up the chaos in the shop, plucking shards of pottery from the floor and wrapping them in newsprint before filling an entire rubbish bag with the remnants of the platters.

Sarah sat back, calculating the value of the stock she'd broken in her frustration. The damage wasn't as horrendous as the time she took out a whole shelf of Royal Albert trios when she was younger, giving her doll a shoulder ride in the shop... her father had been less than impressed at *that* little stunt. But this was the worst breakage she'd had to clean up, although meat platters were not one of the fastest selling items, apart from during the Christmas season.

'Thanks, Trish, you're a lifesaver. Now the shop looks semi-normal again, I might ring the auction guy and get him to pick everything up. What do you think?'

'Excellent idea, but can you give it half an hour? I need to tidy myself up!' Patricia giggled.

Sarah examined her own grimy hands.

'I think I'll need more than thirty minutes to scrub this dirt out of my skin. Let's meet back in an hour?'

The girls embraced, and Sarah watched Patricia practically skip next door to her shop.

'Can you put that outfit aside for me? Don't wash it, I don't trust your laundry skills! And don't go anywhere until I come back! In fact touch nothing!' Patricia shouted.

Laughing, Sarah locked the door after her friend, shaking her head at the absurdity of everything. She made for a peculiar sight, a modern woman dressed as a Victorian lady, covered in dust, heaving a rubbish sack out to the back door. She left it in a forlorn lump, too tired to bother unlocking the bolts and taking it outside to the bin.

'Bloody customers will just have to move around it,' she muttered, limping upstairs, finally ready to wash India from her skin, her hair, and her memories.

It was a good hour before she emerged from the steamy bathroom. A shower, followed by a long restorative bath, had cleaned her both in a physical sense and emotionally. Wrapped in a towel, she scoured her room for something to wear.

Everywhere she looked, there were clumps of historical clothes — a microcosm of the V&A Museum. She scooped up skirts, shirts, and undergarments, folding them into a pile on her bed. Each garment brought back glimpses of memory; a glance from Price, a laugh of Naomi's, the smell of floor polish.

Sarah grabbed the skirt she'd last worn in New Zealand but a rustle stopped her mid-fold. She slipped her hand into the pocket, closing it around a rough rock and a folded piece of paper, and her mind shot back to Bruce Bay, fear twisting in her gut as she recalled the death of Isaac in the miner's camp. This was his note to his mother.

With shaking hands, she dropped the skirt back onto the floor and smoothed open the paper. The spidery words danced before her eyes which filled with tears.

Dear Mam,

I hope this letter finds you and the boys well? I had some luck on the gold fields, which I've enclosed.

Take it into town to get it weighed. I know you will put to good use the money you get.

Tell the boys not to come, but to stay there and look after you.

I'm not sure young Colin could survive here. I was lucky to find gold, but so many of the lads here have nothing, and will die with nothing.

Give my love to the others.

Love Isaac

The sentiment pulled at her heart. He'd written this knowing he might never see his family again.

She flipped it over. In the same cursive handwriting was an address in Wales: Mrs Annwr Lloyd, c/o The Sailors Return, Commercial Street, Newport.

She'd promised a dying man she'd get this nugget to his mother. She rolled the rock in her palm. In today's market a nugget this size might raise about four thousand pounds, based on the current gold price, depending on its purity. With the nugget in her hand, she lowered herself onto her bed. She'd never held a gold nugget before, only gold flakes, the sort you get in little glass vials from souvenir gold panning places like Ballarat in Australia, but this was her first nugget.

Sarah laid the letter on her bedside table, placing the nugget in the centre of the paper. She tried ignoring the letter and its contents as she dressed. Her little apartment wasn't usually cold, but she felt chilled to the bone, so added a Merino sweater to her jeans and T-shirt ensemble. She finished picking up the historic clothes from around the room, piling them on the bed for Patricia to grab later. Ignoring her overflowing laundry basket, she unplugged her mobile phone, scrolling through the missed calls to find a number for Andrew Harvard.

Downstairs, she stared in dismay at the shambles she had to face. She and Patricia had cleaned up the broken stuff, but the contents of the Williams Estate were still spread from one end of the shop to the other, mixed haphazardly with old stock, boxes of damaged bric-à-brac waiting for a date with the auction house, and other stock she'd yet to catalogue and price.

She eased past the remains of Elizabeth Williams' life, sank onto the stool, and called Andrew Harvard at Christie's. The phone had barely connected before there was a reply.

'Hello, Mr Harvard, Sarah Lester here... yes, sorry about earlier, you caught me at a bad time... no, I'm quite recovered now, I think. It's amazing what hot water can do... thank you, yes. But the reason I'm ringing is to say that I'd very much appreciate it if you could pop back in this afternoon to pick up those things I emailed you... no, not any earlier. If we could just leave it till then, that would suit me better, I've got so much to sort here as you're no doubt aware... I understand, but until you pick them up, they are still mine... right, I'll see you later. Thank you.'

Ending the call, she ticked another thing off her list. The nugget and the letter kept forcing their way up that list and she pushed them to the bottom again. *Get out of my head*, she demanded.

Sarah opened the door to let in some fresh air and reorganised the mess on the floor. The best course of action would be to handle everything only once, which meant writing it up in the stock book, pricing it, and then finding a home for it on the cluttered shelves. Forgoing her usual practice of loading photos of new stock onto the Internet, she started, making a noticeable dent in the pile before her first customer came into the shop.

'Hi, can I help you?'

'Hello, yes, I'm looking for a set of hollow stem Waterford glasses. Do you have any?' asked a middle-aged woman, sporting a grey bun and a multitude of gold bangles.

Excellent, thought Sarah, *the perfect start to the day*.

'Yes, I do. I have a set of six here.'

She took the customer over to the wooden shelves, and passed her a one of the set, discreetly using her sleeve to remove the accumulated dust from the glass.

'They are exquisite, but I'm not sure that they are the right pattern. What are the names of the other designs?' she dithered. *Probably aghast at the price tag*, Sarah thought. New Waterford glasses were around a hundred pounds a pair, or more, depending on the design. She had this set priced at two hundred and twenty pounds for six, and the woman seemed hesitant to pay even that, masking it with indecision about the design.

'This pattern is *Lismore*, the others are *Irish Lace* and *Colleen...*'

The woman interrupted her. 'Yes, it's the *Colleen* I wanted. So sorry, do you have any of that pattern?' she asked, shifting from one foot to the other.

Sarah placed the glass back on the shelf.

'Sorry, I've got no *Colleen* pieces left. It's the most sought-after and the most expensive.'

Relieved, the woman replied, 'Well, thank you anyway, I'll pop in next time I'm passing.'

She left, disappearing down the street.

Sarah returned to her pricing, losing herself in the longhand stock records her father had devised, and which she'd continued. Enamel teapots, trinket boxes, and ornamental Indian brassware kept her occupied until Patricia turned up a little before two o'clock, bearing three takeaway cups of coffee in a handy cardboard tray.

'Am I early?' she rushed, placing the tray onto the counter, looking around for Harvard.

'He's not here yet, but thanks for the coffee. I can't tell you how much I needed this!'

She sipped her drink, raising her eyes to the heavens in silent gratitude for the life-giving properties of a great coffee.

THE HANDOVER

*H*arvard took another sip of the substandard coffee and read the newspaper someone had left in the magazine rack. There was nothing as pointless as reading old news to fill in your time. Buried halfway through the paper he found a small article about a Mughal era ruby necklace bequeathed to India's National Museum in New Delhi.

Then his mobile rang.

Afterwards, Harvard hung up, a grin splitting his face in half. Thank God she'd seen sense. He was still certain she wasn't a fraud, but he'd decided she was somewhat nuttier than your average fruitcake.

He finished the lukewarm drink he'd been nursing at the overpriced, over-decorated, 'tourist only' tea shop near Sarah's, and moving at a Usain Bolt'esque pace, he jogged back, dreams of job security and lucrative commissions filling his head.

As he entered, he caught the tail end of the girls' laughter, and the tiny sphere of concern inside him loosened its claws and dissipated in the dusty shop. Ignoring the customers fossicking through the souvenir teaspoons, he approached Sarah and Patricia with a goofy smile on his face, all pretence of a classy Christie's employee gone.

'Hello, ladies! Superb to be back here so soon. You'll never believe the dire cup of coffee they served me at that cafe,' he joked.

'Andrew! Hello!' gushed Patricia.

'Hi, look I'm sorry about before. It was completely out of character. I've...' began Sarah.

At this, she glanced at Patricia, who shook her head.

'I've been going through a few issues relating to my parents. They're both missing...'

Andrew tried interrupting.

'No, it's okay, they've been missing for years now, I'm used to it. But some things cropped up which threw me. So, thanks for being so good about it, and sorry for mucking you around this morning.'

Andrew avoided her direct gaze and offered up an olive branch. 'Looks like you got it cleaned up pretty well.'

'Doesn't take long when you put your mind to it. Do you want to come upstairs and I can give you the *katar* and the sampler?'

'And the Paul de Lamerie candelabra?'

'Oh, they're up there too.'

Leaving Patricia to manage the shop, he followed Sarah up the rickety stairs, where she pointed to a lumpy mound on the floor by a pile of battered banana boxes. Wide-eyed Andrew followed her casual gesture, and gaping like a koi carp, he had to bite back his astonishment at her disregard for one of the world's most famous silversmiths. His surprise was complete when she pulled the atlas from the bottom of the bookcase.

'Here's the sampler,' she announced, her back to him.

Looking around the room, unchanged from that morning, he couldn't see the sampler, and was just about to ask for clarification when Sarah stood with the sampler held in one hand.

'What are you doing?' he yelled, leaping towards her to rescue the colourful embroidery from her hands.

Holding it like a baby, he carried it over to the net-curtained window, cooing over it as you would a newborn.

'Look at the colours! And these stitches, so tiny. How did they get them so precise? What do you know about the girl embroidered did this? Anything?'

Harvard fired questions at her, one after the other, till Sarah's head was spinning.

'Um, Lord Grey used to own it, but before that I don't know, sorry. Do you want the *katar* as well?'

He paused mid-question.

'What? Oh, yes, yes, the *katar*.'

He lay the sampler on the stained wood of the coffee table. If every one of his brain cells wasn't telling him that this was a genuine antique sampler, his eyes would have suggested that it had been made a week earlier. The base fabric was in mint condition, except for four small nail holes, which had been visible in the photos he'd seen. The digital images didn't do justice to the vibrancy of the colours and the minute details on the border.

Reluctantly, he left the sampler, and followed Sarah into the kitchenette where she opened the freezer and pulled out the frosty container with the dagger clunking inside it. She thrust the plastic box into his hands.

'This came from Lord Grey's home too, but originally it belonged to the Raja of Nahan in India, according to the seller,' Sarah said, adding in the all-important provenance, although there was no one left alive who could query her ownership.

In a kitchenette, above a second-hand shop, holding a valuable artefact, was not something Andrew Harvard ever imagined himself doing. But this was his job, and if he wanted to keep it, he'd do whatever was necessary. He placed the container next to the sampler and peeled back the plastic lid. The *katar* was incomparable to anything he'd ever seen; exquisite.

He opened his briefcase and, with his Parker pen, a graduation gift from his mother, started filling in the auction agreement, listing the features of the *katar*, and then the embroidery. Sarah returned with the candelabra and placed them on the coffee table too. Harvard paused in his work. The sight of three very different, but valuable items, would have given any person reason to stop and stare, and he looked from the trio of treasures up to Sarah's face.

'Do you mind me asking where you got these from?'

Unsurprised at the question, Sarah let out the breath she'd been holding, and gave the answer she'd rehearsed in her head.

'I purchased a large deceased estate from up Salisbury way, and the sampler and the *katar* came from there. Believe it or not, I found the candelabra in the basement in a hessian sack. I know it sounds unbelievable, but my father was a complete hoarder, and I'm still going through the stuff he had in storage. I can't believe he didn't sell them straight away, but knowing him, he probably expected the silver market to rise and so put them away until then. But then he disappeared... so I'm just trying to make enough money to keep the business going until he comes back.'

She looked Harvard in the eye, challenging him to question her further.

He turned back to his paperwork, satisfied with the answer which was a lot more plausible than many of the provenances provided with items auctioned through Christie's during his time.

A short while later, Andrew made his way downstairs, the articles stored in a packing crate he'd brought with him. He presented the paperwork to Sarah, who was back behind her counter, talking with Patricia.

'You need to fill in the section where it says what you want the reserve set at and then sign it. Then we're done.'

'I've got no clue what the reserve should be. I'm normally just sending boxes of damaged Royal Albert teacups and dented silver plate off to auction. Can't you give me a suggestion?'

'Well, based on my experience, a sampler such as this deserves to have a reserve set at around the ten to twenty thousand pound mark.'

The room fell silent. Sarah and Patricia froze.

'Don't you mean two to three thousand?' Patricia corrected him.

Harvard raised an eyebrow.

'No, I'd recommend a reserve of ten thousand pounds, and I'd expect this piece to achieve closer to thirty. In fact, I wouldn't be surprised if it fetched more than that. You realise this is a significant piece of history?'

'Right, well, put that down. I'm not sure I can write any more, I've gone into shock. Next you'll be telling me that the candelabras are worth a hundred thousand!' Sarah laughed.

'I'm not the silver expert but, based on the research I did before coming here, and on advice from the Silver Department who saw your photographs, a *reserve* of a hundred thousand pounds is fair. Not long ago we sold a set of four Paul de Lamerie candlesticks for two hundred and eleven thousand. So I'd say your reserve is in the right ballpark. Shall I fill that in too?'

Sarah nodded. *So much for just a new van and shop counter,* she thought. At this rate she'd be able to afford a fleet of vans. She was almost too afraid to ask her next question.

'And the *katar*?'

'Ah, well, that requires more research, so I've filled that one in for you. See here it says, "Reserve to be confirmed with Vendor after examination by Christie's."'

With that, he proffered the agreement and his precious pen to Sarah, and waited for her signature.

Dazed, she signed on the dotted line. Harvard tore off the duplicate copy and handed it to Sarah.

'I would love to stay, but I need to get these back to the office so we can catalogue them for the next auction. Perhaps you could both come? I can send you an invitation to the preview night if you're interested?' he offered.

His question directed more towards Patricia than Sarah.

'Sure,' Sarah agreed, still in shock at the figures he'd quoted.

'Fabulous!' Patricia enthused.

Smiling as if he'd won the lottery, Andrew Harvard left *The Old Curiosity Shop,* and drove back to Christie's, where a great number of people awaited his return.

THE ROBBERY

*W*ith Andrew gone, Patricia declared she had to go to continue working on her collection. She gave her friend a huge hug.

'I believe you, you know, but for now you're stuck here with me. You're going to become a very rich woman, so try to stick around, okay? Besides, nowhere else you've been has had showers!'

That was true.

After a quick kiss on the head, Patricia disappeared back to work and Sarah ambled around the aisles of the shop, straightening stacks of ashtrays, rescuing precariously perched ornaments, and marrying Edwardian vases with their mates. It still astounded her that her customers had an innate inability to return anything to the same shelf they picked it from.

With some housekeeping achieved, she returned to price up the new stock. Customers dribbled in and out: some filling in time, others for a trip down memory lane; a pair of photography students keen to photograph her astounding collection of stock, and lastly a young girl carried a gigantic bottle of Arpège perfume by Lanvin up to the counter, plonking it down.

'I can't believe that they made bottles of perfume this big, and no one has even opened it!' the girl enthused.

'It's a factice,' Sarah explained.

'A what?'

'A factice, a dummy bottle of perfume — used on perfumery counters as advertising. It's either filled with coloured water, or rubbing alcohol.'

'So it's not real perfume? Why is it so expensive then? What a rip off!'

The girl stalked out of the shop, her ponytail swishing angrily across her shoulders.

Sarah rolled her eyes; you could never please some customers. Half the time they asked why something was so expensive, and the rest of the time they queried why it was so cheap. She wasn't sure why she bothered.

But thank goodness she had. Now there was the real chance that at any moment she'd be reunited with her parents. There was the possibility that somewhere in the shop existed the one item which could reunite her family, which was all the motivation she needed to continue.

The day wore on till the changing light of dusk scared away any remaining customers. Sarah reviewed her sales book — a hundred and fifty-nine pounds. Now her worst day ever. Not a single person had even paid by cash, the sales all by credit card. *A sign of the times*, she reflected, before thrusting such negative thoughts from her mind. It didn't matter because she was about to come into lots of money.

She busied herself pulling the jewellery trays from the cabinets, stacking them in size order ready for the safe.

The door opened and two men walked in, the lower half of their faces concealed with scarves, sunglasses covering their eyes. Sarah's heart dropped, only one thought on her mind; armed robbery. The moment took on a surreal hue as she laughed; they were on a hiding to nothing. Her worst day of business in years wouldn't net them much for their effort.

The first man stopped opposite her, and time slowed. He lifted the bottom edge of his dark coloured top, exposing a tight expanse of stomach, and the ribbed grip of a pistol. Withdrawing the handgun, he pointed it at her head.

'Get on the ground.'

THE REFUSAL

*S*arah's mind panicked and her body refused to obey his command. She stood there, holding a tray of wristwatches, incredulous at the scene in front of her.

'You have *got* to be joking,' she blurted out.

'Get on the ground,' the gunman repeated.

Sarah sank to the floor, her eyes never wavering from the dark depths of the pistol barrel. Time froze and nothing existed in the world other than the end of the gun. Later, if anyone asked her to describe the gunman, she'd find she could recall nothing, except what the *gun* looked like.

Her foot brushed against a dilapidated cardboard carton under the counter; another box of stock left over from her father's time. She'd opened it years ago — it was full of a dozen stone adzes, roughly hewn, and of no significant historical value.

In the surreal mist of the robbery, she was barely even registering the words being yelled at her by the gunman. Sarah was cognisant of only one thing. The last time she'd touched an adze she'd ended up in New Zealand. Regardless of how this box got here, or where it had come from, maybe it could take her back?

Sarah reached out, her attention no longer on the ranting lunatic pointing a gun at her, demanding she hand over the *katar*. She tried telling him over and over that it was already at Christie's.

'Liar,' he screamed at her. 'Liar, liar!'

With his enraged, and oddly familiar, voice in her ear, she lunged for the box, grabbing the closest adze. Nothing.

She grabbed another one. Again, nothing.

Third time lucky.

The pistol fired, shattering the shelf behind her head. It would have shattered her head too if she'd still been there.

THE POLICE

*P*atricia heard the gunshot from her workroom — a robbery next door — the one thing she dreaded most. She was too afraid to move, but equally terrified for her friend. Moving to the front window, she dialled the emergency services, and the few seconds it took for them to answer was agony.

She relayed to them what she'd heard, and how, when she'd peered out her window, she saw two men running down the road in the half-light of dusk. Their features indistinct, only their hurried actions marked them as suspicious.

With sirens wailing in the distance, Patricia walked the few paces to *The Old Curiosity Shop*, and stepped across the threshold. She fancied she could smell the black powder from the gunshot.

'Sarah? Sarah, are you here?'

Nothing.

Making sure she didn't disturb anything, Patricia made her way down the narrow aisle to the counter. This part of the store was *not* the same. A mass of splintered wood decorated the array of tiny wooden drawers behind the counter. Of Sarah, there was no sign.

She was still standing in shock when the police arrived. Patricia pointed mutely to the shattered wood where it was obvious a powerful gunshot had caused the damage.

The police checked the premises for any sign of Sarah or the gunmen before the officer in charge took Patricia upstairs to question her further.

'When did you last see your friend?'

'Two or three hours ago. We had a coffee together downstairs, with a rep from Christie's Auctions. He left with the stuff Sarah was sending to auction, then I left.'

He scribbled in his notebook.

'And the men you saw running away — you're certain they came out of this shop?'

'I'm positive they did. That's what I told the police on the phone. It looked like they'd just run out of here, after the gunshot.'

'And your friend wasn't with them?' he probed.

'No, is her van still out at the back?' she asked, hopeful that Sarah had driven off somewhere.

One officer disappeared downstairs to check, appearing moments later to say that Sarah's van remained parked behind the shop.

Patricia's heart sank further.

That left one scenario, a scenario she couldn't share with the police.

'What happens now?'

'The crime scene team are on their way, but without Miss Lester here, or any visible sign of a struggle, there's not much they'll be able to do. Do you have a set of keys by any chance, to lock the door?'

Patricia nodded. The keys were still in her pocket.

'I can't leave you up here by yourself, I'm sure you understand,' the uniformed officer muttered as he stood up from the couch.

'Sure, I'll be next door until you need me to shut up,' she replied.

She found it hilarious they wouldn't allow her to stay in the flat by herself, yet knew she had her own keys, so could let herself in whenever she liked.

That's the bureaucratic way, she reasoned, as she followed him downstairs.

351

She watched the technicians on the floor behind the shop counter as they photographed the splintered wood, took measurements, and bagged a misshapen bullet from the wall. Another officer stood across the road talking to the bakery staff, leaving two other policemen chatting outside, filling in time until the technicians finished.

On the counter was the manila folder Sarah had pulled out of the travelling trunk, with the word 'Family' written in black ink in the centre. Curiosity overtook her, and Patricia picked it up. Hugging it to her chest, she left the shop, scurrying next door before any of the men could see she'd taken something with her. She fled to her workroom and slid the folder under her design books.

Less than an hour later, an officer knocked on her door, and asked her to lock up Sarah's shop.

'This is the place where the couple went missing right?' he asked, as he waited.

Patricia turned the key in the final lock.

'Yes, both Sarah's parents are missing.'

'And now she appears to be too,' he added.

'Then you should be out looking for her,' Patricia retorted.

Pocketing the keys, she spun on her heels and returned to her shop, locking the police, and the evening, outside.

THE PUNISHMENT

*H*arvard arrived back at Christie's late in the afternoon, success written all over his face, and the signed auction agreement in his briefcase. Hannah didn't realise he'd returned until she bumped into him on his way up to Jay Khosla's office, with a cardboard carton in his hands.

'What's in the box, Andrew, more tablecloths for your dolly's tea party?'

'Pretty sure you know what it is, Hannah. We were at the same meeting.'

He brushed her off. Not even Hannah could temper his good mood.

'Wait!' she rushed after him, stopping him at the lift. 'So you got the knife then?'

'I did, it wasn't difficult. It's amazing what you can achieve when you're polite to people. You should try it one day.'

Andrew pushed the lift button, closing the door on Hannah's thunderous face.

She'd mulled over the conversation she was about to have with Grey. Whichever way she dressed it, it wouldn't go well.

Hannah shut the door to her tiny office and dialled Grey. It took her most of the afternoon to summon up the courage to ring him. His displeasure did not disappoint but now the *katar* was at Christie's, there was nothing she could do to ensure that Grey would own it.

Grey had not held back in accusing her of complicity in him losing it. Thankfully, their conversation was brief.

Hannah felt a migraine pulling behind her eyes. The energy and desire to do any further work for Richard Grey diminishing as the pain level increased.

From his apartment window, Grey looked upon the glittering ribbon of the Thames. He turned to gaze at the framed painting of his grandmother.

On the wall next to the oil painting was an obituary. In a simple black frame, it was an odd choice of decoration in an otherwise stark home.

The obituary was for Lord Edward Grey and his wife, Mary, who had perished in a boating accident before the outbreak of the Second World War. Their only child, their sole heir, Elizabeth Williams (née Grey), survived them.

It gave Richard Grey no end of joy that their branch of the family line had finally died out. Although it had taken much longer than anyone thought for Elizabeth Williams to die. *Thieves, every last one.* His grandfather was left nothing. His harridan of a great-great-grandmother had been adamant that his great-grandfather, Benjamin, be left nothing, not even a roof over his head. Even when Grey visited Elizabeth, his great-aunt's house, asking for a share of what was left of the family inheritance, she had thrown him out, tossing back in his face the words of his great-great-grandmother, that Benjamin, *and* his descendants, would get nothing.

He always got what he wanted, and he wanted the *katar*. That he didn't have it now was the fault of other people. The person at the top of that list was Sinclair. He had one task — to retrieve the dagger. Gardiner's failure at Christie's was unfortunate but she was a useful pawn inside the auction house. No, it was Sinclair who would be punished for not obtaining the knife. He owed no loyalty to the man.

THE FOLDER

$\mathcal{W}$ith sleep an unlikely possibility despite the late hour, Patricia made herself a coffee, locked the workroom door, and opened the folder she'd lifted from Sarah's shop.

It was devoid of any markings apart from the word 'Family' on the front. Patricia carefully paged through the fragile papers, some so thin they were practically transparent.

A quarter of the way through the stack, she found a yellowed copy of a marriage certificate, recording the marriage between Philip Antony Williams and Elizabeth Laura Grey at the outbreak of WWII.

Patricia presumed this was for the woman whose estate Sarah had just purchased.

Fascinated, she carried on trying to decipher the writing on the other papers in the folder.

There was an old-fashioned wedding card, with decorative cut-out bells, made out to Phil and Betty, wishing them all the happiness in the world, and signed:

Mother (Grace)

A faded telegram, with its stark typed print was next. The War

Office had sent tens of thousands of almost identical telegrams to families throughout the Commonwealth, the script the same...

DEEPLY REGRET TO INFORM YOU THAT YOUR HUSBAND SQUADRON LEADER PHILIP WILLIAMS NOW REPORTED TO HAVE LOST HIS LIFE AS RESULT OF AIR OPERATIONS ON FEBRUARY 12TH 1944. THE AIR COUNCIL EXPRESS THEIR PROFOUND SYMPATHY. LETTER CONFIRMING THIS TELEGRAM GIVING ALL AVAILABLE DETAILS FOLLOWS.

Checking back on the date of the marriage certificate, Patricia calculated they'd been married four years.

Another war widow.

So many women lost their husbands, fathers, and brothers. She put the two documents to one side to show Sarah when she next... she gulped.

She didn't know when she might see her again. Pushing the thought away, she returned to the file, fighting off the fears about her friend.

At the back was a will, the rust marks of an old staple had left a brown line at the top of the page. Written on a typewriter, someone had filled the gaps with spidery script, listing the beneficiary as Elizabeth Grey of Salisbury. It listed the testator as Lord Edward Grey.

POSTCARD #14

2/2/44

Dear Phil
My uncle was here asking about the Indian dagger. I told him only you knew
where it was, and he left. You would have thrown him out on his ear! I've sent it
to London now. I can't bear to have it in the house any more.
I wish he would just disappear. If he wants it, he can bid on it at auction.
It does amuse me to see him so frustrated.
Stay safe.
B xxx

THE AUCTION

*P*atricia slipped into the packed auction room, joining Harvard, who'd saved her a seat.

The auctioneer's very English tones caressed the crowd as he welcomed the attendees. The cavernous chamber was full, and Christie's staff lined the walls, each with a mobile phone ready to receive the anonymous telephone bids all auction attendees learn to dread. One never knows if anyone is at the end of the phone or if it's an elaborate ploy by the auction house to inflate prices.

Patricia spent the opening moments of the auction smoothing her Victorian-inspired pant suit ensemble and casting an expert eye over the other patrons seated around them. The quality of clientele here was a far cry from those she used to see shopping at *The Old Curiosity Shop*. There wasn't a single pair of jeans in sight, and the value of the diamonds being worn in this room alone was such that they could claw Britain out of its recession if liquidated all at once.

The atmosphere subtly changed from social to businesslike as the clerk carried the first lot onto the stage and the auctioneer began his patter.

Lot number one was a nineteenth century Indian gold betel box, the cover embossed with the scene of a lion eating an antelope, flanked by hounds and a hunter in a turban, wielding a pistol. Spirited bidding around the room saw it exceed its estimate by more than two thousand pounds, with a hammer price of three thousand two hundred and fifty. With the successful sale of the betel box, it disappeared from the stage.

Harvard was making notes in the glossy catalogue. While many of the articles didn't have a colour photograph next to their flowery description, Sarah's *katar* adorned the front cover. Christie's had done a remarkable job of cleaning the knife, and its gemstones gleamed with new life.

Apart from Patricia, only one other person knew the knife had a mate, and he was holding centre court in the front row — Richard Grey.

The next piece was a carved ivory statue of an Indian god. With the recent media uproar at the booming illegal ivory trade and the poaching of elephants, Christie's had announced that after this year they would no longer auction any article made of ivory, regardless of age. A bold move, and one that had sent the prices of ivory skyrocketing, with moneyed Asian clients outbidding each other at auctions around the world.

As predicted, the statue exceeded all expectations, and there was a collective gasp from the audience when the hammer fell, as the piece sold for five times its estimated value to an anonymous phone bidder. And thus continued the auction. Most pieces made their reserve with little effort by the auctioneer. Halfway through there was a brief intermission of sorts where the clerks removed the sold lots from display and carried in the next wave.

Most bidders in the room knew each other and gossiped in the aisles while white-aproned waiters topped up wine glasses to loosen the wallets of the audience.

When the auction recommenced, several pieces of Georgian silverware came up for sale before the *de Lamerie* candelabra.

Everyone knew how unique these pieces were — a pair, in immaculate condition, coming up for auction was unheard of. It was as if Queen Elizabeth II herself had decided to part with a couple of odd bits of the family silver.

None of the research that Christie's had undertaken had found any mention of these items. Sadly, *de Lamerie's* ledgers hadn't survived, and despite being a prolific silversmith it was impossible to know who had commissioned these pieces.

Bidding started strong, and the candelabra reached their reserve after only seven bids.

'And we are on the market. Do I hear one hundred and ten thousand pounds? Yes, sir, thank you... any further advances? We have a telephone bid, one hundred and twenty thousand pounds, and straight back to you, sir. One hundred and thirty thousand? Thank you... any more bids for these two magnificent examples of Paul de Lamerie's work? Oh, I have one hundred and fifty thousand pounds on the phone, thank you.'

The auctioneer slowly made eye contact with all the early bidders.

'No further bids? Going once... going twice... sold to the phone bidder. Thank you.'

An appreciative hum filled the room, and Patricia and Harvard grinned at each other like Cheshire cats. Although Sarah wasn't with them to enjoy the show, Patricia knew her friend would be delirious at the result.

A clerk carried the final item for the night's auction, Sarah's *katar*, onto the stage. The auctioneer's spotlight picking out the fire in the rubies silenced the room. Expectations of another stellar performer were high.

As the bespectacled auctioneer leaned into his microphone to begin his well-oiled patter, Grey stood up and announced, 'No. No, this piece is not for sale. It belongs to me and was stolen from my family.'

Patricia shot to her feet.

'Liar!'

There was no way she would let him accuse her friend of being a thief.

The crowd parted as everyone spun in their seats to watch the show. Ryan Francis moved to the back of the room, joining Gemma Dance as Grey made his announcement.

'Too late,' she whispered to her partner.

'Let's see how this plays,' Ryan replied, taking in the scene and all its players.

Ryan shuffled through the papers in his folder, pulling out a copy of the sales agreement for the *katar*, the one sold by Christie's in 1944.

The auctioneer tried placating Grey and to continue the auction.

'Mr Grey, could I please ask you to sit down.'

'You may ask, but I will not sit until you have given me that which is mine.'

Don Claire and Jay Khosla were standing on the side arguing over the best course of action. The paperwork held by Christie's showed that Christie's sold this very *katar* in 1944, with the purchaser recorded as Benjamin Grey. Further digging had shown that Benjamin Grey was none other than Richard Grey's great-grandfather, the brother of Lord Edward Grey.

Richard Grey interrupted their discussion, 'Mr Claire, tell your employee that this *katar* belongs to my family. Stolen from us when my great-grandfather was still alive.'

Conscious of trying not to upset one of their best customers, Don Claire replied. 'Are you suggesting that someone stole it after your great-grandfather purchased it at auction in 1944, Mr Grey?'

The heads of the audience were swivelling backwards and forwards between the protagonists.

Grey, who had all the facts of the earlier sale and purchase of the knife by his great-grandfather, from Hannah, responded.

'That is not what I was suggesting, Mr Claire. They stole it before that.'

Claire looked incredulous.

'Before 1944? Where is your evidence? For I believe that we are auctioning off the very same *katar* your family purchased then, and, unless you have a police report for the theft, we here at Christie's believe that your great-grandfather, or perhaps your grandfather, sold it after that date. I'm sorry Mr Grey, but the auction will continue.'

He nodded to the auctioneer.

Grey's face took on the hue of a man in the grip of a heart attack, the colour draining as an enormous rage overtook his sensibilities.

'How *can* it be the same knife, when I have it here!'

Leaping towards the stage, Richard Grey withdrew the second dagger from within his coat and was waving it above his head, screaming obscenities at the auctioneer who'd already pressed the discreet panic button under his lectern. As Grey stormed the podium, the poor clerk with the *katar* stood transfixed with fear, while the auctioneer leapt from the stage, falling awkwardly into the panicked crowd, his screams adding to the confusion.

The clerk took his chance and tried rushing past Grey.

Wildly brandishing the *katar*, Grey eviscerated the clerk, slicing straight through the decorative velvet cushion. His death was as instant as Grey was terrifying.

Grey rescued the second *katar* from the floor and stood on the stage, armed with both knives. The audience trampled each other in their panic, champagne glasses smashing underfoot mixed with Grey's cries of rage. Don and Jay slipped out a side door, locking it behind them. White-faced they waited for security to handle the disturbance.

Harvard bustled Patricia from the sales room as soon as he saw Grey brandishing the first *katar*, using his staff card to swipe them both into the safety of the corridor. Gemma and Ryan followed them, and the quartet stood in shock as they listened to the screams on the other side of the locked door.

THE RECIPIENT

*P*atricia filled the void from Sarah's disappearance with Harvard and her new collection. The dust in Sarah's shop grew thicker without the customers to disturb it. The success of the sale of the candelabra, and the mayhem over the *katar*, meant the sampler had flown under the metaphorical radar. It had reached its reserve, purchased by the Victoria and Albert Museum, just as Sarah expected, earning Harvard a healthy commission.

Periodically, the police appeared at Patricia's shop to question her further about Sarah, and the men she'd seen running from the scene. But without a body, there was no crime, and they officially listed Sarah as a missing person, padding out the hefty file already held on her parents.

With the launch of her collection imminent, Patricia started worrying about the props for her show. She'd been relying on Sarah to give her what she needed, and after pondering the dilemma for the best part of a week, she discussed it with Harvard.

'Do you'd think she'd mind me helping myself to a few things, for the launch?' she asked over curry one night.

'Won't the police be angry with you letting yourself in with Sarah still missing?'

'They know I have a key, so I don't expect they'll worry about me borrowing half a dozen vases and stuff. We'll pop in and look, yes?'

Andrew nodded, trusting her judgement.

THE POSTCARD

*W*hen Patricia took the folder from *The Old Curiosity Shop*, she never noticed the pile of postcards. She didn't see it totter over, spilling onto the counter. The topmost card was the only one without a stamp or postmark.

Never sent and never read.

POSTCARD #15

12/2/44

Dear Phil
I received a telegram today, but I guess you know that.
I love you.
B xxx

THE DELIVERY

The boy delivered the paper-wrapped parcel to the wooden two-storey building on Princes Street in Dunedin, after narrowly avoiding falling into one ditch on the side of the carriageway when a horse took fright and ran him off the road. He dropped half the packages he was to deliver, leaving them covered in the muck and manure from the roadway.

The woman who'd answered his knocking appeared not to notice the mud, and the torn corners on the packaging.

'Yes?' she queried.

'You Mrs Lester?'

'Yes, why?'

'This here parcel is for you. Sorry 'bout the dirt, but they knocked me over. Dangerous street this…'

The woman put her hand in the pocket of her starched white apron and pressed a farthing into his for his troubles. She closed the door, turning the parcel over in her hands.

There was her name: *Mrs Lester*, and her address, *27 Princes Street, Dunedin*.

The handwriting was unfamiliar, and a package was the last thing she'd expected to receive here. She carried it into the kitchen, unpicking the knots in the string; string was too useful to waste by cutting with a knife. The paper fell away revealing a black leather bible.

As with anything new she came into contact with, she hesitated, before she reached out to open the cover.

Nothing untoward happened, but the chill that shot through her was enough. Fate was playing a cruel trick on her. Someone made the inscription inside the bible to Sarah, and the only Sarah *she* knew was her daughter.

A daughter she'd left in another time...

**The story continues with *The Last Letter* —
Book #2 of *The Old Curiosity Shop* trilogy.**

REVIEW

ear Reader,

If you enjoyed *Fifteen Postcards*, could you please leave a rating (or review) on your favourite digital platform?

Ratings (or reviews) are invaluable to authors.

Thank you.

Kirsten McKenzie xxx

CAST OF PLAYERS

THE OLD CURIOSITY SHOP SERIES

Sarah Lester
  (Sarah Williams
  Grace Williams
  Betsy
  Sarah Bell)

Art Loss Register
  Gemma Dance
  Ryan Francis

Auckland, New Zealand
  Aroha Kepa, wife of Wiremu Kepa
  Henry Neumegen, a pawnbroker
  Jimmy Jowl, a publican
  Joe Jowl, a publican
  Moses Robley, collector of artefacts
  Sophia Kepa, daughter of Wiremu
  Wiremu Kepa, a miller

Bruce Bay, New Zealand

Bryce Sinclair, ferryman
Christine Young, wife of Reverend Young
Felicity Toomer, daughter of John Toomer
Frederick Sweeney, publican
Grant Toomer, shopkeeper
Isaac Lloyd, gold miner
Margaret Sweeney, wife
Samuel Sinclair, son of Bryce Sinclair
Saul Hunt, ex convict
Seth Brown, gold miner
Shrives, a bullock driver
William Price, Warden
Reverend Gregory Young

Christies Auction House
Andrew Harvard, Costumes and Textiles
Don Claire, Senior Partner
Hamish Brooke
Hannah Gardner
Jay Khosla, Manager of the Indian Art Group
Leo Hayward, clerk

Dunedin, New Zealand
Amos Wood, army deserter
Annabel Lester, mother of Sarah Lester
Colin Lloyd, younger brother of Isaac Lloyd
Edwin Sutton, Sutton's General Store
Graeme Greene, police constable
Howard Cummings, clergyman
Jack Antony, army deserter
Jock Crave, police sergeant
Mervyn Kendall, Collector of Customs
Norman Bailey, assistant to Bishop Dasent
Thomas Dasent, Bishop of Dunedin
Una Neville, on the boat with Colin Lloyd

England

Adelaide, maid to Lady Laura Grey

Arthur, a silversmith

Arthur Sullivan*, composer

Audrey Grey, mother of Richard Grey

Barry Wentworth, a farmer

Benjamin Grey, brother of Edward Grey

Daniel Shalfoon, a clergyman

Edith Grey, ancestor of Richard Grey

Elizabeth Williams (née Grey), daughter of Edward Grey

Grace Williams, daughter of Robert Williams

Jessica Williams, sister of Robert Williams

Jonas Williams, foster father of Robert Williams

Josephine, a prostitute

Lady Laura Grey, mother of Edward and Benjamin

Lord Edward Grey, brother of Benjamin Grey

Lord Henry Grey, husband of Laura Grey

Mary Grey, wife of Edward Grey

Melissa Crester, an American

Mr Sutcliffe, manservant to Lady Grey

Mrs Phillips, housekeeper to Lady Grey

Nicole Pilcher, antique shop manager

Patricia Bolton, fashion designer

Paul de Lamerie*, a master silversmith

Philip Williams, husband of Elizabeth Williams

Ravi Naranyan, security guard

Rebecca 'Betsy' Jane Williams,

Richard Grey

Robert Williams, illegitimate child of Sarah Williams

Samer Kurdi, a trader

Sally Glynn, a Muslim in Liverpool

Stokes, goon employed by Richard Grey

Tracey Humphrey, Royal School of Needlework

Wick Farris, a knocker

W.S. Gilbert*, dramatist

Customs and Excise
  Alan Bullard, Surveyor of Customs in London
  Clifford Meredith, a customs officer
  Mervyn Bulford, the Collector of Customs, Liverpool
  Paul Shaskey, a customs clerk

France
  Clara Bisset, resistance fighter

London Police
  Fiona Duodu, Constable
  Owen Gibson, Detective Sergeant
  Sean Jones, Corporal
  Tania Foster, Sergeant
  Victor Fujimoto, Inspector

India
  Abe Garland, army officer
  Ajay Turilay, assistant to Patricia Bolton
  Albert Lester, husband of Annabel Lester, father of Sarah Lester
  Alice Montgomery, Anglican Missionary School
  Amit, servant to Simeon Williams
  Christopher Dickens, army officer
  Elaine Barker, Anglican Missionary School
  Jai Singh*, the Maharaja of Jaipur
  James Doulton, army officer
  Kalakanya, servant to Sarah Williams
  Karen Cuthbert, Fishing Fleet Girl
  Layak, servant to the Raja of Nahan
  Madame Ye, opium dealer
  Maria, Fishing Fleet Girl
  Naomi Abbott, wife
  Navin Pandya, a stonemason
  Nirmala, servant to Sarah Williams
  Raja of Nahan

Ram Singh II*, the Maharaja of Jaipur
Reverend Montgomery
Sally Brass, Fishing Fleet Girl
Sanjay, a street urchin from Jaipur
Saptanshu, driver for the Raja of Nahan
Simeon Williams, brother of Sarah Williams
Warren Brooke, army officer

Victoria and Albert Museum
Brenda Swift, curator
Eliza Broadhead, Department of Furniture, Textiles and Fashion
Jasmine Gupta, manager
Steph Chinneck, intern

Wales
Annwr Lloyd, mother of Isaac and Colin

* Real historical figures. Their names have been used in a fictional sense, although the notable achievements mentioned in this novel are real.

BOOK CLUB DISCUSSION QUESTIONS

1. What was your favourite part of the book?
2. Did you race to the end, or was it more of a slow burn?
3. Which scene has stuck with you the most?
4. Would you want to read another book by this author?
5. What surprised you most about the book?
6. How did your opinion of the book change as you read it?
7. If you could ask the author anything, what would it be?
8. Are there lingering questions from the book you're still thinking about?
9. Which characters did you like best? Which did you like least? And why?
10. If you had to trade places with one character, who would it be?
11. What do you think happens to the characters after the book's official ending?
12. How did the setting impact the story? Would you want to read more books set in that world?

ACKNOWLEDGMENTS

Thank you for reading *Fifteen Postcards*. It would be wonderful if you could post a review on Amazon or BookBub or Goodreads, or any other digital platform you use to record the books you've read. Reviews really help authors.

I would like to thank Andrene Low, for all the advice she has provided over the years. I've been following in her footprints, and I am eternally grateful for her guidance.

When I told my brother I was writing a book, he replied "You never finish anything." That was enough motivation for me to finish this book, and the sequels. So I want to thank Gareth for encouraging me in his own special way!

ABOUT THE AUTHOR

For years Kirsten McKenzie worked in the family antiques store, where she went from being allowed to sell postcards in the corner, to selling Worcester vases and seventeenth century silverware, providing a unique insight into the world of antiques which touches every aspect of her writing.

Her historical time travel trilogy, *The Old Curiosity Shop* series, has been described as *"Time Travellers Wife meets Far Pavilions"*, and *"Antiques Roadshow gone viral"*. The audio books for the series are available through Audible.

Kirsten has also written the bestselling gothic thriller *Painted*, and the medical thriller, *Doctor Perry*. Her latest novel, *The Forger and the Thief*, is a historical thriller set in 1966 Florence, Italy.

She is currently working on her next time travel trilogy, which begins with *Ithaca Bound*, and features many of your favourite characters from the *Old Curiosity Shop* series...

Kirsten lives in New Zealand with her husband, her daughters, and two rescue cats. She can usually be found procrastinating online.

You can sign up for her sporadic newsletter at:
www.kirstenmckenzie.com/newsletter/